Angels
and their
HOURGLASSES

Angels
and their
Hourglasses

J.M. Surra

J.M. Surra
Visit his website at: http://www.jmsurra.com
First Print Edition June 2012
First eBook Edition: April 2011

21 20 19 18 17 16 15 14 13 12   1 2 3 4 5

Published or pending publication under the following ISBN numbers and formats:

Paperback format: 978-0-9834647-4-7
Kindle eBook format: 978-0-9834647-0-9
EPUB eBook format: 978-0-9834647-1-6
Google Edition format: 978-0-9834647-2-3
Multiple Formats: 978-0-9834647-3-0

Print and eBook formatting by Erika Q. Stokes http://erikastokes.com

For Gary O.

My greatest privilege was being your friend.

Preface

At six years old, I could look up or listen to the sky and identify a C-119 Flying Boxcar, or a Corsair, or a P-51 with a Merlin up there. Because my Dad loved planes, I loved planes. I thought I was a typical post-war kid. I grew up playing the pop-quiz game with him; he'd pop the questions, and I'd have to answer them. Planes, Golden Age Racing, Warbirds, World War II, and more. It didn't matter what the subject; I couldn't get enough. He taught me so much about aviation this way, and directly or indirectly, I owe most of my knowledge to him.

Fiction or not, *Angels and Their Hourglasses* is a remarkable, inspiring story. Before I tell it to you, I think it's important first to tell you his story.

I believed from an early age that Dad was a fighter pilot, or a bomber pilot. He was a pilot; I was sure of that. A high school teacher, he had a photo on his desk—a wartime photo of him standing by the nose of a P-51 Mustang. Though I didn't know it then, a million other guys had very similar photos. This one was painted up like the Tiger Sharks, with a big mouth full of sharp-looking teeth. I listened to his stories, transported to far away airfields and riding along inside the planes he flew.

The considerable mechanical knowledge I accrued came from Dad. In my late teens, I somehow learned that instead of a pilot, my Dad was in fact a crew chief, a lowly mechanic. I was devastated, and that bitter disappointment stayed with me. I wanted nothing further to do with talking about airplanes. Soon after, I discovered the female of the species, and became otherwise occupied. One thing led to another; I went off to college, took a job in another state, and eventually got married. Dad took a good job with the state and spent many more hours at work. Just like Harry Chapin's song, *Cat's in the cradle*, we intended to spend more time with each other, but life intervened. As my disappointment softened, my love of airplanes resurfaced. I learned how to fly radio-control planes, which lent fresh fuel to my passion for Gee Bees and other Golden Age Racers, and all things World War II. Studying these became an important part of my life.

Flash forward three decades. Dad had developed some health problems, so we made the decision to move where we could be near him. He was eighty-four, and had grown old and quite frail while I was off living my life. Just two miles up the road, I checked on him every day, and we visited. To my delight, the stories resumed. Now older and a much better listener, I learned the whole story. Dad was indeed a wartime mechanic. His vision was not good enough to become a military pilot. But he was not just any mechanic. He was an amazing mechanic with incredible diagnostic capabilities. His crew traveled to whatever distant field or patch of dirt a disabled multi-engine aircraft managed to land on. In order for the plane to be ferried to the nearest base, his crew had to perform whatever repairs were required first. After that, they loaded up the tools, hopped in, and he flew the aircraft and his crew to the base. Yep. Dad was a pilot after all. Like hundreds of other capable men and women pilots in the country during WW II, Dad was rated to move planes around. As a specialized crew chief ferrying them around, he was the pilot. His name was John, but he was often called Jack, and had acquired a lifelong nickname—they called him "Jackson." After the war when they phoned him, I could hear them as they yelled "Jackson!" over the phone line.

In the common ferrying of planes, he and his crew differed from most other crews significantly in one respect—the element of danger. The planes they retrieved were already broken down, and as often as not were worn-out flying buckets of bolts. More than once they had to make an emergency landing and re-patch whatever they had patched to get it in the air in the first place. They were always under the gun for time. Sometimes they moved planes from one base to another. Their filed flight plan would be posted, and personnel invariably flocked to the ramp to catch a ride. It didn't matter; flying deathtrap or not, they wanted a ride home for the holidays or whatever. He and his crew objected, but as often as not they were overruled and had no choice.

You can't fight city hall, but they decided they could have a little fun with it. Dad dug around in a box one day and produced a hilarious photo of them messing with prospective passengers. They'd fabricated some glasses using lenses made from the bottoms of old (Coke?) bottles. They wore them while greeting their passengers on the ramp, smiling and offering a warm welcome aboard with a handshake that missed the passenger entirely, taking three or four tries to find the person and their hand. Then they would announce it was time to load up, turn around, and walk headfirst into the side of the plane and fall down. Any number of those passengers must have seriously considered waiting for another plane; any other plane at all. After he finished that story, my sides ached for days.

Their 'navigator' was much better at his day-job as a mechanic, and notorious for sending them the wrong way. I can't remember the man's last name (nor would I say it here), but they affectionately dubbed him with the nickname "wrong-way" spoken before his name. After angry Mexicans chased them from Mexican airspace for the second time in one year, Dad sought help from another pilot in learning "dead-reckoning." This was his term that referred to using the time of day, the time of year, and the position of the sun to establish a good approximate heading. It's an easy, common-sense method. He taught me dead-reckoning before I was ten. I still use it.

Often, his crew would patch up an old hulk and manage to bring it back to base, only to have it condemned, permanently removed from flight status the next day. Dad described the big red X the safety officer would draw across the whole form.

One day, the dangers of the job caught up with them. They retrieved a Mitchell B-25B bomber, which developed a series of problems. A number of options were discussed, including bailing out. Time ran out on them, and, trying to save the bomber, Dad rode it in and did what he could to control the crash. The cockpit caught the worst of it, and

Dad's leg was badly injured, signaling the end of his career in the military. Though he tried not to show it, he limped, and it hurt him for the rest of his life. One of the characters in this book will suffer this same injury.

He never lost his love for planes, and over time the love he had for them became deeply ingrained in me. I once wondered why men would continue to climb into them, with all the stories of the danger, the lives lost, the bailing out, the crashing and injuries sustained. These adventurous men loved the planes, loved aviation, loved flying. It was all worth it. The undercurrents of the stories played to me. The reasons why always mattered, and the friendships he made lasted a lifetime. Those were treasures. He loved those guys. How can you not envy that?

Dad's health problems were diagnosed as cancer just over two years ago, and three months later it claimed him at eighty-five. I was bereft. Near my father again after so long, and transported by his stories once again, I was not ready to let him go.

Though unwilling himself, he finally had to let us go.

And with that, he was gone. The silence was deafening. I had nowhere to go to change that, and grieved mightily.

The stories were not lost forever; simply placed on the shelf during my time of grief. But I had not been left without them, or without him; he had cunningly passed the torch on to me through his wonderful story-telling genes. I had learned so much from his colorful stories of Golden Age Aviation, WW II, mechanics, and writing.

I'd been left a treasure, and an all-encompassing need to share it with others. I don't know exactly how long it took me to realize that, but I vividly remember the moment I knew what I'd do with it. I spent the next hour scribbling like a madman on a legal pad, and two hours after that I printed the complete storyline/outline for this book, from beginning to end. I had so much fun writing *Angels and Their Hourglasses* that I wouldn't discount the very real possibility that Dad and I wrote this book in a final marathon story-telling session together.

I dedicate this book solely to a man who, during my youth, was first, foremost, and happiest as an educator. He taught me so much—about the world, about learning, about writing, about flying, planes, and every exciting thing that goes with that. He taught me that there can be value in every life, every person on the planet, whether that person is Japanese, Chinese, German, or Russian—skin colors and nationalities don't matter; we're all in this together.

It's easy to see why he was a hero when he held the hand of a little boy and introduced him to the wonders and denizens of the sky above, and why he was still my hero when I held his hand as he left this world. I can only assume he was soaring skyward.

Though this volume is a far cry from being a summary of the wealth of knowledge he conveyed to me; without a former Army Air Force Lt/Captain named John W. Surra, this book would never exist.

This one's for you, Dad.

I love you.

Chapter One

Archangels settled matters with swords. That's just how it was. That's how they were built. When the battles of biblical legend ended, the battle-hardened seraphs could only hope for assignments that suited their nature. Many tasks could be found. Humans are a busy lot, and there are no unemployed archangels. All too often, the match was a round hole and a square peg.

The garden's original intent had long since fallen by the wayside. Humans, designed with the intelligence to do great things, and placed lovingly on a garden planet with everything they would ever need to live in bliss, chose instead to embrace war. The killing continued, and wars grew bloodier by the century.

Warriors themselves on a celestial scale, archangels remained unaffected by the relatively minor spectacle of human wars. They understandably were unable to equate war with tragedy. And so, their presence made little difference.

One quiet, reserved individual dwelt among them. This archangel, once held in wide renown for healing, wisdom, and teaching, had experienced a number of difficult centuries because of the humans.

As slowly and surely as the drops of water from a cavern ceiling will form a monumental stalagmite, a cynicism of humans and human nature formed in his mind. Eons upon eons passed before the moment arrived. When it did, he decided that the humans had lost their capacity to learn. From that day on, he avoided them, eschewed and disdained them, wanted as little to do with them as possible. He hardened himself and turned away.

Sadly, he didn't realize—he had forgotten—that he was the best-equipped of his kind for the assignment, the only archangel created for that purpose: a sublime creation, most cherished by his maker, and unique; like an author's inspired passage or unexpected timeless line, a treasured masterpiece among works of great beauty.

And for all of that, fragile beyond description.

He had lost sight of his own past. A past of enlightenment. The majesty of the written word, his quill, his passion for imparting wisdom and knowledge; these were once his mightiest weapons. Mightier still when wielded with a characteristic now scarcely evident—perhaps his greatest attribute—his compassion for humanity.

Summoned by his maker, he knelt, looking not up into the face of his creator, but downward, silent and surly, sure of what was to come.

"You are here with me, yet you are not. Why is this?"

"I am here as you commanded, Father. What is your bidding?"

"I bid you look into my eyes, dear one. Is this so much to ask of you?"

Slowly, the angel's head lifted, and his sullen eyes met his creator's. "As you wish."

"You turned away on your last assignment. This is the third time. Have you forgotten who you are? Have you forgotten the importance of what you do?"

"What difference does it make, Father? The humans forget their teachings. In all your names, they kill one another. They do not deserve your love," he said, his voice flat and morose.

Disturbed, the maker's eyes flashed, and his voiced rumbled like threatening thunder. "Now you decide who deserves my love?" A moment later, a sigh of disappointment was heard through the rumble. "You leave me no choice. You need to remember who you are. You will take this assignment. You will attend. You will watch from the first moment to the last, and you will not turn away. Do you understand?"

"Yes, Father. I will watch, and I will not turn away, from the first moment to the last," he said, bowing his head before he rose and turned to leave, taking for granted his privileged status. For only an archangel would dare to turn his back in the presence of the creator of all things.

Remember who I am? What is that supposed to mean? This assignment is nothing more than a punishment. Depending upon humans for anything was a mistake. Charged with one, and then another, time after time he had watched them fail. *Another young one. How much could this one possibly know? What difference could he make? Wasted effort, that's what this is; time that could be better spent elsewhere.*

It was no use. His was not to question why (though question he did). He had his orders and would follow them. With a decided lack of enthusiasm, he set about making the preparations for his assignment.

Chapter Two

June 20, 2010
The Lodge at Moosehead Lake – Greenville, Maine

It wasn't that he didn't love her. Benjamin Ryan had loved Katie Lynn Spencer since he was eighteen, from the first moment he met her, six years ago. He couldn't imagine life with anyone else. The prospect of marrying her exhilarated him. At least, it had until recently. He couldn't put his finger on just why he avoided all talk of marriage, but for months he'd done just that. An ominous feeling beset him each time he thought about it, a feeling that a storm was coming. Not like the days Gramps felt his bunions kicking up, or when the grass and trees moved around more than they should; those told him to expect some wind and rain. This was a feeling like no other; it made his teeth grind. It twisted his stomach into a knot.

Though he wouldn't say so, it terrified him.

For his birthday, she'd insisted on a weekend trip to Maine so they could talk it out. The Lodge at Moosehead Lake was a wonderful place to relax and unwind, and their room—the Moose room—was a delicious combination of rustic, cozy and romantic. That, and her persistence, made the getaway successful. Now, their wedding plans were back on, but their weekend was rapidly drawing to a close.

Pleading puppy-dog eyes followed her. "You have to leave?"

She felt herself waver, but said, "You know I have to get back to school. It'll take me a few hours to get back to Framingham," then she whispered, "You know I love you, sweetheart." She softly kissed him, leaned her forehead against his for several moments before she forced herself to climb into the car, and then said, "I'm going to miss you."

As she drove away, he breathed, "I already miss you."

Outside of his family's hangars at the small Greenville airport, Ben performed a thorough pre-flight as the Ryan Aviation ground crew fueled and serviced his plane. The magnificent antique 1938 Waco bi-plane was ship-shape, as expected, so he filed his flight plan for Springfield and climbed in. Tucked between the gauges on the dash, in imitation of many World War II pilots, he had Katie Lynn's photo. He kissed two fingers and gently pressed them to her photo. A few minutes later he was airborne.

Such magnificent weather. He loved taking deep breaths of the cool, sweet mountain air. He never failed to find inspiration in the azure of a Maine summer sky.

An hour or so had passed when a nagging feeling of apprehension gnawed at him. Looking around, he saw only fluffy clouds; he was alone in the vast blue sky. Whatever it actually was, storm or not, it wouldn't hurt to keep a weather-eye out. When he passed the two-hour mark, Manchester lay in his wake and to his left; he was on the home stretch for Springfield.

The eerie feeling of impending danger swept through him again, but this time much stronger; he grew anxious, on-edge. Quick glances all around revealed nothing but blue sky and small, fluffy clouds, same as before. The radial engine continued to run flawlessly, and its distinct throaty sound bore resonant witness to it. The beautiful white and red Waco showed perfect pressures and temps on all the gauges. But he couldn't shake it.

Leaning out and looking the bipe over from front to back, he saw nothing out of order. As he wondered whether he might have something wrong with him, he sensed an ominous presence behind him. He chided himself for being so jumpy; but as he wasn't far from Manchester International's heavy air traffic, he took one more glance just to prove to himself that nothing was there.

The entire sky behind him and extending to the east was filled with a massive dark cloud, either black or devoid of light, and sinister in appearance, rolling and moving fast . . . straight at him.

He stared at it, uttering a string of expletives. Three minutes ago, the sky was clear. Yet there it was, a mammoth cloud, too close, and gaining on him at a phenomenal rate. Worse yet, he recognized it.

Twice before, on his trip up from Springfield, a similar cloud had appeared at a distance; as though stalking him, waiting for the right moment.

No longer stalking him, it was now bearing down upon him like a freight train, and fright momentarily seized him. Twisting, roiling blacks and browns laid a stark, frightening background for the strange, ball-shaped, blinding lightning bursts tearing across it; yet for all the lightning, there were no familiar cragged tentacles reaching for the ground. Like a set of massive, churning rollers from an antique washing machine, the unearthly cloud pulled in everything in its path. Sheets of metal roofing, old barns, trees and telephone poles were ripped from the earth and devoured as it gained velocity; and it moved with a singular, horrifying, dreadful purpose. The inconceivable entity wasn't alive—he knew it didn't have a brain—yet there could be no mistaking its purpose. He knew beyond all doubt that it was coming for him.

Tearing his eyes away, he acted. Banking the plane hard right, he dove to the southwest, trying to coax enough speed from the graceful old girl to elude the monster. The Waco was powerful and aerobatic, but she wasn't built for extreme speeds, so he tried to travel far enough to put a safe distance between himself and the terrifying, voracious cloud. Glancing back over his shoulder to check his progress, he felt the blood in his veins flow cold as ice.

The storm cloud had changed course. Impossibly, it had pursued him, moving faster yet. Behind and now even above him the sky was gone, consumed by the screaming banshee that filled his entire field of vision. His stomach churned and tightened into knots. He banked southward but it was clear he'd never make Springfield, and no way could he survive this monster in the air. Out of options, he pointed the nose down and dove hard, willing the ancient biplane to gain all the speed she could, heading for the ground to find a place to land, any place at all. If he could reach that pasture below, maybe he could wedge it in between some trees. He prayed he would make it.

Four hundred feet above the pasture, the storm snatched the Waco up as easily as a vacuum cleaner would suck up a small toy.

The pasture grew distant as the biplane was pulled inexorably back into the sky, into the mouth of the monster. Like a rag doll in the roiling blackness, he tried to hang on as he was tossed violently about the open cockpit. He wanted to be terrified, wanted to close his eyes, but found himself drawn in, helpless, compelled to watch.

Seconds later the noise abated, and still breathless, he found himself flying level at some altitude, deep inside of the storm. The violent exterior belied this interior; here it was quiet, serene, and although there was little light, the range of vision had improved. The plane around him, the ground below, all of it was visible in an iridescent red light. The biplane droned on through bits of misty turquoise-colored clouds. The light wasn't bright, but its red-orange glow touched everything. It pulsated, illuminating even the dark corners of the cockpit floor, and he could clearly see his feet.

It was then he realized there was no light glowing around him; it was emanating from the plane, from him, from the ground below, and the intensity increased by the second. His feet and the floor glowed brighter and brighter, and he had to look twice, but yes; he saw the bones in his feet. In wonder he watched, surprised that he felt no pain. Seconds later he saw through the feet, through the floor, saw the landing gear and wheel pants passing over the patchwork quilt fields far below, all glowing like himself, pulsing and fading, in and out, one second red, visible, and iridescent, the next second as transparent as glass.

Looking up, he saw the Waco pass through a foggy blue bank, or more precisely, he saw the light blue cloud pass through his plane. Everywhere the misty fog touched, parts of both he and the plane became transparent for a time, and each time they flew through another patch the areas increased, as did the length of time. Each new cycle of the event lasted longer than the previous cycle. He should have been terrified, but he was more astonished than alarmed.

Leaving the scattered clouds, they entered a more condensed shroud where all he could see was blue. By then he and the entire Waco were transparent, with barely visible glass-edge outlines. Amazed by it, and caught up in it as though in a dream, he was filled with a sense of well-being and security, captivated by the serene surroundings and the beautiful turquoise color. On a sudden impulse, he spread his arms and experienced a few precious seconds where he flew like a bird, seemingly alone in the mesmerizing blue of that tranquil sky.

The capricious moment ended with a scream of rending metal and a great heave as the tortured, ancient airframe succumbed to the strain. Wings and airframe snapped and buckled, and pieces of framework and fabric tore away with a loud ripping sound. The overstressed Waco abandoned the azure and plunged again into the lightless void; bucking, twisting, and gyrating, an enraged bull that wanted him off of its back.

He felt himself slipping from the cockpit into the void, and realized with renewed terror that his belts no longer held him; they had simply slipped through him. He tried to hang on, to hold onto something, anything, but nothing was solid enough to grab, nor was he solid enough to grab anything. As the storm celebrated its victory, its fury reached incredible levels. Lightning flashed everywhere, reaching a crescendo when thunder exploded; blast after blast, and chaos heaped upon chaos. The noise was so percussive he cried out, but could not hear his own voice. He and his trusty old Waco were to be left in ruin, torn asunder by this insanity.

He could never have imagined anything like the violent, mad cacophony of wind, noise, and electrical flashes and explosions. He slipped out the side of the Waco, falling away into the void, when just as suddenly he was lifted and buffeted, tossed about the sky at the whims of the churning monstrosity. He tried to resist, but the stresses upon his body increased beyond all human tolerance.

Then, without warning, the chaos of the void around him wound down into slow-motion, the screaming winds reduced to tortured, waning moans as the wild twists and gyrations slowed to a deliberate, placid circular motion.

The terrifying falling feeling settled into a gentle floating sensation, and as the noise faded, a feeling of some clarity returned to him.

Time around him slowly returned to normal speed, and the storm was decreasing in its intensity; its retreat every bit as stealthy and unexpected as its arrival.

Not a drop of rain had touched him; nor had any dirt flown into his open mouth or eyes. It grew quiet and still, and to his surprise, he found he was flat on his back, and somehow safe on the ground. He felt shaken but unhurt. Tentatively, he sat up.

One last vicious blow struck him through the blackness, smashing down upon him with terrific force.

The malevolent, vindictive storm had re-established its jealous claim on him. He now knew how it felt to be a house fly introduced to a rolled-up morning newspaper.

Those were his final, painful thoughts as he spiraled into the merciful blackness.

Chapter Three

It was dark. Too dark. He could see nothing, and tried to move, but found himself pinned to the ground from head to toe. It was possible to move an inch or two, though it required a tremendous amount of effort and pain. Though it seemed to take forever, he somehow managed to crawl and squirm his way out from under the object, which turned out to be a large section of the Waco's top wing.

Once again he sat up, then tried to stand up, only to cry out in pain as he fell back again. Not much was visible in the half-light of predawn, but he could see his right ankle bent at an alarming angle. When he saw his foot would not turn with his leg, he felt nauseous and lightheaded for a moment, but managed to fight it back. By some small miracle no bones protruded. The pain, searing and throbbing, was tremendous, and he gritted his teeth against it. Dried, crusted blood from a small head wound just above his hairline had sealed his left eye shut. The dried blood was a good indication that he'd been unconscious under that wing for some time.

Once he removed enough crust so he could see with both eyes, he took stock of his situation. He'd ended up next to a single tree in the middle of a pasture. Not far away, he could make out the twisted fuselage. The engine was gone, as were the wings and landing gear. The empennage, not far away, was shredded and broken.

Scattered about the ground were several sticks. One looked like it might hold him. He tested it, and used it to lean on and push himself upright. Unable to place even the slightest weight on his right foot, he hopped on his left. He thought he could grit his teeth against it once more, but cried out as each hop brought fresh agony to his dangling right foot and ankle. He endured the few dozen torturous yards to the fuse, where he was relieved to find no smell of gas. The fuselage was upright and stable, so he opened the luggage compartment behind the cockpit and pulled out his sleeping bag and ground cover, which he opened and laid out. He tried to take stock of his situation.

He was growing fainter by the second, with no way to tell how severe his injuries were. Having survived the freak storm, the strange lightning, the thunder, being tossed about like a rag doll, and the crash, he now had no idea exactly where he was or in which direction help might be found. If he didn't rest, he soon would not be able to make rational decisions. Climbing into the sleeping bag, he huddled close against the fuselage.

With his cell phone, he tried calling 911 for help. There was no signal. "That figures," he mumbled. His words were slurring, and he was experiencing bouts of uncontrollable shivering, unable to warm up. That was a bad sign. The broken bones were grinding and providing plenty of searing pain, so he could be certain the leg would swell. All the signs were there. He was slipping into shock from his injuries, and was powerless to do anything about it. Climbing into the sleeping bag to keep warm was all he could do, and it was a small miracle that he'd succeeded in that. The rest would be left to providence.

"Easy, now. You're hurt. Can you understand me, Benjamin?" the voice said through the fog. Swimming in pain, Ben opened one of his eyes. Everything was out of focus, but slowly his vision cleared, and he saw the faces of two men hovering over him. The concern showed in their faces. He saw that the men were dressed strangely. He found it curious that these fellows were dressed rather like the gentleman in the Lennox heating commercials; they even wore the same type of cap. No matter;

he appreciated their concern for him. Hmmm . . . why did he need help? He had no idea. He recalled something about his Waco strewn about, all in pieces; that couldn't be good . . . and faded away.

He awoke with a yell to a sharp, searing pain, and found a man working on his lower leg and ankle. The old gent was wearing a rumpled vest and wire-rim spectacles. He had a head of gray hair and appeared to be doctoring Ben's leg. The same two men were with him. And he hadn't imagined it; they were dressed in blue-collar 1920s clothing. There were more men in similar garb moving around the building beyond them, performing various tasks in what appeared to be a large workshop.

"I think I got the smaller bone lined up, but with all this swelling it's hard to tell. And look who's decided to join us!" Doc Perkins exclaimed, and Ben's attention returned to the foot of . . . whatever he was lying on.

He could only manage a dry, croaking voice, "Hello. Wh . . . Where am I?"

One of the men spoke, "You're here at our shop, Benjamin. We brought you here when we found you, and other than your name, we couldn't make heads or tails of the papers we found on you."

Activity in the shop ceased, and the workers came over to meet the strange young man who had at long last awoken. The speaker appeared to be the accepted leader of the other men. With the others present, he began. "I would say that introductions are in order. I'll start with myself. My name is Zantford. Zantford Granville."

Ben stopped, stunned. Had he heard the man correctly? His mind raced as he looked at the men.

Doc, who had been working to set the broken bones, took advantage of the young man's momentary distraction to give a hard yank and finish setting the leg.

Still weak, Ben could not endure the blinding pain, and passed out again.

Chapter Four

The two passed many a long, lazy afternoon in animated discussions about World War II, Golden Age Air racing, or the Granville brothers and their marvelous Gee Bee racers; the men who came to fame right there in Springfield around 1930. It had been some time since Gramps could trip him up with pop-quizzes about his heroes.

Ben often dreamed of being there as they made history, imagined creating race planes that were so fast for the time. Living in that exciting era when flying was largely an unexplored frontier.

There was little about the Granvilles he didn't know. He'd spent his life reading anything and learning everything that had ever been set to print about them. The Granvilles were celebrated heroes in Springfield's history, and every local history museum contained some sort of Gee Bee exhibit, which usually included a mock-up of one of their R-1 or R-2 racers, if not an actual reproduction.

Gramps asked, "Which crash was the worst for them?" Today's pop quiz had begun.

"That's easy. Russell Boardman stalled the R-1 racer from over fifty feet in Indiana, and it flipped over and landed upside down, killing him. The FAA inspectors descended upon them and grounded all their planes, including Granny's Model Y, which he'd arrived in afterward."

Gramps feigned a frown. "Not bad, not bad. . . . Who were the best pilots they had?"

"Jimmy Doolittle, Lowell Bayles, and Bob Hall."

"What about Boardman?"

"Good pilot. But a loose cannon."

"You think so?"

"Yeah, I really do. But it's just my opinion."

"Hmmm. Interesting take on that. What single person was the glue that held the Granvilles together, that made them into a force to be reckoned with?"

"WAY too easy, Gramps! Zantford 'Granny' Granville was the glue, there's no doubt about it."

Gramps nodded, satisfied. Ben had learned well. That was good.

He would need it. All of it.

Gramps said something, but it sounded like somebody had changed the speed on a record. Ben strained to understand it.

"Gramps?" he said, leaning toward him, but Gramps's voice sounded slow, slurred, distant.

"Ben? Bennnn . . . . . . " the room was spinning, swirling.

Chapter Five

"Ben? Ben, can you hear me? Ben, wake up, now. Ben . . . ah, there he is, he's back with us." Doc was gently slapping his cheek. "You fainted, Ben. I don't blame you; setting a bad break can be excruciating. I think we got it this time."

He nodded; his mind still foggy, mired in quicksand.

Once Doc finished the splints and was sure the young man was otherwise in good shape, he picked up his black leather doctor's bag. He had to get to his next house call.

As the fog subsided and Ben grew more lucid, he inspected his surroundings again. The attention to detail was remarkable. The old-style tools these men were working with were amazing. Never mind the vintage hand-drills hanging on the wall, and the saws, mallets, and old-style clamps all over the benches. It went far beyond that.

Their clothes. The men wore clothing that was perfect down to the last detail, to details he never even knew existed. Something wasn't right. No, that wasn't it. It struck him that everything he saw was far *too* right for this to be anything other than it appeared to be.

Zantford saw the look on his face. Watched him taking stock of the shop and inspecting the crew. There was considerable alarm in Ben's expression. "Benjamin, are you all right?" he asked. Ben's scanning stopped, and he scrutinized Granny, looking for a detail out of place. Any detail to give it away, to expose an elaborate hoax or joke. He saw none.

"Zantford Granville. *You're* Zantford Granville? *You're* Granny?" He asked, his voice still a raspy whisper; knowing as he said it that this was indeed his hero of history. He'd seen far too many old photos not to know that this was him. He'd seen him on the old film, talking about and then flying the Ascender. His voice was the same. His "Downeaster" northern New England accent was the same. He pronounced 'Mister' more like 'Mistah,' and 'Manchester' as 'Manchestah,' or Lobster as 'Lobstah,' 'can't' as 'cahn't,' and placed the occasional 'r' where one didn't belong, as in 'Auguster' instead of 'Augusta.' Ben knew the accent still existed in 2010, but in a washed-out, milder form.

The trademark pipe was even stuffed into Granny's shirt pocket, along with a Prince Albert tobacco pouch. Ben held up his hand before Granny could say anything, and in a hoarse voice uttered, "No, you're Granny, all right." He scanned the other suddenly-familiar faces, and said, "You're the Granville Brothers." He moved from face to face. "Zantford. Thomas. Robert. Mark. And Edward."

His voice full of wonder, he muttered, *"I don't believe it.* I'm right here in Springfield. I made it home. Well . . . sort of."

The brothers looked at each other in surprise, and Granny said, "It would ('twould) seem that Benjamin knows the lot of us far better (fah bettah) than we know him."

"Call me Ben. Everybody calls me Ben. I'll tell you what; I'll answer all the questions that you have, if you'll answer a couple of questions I have first."

Granny spoke for the brothers. "Agreed. Ask your questions."

Ben started in, "What's the date?"

"The twenty-fourth of June."

"Well, that's about right. What year is this?" Ben asked. A few eyebrows were raised.

Granny said, "1929," and waited.

Ben did some quick math and muttered, "Eighty-one years." Just saying it aloud, he felt his chest tighten in panic. His eyes blinked rapidly as his mind struggled to fight back panic, but he couldn't grasp all of it; not fully, not yet.

Granny heard him and said, "I had a feeling you might ask what year it is." He reached over to the shelf above Ben's head, and brought down a number of items; Ben's wallet, a thin steel plate, and his blue jeans. He started with the jeans. "I'm familiar with these waist overalls. Exceptional quality. But . . . what is this?" he asked, pointing to the front of the jeans.

Ben identified the item in question. "That's a zipper."

"A . . . zipper?"

"A zipper. You haven't seen one before?"

"Well, Goodrich has those rubber 'Zipper Boots,' now that you mention it, but I've never seen trousers or overalls with them before."

Ben raised his eyebrows, contemplating the stir his zipper had caused. "They're quite . . . common where I come from. They'll catch on here . . . pretty soon."

Granny nodded, and said, "I should like to see this place you come from."

Ben knit his brow, thinking, *Right now, I wouldn't mind seeing it either.* "Here, Granny. I come from here. I come from Springfield. But not from . . . now."

They fell silent. He could have heard a pin drop.

Granny, unfazed by that, opened the wallet and removed a ten-dollar bill from it, which he handed to Ben. "It's American currency, yet we're all quite sure we've never seen one like it before. I can't find a date of print on it."

Ben inspected it and handed it back to him, pointing at the date.

"Series Two-zero-zero-three?"

"Two thousand and three. That's the year it was designed, probably the year it was printed. To me that bill is seven years old."

Seven years old! 2010! Everybody in the room began talking at once. It took a few minutes for Granny to calm them down and assure them he would get answers to all their questions.

"All right. Let's move on. . . ."

Ben said, "Could I interrupt you? I'm starving, fellas. Could I maybe get something to eat?"

Robert answered, "Of course. You must be. It's been three days since we brought you back here. We managed to get a few mouthfuls of soup down you each day, but that was all."

A couple of the brothers left the room to find some food for him. They came back several minutes later not with bowls or dishes, but with two Pennzoil cans. Steam rose from the top of one can. "Here's some soup, and some water," Edward said as he offered Ben the two Pennzoil cans. "Sorry it's not more. We . . . we don't have a lot right now."

He waved off the apology, thanking Edward profusely for the generous offering of their food. He did, however, pause for a moment before putting the Pennzoil can to his lips and drinking some soup. He'd never eaten or taken a drink from an old oil can before. But the cans had obviously been used many times before. Around the shop here, the metal oil cans took the place of cups and plates, and judging by their appearance, probably even cooking pots. He remembered grimacing when looking at an old race photo of Russell Boardman, drinking water from what was clearly a Pennzoil can. Perhaps it was one of these cans right here. He could vaguely recall being barely conscious and drinking those first few mouthfuls of soup from these.

The water was cloudy.

There was no fooling himself; he was over the rainbow, and he would have to adapt if he was to get along. Gone was his easy access to his immense wealth, his influence, his Gramps's guiding hand and his Mom making sure he had what he needed. He was lying on a fold-up World War I cot in the back of some sort of airplane hangar or shop. His lower leg was shattered, and splinted with two wooden slats and some strips torn from an old blanket.

He drank the water.

Chapter Six

History was his hobby, and his forte, and he knew their history better than he knew his own, if that was at all possible. The Granville Brothers were not wealthy men. They were hard workers and did whatever they could to get by. They were thin as rails, though he knew from his research that these men were "Type A" personalities many decades before that term had ever been uttered by any psychologist. They were living in the Depression; money and food were both scarce commodities.

And here he was, lying on a cot, eating up their time and their food, at the very time when they were supposed to be making history. June 26, 1929. They had only just moved to Springfield from their former digs near Arlington. They hoped to design and build racers to compete in the Air races, hopefully the National race circuit and Bendix Races, compete for the Thompson Trophy, and to get some orders, perhaps contracts to build planes.

The field was wide open. Enterprising people just like them were developing aviation technology all over America. They did the best they could, and never complained. In light of that, he made up his mind that he wouldn't complain about cloudy water. He literally owed the Granvilles his life. He would gratefully sip any soup they offered, he would drink the water, and he wouldn't grimace. And in those next quiet moments alone, he wondered how the hell he ever arrived here, and what the hell he was going to do about it.

After his meal he felt much improved, and was able to sit up and look around. The realization of his plight had settled in, but rather than tumbling into depression, he found himself so stimulated that he could barely sit still. To be in the shop with the Granvilles at this time in their history! To know what he knew, what nobody else could know about them. To know what *they* could not know about themselves! Weeks, months, even years he'd sat mesmerized, reading everything he could find about this tight-knit family of brothers who had come to fame right there in Springfield . . . his own area. Men who, controversial in their time or not, ultimately came to be recognized as pioneers in aeronautical history.

The Granvilles filtered back in and sat down. Something big was afoot, and they needed answers. Granny started again. "You said you're from here. But we're not from here, we've only been here a few weeks. So, how can it be that you know all of us, just like that?"

"From my history books. The Granville Brothers are some of the most famous names in aviation history, from the times of the Golden Age Racers."

"Golden Age Racers? What are those?"

"The racing planes. The planes that flew—sorry—will fly—in the Bendix and Thompson Trophy races, flying across country, setting and breaking records."

The brothers looked at each other, whispers flying back and forth. That's why they were here; that was what they hoped to achieve, to be certain. Could this be a glimpse of their future? Talk about exciting stuff!

Ben continued, "The next few years and through the '30s come to be known as the *Golden Age of Air Racing*. It's the source of many important advances in America's air technology. The Granville Brothers laid some of the most solid and advanced aeronautical groundwork for their time."

A couple of the brothers scoffed; this seemed a little far-fetched. They were not in the mainstream. They had some ideas, but had yet to be in any position to be competitive. Honest, hard-working men to the last one, they couldn't picture themselves as heroes in history books. Indeed, their recent projects were a bit lackluster in that respect—too much of their time had to be spent on bringing in enough money just for rents, bills, and food to feed the clan. The Granvilles were barely out of the starting gate here in Springfield. And to be spoken of in the past tense felt a little spooky to them.

Granny was the leader precisely because he was a man of vision, and he didn't scoff. Had he not been a man of vision, the Granvilles would not have made it this far. By nineteen years of age, Granny Granville had been the youngest person ever to own and run a Chevrolet dealership, and he brought his brothers to Arlington to work the dealership with him. By the time he was twenty he was already working on planes and making advancements in the technology of almost anything he worked on. The dozen or so Biplanes that they had developed and sold were not highly competitive race machines, but the technological advances that Granny designed into them were astounding.

He alone pictured a plane in the 1920s where the pilot could release the controls in flight, swing and lock them to the other side so the person next to him could fly the plane. Granny was a mechanical and entrepreneurial genius. At the tender age of eleven he converted a Model-A truck into a combination truck / portable log sawing mill. That was how he made his first money.

Here before him was a scenario that could challenge even his belief. But Granny was never one to set limits. Not on anything, least of all his imagination. He saw everything. He heard the honesty in Ben's voice. He was no pushover; he could be as cynical as any man. So much information could not have been invented on the spur of the moment. And though not inexplicable, the young man's strange possessions were nothing short of astounding. The truth rang in Granny's ears like a church bell. Holding up his hand, he stopped the chattering amongst the brothers so he could continue questioning Ben.

He tossed the driver's license on the bed. "We know what this is. I guess we should wish you a happy birthday. So, you would be . . . ?"

"Twenty-four years old. A couple of days before I . . . came here."

He tossed a small, shiny flat rectangle onto the bed. "Tell us about this."

"That's called a credit card. That's a good one . . . okay. You, ahh, you know what a line of credit is, right? Let's imagine that I've got a line of credit at my bank. When I go out and about, I present this to make purchases with it, and the bank sends the money to the business to pay for my purchases. The money is moved electronically . . . no, wait, that's not invented yet. Picture that the money is moved from my bank account to the store by telegraph."

This brought a dozen more questions from them. What if the store doesn't have a device or a telegraph to use?

"In 2010, all stores have the devices. People who carry these cards have no need to carry much cash, although I usually carry a small amount in my wallet."

He prayed the conversation wouldn't turn to phones. He'd hate to have to explain cell phones to them. He thought briefly of his own cell phone. It wasn't here amongst these items, so it hadn't turned up. It would eventually be found in his sleeping bag, but no matter; in 1929, it was useless to him.

Granny got the discussion back on track by tossing a thin metal plate onto the bed. Ben picked it up and inspected it. The shiny plate had some dings in it, but the writing on it was still readable for the most part. It was the manufacturing plate for his Waco. "Ahhh, my Waco." Clearly stamped was the date: 1938; it would be built nine years in the future. "This biplane was mine. It was a beautiful antique aircraft. This year it was seventy-two years old, a real classic."

Murmurs ran through the group. Granny spoke up. "I sent a wire to the folks from the company that used to be Waco and told them about this. They're on their way to see it. They should be here in a couple of days. I guess the question is: what do I tell them about this?"

Ben nodded. "I'd like to talk with those folks, if you don't mind. Did you tell them the date on the plate?"

"No. I just said that their company name was on it. And the model, which their return-wire said they didn't recognize, though it's similar to their designation numbers."

"Was the radial engine anywhere to be found?"

Granny nodded. "We found it a hundred yards from the fuselage and brought it back here. Apart from some dings in the tin covers and a lot of packed-in dirt, it looks salvageable."

"That's a little good news," Ben said.

"When we're done here, the boys and I will make another run out there and recover the rest of the aircraft. Do you need anything from it?"

"There's a photo in the cockpit, or at least it was there before the crash."

"You mean this photograph?" Granny asked, and tossed Katie Lynn's photo on the bed. Ben grabbed it up with profuse thanks. *Oh, Katie Lynn. . . .*

"I've never seen a photograph like that," said Granny. "Those colors. They're so . . . bright!"

"Where I came from, this is what all photos look like. Within a few years you'll be able to get expensive color film for your cameras. It's not very good. All of the photographs of Gee Bee Racers in existence are in black and white. By 2010 the colors are perfected."

He decided to save the talk on electronics, digital graphics, computers, laptops, and everything else for later. Much later. Years later.

Chapter Seven

Long before he arrived in the past, he'd identified distinctive personalities and traits for each of the Granvilles. Watching them now, he could hardly sit still or refrain from whooping and clapping his hands with glee when they turned the air around them blue with their cussing, or displayed their amusing tendency toward irreverence.

Few, if any, of the Granvilles had graduated the eighth grade, but that was not uncommon in their day. Growing up and working on a small, hardscrabble farm in Madison, New Hampshire, life at the best of times was hard. Foul language came with the territory; they all knew their share of cusswords and did not hesitate to use them should the situation arise. Indeed, most any situation that presented itself seemed a prime opportunity to let flow a barrage. Even so, one needed but to look past those rough edges to see the genius that shone through. From an early age, with no money but lots of energy, Granny created something from nothing, or anything. There was little money, and an endless list of things that needed doing.

As a young boy, Granny built toys from bits of this and that, toys that held together so well that his brothers and their children still had them to play with many years later. Even in these rudimentary toys, the genius that was Granny Granville was already making itself known. With his Errol-Flynn looks and smile, and his engaging way with people, Granny's potential was virtually unlimited.

Robert was another story. When it came to machinery he was not recognized for any particular mechanical genius. He was actually an excellent mechanic, but as the slow and steady constant within a crazy herd of fast-moving wild men, he took his share of good-natured ribbing from the others. His 'hands-on work' was often shelved while he handled the paperwork the others avoided. From the time he arrived at Granny's Chevy dealership, Robert's unique form of genius served the business in one critical way—by taking meticulous care of the books, ordering and maintaining tools, parts, material orders, and payroll, he brought a crucial skill that kept their work on track. It was his niche, his forte. To put it quite simply, they all knew he was the best.

Edward, the dark-haired youngest brother, often worked as a gopher and odd-jobs man earlier on. But place a welding torch in his hand and he had the knack; he and the metal became one. When a really important welding job came up, it defaulted to Edward. With the skills he honed working with his brothers, Edward went farther than any of them later in life.

Perhaps the most brilliant feature the band of brothers displayed was that no matter what task arose amidst the beehive of activity that was their shop, each had a particular skill that the others never questioned. When something important came up, without so much as a word they all knew who that task would default to. Should an argument arise, it was rarely serious and quickly settled. That highlighted the awareness, dedication, and serious nature that ran through all of them, like an undercurrent, driving them as one.

More than just a thread of mechanical genius ran throughout them. There was something else between them, like a form of telepathy. Though it was strongest between Mark and Edward, they could all work together in complete silence. On the occasions he was fortunate enough to witness this, Ben watched in near-veneration. Without asking, each one would know which work they were responsible for.

Granny stepped up as the leader when it became necessary; otherwise the brothers worked with minimal supervision. If there was any doubt in Ben's mind as to just how remarkable these brothers were (there never was), it would have been erased in a single day of watching them work together.

The brothers found they liked Ben very much, and three days later he was out of bed and moving about. Thomas, Mark, and Edward, exercising some of the aforementioned mechanical genius, contrived an interesting-looking but very sturdy, comfortable, and serviceable set of crutches from some old wing spars. He was grateful; it saved him from the embarrassment of being helped out to the outhouse several times each day.

He fretted and worried that he was a burden to the Granvilles. These kind, generous men barely scratched out enough to survive, yet they shared their meager fare with him without comment or complaint, while he contributed nothing. Worse yet, he had learned that the brothers paid the doctor for his services out of their own pockets. The Depression was upon them. It was money they could scarcely afford to lose.

On the fourth day, he was returning from the outhouse when he passed a stranger alongside the shop. Their eyes met, and he looked away in shock. He knew the man, recognized him, and although the man's clothes were era-appropriate, he wore the same handsome, well-worn brown leather jacket Ben had seen him wearing before. He'd seen his grandfather talking to him on several occasions. *How could that be? That was eighty-one years in the future.* But there was no mistake. The two had always kept their heads close together, speaking in whispers.

Well, Gramps had always spoken in a whisper, and always looked unhappy that the man was there. The man rarely said anything, and always seemed to answer in as few syllables as were needed. Gramps abruptly dismissed the man as "nobody" whenever the boy asked who he was, so Ben named him "the quiet man," and without knowing it, he bestowed upon the man the same moniker Gramps had dubbed him with many years before.

He fought back his panic as he continued walking. His gut twisted into a knot, because he felt sure the man had stopped. He felt the stranger's gaze burning into him from behind. He did not turn and continued on his way, hoping and praying he might make it away from there. *Please, just let me get around the corner.*

The man spoke, "Benjamin."

He stopped short, full of dread, closed his eyes and let out a breath, and then turned clumsily with his crutches to look at the man. When their eyes met, all doubt was gone. Ben said, "It *is* you."

The quiet man looked at him, his face inscrutable. Saying nothing, he held up his hand with the back toward Ben and his ring facing Ben, as Gramps had done every day. Ben did the same and they both nodded the "secret nod," as Ben had named it.

Aw . . . Damn, he thought, dropping his hand to his side. *Who said things couldn't get any worse?*

His stomach did a flip-flop. Not good. "Over the rainbow" had just become "through the looking glass." He wasn't sure how much more of this he could handle. Surprises seemed to be the order of the day since the moment of his arrival here, and he had a bad feeling about this. Ready or not, he was pretty sure he was about to be treated to a surprise or two.

Chapter Eight

True to Ben's recollection, the quiet man wasted few words.

"We don't have much time, and we have a lot to discuss."

Ben could picture Gramps saying, "Should you meet any man wearing the same ring as yours; it will not be a chance meeting. Listen closely to whatever he has to tell you. Never take it off, for any reason. And remember all I have said here today."

He closed his eyes, and shook his head slightly, recalling in dismay how he had chuckled at Gramps's theatrics the day he received his ring. He looked again at the quiet man, took a deep breath, and just as he did the day he first was given the ring, he nodded and said, "I understand." He couldn't even venture a guess as to what was coming.

"I know you have a lot of questions, Ben. I can't give you many answers. I have some specific information I must provide you with, and then I have to go."

"Go? Go where? Back home to my time? You *are* from my time, aren't you? You're the man I've seen with Gramps."

"I can't answer that. Please, listen closely to me, and believe me when I tell you that we are both here for a good reason. You *could* make a real difference. You could change the *world*. The lives of millions of people depend on what you do with what you know. Do you think that's a real difference?"

Ben took another big breath and released it all at once. He nodded. "Yes, I do, and I'm listening." *Oh, Gramps, you knew. The ring. The*

31

damned ring. You knew the whole time! He looked at the ring. Like Gramps's ring, the entire top was a gold rectangle. An intricately carved set of platinum wings stood in relief above the rectangle. For years he'd asked if he could have one. Gramps never wanted to give him one, so he was surprised to receive this ring on his eighteenth birthday. He used to think it was quite beautiful.

He wondered if he would still think so after today.

Perhaps the quiet man could read his thoughts. Perhaps he spotted Ben looking at the ring. Whichever it was, he addressed what Ben must be feeling right now. "Don't blame your Grandfather. This is bigger than him, than you, than us all. He hated to do this, and he wasn't permitted to tell you about this. There's a reason for that. Anything he said you would find might not have been true when you arrived. Time is a flexible, changeable thing; nothing is set in stone. Throw a pebble in a pond; and watch the ripples it creates. The ripples act much the same way time does; moving outward from that point in all directions. One small thing changes and the effects are exponential as time ripples outward from that point, touching everything. Are you with me so far?"

Right. Flexible. Changeable. Pebble in a pond. Ripples from the pebble. Exponential effects. No problem. He was listening so intently that on a scale of one to ten, his focus was about a seventy-two. Tension gnawed at him. He nodded and said, "Every word. You wear the ring. I know I'm to listen closely to you."

The quiet man nodded at the deference his ring commanded, and continued. "You're here to correct historical errors. You're the pebble, Ben. The future depends on what you manage to do with what you know. What you already know is the reason that I can't tell you anything about what will happen. You see, every move you make has the potential to change the future. Armed with your knowledge of history, you have the potential to effect profound change. And the potential to cause terrible tragedies through those same actions or inactions."

"What historical errors? And why me? I'm just a guy from Massachusetts. I'm nothing special."

"No, Ben. You're very special. Living matter passing through a temporal rift is torn apart at a sub-molecular level. Your unique makeup allowed you to be put back together in the proper order again. You came through, and your DNA reassembled within a few seconds. Once you're 'solid' again, you're susceptible to things like . . . wings falling on you," he said, and knitted his brow. "That was . . . unexpected."

Ben thought about that for a few moments, then asked the quiet man something he wanted to know above all else. "There's one thing I need to know. After we're done with this, I can travel back home, right?"

The quiet man said, "I think you know that I can't answer that."

Ben grew angry. "What do you mean you can't answer that? YOU get to leave. I'm eighty-one years from my own time, my life, my girl, and my family. You're laying all this cryptic "temporal rift and correcting historical errors and pebbles in a pond" stuff in my lap. I'm supposed to do something with all of this, and oh-by-the-way, I have no God-damned idea what it is I'm supposed to do with it or HOW. And you can't answer that for me?" He was waving his crutches around angrily now, thinking of using them to do something he'd probably be sorry for. "Well, the hell with YOU, quiet man! Fix your *own* time problems. I want to go back, and I want to go back *now.*" His eyes flashed with anger.

The man looked at him, his face still unreadable. He didn't move at all. When he spoke, his tone made it clear his patience was ebbing. "You forgot to *listen.* I'm not some waiter who brought you an undercooked steak. I'm not in control of this. I'm here to give you what help I can, so stop wasting what little time we have left. This can't be undone. It's a one-way trip, Ben. You can't go back now. The rest of your lifetime will be spent in this time."

Ben's challenging tone turned frantic. "Who gets to decide that for me? Why don't I have any say in the matter? You said I was built for it. Please, just send me back. Please." His voice shook on the last word.

"You're built for one trip. *One way.* You couldn't hold up to a repeat trip. If you were sent back now, you'd arrive as a small pile of sand."

His anger deflated, his heart sank. Here forever. . . . *Oh, God.* He was scared, shaking, fighting his burgeoning desperation.

"Mom and Gramps . . . they're going to be frantic. My Mom has lost so much in her life. She lost my Dad when his fighter went down in Iraq; his body was never recovered. She went through YEARS of waiting to hear something. You can't do this to her. She won't be able to handle losing us both. This will break her heart!"

For a moment, the quiet man didn't move; he didn't look like he was going to say anything at all. Then he said, "If that *does* happen, it won't happen for eighty years. Eighty years, you understand that, don't you? Anything you experienced in the future, anything you loved, hated, anything you treasured or despised . . . any of it, all of it has the potential to happen, or NOT to happen."

The man continued, for the first time with a sense of urgency in his voice. "Ben, I have to go now. Please remember these things I've told you. Your grandfather prepared you for this in the only ways he could. You *have* the knowledge to succeed. Remember that NOTHING in the future is set in stone. The knowledge you have is more powerful than anything on this earth," then he said with finality, "I have to go now." With that, he wheeled and walked off, and seconds later rounded the corner.

Ben hollered, "Hey! Wait!" and hobbled after him. "Does my Gramps know I'm here? What's your name . . . ?" He turned the corner and stopped, confused. The quiet man was nowhere to be seen. He stared at the empty field. The grass, tall and green in late June, flowed like waves in the summer breezes as butterflies fluttered lightly from flower to flower. Nothing else moved out there but a dust eddy.

Granny and the brothers came up behind him. In the natural course of protecting a family member, they surrounded him. Each one touched him in some way—arm against arm, hand on shoulder. They all looked for the quiet man. They'd seen him, heard him, heard everything he'd said. He should have been there, within sight. There was nowhere he could have disappeared to. Yet he'd vanished just the same.

Granny turned and spoke to him. "Forgive us for eavesdropping, Ben. For what it's worth, we'll never question your word again. Is there anything we can do?"

Through the swirling morass of thoughts and heartbreak, he responded, and was surprised when his answer made sense. "Yeah. You can build the R-2 *first.*"

He turned and hobbled away, leaving his new brothers baffled in his wake.

Together, Mark and Edward asked, "What's an R-2?"

Chapter Nine

Vexed by his circumstances, he sat in his room in the back of the shop, trying to gather his thoughts, to make real his surroundings and situation. He took in the details of his humble new abode. The little room was originally a broom closet, but it was all the brothers could offer him. They were out front talking about this, and like him, they tried to make sense of it all.

After a while, Granny came back to see if he felt up to discussing the situation with them. The way they saw it, Ben needed them. Just as importantly, Granny had a feeling they needed him, though exactly why wasn't clear . . . yet. But they all liked him. They liked him a lot. For now that would have to do; they would take the rest as it came.

Ben hobbled out through the workshop, into the shop area, and sat with them, still glum. Granny wanted to address some of what they had overheard.

"What was all that, about the knowledge he said you have?" Granny asked, curious as to what Ben might know. They were all curious.

"I've been thinking about the things this guy said. He said my Grandfather prepared me for this, but I don't know what he did to prepare me."

"What's the deal with the matching rings?"

"I don't even know *that*. When Gramps gave me this ring, he told me never to remove it, not for any reason. I thought he was just being dramatic."

"What historical errors? And how are *you* supposed to repair them?" Granny asked.

Robert, accurate and precise as usual, interrupted, "Not repair, he used the word *correct.*"

"Ahh, yes, thanks. *Correct* the historical errors. How does he expect you to do that?"

Ben shrugged and said, "I don't have a clue. I can only guess. To correct an historical error, wouldn't one have to go back in time and change the circumstances? I'd have thought that going back in time would be the hardest part, but somehow I managed it . . . or somebody managed it for me. I'm here, so . . . changing the circumstances comes next, I guess."

Granny nodded his head in agreement, and pursued the same train of thought. "How is it you have been prepared for doing this? Are you a master historian?"

Ben shook his head. "Hardly. Are you kidding? I just finished college, I'm an Aeronautical Engineer." He began to wonder what he might know. Where he might have become an historian . . . of sorts.

He recalled the endless pop-quizzes his Gramps gave him on history. He never let up until the boy knew the historical details relevant to any aspect of this era. Gramps often referred to something that *his* Gramps loved to say, "Time travel is the realm of angels and their hourglasses." All the years, all the time and trouble he went through so Ben would be prepared when he arrived in this era; now it all made sense. It wasn't fun and games; it never had been.

"Wait. Yes, I am . . . well, sort of. I'm kind of an expert in the history of the Granvilles and their Gee Bee Racers, and other aeronautical history. Also, World War II, and some other subjects." He continued to ponder. *Could it be that simple? I take what I know and I change the world for the better?*

The switch was thrown, and on came the light in his head. He looked at them and said, "Pop quizzes. My grandfather drilled me on World War II . . . drilled me over and over until I knew details nobody else even cared about. He was always giving me pop-quizzes on the history of warbirds, about Robert working on design prototypes that ended up in the hands of the Japanese. The Zero was the plane that in the end became their main fighter aircraft, which they used against us at Pearl Harbor. Why they attacked Pearl, and how we recovered. And all about nukes . . . how we developed nukes and finally won the war. I gave a physics presentation on nukes in college."

Granny spoke up, "Whoa, whoa. World War II? Now, that's an important detail, Benjamin."

Robert chimed in too, "I helped design the . . . Zero? Was it a good plane?"

"You *may* have helped design it, yes. Or just as likely, parts of your design may have been incorporated into its design. The Zero's design focused on using minimal materials. It reflected their situation. As an island country, Japan had material shortages."

Thomas had a question. "Wait . . . Japan is going to attack us? How did they get the jump on us?"

Mark and Edward asked together, "What are nukes?"

Ben's head was spinning. *Oh, how could I have been so thick!* He realized that all of those quizzes, all of that information, it meant something, it mattered, it could change history dramatically if even a few of those things changed. Sixty-one million people died as a result of World War II. Adrenaline began pumping as he realized that America . . . no, not just America, the whole *world* . . . could have a chance at a do-over.

"I know why I'm here!" he blurted out. "I can't believe it. It's been here in my head all along. I knew it without knowing it. Remember when I said that you needed to make the R-2 first? I was talking about a series of racers that the Granville Brothers—you guys—built and raced."

His mind raced as he continued on. "Stay with me, okay? Next year . . . 1930 . . . the US, Britain, and Japan will sign an arms reduction agreement. The United States will fall behind in the development of fighter aircraft. Japan will *not* abide by it. They'll build an entire navy and air attack force, and then claim they have the 'Divine right' and go out and try to take over all of Indochina to expand their Colonial Empire. On December 7, 1941, the Japanese will attack our Pacific Fleet at Pearl Harbor, Hawaii. Because of an unfortunate series of events and mistakes we will have very little with which to stop them. It's one of the most devastating attacks in the history of our country."

Granny asked, "But what does this have to do with us?"

37

"Everything! The air races provided advanced airplane technology that the US military failed to recognize, technology that Japan may have acquired and used in their fighter aircraft. We need to keep your organization from making the same mistakes you made.

"I don't believe any of this is random. The way I see it, the Granvilles are the keystone to changing history for the better. If they weren't, why would I be dropped in their laps? It makes sense, doesn't it?"

He grew excited. He knew what he needed to do, if not exactly how he planned to accomplish it. "Okay, listen up, guys. We have a lot of ground to cover here and you're going to need to listen to me. I'm going to tell you a story, and you won't like most of it. Just remember that everything I'm about to tell you is only a possible future. We can change that future and make it better and brighter. History books are full of mistakes that ultimately help people avoid those same mistakes. For some reason, the Granville Brothers—my heroes—are getting a chance to do it differently this time. We're going to make sure you do."

Chapter Ten

"First, Howell Miller." He held up two fingers on each hand in quotations. "Howell 'Pete' Miller, is he working on your plane designs yet?"

Granny shook his head. "I don't know who that is."

"*Yet*. You don't know who that is *yet*. Historically, he started working with you starting in 1932, after Bob Hall leaves, so let's catch up. He lives in New Hampshire, I think."

"Who is Bob Hall?" Granny inquired, and Ben stopped short, caught off balance. He knew that Bob Hall should be here right now, designing the 'Z'. Obviously, there was already a shift from the history he knew. *How did that happen? This is tricky stuff. I'm not going to be able to take anything for granted.*

His arrival alone could have profoundly affected history. The "pebble and pond" parallel was more than applicable to the situation. Anything that happens is a pebble dropping into the water. The ripples flowing outward affect other things in ways nobody can predict. Ripples from other pebbles could change the course of any other ripple. The realization that Bob Hall was not in the picture was testimony to that. Clearly, he was not going to be able to do this alone. Moreover, his simple presence had so far seemed to change their course for the worse, not the better. Would it be that way with everything?

He had paused for too long; they'd grown silent waiting for him. He started again, "Bob Hall is an aircraft designer that worked with you for a while, but in the end he left and was replaced by Howell 'Pete' Miller. Pete helped you to make some important advances in your planes. He's obviously not with you yet, so let's skip that chapter and move on." Ben didn't want to alarm them with an unexpected historical change. Not yet, anyway.

"Next. Jimmy Doolittle. Aeronautical engineer and the finest pilot around. We need to find him. We'll need him as a pilot. You built fast, cutting-edge Gee Bee racers, and the pilots you found climbed into them, but some were not capable enough. Several killed themselves, others wrecked your racers, but the effect was cumulative. One-by-one the crashes wrecked your future.

"Jimmy Doolittle was a great pilot, but the Gee Bees had already been labeled killer planes. You lost your funding and you went under. Your luck could have been better all around."

The normally ebullient, oft-cussing and unstoppable crew fell uncharacteristically silent and still. *Killer planes? Lost our funding and went under? Wrecked future?*

Out in the front office the gals and guys had learned bits and pieces of Ben's story, and before long they had migrated in, and they too were listening to him. Ben moved ahead with his story, knowing full well that human nature would not allow the story to remain within these walls. By nightfall, although it might only be whispered, it *would* be repeated somewhere, to somebody.

Another pebble would drop, and a new ripple would form in the pond of time.

Chapter Eleven

Ben continued. "Let's start at the beginning, shall we? Bob Hall helped you design and build the Gee Bee Z. The Z most everybody assumes stood for Zantford."

Granny took the pipe from his mouth and grinned his Errol-Flynn grin. He liked that.

Ben went on, "You developed a fondness for the Pratt & Whitney radial engines because of their power and durability. For these times, it's a great choice. Pratt & Whitney radials will be used in almost anything of importance for the next fifteen to twenty years. You use them in most of your designs. But the radials have a problem. Their size and shape creates a blunt nose. On the Z, a cowl is created that curls around the edges of the radial to streamline the engine somewhat, but it's still a fairly blunt-nosed creation. It can't be *too* closed in because the radials need a lot of air for cooling. Add to that the stubby body, and the Z is a little touchy."

Granny raised an eyebrow. "Touchy?"

Ben nodded. "It's about choices. When designing these planes, you had engineers, and you had pilots. The engineers approached it from the perspective that the plane should have a little bit more wing, be a little longer in the body. The pilots would have less to contend with because the plane would compensate for more; it's fundamentally safer. But the added features and area create a touch more drag, the extra weight also

41

slows the aircraft down. The pilots figured they could handle whatever comes; and from their perspective they'd rather have a much faster aircraft to win the races. When the final choices were made, the pilots won out. What had not been factored in was the skill of the designers—that would be you, Granny—and Pete Miller. The advanced designs you create, and the balls-to-the-wall speeds at which these planes would fly were beyond the skills of the pilots."

A few smiles and chuckles went through the group. They liked hearing that they could create that kind of plane. That's why they were here, after all. Granny smiled too, but now that it had been said, he couldn't pry the label "killer planes" from his mind. "Go on, Ben."

"These pilots were all good pilots, but that wasn't enough. There was no room for error, and just a moment of inattention or the smallest incident meant mortal danger. And you folks hadn't factored that in yet. Or more to the point, you'd factored that out when the pilots' preferences won out. Now, you did have an excellent first pilot, Lowell Bayles."

Thomas smiled. "Lowell! He's an excellent pilot. We've been thinking about approaching him."

Granny nodded. "Lowell is practically one of us. He's one of my best friends."

"Well, you could do worse, I can tell you that much. You developed the number four, 'City of Springfield, Gee Bee Z' and it was flown by both Bob Hall and Lowell Bayles to wins wherever she was run. Both were excellent pilots and had the right touch for the racer. The investors were pleased at the excellent returns on their investments. Springfield threw parades, testimonial dinners, and the Granvilles did fly-overs. The Granvilles were the toast of Springfield and soon Lowell was considered a national hero.

"Early in December of 1931, Lowell was trying for another speed record in the Z. He was diving to increase speed, and as he entered the course the Z suddenly pitched up. Nobody knows for sure what caused it, but at the sudden pitch-up the right wing folded and simply snapped off. The plane rolled into the ground, creating a spectacular fireball and killing Lowell instantly. They believe the gas cap came loose and went through the windscreen."

The whole room was silent, not a sound was made for nearly a minute. Their dear friend Lowell Bayles—practically one of the family—was going to die in *their* racer.

"I guess this is a good time for a break," Ben said.

Granny, aghast at the prospect of his friend's death, removed his pipe from his mouth, dazed. Twice he opened his mouth and started to say something. Twice he couldn't speak. Overwhelmed, he remained silent.

Chapter Twelve

After about a half-hour, the story continued. "You were traumatized by Lowell's death. There was some speculation about Bob Hall, who had designed the Z with a laminated wooden wing strut. Would it have saved Lowell if the wing had been braced to withstand more Gs? Who could know? Probably not. He was hit hard enough to have his goggles torn off and flung from the aircraft, while introducing wind at nearly three hundred miles per hour through a smashed or missing windscreen. There's just no way to know how bad that was or if Lowell could have recovered in time to avoid the crash."

"Since nobody knew for certain why the Z crashed, orders for aircraft built by the Granvilles virtually ceased. Things were tough. Bob Hall left the organization to start his own aircraft building concern across the river. That left you, Granny, as the chief engineer. Russell Boardman then bought fifty-one percent of the organization when he placed orders with you for two winning racers. You had ideas, Granny, but you also needed another engineer, so in the spring of 1932 you were fortunate to find and hire Howell W. Miller, or as you all knew him, 'Pete' Miller. Pete and Granny worked closely together and designed two purpose-built racers called the R-1 and R-2, one designed explicitly for pylon pacing, one designed just for cross-country races. They started winning races everywhere they went."

"Wait! That's IT?"

"What did they look like?"

"What did the R stand for?" one of them hollered out.

Robert stood up and said, "It was MY turn! It stands for *Bob!*"

Mark and Edward found that hilarious and almost fell off of their chairs, whooping with laughter.

"Okay, Okay, settle down. . . ." Ben said, smiling. "The R stood for racer. Sorry, Robert. What did they look like? Stubby. Round. Fat. Granny and Pete Miller had followed Granny's hunch and proved the teardrop shape to be the most Aerodynamic shape in nature."

"Aero . . . what?" Somebody asked.

"Aerodynamic. It means the air flows as unimpeded as possible over this shape. Very little drag."

"AERO-DYNAMIC!" Granny exclaimed, trying out the new word. "Is it me? Or is that a great word to describe our racers?"

Aerodynamic! The brothers and office staff tried out the word on their tongues. It had a nice feel to it. Amidst murmurs of approval, a new and exciting word was born to them. Nothing would ever be the same again.

"Aerodynamic or not, if the Z was equipped with balls-to-the-wall power—excuse me, ladies from the office—then the R-racers were twice as much so."

"The aircraft were designed and built for one purpose: racing. They demanded respect and total concentration from their pilots. Jimmy Doolittle equated flying your R-1 to 'Balancing a pencil by its point on the tip of your finger, and then just keeping it there the whole time you're flying.'"

Murmurs abounded as they discussed what these planes must have been like. He continued. "There's too much story there for one sitting, so let me cut to the chase. Russell Boardman crashed a racer and died during a bad takeoff, and several other pilots busted up or crashed the various aircraft, but the ending is the important part. Your funding was pulled and your company went onto the auction block. You brothers ended up scattering to the four winds and the Gee Bees became unrealized dreams. They briefly sparked America's imagination . . . then faded into obscurity."

At the end of the meeting, they all agreed on one thing. If ever there was a future with historical errors that needed "correcting," the Granvilles' history—which loomed now as their bleak future—seemed the perfect place to start.

Chapter Thirteen

As the hangar area emptied, one young woman remained in her chair. When she finally stood up, Ben saw she was about his age, and using crutches. She tried to navigate through all the chairs scattered by the departing staff. Ben grabbed his crutches and hobbled over, using the sturdy old spar pieces to push chairs aside to give her safe passage.

She looked up and saw him using his crutches as a plow to clear the way for her, and she smiled. Her smile set off her red hair, and her red hair set off her pretty blue dress. She had a beautiful smile. One tooth was not quite perfectly aligned with the others, but if anything it added to her beauty. Ben knew every curve of her face, and stopped short, breathless. She was identical. Perhaps an inch shorter. Her shape was slightly different, her chest was somewhat larger. But those eyes! He knew those eyes, a green so vivid that it drew his gaze and his heart like a magnet. He knew Katie Lynn would not be born for sixty-something years, yet here she was. This woman was her twin. She stopped at his long gaze, curious about his expression. "Benjamin, are you all right?"

He wrenched himself from his thoughts. "Huh? Oh, yes, yes. I'm Ben Ryan." Then he thought, *Well aren't you smooth! She already knows your name; she works here, remember? And oh, yeah, she just sat and listened to you talk for the past half-hour!* His face reddened.

But if she had noticed, she didn't let on. *Besides, oh my, he is handsome!*

"Laney," she said, "Laney Perkins, short for Elaine. I believe you've already met my father, Doc Perkins?" She held out her hand in a 1929 version of a lady's introductory handshake, arm offered and extended slightly up, palm down. He thought for a second that perhaps he should kiss her hand. For all of his knowledge of history, he was woefully unprepared for this. Unsure of exactly what to do, he reached out and took her hand, gave it a bit of a shake and bowed a little, still gazing into her eyes.

Red-faced, he thought, *I feel like an idiot! What the hell am I supposed to do now?*

Laney realized he was unsure of himself, but she sensed his keen interest in her. So she did what a lady does best; she complimented him. "Why, Benjamin, what a wonderful introduction! The ladies of your time are so lucky to have such attention paid to them!"

She was lying and he knew it; even so, it helped him to relax a little, and he found his tongue. "You're very kind. I suppose you can tell I'm out of my element here. I don't know how men and women interact—now . . . in this time." His breath exploded from him in frustration, and, exasperated with himself, he shook his head and shifted his gaze out the window. She could sense his frustration, and made light of it.

"You're doing just fine, Ben . . . may I call you Ben?"

"Oh, I prefer it. When somebody calls me Benjamin, I get that feeling that I'm about to be called into the kitchen and straightened out." They both laughed at that. "I'm afraid that I'm going to be a social klutz for some time. I know planes, and I know the Granvilles, but I know very little of 'polite society' in this time."

"A . . . klutz? What is that?"

"Oh, I'm sorry. It's German—in America it's slang for 'inept' or 'fool.' You'll start to hear it more in about . . . oh, fifteen, twenty years."

"I like it. It's a good word. It sounds right. Maybe I'll start using it."

He relaxed a little more. "Laney. That's a pretty name. If you don't mind me asking, how did you earn your crutches? I think you probably know how I got mine."

"I do. You must have been petrified, I don't know what I would have done, I can scarcely imagine it. What was it like?"

"I've thought about it a lot, and there was nothing I could do but

50

ride it out. According to that man who came to talk to me, the storm did something to me. It made me less than solid for a few moments, then left me flat on the ground, unhurt. Once I became solid again the wing fell on me; I think the edge hit my leg first. That was a bit of bad luck. But, let's not forget, I asked you about how you earned yours."

Laney knitted her brows in frustration. She'd turned the conversation back around to him, but the diversion had failed. So, she fessed up. "I . . . I fell off a horse."

"Oh, you own horses? You ride?" It was an innocent question; and he was genuinely interested in both her and her story. He had no idea he was cornering her.

She felt her face redden with embarrassment. She wasn't getting around it. "No, I was riding a horse outside of town a ways and it threw me. I hit the fence on the way down and broke my leg."

Ben smiled, trying to lighten the moment. "Well, thank goodness for that!"

"For what? Thank goodness that I broke my leg? What do you mean by that?" Suddenly she wasn't sure she liked the way this Ben Ryan fellow thought. And she was in no mood for any sort of humor now, anyway. She thought, *How could he think that breaking my leg was a good thing? That was a rather mean-spirited statement.*

He delivered some dry New England humor. "Well, if the horse had broken its leg, we would've had to shoot the poor thing now, wouldn't we?" He clearly was trying to hold back a smile. His eyes were laughing.

She lashed out at him, so angry she never met the twinkling blue eyes that would have disarmed her. "Benjamin Ryan, you're a very strange man indeed, to think this is funny. This is a terrible thing for me to endure. By the time this plaster-cast comes off, the snow will be very nearly ready to fall again!"

"I'm sorry, Laney. I . . ."

Furious as she spat out the last few words of her tirade, she turned and hobbled away as fast as her crutches would take her, leaving a bewildered young man in her wake.

It was bad enough that she had to work every day at this job her father had forced her to take. It was worse yet that she had to do so in this massive leg cast. To be teased about it by some strange man she just met, that pushed her beyond the limits of her already sorely-tested tolerance; even if he was breathtakingly handsome, and even if it *did* make her heart beat wildly and her stomach flutter like butterflies when she looked into his blue eyes.

As much as Laney Perkins looked like Katie Lynn, her behavior was the exact opposite in almost every important way. Doc Perkins was not rich, but he was an important, well-respected man in the Springfield area, and Laney had been raised as a privileged girl, with few limits placed upon her. She'd never been away from home. Working in these dingy offices depressed her; she felt it was beneath her. Doc wouldn't budge on that point, though. She was a young, naturally-beautiful woman of substance, and many men had come to call on her in the hopes of courting her. To the last man, her sharp tongue and bad temper had driven them away by the end of their second call.

As Doc's lovely daughter seemed destined by her own temperament to become an old maid, he decided she would need to be able to earn a living, as a simple matter of practicality. Resigned to her plight, he struck a deal with Granny Granville to get her the office job.

Though she had been schooled in the art of being a lady, getting her to wear a dress was near-impossible. During her school years, every day without fail, as soon as she returned home from school the dresses came off. She reverted to tomboy and disappeared to goodness-knows-where. Doc did his best, but he had patients to attend to. Mrs. Perkins tried to gain some control over the willful young woman, but couldn't handle her. She was a wild one; always slipping out and getting into some sort of trouble.

Just a month or so ago she'd gone and tried riding that horse over at the Woodman farm. She knew full well that nobody was allowed to ride it. As one might have expected, it bucked and threw her right over the fence, and she broke her leg. It was a miracle she wasn't killed. Thank goodness her father was the town doctor.

What Mrs. Perkins didn't know was that it may have been Laney's idea to ride the horse, but in order for her to find the farm and mount the massive, unwilling beast she'd had a little help from the same two young men who had helped her home again after her fall. Fortunately for Mark and Edward, Mrs. Perkins wasn't much for puzzles. Had she spent any time thinking about it, she might have noticed a pattern in the girl's recent choice of companions. It wasn't that the boys were looking for trouble, or any sort of bad influence upon Laney. Like her, they were smart, and if they couldn't find enough to keep their minds occupied, they grew bored. As a result, all three often found themselves wandering in the same direction.

Laney was furious. Did this Ben Ryan think that just because he was handsome he could get away with ridiculing her? It wasn't HER fault that she'd ended up in a cast. Well, maybe it was her fault a *little*. Of *course* she regretted doing what she did to get the broken leg. She'd certainly learned her lesson, and learned it well. It wouldn't happen again. Next time, she was going to pick a better horse, and that was the end of it.

As for Ben Ryan, he'd better stay clear of her or . . . or she'd give him a real piece of her mind. She'd crutched her way nearly all the way across town, simply *livid* over that smug, smirking, irritating man. Furious over the situation, she'd hobbled straight out of work early and without her purse, hadn't called home for her ride, and by the time she hobbled up the steps to her house, her armpits, hands, and good foot were sore and blistered.

But not nearly as blistered as her opinion of Ben Ryan.

Chapter Fourteen

Soon after Laney stormed out, the folks from Advance Aircraft Company showed up to inspect the UMF remains. Ed Weaver, the lead man and owner, inspected the biplane. "This isn't one of ours. It isn't anything we manufactured. But a number of these assemblies look identical to parts we presently manufacture. I can't see how they got their hands on this volume of them without my knowledge."

Advance Aircraft had formerly been called Waco, which stood for the Weaver Aircraft Company. But they hadn't built it; he was certain of that. He was intrigued, and it showed.

As predicted, Ed asked Ben if he would consider selling the wreck to them for "research." They made a more than reasonable offer and Ben accepted, folding up the money and pocketing it. As they prepared to leave with the wreck, he took Ed aside for a few minutes and spoke in whispers with him. He took something out of his wallet and handed it to Ed, who looked amazed. Then he removed something from his pocket and handed it to the man. They spoke in quiet, terse whispers for some minutes. Before they turned away from each other, they held their index fingers up to their lips to indicate "silence," and both nodded. Ben shook his hand. Whether these folks had recognized his biplane as theirs or not, they would change their name back to the Waco Aircraft Company that year, and the first Waco UMF would roll off the line the next year, right on schedule.

The ball was rolling. Like it or not, the world was one big pond; therefore Ben planned to become one big pebble. And he had an inkling of how he might go about it.

He walked inside and handed Granny the money; it was more than enough to cover the doctor, the meals, and the lodging. The others were quietly talking as they digested their history lesson.

Ben called them together again. "I want to say again that I wouldn't have revealed all of this dismal history to you unless I believed that we could work together to change all of it for the better. We're armed with the knowledge of history's mistakes. We don't have to make those mistakes again."

That helped to relieve some of the stress. Granny dismissed the crew for the day, and after the office staff left for home, he called the brothers over.

"Tonight, we eat!" he exclaimed, holding up the money, and the mood lightened almost immediately. Nothing helped to fade troubles away like a full stomach!

Chapter Fifteen

A busy and exciting month followed. They found Howell W. "Pete" Miller; he was available and excited to be a part of their new enterprise. Pete sketched and drafted as Ben gave him the crash course on the costly lessons that Pete and Granny had learned during the last history of the Gee Bees. The airframe incorporated Granny's influence and eighty years of future aeronautical knowledge. To Ben, the racer had a look reminiscent of their 'first' Gee Bee racers from certain angles, from others it looked nothing like them. To Granny and Pete, it was all new.

Ben was excited that, true to history, the first racer off the drawing board was a Gee Bee Z. But this time with a twist; the new Gee Bee would be named the Gee Bee ZR-2 racer. Granny, Pete, and the brothers, in deference to their history, all felt the racer's name should be a fitting tribute to their Z, R-1, R-2, and R-1/R-2 racers, even the QED. Those racers would never be realized in this timeline. Though they all became obsolete the day Ben and his Waco fell from the sky, their spirit and the lessons learned from each of those racers would be very real and tangible building blocks in making the ZR-2 into a bit of each, but the best of them all.

Granny, Pete, and Robert sat in conference with Ben. Ben took out his notes. "We have several subjects to address today. When the original Z was built, many of the parts were given to you by the manufacturers.

As a result, you didn't have a lot of cost into the plane, and you had great results. Our ZR-2 racer is much more advanced, so we can't use many of those items. We'll require more financial backing. How are we doing with that?"

"Funny you should ask. Remember that Boardman fellow you talked about? He dropped by and flew my Senior Sportster. He wants to invest with us, and order two racers from us."

"Don't tell me. He took off, and after he got into the air he pulled a loop?"

"Yes he did, how'd you know? I was a little perturbed, I don't mind saying. The Senior wasn't damaged. If it gets us those orders I guess I can get over it."

"Granny, we should have talked about this before. I know Russell Boardman has the money, and he's a good pilot. But we need to look to the future. We need to avoid situations that hurt you before. We're trying to change your luck here, to keep it all good. In August of 1932 he wrecked himself and your Model E pulling a loop right after takeoff, which, by the way, is one of his trademark moves. It landed him in the hospital through the whole racing season and you had to find replacement pilots at the races. That cost you.

"The next year, when he was angry, he yanked a fuel-heavy racer off the ground too early. It stalled, flipped, and crashed upside-down next to the runway. He didn't make it out alive. The federal aviation inspectors descended on you and grounded all your aircraft . . . they even grounded the personal plane you flew down there in."

As Granny processed all that, his face fell. In this economy, it would hurt to lose an investor. Conversely, he didn't relish the thought of the Federal inspectors descending upon them with the sole intention of shutting them down.

Ben said, "I know he has money, but it's crucial that we avoid anything bad in your history which we know could possibly occur again. We need to change other things around if we can't. If nothing else, leave him as a last resort."

Pete spoke up, "But you said he's a good pilot."

"He's an excellent pilot. When he's paying attention. When he's angry or distracted, he's got a history of having issues, or . . . he *will* have a history of it . . . you get what I'm saying. It's my own opinion, but I feel he's a loose cannon. Think of it as us saving his life. I can't force you to change your minds, and I know these racers are much more advanced. I'll leave the decision up to you."

Granny looked at Pete, then back to Ben. "We'll find another way to get our funding, Ben." He sighed. "It sounded attractive, but I felt it was reckless of him to pull that loop in the Senior. And I don't have to tell you, my Model Y is my favorite. At the very least, I feel he should have asked first. I know you have your eye on our future, Ben."

"What about Lowell Bayles?" Pete asked.

Ben nodded in approval, adding, "Absolutely. He's an excellent pilot. And I've got a feeling he'll be willing to pay at least five hundred dollars to be involved in the organization as the pilot of one of our new racers. Call it a hunch." A grin spread across his face.

Pete asked, "But didn't he die flying the Z?"

"Yes, he did. But the Z failed him; he didn't fail the Z. His piloting of the Z was nothing short of superb. One of the first things we did on this design was recess the gas cap and make sure it's secured, right? And this wing design will handle six times as much stress as the original Z wing, and will weigh just a little more than half as much. He'll be safe. Granny trusts Lowell, and to me that's a big deal."

Pete said, "Then I say yes; I'm okay with Lowell. I've heard only good things about him."

"Then Lowell is in," Granny said with a smile. He looked forward to telling Lowell himself.

"Perfect. So we have a full-time pilot for one of the racers if Lowell accepts. You could check with Bob Hall too, he was very good. I've had an idea about potential funding. I'd like to try to find my great-great-grandfather. Maybe he'd be willing to invest with us."

Pete chuckled, and said, "I don't suppose you realize how strange that sounds, do you?"

"Actually, I do. I've been trying to figure out how to get around the issue that we both have exactly the same name, without letting the cat out of the bag."

Granny did a wide-eyed Ben imitation. "Hello, sir, I'm your great-great-grandson, and we have the same name. I've come back in time and was wondering; would you like to invest some money in this racing-plane business I'm involved in?"

Ben winced, and Pete laughed.

"Yeah, should be *real* easy!" Granny said, shaking his head. "Good luck with that."

Ben shrugged and said, "Well, the worst he can say is no. But first I have to find him, and that's a detail I never knew. I already checked around Springfield; he's not here. Where the Ryan estate was . . . er . . . will be, it's still just hills, woods, and fields. He could be anywhere. I'll let you know how that goes. Any word on Jimmy Doolittle yet?"

Granny reached into his pocket; the look on his face said he had some bad news. "He answered you. I hate to bring you news like this. Here, you'll want to read it for yourself."

Ben sighed and thought, *Boy, this doesn't get any easier, does it?* He read the telegram.

Chapter Sixteen

Jimmy Doolittle was already famous for his exploits, breaking transcontinental flight records. Under Colonel Billy Mitchell, he had been a member of the too-successful Bomber-versus-Battleship test team. Like his boss, he was a staunch advocate for the development of American air superiority. Mitchell had already ticked off the wrong people when his bomber-versus battleship tests sunk every naval vessel they were put up against. His comments that he viewed their refusal to develop air superiority as "tantamount to treason" brought his superiors down upon him with a vengeance. Mitchell took full responsibility for his actions and statements at the subsequent court-martial. That's not saying that his beliefs ever wavered.

The members of his team were for the most part unaffected. But the tone had been set, and the message was clear. Those foolish enough to pursue air superiority literally risked their military careers. America's development of military air technology fell stagnant.

Jimmy Doolittle was a man small in stature. From a young age growing up in Alaska, 'scrappy' was the word most often used to describe him. Under the present military leaders he'd learned that 'scrappy' wouldn't facilitate the pursuit of air superiority. He maintained a quiet advocacy from behind the scenes, and pursued an advance in air technology in the only way he could; he attended the new Army program at MIT and received his Doctorate degree in Aeronautical Engineering in 1925.

Something of a genius as well as a patriot, Jimmy saw everything there was to see, and he always saw more than others did. His genius was his open mind, his broad vision for the future of aviation. In the 1920s he was already aware of something that few others would recognize for another four decades. Inspired civilians could—and would—advance technology faster than the military could ever dream of doing.

All over America, air racing had captured America's imagination. The Thompson Trophy races already drew huge crowds to see the next best, fastest racers of the day. The Bendix Trophy races were run across the country.

In 1929 he prepared to resign his commission so he could take a position with Shell Oil in 1930. And historically, he did just that. This time around, he received a cryptic telegram from a man named Benjamin Ryan. The wire asked him to re-think his move to Shell Oil in favor of coming to Springfield, where they hoped he would become a valued part of the greatest leap in the advancement of American aircraft design and the most promising potential to develop air superiority in US history. Ben knew what bait to use to get Jimmy to come to Springfield, because he knew what made Doolittle tick. Shell Oil had offered him good money, to be sure, and good jobs were scarce. But being a part of something like this meant more to Jimmy Doolittle than almost anything. He sent a return wire: *"I am interested. Immediate plans to be there ASAP. Jim."* He rarely wasted words on telegrams.

Ben looked at Granny.

"Gotcha," Granny said, smiling his most devilish smile.

Jimmy arrived at the Granville facility unannounced. The plain, faded exterior of the old former dance hall gave away nothing, and the hangar doors were closed against the hot afternoon sun. Jimmy walked around the side, where he found an entry door and stepped inside. A smile slowly spread across his face as he took it all in.

Men were hard at work on all aspects of aircraft construction, and milling around the subject of their industry. A long, streamlined, bullet-nosed fuselage graced the center of the shop. As though she were a queen bee, matriarch of the nest, the industrious workers swarmed over her as they saw to her every need. She was a dream. Her lines were striking, like those of a beautiful woman; streamlined, graceful, and for one who understood flight on a level as visceral as Jimmy Doolittle did, emotional to behold. Before he had spent five minutes in the Granville's facility, Jimmy Doolittle saw the future. As an aeronautical engineer, his instincts told him that this was the direction that America's military would need to take to remain powerful and viable in a changing world. Drawn to the fuselage like a moth to a porch light, he made his way through the shop to the nose, and placed his hand up against her cowl in a loving touch. He looked alongside her; followed the lines back to the tail. He imagined the sleek aircraft slicing without effort through the skies. As he slid his other hand down alongside it, he could almost feel what it would be like to fly her . . . fast. Oh, SO fast. "Somebody *please* tell me that these folks are looking for a pilot for this lady," he said to himself in his reverie.

"They are. Oh, and *SHE* is called the Gee Bee ZR-2 Racer!"

As the voice behind him spoke, Jimmy wheeled, embarrassed by his daydreaming. "I'm sorry. I . . . I didn't mean to be poking around in here. I came in the door and saw her, and I guess I just ended up over here. She . . . she's just gorgeous. Exceptional. You say she's the, ahh . . . ZR-2?"

"The Gee Bee ZR-2 Racer." Granny reiterated, with a proud smile. "She's sleek and Aerodynamic!"

Jimmy smiled and nodded in agreement. He liked Granny already. Granny shook hands with Jimmy, and the rest of the brothers walked over to meet and greet him, animated and chattering away. This was a big moment for them; Jimmy Doolittle really *was* famous, and they knew it.

Granny introduced himself, and next he made introductions all around. Jimmy was, as always, a gentleman and as fine a fellow as you could find anywhere. He made a point of trying to remember the names of all of the Granville brothers and staff, and there were a lot of them.

By the time those introductions were made, Ben arrived from the drawing room, hobbling along as best he could on his crutches. Granny introduced them. "Jimmy Doolittle, I'd like you to meet a very special member of the Gee Bee crew. Ben Ryan. Ben, this is Jimmy Doolittle!"

Ben, thrilled beyond his wildest dreams, extended his hand. "Sir, this is an honor indeed. I'll never forget this moment for the rest of my life. Thank you SO much for coming, we're in your debt." He felt chills run up and down his back and neck.

Jimmy was gracious and modest. "Ben. I remember your name from that wire you sent me. You seemed to know just what to say to get me to come here. If this is the sort of thing I can expect from working with you folks," he said as he gestured along the ZR-2. "Then I'm probably going to be the one in YOUR debt."

Granny sent Thomas off for something, then turned back to Jimmy. "Mr. Doolittle. . . ."

Jimmy interrupted. "Jim. Call me Jim."

"Of course. Jim, would you follow us into our offices? Ben has . . . an interesting story we think you'll want to hear. And we'd like to talk to you about a few things as well." Granny finished by also gesturing along the length of the Gee Bee, and smiling his all-knowing 'Granny' smile.

Thomas hurried back to Granny and handed him the items as they entered the office, and Granny handed them to Ben. Ben saw the manufacturing plate from his Waco, his Massachusetts driver's license with a color photo, and the ten-dollar bill that Ben had arrived with. They walked into the office and all sat down in a circle in front of the desk and Jim. Nobody wanted to miss the look on Doolittle's face when he learned Ben's story.

Instead, Ben laid the items in front of Jim. "I'd like you to look these over. Take your time. Once you've had time to take it all in would you humor me—us all—by telling us the story that these items tell you?"

He also took Katie Lynn's photo from his wallet and placed it with the other items.

Jim focused first on the color photo. There were a number of smiling faces throughout, and a few chuckles slipped out when Jim did a double-take on the manufacturing plate of the Waco. When he read the 'Series 2003' on the ten-dollar bill, they all expected him to say something. Jim said nothing; he just turned back to the other items, and once or twice glanced up at Ben, then back to the items. His gaze wandered off to the side with a pensive look, and then the pieces came together in his head. Jim spun his head toward the shop and the Gee Bee and stared for a full five seconds, and then to the floor, lost in thought for a full half-minute. He mentally put the pieces of the puzzle together again, seeing if they truly fit the way he had them laid out. He turned and his eyes locked with Ben's. He saw the truth in the blue eyes.

"NO!"

Ben nodded. "Yes."

Chapter Seventeen

Jim's eyes were wide with wonder. "How did you get here?"

Ben shook his head, shrugged, and answered honestly. "I don't know, Jim. I was flying, and then there was a freak storm, the likes of which I've never seen before. It overtook me, and I was pretty sure I was done for. The next thing I know I'm lying in bed all busted up, and these fine gentlemen had rescued me. They've taken care of me ever since. There are a few more details, but that's pretty much all there is to know about it that counts. Except . . ." he added, knowing he was going to hate saying it out loud, making it real. "except that it's a one-way trip for me."

Jim shook his head, and looked down at the items. Without looking up, he asked, "What year did you start?"

"Two thousand and ten."

Jim looked up at him and gave a low whistle. He'd read the years on the license, but hearing them was a shock. He thought about that for a minute or two. He shook his head slowly and sadly, and picked up one item. "Then this is a tragedy for you, Ben." He held up Katie Lynn's photo.

Ben saw the photo Jim held up, felt the deep sadness, felt his eyes sting and redden as tears threatened, and choked up. He tried to avoid thinking about it. He could barely stand it when he did. His eyes moistened and he blinked it away as best he could, hoping to maintain his composure. All he could manage was a nod of affirmation.

Jim understood, and continued, "You're being forced to pay a terrible price for this."

Ben looked a bit confused. "For . . . what?"

"For coming back to help us." Jim stated it as a fact.

He could have heard a pin drop. He couldn't have known that. But that was what made Jim Doolittle what he was. When he looked, he always saw more than others did.

"That's the story, isn't it?" he pressed on. "You're here and you know things, things from the future, from your past. And whatever you know makes it critical that I join you. If you've been asked to pay this price, then something vast . . . perhaps beyond our comprehension . . . must be at stake. Lives, maybe more than just lives. How big is all of this, do you know?"

"Well, some idea. I was told that millions of lives hung in the balance. I've thought about it. I think I know some of the wheres and hows."

"I'm listening." Jim said.

After a moment to collect his thoughts, Ben slid up on the edge of the desk. "Let's start with the United States, Japan, and Pearl Harbor. Also Billy Mitchell, your ex-boss, the man of vision who was right all along."

Several of the brothers had become a bit restless. They'd seen what they came to see, and they'd heard some of these "history of their future" stories before. They had a lot of work to do and guessed this would be a recap of what they'd heard.

Most of them rose and made their way toward the door. Granny stayed put. His brain was just starting to wrap around all of the "former history" and "this time around" dialogue, and he found it as inspiring and compelling as anything he'd ever known. He could foresee one thing already; nothing would ever be the same. And he could hardly wait.

Moreover, he had no intention of walking into that future unprepared, not when the best tools and information were available to him right here.

"Oh, and one subject I think you'll find interesting," Ben added, "Doolittle's Raiders."

Chapter Eighteen

Jim raised both eyebrows in surprise and sat a little straighter in his seat. Ben had his attention. The brothers who had been leaving stopped in their tracks, mumbled between themselves for a moment, and as one they all returned to their seats. The work could wait. They settled in for a history lesson with the newest kid in class.

Granny grinned, sat back, clapped, and rubbed his hands together. *Oh, yes. Here we go!*

The Doolittle's Raiders story had them captivated. Nobody moved.

"Six hundred and twenty-five miles off the coast of Japan. So far, un-detected. Still two hundred and twenty-five miles from their designated launch point. A Japanese patrol boat spotted the task force, and man-aged to transmit their coordinates before our destroyers sank it. They were exposed. Colonel Doolittle had to make the call as to whether they should scratch the mission or proceed. Calculations showed that they would likely NOT have enough fuel to make it to Mainland China."

Except for Ben's voice, the room was still and silent. Every man in the room was leaning forward on the edge of their chairs. One man above all. The tension showed on Jim Doolittle's face as he listened to this in-credible story of his own future. Ben imagined the stress that Jimmy

Doolittle would have felt at this point in the mission. He could only imagine the thoughts raging through Jim's head right now. Jim said nothing.

"If they launched now, there was no way to make contact with the Chinese working with them. They would be leaving a half-day early. Their landing beacons would not be in place. They'd be flying blind, they'd have NO fuel left and if they made it to the mainland at all they'd be landing . . . probably crashing . . . in Japanese-occupied territory at night."

Jim sat silent, the strain clearly evident on his face. *This isn't just a story. I'll be responsible for all these men and planes, for making this life-and-death decision for them all.*

Ben went on. "Jimmy made the decision almost instantly. He told the men: "We're going to Tokyo!" The planes had to be lightened up; the already-stripped down planes had to be stripped down further so each could carry ten more tins of fuel. They worked frantically. Armor plating was pulled out. Guns were removed. As soon as this could be accomplished, they took off, twelve hours ahead of schedule."

"Jimmy's B-25 led the pack off the deck of the flat-top. He very nearly ended up in the sea. After he managed to attain enough airspeed to recover and climb up from skimming the waves, he suggested that the other crews might want to remember to use *their* flaps when they took off," Ben said wryly, with an amused grin.

Jim looked up in surprise with his mouth open, amusement and embarrassment evident on his face as the other men chuckled. The timing was good for a little relief from the stress.

"They all made it into the air and flew on the deck all the way to Japan. Most of them ended up right on their targets in Tokyo and four other cities. They dropped their bombs, doing quite a bit of damage. Nothing the Japanese couldn't recover from. But the intent . . . the *real* damage done by Doolittle's Raiders . . . was to let the Japanese know that we could—and *would*—get to them. Jimmy Doolittle and his Raiders gave America the willpower, the pride, that first push and the inspiration to carry on, to overcome, and to win the war."

Jim looked up at Ben. "That can't be the end. What happened to . . . the Raiders? Do I want to know?"

"I can give you my version. Want to hear it?"

Jim's face was expressionless. His thoughts raced. After a moment, he said, "Yes, I do."

"They never had to fly that mission; they never had to risk it all. Japan's Hail Mary surprise attack was repelled at Pearl Harbor and the war was short. We won it. That's my version."

"Really?" Jimmy responded, still curious about the Raiders.

"Yeah, I think we can make that happen. Are you with us?"

"Do you even have to ask? I'm in."

"Well, all right then."

"And don't think for a second that you're getting out of telling me what happened to the Raiders."

"Agreed," he said. He expected nothing less.

Late that week, alone out back, Ben took out his wallet and slipped Katie Lynn's photo out. He couldn't look at it without choking up; the photo represented his whole world, the world that was now gone, beyond his grasp, snatched away from him. At times the sorrow was nearly unbearable.

There won't be any wreckage to find. The Waco came through with me. Mom must be beside herself, looking for me everywhere. Katie Lynn will be searching too. Oh, God, what if Katie thinks I ran off to get away from her? He couldn't stand it, yet he was powerless to do anything about it. *Will the quiet man tell Gramps what happened? Does Gramps already know about this? Of course. He MUST know, right? But, will he tell Mom? Or will Mom have to live forever, thinking I'm dead and not knowing where my body is, suffering like she did year after year while Dad's remains were never found, never repatriated?*

The thought of his mom suffering more than she already had was maddening to him. Just as bad, perhaps worse, was the thought of Katie Lynn giving up on him and finding somebody else. None of it would happen for another eighty years, and he knew it. But in his mind, they were not twenty miles from here. And frantic over him.

He sensed there was something more, some aspect he didn't yet understand, more he needed to wrap his head around. That didn't make it any easier.

Furious, he yanked his crutches out from under his arms, tangled and untangled them from one another in frustration. Then he heaved each of them as hard as he could at the side of the building, accompanied by some choice words. He turned and limped away, his leg hurting. He didn't care; he needed some kind of distraction right now. Pain was better than nothing.

Mark and Edward, eavesdropping as usual, quietly retreated back into the shop. They often watched Ben go out back and look longingly at the photo of his girl. Other than to reveal her name, Katie Lynn Spencer, he never talked about the girl in the photo, despite their best efforts to get him to open up about it. They had their reasons for asking. They'd seen the woman was identical to Laney, and they wanted to talk to him about it. Occasionally, when talk was high, he'd start a sentence with: "When my Mom, . . ." or "Katie Lynn likes, . . ." and then he'd cut it short.

They felt his sadness, his loss. Everyone felt for this young man. He wasn't much older than they were, so it was easy for them to identify with him. The boys knew he had a good heart. It had to be tough, tossed through time and landing here, busted up, far from everything and everyone he knew, and worse; everyone he loved. The brothers had become his family in nearly every sense of the word, but they knew. It wasn't the same.

Mark looked at Edward and said, "I have an idea."

Edward looked back at Mark, and he saw a gleam in those eyes. He knew exactly what Mark was thinking. With only four years between them, the two gravitated toward each other. Away from the shop, they were inseparable. The others commented on how the two seemed to live inside each other's heads. Yet there were no complaints; it suited them well, and still being young and single, they couldn't imagine it being otherwise.

The two turned on their heels and headed out the door and for town, laughing raucously. They pushed and slapped one another, congratulating each other for having had such a fine idea.

Chapter Nineteen

Granny wondered what Mark and Edward were up to. With the day almost over and the dance in town going on tonight, they were probably getting a head-start on it. He decided to leave them to it. A minute or so later, Ben came limping in the door without his crutches. *That's odd,* Granny thought. He was about to question him about it, when he caught the troubled look. *Let him go. Sometimes discretion is the better part of valor. Sometimes a man just needs to be alone with his thoughts.*

Noises from the office indicated that the workweek was at an end. The conversation had turned to the dance-social in town. The dance-social was an important part of small-town life. Maybe you had a girl. Maybe you were looking for a girl. Perhaps you looked forward to drinking a little punch or having a good time socializing. No matter what, the dance-social was the place to be each month.

After the others walked out the door, Granny walked back to Ben's room.

Ben had done a nice job turning his old broom closet into a homey little abode. He'd taken the time to give it a nice coat of enamel paint and brighten it up, and had built some shelves. Now, Ben's gloomy mood made the room a very lonely place indeed. Granny's heart went out to Ben. Had their positions been reversed, he wasn't sure that he would have been able to forge onward as Ben had thus far.

As if Ben didn't have enough trouble, Doc Perkins had dropped by today to check up on Ben's leg. Doc was apologetic. He had done his very best to reset Ben's leg after he crashed, but sometimes with a badly broken lower leg near the ankle, you can't get both bones to line up as they should. Had it been a protruding compound fracture, Doc would have cut open the leg surgically and used screws and/or plates. Even if the brothers could have afforded it—and they couldn't have—most doctors avoided opening up any patient if they could. In 1929, infections were far too easy to come by, and often too difficult to stop. There was no such thing as antibiotics yet. Sulfa drugs were the latest and the greatest, and only just so effective. Subsequently, the breaks had healed solidly, but they had not healed straight. He would always have pain when he walked. He would require a cane and he would have a pronounced limp.

According to Ben, he had come from great wealth, which had surprised Granny. Ben's great-great-grandfather, Benjamin Ryan—his namesake—had made some investments in the 1930s with a number of companies that grew into conglomerates. Simply put, the Ryans were wealthy beyond imagination.

Farm born and bred, the Granville brothers were the complete opposite. Times were often lean. Complaining did them little good, so they didn't. Swearing helped to vent their tension, but that didn't count as complaining. In Ben, Granny didn't see the spoiled, immature young man one might expect. He found him to be considerate, compassionate, and responsible.

Granny loved the story about Ben painting several miles of three-board fence to earn the money to buy his Waco biplane from his Grandfather. Indeed, Ben had come from money. Any farmer knows that three-board white fences are very expensive. Although reasonably functional, most three-board fencing is for show. Farmers usually watched their dollars and opted for barbed-wire or box fencing. Few folks with money would paint their own three-board fences, much less miles of them. Somebody must have cared how Ben turned out. They hadn't made things too easy for him, and had taught him that wealth is not the most important thing.

Granny cleared his throat, and Ben looked up to see him standing there in his doorway.

"Oh. Hi, Granny. I didn't hear you come back." He was glad to see Granny. They'd grown close as they'd worked together and talked about their future, and Ben's past.

"I was thinking about the dance-social in town tonight, and I wanted to make sure that you were going with us."

Ben paused, then said, "I'm not much for dancing, Granny. Looks like that might be the way of things for me from now on."

Granny sat down on a chair, and pulled out his pipe. This might take a few minutes.

"Benjamin, you've done a remarkable job teaching us about the future. You've taken us places we'd otherwise never go. You've taught us how things will be done in the future. Shown us ways we can change our own future." He lit his pipe, and took a thoughtful draft on it, then continued, "We're all thankful to you for that."

Ben nodded, patiently allowing Granny to go through the motions of explaining life to him, though Granny was maybe three years older than he. In any case, the wisest move was probably to continue listening and letting him maintain his train of thought.

"Might I ask how you are planning to learn about how to live, have a home, a wife, and family in our time, when you have social skills from another time altogether?"

Ben said nothing, he knitted his brow and his eyes searched the floor, as though he might find an answer there. Granny was right, of course. As if he needed any more proof. After his ill-fated first meeting with Laney, she hadn't spoken to him. Since that day, she'd made a point of offering him the coldest of shoulders when they found themselves in the same proximity. She KNEW he was from the future, and that still earned him no mercy. He didn't know what he'd done wrong or what to do about it. He was lost and frustrated anytime he was around her, which was fairly often. It felt to him like Katie Lynn herself had decided to hate him, rather than Laney, and it was terribly confusing to him.

Each time the other office personnel witnessed her arctic demeanor toward him, the ensuing whispers of speculation left him red-faced and fleeing the office. What could he do? He lived right there in the building—there literally was nowhere else he could go.

Granny stood up, inspected his pipe as he stepped outside of the door, where he tapped the contents of the pipe out against the sole of his boot and gave a cheerful smile that, for Ben, bordered on downright irritating. The oldest Granville wasn't taking no for an answer, so Ben didn't put it in the form of a question. "I left you some clothes there on the chair next to your crutches. You'll need them to wear out tonight. We'll pick you up at seven o'clock sharp, Benjamin!" Before Ben could object, he turned on his heel and was gone.

For a few minutes he remained on his bed, pondering his situation. It came to him that he did this a lot, and it struck him that perhaps his pondering was part of the problem. Like the historical errors he'd been tasked with correcting, he'd approached his new life as a problem to be solved. *It isn't a situation that needs to be corrected. I'm not going to find a way out of it. It can't be changed, and there's no way out; the quiet man made that clear enough. Maybe I'm grieving, but I have to face it; mostly I'm in denial. I need to get a handle on this.*

There were any number of things he'd have to reconcile himself to; of that he had no doubt. He started by resigning himself to attending the dance tonight.

I guess I'd better get a move on, then, he thought, and started to wash up.

Chapter Twenty

"My goodness, what brings you two boys by here right now?" Margie Perkins asked the two youngest Granville brothers as they stood on her porch. Mark's face went from the slight red from having run there to a deep burning red; normally garrulous around his brothers, he'd forgotten in his excitement that he was excruciatingly shy in public. Edward, exactly the opposite and more the public speaker of the two, stepped up and covered for him. "Good evening, Mrs. Perkins, would it be possible for us to speak with Laney for a moment?"

"Oh, I don't know; it's almost dinner time and there's still so much do to before the dance social—oh, wait—are you boys here to convince Laney to go to the dance tonight? I'd be so grateful if you could; she simply refuses to go, and she's been up there lying abed since Doc brought her home from work. I just don't know what to do to get that girl to go out tonight."

"Why, yes, Mrs. Perkins, that's exactly why we're here," Edward said. It wasn't really a lie.

Excited, Mrs. Perkins bustled back into the house and called for Laney. "Laney! Those young Granville boys are here to see you! Hurry down now. Your father will be back from his calls any time and we'll need to hurry to make it on time. Hurry now!"

She hustled back into the kitchen. A couple of minutes later, Laney hobbled out on a single crutch, looking miserable and forlorn. When she saw her two partners in crime, a smile crept across her face as she recalled the last time they'd all ventured out together, and as buddies do, she chose not to remember the painful results. She made her way down and off the porch, hobbled over and sat on the bench under the tree with the boys. When they presented their idea, she became angry, and for several minutes they were embroiled in a heated argument. But they persisted, and finally she listened to them. After hearing all they had to say, she relented, and agreed to what they asked.

With that settled, they took off at a run, and Laney made her way inside to start getting cleaned up. To Mrs. Perkins's delight, Laney told her she needed help to decide which of her dresses was the prettiest. She was going to the dance social!

She stood looking in the mirror, holding the lovely blue dress they'd chosen in front of her and swishing it back and forth. It was the perfect choice.

She sighed and thought, *Now, if I could only do something about this horrible plaster cast.*

Chapter Twenty-One

At seven o'clock sharp, Granny stopped by and picked up Ben, who by then was quite presentable. His splints were off and he was walking, but he required one of his crutches to walk any distance. The hastily-improvised crutches the boys built were intended to be strong and functional, and to be certain, they were, but they were not aesthetically designed for the night-life. He had to use one; otherwise the leg hurt too much when he moved about.

That would never change.

Granny's road truck made the rounds, picking up brothers, wives, and dates. It was the large, roomy, tarped-over truck that he took on the road. Created to be a portable workshop to repair planes so they could be flown home, it was also a plane-hauler if on-site repair was not feasible. Since the folks from Waco had picked up Ben's Waco, the truck was empty and the boys had thoroughly cleaned it out. Short of a bus, what better mode of travel was there? Perhaps not quite what their ladies would have preferred, but they lived in a Depression-era New England town. Folks all over America were getting by with very little, and things could have been much worse here. Adventure awaited them, and the truck-ride became a point of excitement rather than disappointment. Spirits were high, and even Ben started to enjoy himself, joining in the laughter and fun on the way, helping others up and greeting them.

When they arrived at the Grange Hall, everybody piled out. They all waited while Granny parked the truck out at the end of the lot. Then he and his wife Alta returned to the group. Granny held up a hand. "Before we go inside, I think there's something we need to do. Ben, could I have that crutch of yours for a moment?"

Curious, he stepped up and handed over his crutch. Granny thanked him and stepped out of the group. With a few violent swings into the ground, he smashed the crutch; quickly reducing it to nothing more than a pile of kindling wood. "There, that should do it!" he said, as he tossed the splintered pieces aside, looking smug as he sauntered back to face a dumbfounded Ben. Everybody was smiling in a most peculiar way, as though they'd thoroughly enjoyed the sight of his only form of mobility being smashed to smithereens, leaving him high and dry.

His mouth gaped and shut a few times, looking very much like a goldfish on the counter, no longer safe in the confines of its fishbowl. Finally he found his tongue. "Wha . . . Granny, why'd you do THAT?"

"Yeah, Granny, why'd you do *that?* That was just MEAN!" Thomas mimicked, and everybody burst out laughing. Ben's face reddened. He didn't enjoy being picked on.

Granny, still smiling, held out his hand toward Alta. She could barely contain her smile as she pulled something out from behind her back and slipped it to Granny, who turned to Ben.

"The doctor told us today that you can walk from now on, but that you'll need a cane. Now, it's not that those crutches weren't *handsome* pieces of work. Even so, we all thought that you'd like something a bit more distinguished to meet the community with. Ben, it's not much to repay you for the future we now can look forward to. But it's from the heart. We would like you to have this."

At that, he held out a cane made of a red-brown wood. The wood was striking, but the head of the cane is what caught Ben's eye. His anger melted away into wonder.

The head of an eagle was carved into the brass head of the cane, with intricate feathers carved around the neck and head. Accepting that his experience with canes was limited, he still thought it was the handsomest cane he'd ever seen.

"It was used. But it's solid and in excellent shape, and we had a fresh rubber tip put on it. We hope you like it, Ben."

"I . . . I don't know what to say, guys," Ben said. He felt himself misting up a little, as did several of the brothers and their ladies. Putting some weight on the cane, he got the feel of it. Nice. It felt nice.

"Maybe you could say . . . Let's go to the dance?" Edward and Mark said in unison, impatient to get inside. Everybody laughed, and Ben walked with his new cane as they headed for the door. It was so nice that he almost hated to use it. He had to admit, he felt dapper with it.

Walking into the Grange hall for the dance was like arriving at a church picnic. Everybody knew everybody. Granny told Ben he should count on being introduced to everybody in the hall before it was over. Before the night was over, every soul in the place would know exactly who he was. A new face at any community event garnered more than its share of attention, especially a handsome, unattached young man. And in Ben's case, a man of some mystery. The Granvilles had put together a cover story to offer folks. In a small town, the less that was known about a person, the more folks wanted to know. Simply refraining from talking about something was the surest way to stir the curiosity to a fever pitch. Gossip and speculation would abound. They kept the story simple. Ben was a third cousin on their mother's side that they hadn't seen since childhood. A fortunate coincidence; he was a pilot himself (it must run in the family!), and he had heard about the brothers starting into the racing planes. He'd decided to fly down to meet them and see if they might need another hand working with the racing planes. Jobs were scarce around his home in northern New Hampshire. He was family, and he'd been injured coming to see them; how could they turn him away? All the brothers found they liked him a lot. So now he was just another one of those crazy Granville brothers working on their planes over there at the Liberty Street airport. It wasn't such a stretch. They were starting to believe it themselves . . . more or less.

As they all spread out to socialize, Ben found himself a chair strategically tucked away off to one side. He hoped—no, he *planned*—to avoid too much attention. That strategy backfired on him immediately. These friendly folks assumed that any person sitting alone at a social was in need of plenty of company and conversation. As the Grange Hall filled, there were soon people everywhere. It didn't take long to learn that when folks did not know him, they made a point of introducing themselves. There was a constant crowd of people milling around him.

From that first day he'd woken up and found himself there, he'd noticed that people in that time had a certain . . . aroma. Showers and baths were luxuries. Although deodorants existed, it was a new concept and most folks didn't use them. Somewhere in his studies he'd come across this information, but experiencing it firsthand was far more memorable.

In fairness to the folks of the 1920s, a person's scent was accepted as an integral part of their personality. Washing up removed some of the smell, but the primary intent was to remove the dirt and leave them cleaner. A woman of some means could afford perfume, the original deodorant, which masked her scent. A man could use cologne. In a small town, cleaning up for a dance consisted of wearing carefully dusted-off dress clothing and scrubbing with soap to remove the majority of the smell from their body. Unless they took a full bath, almost invariably some personal scent remained. Dry-cleaning dress clothes was expensive, so as long as they could be dusted off and *appear* clean, they were worn any number of times between cleanings. In a crowd like this one, the air was pretty thick at times. He figured he'd grow accustomed to it in time.

From his chair he could see the folks dance. The music was foreign to him, as were the dances, with the exception of the waltzes. The couples had space between them almost all the time, and were very precise in their footwork. Dancing to slow music before had been called waltzes or slow dancing, but he could see he'd never danced a true waltz like this.

Though nothing was what he expected, he soon found himself relaxing. As he pondered some boards in the floor, three pairs of feet appeared before him. The feet in the center were attached to a lovely pair of legs and the skirt of perhaps the prettiest blue dress he'd ever seen. Looking up to greet these new folks, he found Mark and Edward smiling at him. Between them he saw Laney, one arm crooked through each of theirs. The fit of her dress was exquisite. Blue was definitely her color. Another quick glance down to be sure, and indeed, there was no cast on either of her rather attractive legs. She was looking at him, and her beautiful smile took his breath away entirely, and doubled his heart rate. Mesmerized, he was helpless to look away.

She initiated the conversation. "Good evening, Mr. Ryan. These two gentlemen have been helping me move about the Grange Hall. It seems

I have no escort for the dance tonight, and they mentioned that you appeared to be in need of a lady to escort. Could I impose upon you to be of some assistance in my hour of need?" She smiled again.

She . . . wants to be with me? His heart raced so fast he thought it might explode. She was so beautiful, he had no idea what to do or say. Frozen, he looked to Mark and Edward for help. They looked at each other and rolled their eyes upward, wondering if this idea was as good as they'd thought. Ben was dropping the ball, no doubt about it. This was their idea, and it looked like Laney would be on their arms all night now. Pretty as she was, and as good friends as they all were, the boys had other ideas of fun tonight. This plan was losing that brand-new shine of genius by the second.

When he opened his mouth, nothing came out.

Laney sensed he wasn't going to speak without some prodding, so she spoke up, her tone on the chilly side. "Perhaps these two gentlemen misunderstood you? Then you are not in need of a companion this evening? I apologize for disturbing you. Good evening, Mr. Ryan."

She turned with her two escorts and departed.

Chapter Twenty-Two

He stood up, which perhaps had something to do with his mouth, as it suddenly began working. "No! Wait! Please. I'm . . . sorry, Laney. *I am* in need of a companion tonight. Won't you sit down and we can discuss the possibility of . . . ahh . . . me . . . escorting you for the rest of the evening?"

Though that probably could have been worse, he didn't know how. Who knew hands could sweat just from talking? He tried to look casual as he wiped them on his pants.

Before she looked back over her shoulder, a smile of satisfaction crept across her face. She winked at the boys and nodded, and they turned back toward him. "Why, thank you, that would be lovely, Mr. Ryan."

The boys looked at each other in relief, and quietly started to make good their escape.

"I'll talk with *you two* later on," he murmured to them, giving them the evil-eye as he hooked a chair with his cane and dragged it beside his. They looked at each other with pie-sized eyes, mouthed the words "uh-oh!" and wheeled, vanishing into the crowd.

Laney sat down, and he took his seat beside her.

Sitting here with her, still not knowing exactly what to do, the situation brought to mind a favorite scene and a line Richard Dreyfuss spoke in the movie *Always*, *"This is good. I needed this. I was rusty on panic."* When he heard it in the movie, he thought it was hilarious.

Laney looked at him and smiled expectantly. Perhaps he should say something? He tried not to look terrified, but at best he looked like a deer in the headlights.

This could take all night. Besides, she knew she had something to get off her chest, so she took the initiative. "Ben, I owe you an apology. I'm afraid I've been terribly hard on you for some time now. Mark and Edward told me about everything you're dealing with. I'm ashamed of the way I've behaved toward you. You were sent here against your will to help us, and lost everything and everyone. You can never go home. It makes my problems seem paltry in comparison."

Breathing a sigh of relief, he said, "Thank you, Laney. I *am* having a rough time. I have no idea how to act or what to say much of the time. I know I couldn't dance the simplest of these dances. I worry constantly that I'll make somebody angry."

"You mean me, don't you? But you're too kind to say it."

She was correct; he did mean her. "I was trying for funny and light-hearted conversation that day, but it all went so wrong. What's worse is that I don't even know what I said to make you so angry with me. I worry about it every day."

"I've not been very kind to you, Ben Ryan." She took his hand and turned herself toward him, and he did the same. "I was *so* frustrated on the day we talked. I was dealing with a broken leg and that heavy cast. And my father had just forced me to take this job, because I had discouraged a whole string of utterly *vile* suitors I'd rather have died than marry. He was certain I was to become an old maid. I was simply livid. And I do have a temper . . . as you might have noticed," she said, with a slight cringe of embarrassment. "I'm afraid I took out my frustrations on you because you're a man. You didn't deserve it. You didn't deserve any of it. In fact, you were quite kind and decent, and very charming, which I think may have scared me a touch."

"A touch?" he asked, holding his thumb and forefinger a half-inch apart. This time he didn't hide the smirk.

Laney blushed and looked down, amused, and smiled in agreement. The way he accepted her explanation was so gracious. "Yes, just a bit. I have to confess, I was appalled by my own behavior. After I'd behaved that way, I didn't know what to do to change it. I pretended to stay a bit cross with you to . . . avoid having to face the music, I guess you might say."

The fingers remained in the same position. "Just a bit?" he asked, smirking openly now.

"Oh, stop it!" She said, blushing and laughing as she pushed his hand away. And with that, the ice was broken. They talked all evening, and as she remembered, he was an interesting man, so different from the other men she knew. He was kind, decent, and intelligent. Obviously educated. From that moment on, they never left their chairs. Their heads were close together and the talk flowed. Before the night ended, he asked if she might allow him the privilege of walking her home. After asking her mother, she accepted.

Everybody commented on what an adorable couple they made as they limped off into the night together. They were the main topic of discussion as Granny's truck made its rounds around town. It was a fine end to a good evening.

The last swing Granny made was along the way from Laney's house to the shop. There he found Ben limping along with his new cane, a silly smile on his face, and what must be by now a very sore leg. He was delighted to see Granny, and climbed in. He stared out the window and continued to smile his silly smile. Much of the way home he was in a world all his own.

He only looked over at them once. Alta leaned against Granny, wrapped around his arm, laid her head on his shoulder and they enjoyed one of their rare quiet moments alone. They looked at each other and their eyes twinkled as they remembered their first night out, and their own silly smiles. It wasn't so long ago.

Abruptly, the smile left Ben's face.

He paled, turned, and looked out the window.

Chapter Twenty-Three

Back in his room, Ben tried to sort out his thoughts. He was angry with himself for cheating on Katie Lynn; at the same time he felt as though he'd been with Katie Lynn tonight and nobody else. He knew he had to get a handle on the situation. . . . *Why am I so upset, anyway? I have to face facts. Katie Lynn Spencer won't even be born for another sixty-odd years; I won't meet her for the first time until seventy-five years from now. I'll be ninety-nine years old by then. And eighty-odd years from now, my young self will disappear from her life forever, without a trace, leaving her to wonder where I went, why I broke my promise to her not to run out on her. I have no way to tell her. I have no way to send her a message. I can't go back. I'm here forever. There isn't one damned thing I can do about it.* It was so confusing; he looked at Katie Lynn's photo and he saw Laney. He looked at Laney and he saw Katie Lynn. *DAMN it!*

Still agitated, he slept at last; dreaming crazy, wild dreams of women and canes and aircraft and war. Sometime late in the night he fell still, and didn't move again until morning. Saturday morning he rolled out of bed, surprisingly well rested for all his nocturnal activity. In the midst of his dreams he had managed to reconcile himself to his situation. He'd come to terms with his self-division over Katie Lynn and Laney, and now he knew what he would do.

The brothers and production staff worked on Saturdays, and he worked with them. The office staff didn't work on the weekends, so it was a surprise when Laney walked in the front door and back through the shop to him, amidst low wolf-whistles and jabs aimed at him by the boys.

He was happy to see her and his smile showed it. "Hello, Laney! You look bright and chipper this morning."

She smiled. "Why, thank you! I was wondering; do you have a minute?"

He turned and looked at Granny, who waved him out the door, joined by the rest of the hooligans who yelled out that they didn't need him there; he'd just be in the way. Giving them a grin and a nod of thanks, he grabbed his cane and walked outside to the sounds of their laughter and a few more wolf whistles.

"Sorry, you'll have to forgive them; they don't mean anything by it."

"You forget, I work in the office with the door open and listen to them pinch their fingers and pound their thumbs every day. I've learned an entire vocabulary of brand-new words since I started here," she said, and laughed. "But I like them all, they're all good people. I never thought I'd say this, but I like it here. I like it here a lot. I like my job, too."

"I'm glad to hear that. As you can probably tell, you're pretty well-liked around here yourself."

"Oh! Do you really think so?" she stopped and asked, surprised. "After the way I acted toward you, I thought maybe I wasn't so well-liked at all."

"The way they figured it, you were sweet on me and playing hard to get."

She felt her face do a slow burn. There was more truth to that than she cared to admit.

He waved it off. "Don't let it bother you. People talk. I realize now that they were hoping we'd find a way to patch things up, and maybe even hook up."

"Hook up?"

"Oh, That's . . . that's . . ."

"Slang?"

He chuckled and nodded. "Yeah, slang. It means umm . . ."

"That we find that we like each other and get together?"

"Umm . . . yeah, that's right. That's exactly right."

"So, Mr. Ryan, have we . . . hooked up?"

He looked at the summer dress she was wearing this morning. Cream with little flowers. Simple and elegant. Along with a fetching figure, she had stunning taste. Never before had he given much thought to women wearing dresses all of the time, as they did here. It added another dimension to her femininity. He liked it, and he liked her. A lot.

"Well, Miss Perkins, if you ask me how I feel, I'd say yes, we have. But I can't speak for you. Do you feel like we have?"

"I think so. I know I couldn't wait to see you this morning."

"I was glad you showed up too. Sooo, yes, I think it's safe to say that we've hooked up."

She smiled and asked, "Sooo, what comes next?"

"I'm afraid I'll have to depend on you for that. I'm still learning my way here, and it's clear that I don't know my way around social situations. I had no idea it would be this tough."

She took his arm, and they strolled for a while, just chatting about everything and anything, spending time getting to know each other. After some time, she brought up the reason she had come to talk with him.

"There *is* something I need to tell you about. It may not be a serious problem, but I think since we've 'hooked up,' you have the right to know about it."

Ben nodded. "Okay. Whatever it is, I'm sure we'll be okay."

She didn't look convinced of that, but she proceeded. "There's . . . this fellow Michael, and we used to spend time together."

"You dated?"

"No, not dated. He came courting me. But then jobs became scarce, and he went into the Navy. He asked me to marry him."

He faltered, disappointed. "Oh. I see. You're engaged. I guess we're not hooked up after all."

She shook her head. "No, it's not that. I wasn't sure about it. I told him that if he still wanted to marry me and if I was still single when he got out, I would. That was three years ago. He'll be out next year."

"Is he still talking about the marriage?"

"We exchange letters, usually about six or eight of mine for every one of his. He's not well-educated and not much for writing. He mentions getting married . . . now and then . . . I can't tell if he's serious about it, or if he's dreading it."

He raised his eyebrows hopefully. "I vote that he's dreading it. Does my vote count?"

"If only it did. I'd make the majority."

"So you're saying you'd vote my way?"

She put on her best 'I am offended' look and took on a comic sophisticated air. "Sir, after everything that we women have gone through to earn the right to vote, do you think I'd sully such a sacred institution by revealing my intentions to any passing stranger?"

He didn't stand on ceremony. "I'll take that as a YES. Democracy at its finest."

She laughed and looked in his eyes. She tucked her hair over her ear. "I think you could sway any woman's vote, Ben Ryan."

"I'm counting on it."

Contented and happy, she slipped her arm through his and they started strolling again, and looked out over the fields. A few moments later, her smile faded and she knit her brows. Dismay showed on her face, and in a quiet voice she admitted, "I may have no choice."

"You didn't leave each other any way out?"

"Just the one. If either he or I get married in the meantime."

"I see."

"What do you think?"

He did not turn to look at her. They walked on for a long time, and without stopping, he spoke to her. "I've known you a total of one night and half of a morning. Ordinarily it wouldn't make sense to say what I'm going to say. I want you to see something before I tell you."

He pulled Katie Lynn's photo out of his wallet and handed it to Laney. She took it and looked at it. She stopped in her tracks. The first thing she noticed was the incredible detail and the color, both of which impressed her. Then she looked at the woman in the photo. It was her. Not exactly her. More like a twin sister who looks so much like you that nobody can tell you apart, except maybe your mother and siblings. Even her own father would mistake this woman for her.

"Ben! Who is this? She's . . . she's ME. Where did you get this?"

"You remember that fellow you were telling me about? The one who you said you would marry?"

"Michael? Yes."

"Well, I'd like to introduce you to Katie Lynn, the woman who promised to marry ME."

"She's . . . I . . . why does she look so much like me?"

"If I could answer that, I'd probably be good enough at this time-travel stuff to know what the heck I'm doing here. Maybe I'd even know how I'm supposed to get it all done."

"She's from . . . your time? She's in the future?"

"Yes." He said.

"What must you have thought when you first saw me! This is . . . why, Ben, this is amazing! Are we alike other than that?"

"Yes . . . and no. No offense, Laney, I'm just making this comparison. You . . . are a little on the spoiled side, whereas Katie Lynn grew up with very little, on a small farm. Her whole family worked very hard to keep body and soul together. In your looks, you're identical; and the way you move, it's a little scary for me. I see you do little things just the same."

"Oh? Like what, for instance?"

"Ah, I don't know if I should be telling you this. I never told her in the whole six years."

"Six years together! Oh, Ben. You must be devastated!"

He nodded, sad at the thought. "I am. But I have no options. I'm here forever. Anyway, when she would look in my eyes . . . like this . . . her right hand would come up and do what you're doing right now; she'd tuck her hair back over her ear."

Laney stopped in mid-tuck. She felt as though she'd been apprehended.

"Don't be embarrassed. I *loved* that about her. I think it's great that you do it."

"Oh, thank you, Ben. Maybe . . . maybe I'm her . . . ancestor? That would make sense."

He nodded in agreement. It would make sense. "I was glad to learn your name was Perkins. If your name had been Katie Lynn or your last name had been Spencer, I would've been pretty confused."

Laney didn't respond to that. He looked at her face. The color had drained from it. She looked distressed. Something was wrong. Very wrong.

"Spencer. You said . . . Spencer?"

"Yes. Her name is Katie Lynn Spencer. Laney, what is it? What's wrong?"

She turned and looked up, her breath gone, her skin now pale as rice paper. "Spencer. Michael . . . Michael Spencer . . . his name . . . is . . . Michael Spencer," she said, dismayed.

Ben took a deep breath, and held it for minute. He was caught off-balance by that, and he thought, *This just keeps getting better and better.*

He said what he could. "I don't know what it means, Laney. I'm going to have to give it some more thought. In the meantime, I think we'll be fine. We'll figure it all out."

She nodded, still worried. "Oh, I hope you're right. You had something you were going to tell me?"

He hesitated, wondering how—or *if*—he should proceed now. He decided to forge ahead. "I'd like to get to know a lot more about you. It can't be a coincidence that I'm tossed eighty years back in time, only to land here with the Granvilles, and here I find you, of all people in the world. You're here, you're my age, available, and kind of cute, I should add."

Thrilled, she couldn't keep from saying, "Why, Ben Ryan, are you telling me that you would like to come calling?"

"Does that mean would I like to date you? I sure—"

"No," she interjected firmly. "That means, are you stating your intent to court me?"

"Court you?" he asked, though he'd heard every word.

She sighed patiently. "You would court me if it is your intention to marry me."

"Oh. I see. Things are a bit more complicated in this time, I guess," he said. *If it is your intention to marry me.* The more things changed for him, the more they stayed the same.

Katie Lynn and he had gone through a bad time just before he'd been transported to 1929. He had no way of knowing then or now that he'd sensed his connection with the temporal rift as it sought him, closed in on him. The feeling that a "storm was coming" had haunted him so that only Katie Lynn's unrelenting devotion and resolute focus had held the wedding plans together. He hadn't taken the time to think about all of that since his arrival in this time. Had he taken the time, he'd have realized that it had never been the wedding that bothered him.

Marrying Katie Lynn was the one thing he'd ever truly wanted. Nevertheless, he'd developed a knee-jerk reaction where he backed off at the word "marry."

The obvious ancestry between Katie Lynn and Laney added to his confusion, as did the obvious implications with Katie Lynn Spencer and Michael Spencer.

Laney asked, "Is something wrong?"

"Wrong? Oh, no . . . no," he lied.

With that, he and this woman, who in all likelihood was Katie Lynn Spencer's great-great-grandmother, silently resumed their walk, hand-in-hand, down by the riverside.

Chapter Twenty-Four

It frustrated Laney. The rest of the afternoon had been nice enough, but she sensed the tension. As a woman, she normally reserved the right to become vague any time a conversation should take a direction she wasn't pleased with. So far, her discussions with Ben had gone awry. *I led him right up to the issue of marriage, pushing the subject as far as a lady could; I couldn't go further without crossing the lines of propriety. I couldn't very well ask HIM to marry me, now, could I?*

She'd impressed upon him what a small window of opportunity they had available to them, and she was certain he was about to say that he intended to court her. She'd even led him straight through the confusion of their conflicting customs to say he needed to court her to marry her, so he couldn't make a mistake. Yet, just as he was about to say it, he instead said nothing, then became vague and detached. *I couldn't have run the conversation off the road better myself. Doesn't he understand what I'm up against? He seemed so interested; he even indicated that he hoped Michael would not want to marry me.*

She had some misgivings herself. If she didn't marry Michael, would it mean that this girl Katie Lynn Spencer might never be born in the future? This girl almost certainly must be her descendant, a baby of her own child or grandchild or *their* grandchild. *Maybe I'm supposed to marry Michael, maybe Ben knew that somehow. If he did, wouldn't he say so? If he wasn't interested in courting me, why was he so attentive to me? Men can be so infuriating at times. Michael was never obtuse; he said what he meant.*

But she knew that wasn't entirely true; mostly Michael didn't say anything at all. Not to her, anyway. She'd never known the way he really felt, and he'd never made her feel welcome to ask about those things. Had she known what he truly thought of her, about women in general, she'd have stayed as far away from him as she could get. She'd have run. As it was, she sensed something wasn't as it should be. But a woman of marrying age in 1929 was under tremendous social and family pressure to marry.

Even before Michael Spencer left, Laney knew they had little in common. When her father allowed her to start accepting suitors who came to call, she allowed herself to hope. *Surely there must be some eligible, educated men in the area.*

Doc Perkins had made sure she was educated through all the grades and had some training on being a proper lady and a woman. She was a beauty, and for all intents and purposes, considered to be a real catch. With no money to be found anywhere, even a small dowry looked good. Since her father was a doctor, rumor held that it was sizable. This brought an endless procession of suitors—in large they were vile, ignorant, smelly, toothless, illiterate men—both young and old. That continued for over two years before she called an end to it.

Then, out of the clear blue sky, this young man Ben Ryan had arrived. *Very* nice looking, blue eyes, well-built, polite, serious, educated, gentle, warm, and kind . . . he was everything she'd wished for and thought she'd never find. And when he looked at her, she *felt* it. The closest thing to it she'd ever felt was a few years back when her arm brushed up against that electric fence. That was a good way to describe it. Looking into his blue eyes was like electricity flowing through her whole body. And she thought he was interested in her too. She was sure of it. He'd seemed ready to say that yes, he'd like to come courting her, that he would state his intentions. Instead, he made a point of backing off and *not* saying it at all; he even avoided the subject for the rest of the day.

She looked at the calendar, worried. *I was wrong when I said three years. Michael has been gone three years and seven months. The time passed too quickly. He'll be coming home next year . . . early next year . . . in a few short months.* Things were closing in on her, and fast. She didn't know how to tell Ben and not seem desperate.

So, she didn't.

Chapter Twenty-Five

Ben walked around town for a while after he walked Laney home. He had a lot on his mind. After reconciling himself to his situation, and realizing he had no way back to 2010, he'd made up his mind that he was going to let her know that he wanted to continue seeing her. But when the dating discussion suddenly became the marriage discussion, he freaked out a little. *Freaked out. Great words for 2010, but I can't use them here without folks thinking I'm from another world. Which, I have to face facts; I am.*

He couldn't say half of what he knew. There were so many things to think about, and some he couldn't talk about, or at least his instincts told him he shouldn't. The Katie Lynn Spencer thing had them both off-balance, and neither seemed to recognize that Katie was clearly Laney's descendant, and if Laney's life changed, Katie's last name might be different, but she'd still more than likely exist. Time had shown him how resistant to change it really was. After some thought he decided not to give up; he'd make sure she understood he had feelings for her, and he felt certain that they'd be able to work their issues out in good time.

He had more on his mind than just that. For a brief moment riding home last night, when he saw Alta and Granny together and looking so close, he couldn't get the date out of his mind; *February 11, 1934. That's the day that Granny is supposed to die.* He had no idea how to broach the subject. Not having any brothers of his own in 2010, he'd come to love

99

Granny as though he were his own brother. He couldn't stand the thought of Alta and their two children being without Granny, struggling to carry on. *I could do something about it. I have to do something about it.* At that moment, he swore an oath that he would never let that happen. *I'll burn the Model E to keep Granny out of it.*

Already, things had changed enough that Granny would likely never need to sell the plane due to a need for money, so he shouldn't have a reason now to make that trip. But there was always the possibility. As a whole, the organization had come a long ways in a short time.

Jimmy Doolittle had signed on as the Granvilles' main pilot. Additionally, he was tasked with finding any experienced flyers he could and honing their skills; making them into the best pilots anywhere. The Granvilles would need top-notch pilots to be able to handle the Gee Bee ZR-2 racers. No pilot would sit in a Gee Bee racer until they completed training with Jim Doolittle. In the future it was possible—even probable—that these pilots would be re-trained so they could train military pilots.

With the combination of Granny, Ben, Pete Howell, and Jim Doolittle, the Granville team had become a force to be reckoned with. They had Granny, a man with real vision and the instincts of an aeronautical engineer, Pete and Jim, two men with current Aeronautical engineering degrees, and Ben with an aeronautical engineering degree from eighty years in the future. The latter came with the answers to current mysteries and misbeliefs, and knowledge of the advances made in the next eighty years. Together they comprised the most formidable racer-design team ever assembled. Ben couldn't think of another thing they could have done to advance their situation further. Winter would be winding down in a few short months, and they would be ready for the Thompson Trophy Races.

Chapter Twenty-Six

The Nationals

The crowds were amazing. Folks came from every corner of the country and even Canada to see the 1930 Thompson Trophy Races in Chicago. The first races were held August 23, and the air was charged with anticipation and excitement.

Ben thought, *Somebody pinch me!* Only in his dreams did he ever picture himself at the Thompson Trophy Races. Racers he knew well—famous racers and their pilots—had leapt from the pages of the history books, and were all around him. Not the grainy black and white images he'd studied in such detail; these racers were ever so much more vivid, adorned with bright, clear colors and designs. Charles "Speed" Holman and his new Solution, just completed and fresh from the factory. Jimmy Haizlip and the Travelair Mystery Ship. The Navy had returned, determined to settle last year's score with their modified Curtiss Hawk. The black and white photographs from his books could never have done justice to this rainbow of racing history. He was so excited he could barely contain himself.

Bright banners of every color were strung along the grandstands and fluttered in the breezes. The grandstands were massive—a single, long, white wooden structure, filled to capacity with tens of thousands of spectators. The noisy, excited crowd maintained a constant medium-volume roar. But once the flag dropped on a race, the crowd noise reached deafening levels.

The flat, open area was massive; far larger than he had ever imagined. The course was ten miles long, flown at low altitude around red-and-white checkered fifty-foot pylons so the crowd could see most of the race as it progressed. At speeds of two hundred miles per hour, a lap took only three minutes. Three minutes of pilots jostling and positioning their racers for the best position to go around the next pylon, and then the next. Three pylons in three minutes. That next pylon caused a sort of tunnel vision in the pilots, which made things interesting for the whole pack. One bump, one wrong touch from another racer, one propeller too close to another racer's tail could—and upon occasion did—mean certain death. Air racing was not for the faint of heart. The pilots needed to have the reflexes of an athlete and nerves of steel. During interviews and conversations, some pilots hinted that it didn't hurt to be a little crazy.

Ben was there for a purpose, however, and his historical fanaticism had to be put up on the shelf. The Granvilles had entered one of their Gee Bee ZR-2 racers in the pylon races, and it was crunch time. Now they would see whether their hard work had paid off; they would see firsthand if their superb racers were as fast as they believed.

The competing racing crews cast nervous glances in their direction. Nobody had ever seen aircraft such as the ZR-2 racers; the sleek Gee Bees looked as formidable and fast as the newspapers articles and interviews had claimed, perhaps faster. Granny's idea, the teardrop shape, was there, but modified and lengthened. The tail might have been described as resembling the tail of a large Moray eel. The wheels were impossibly small; the product of a cooperative effort between Ben and BF Goodrich. They'd wanted his more advanced zipper, and he'd needed a supply of small, high-performance tires and wheels to be created under exclusive contract for the Gee Bee Corporation. As a result, the ZR-2 wheel pants, or "spats", were small, beautifully streamlined assemblies, and the rear steering gear tire and pant were positively miniscule. The struts, tall and lean, reached down and forward to the wheel pants, an engineering marvel for the day. The dreaded "floating" curse of the original Gee Bees had been addressed by shaping the belly like a "V" under the pilot, and curving it up, much like a lean dog's belly curves upward toward the back. That was sufficient to reduce the lift upon landings, and taking that much out of the airstream helped to reduce the drag created by lengthening the fuselage. An aluminum spinner topped off the propeller, streamlining it even more and increasing the cooling air flow to the radial engine. This enabled them to further tighten the front opening of the cowling, reducing drag further. Every aspect of the ZR-2 racers complemented every other aspect; nothing was left to chance. It was painted a bright red color on the bottom, extending two-thirds of the way up the sides, finished off by a bright white top, and flat black in front of the pilot. The cowl was a flashy black and white checkerboard all around. Black pin-striping set off the colors, and the wheel pants mimicked the scheme. The familiar words "Gee Bee" adorned the tail in script, and a large, bright Texaco Star logo was splashed across the nose. It was a vision of promised speed and grace. But would it beat the fastest in the nation?

They wouldn't have to wait long to find out. Thirty minutes until race time and they were double and triple-checking everything. Jim Doolittle was piloting today. Once he strapped into that cockpit, Jim became Jimmy Doolittle to the crowds. Lowell Bayles was standing by as backup for Jim, or if they needed to run the other racer. They'd brought the second ZR-2 along for a show of force. It was set up for distance racing and not for pylons, but that fact wasn't broadcast. If entered, it was so fast they felt it would still beat them all. Indeed, they would run it if worse came to worse. They were here to compete. But so far, no troubles had plagued them, other than a sizable case of nerves all around. They were ready.

Ben looked over at the Curtiss-Hawk. Earlier that morning he'd given a kid a dime to deliver an anonymous note to their crew, telling them that they needed to check out their racer, because if they didn't find the problem their plane would crash on the seventeenth lap. Since nobody had ever found what the cause was, he couldn't give them any more help than that. He didn't care about the racer, but Captain Page dying was something he couldn't stand the thought of.

With fifteen minutes to go the horn sounded, indicating that they were now to move their racers to their designated starting point, where they would wait for the final countdown. With a little less than eight minutes to go, Jimmy and the ZR-2 were waiting at the starting point, the engine shut down. The planes were all lined up side-by-side with about a hundred feet between them. The crowd noise grew louder by the minute; the anticipation had grown to such a fever pitch that it could be felt in the air itself. Out on the course, the face of every crew member was etched with concentration, making sure every detail was attended to. Three minutes to go, and the teams prepared—engines were started, last minute checks were made. They'd done everything they could; the rest was up to the racers and their pilots.

They didn't use cannons to start the air races. They used bombs, and when the thunderous explosion rolled across the grounds it shook the air and whipped the crowd into a frenzy. The racers were off, ungainly creatures of the air bouncing along the ground, rolling across the grass, struggling to gain enough speed to become airborne, each pilots' singular focus to put the rest of the pack behind them. Each time another racer clawed its way into the air the cheering from the crowd grew louder. The ZR-2s takeoff run was effortless and graceful. Soon all the racers were in the air and gaining speed, but as Granny and Ben watched, there appeared to be a problem. Instead of breaking away from the pack, the sleek ZR-2 matched the pack and stayed a little wide on the first pylon, when all the other racers bunched up. It looked to the crowd as though they might pile up and come down in a tangled mass of wreckage. The cheering of the crowd reached a crescendo when somehow they all pulled through without damage or entanglements, and then sprinted for the second pylon. Jimmy and his ZR-2 didn't fall behind, but he didn't appear to be mixing it up either. Some started to fall behind, and Jimmy didn't seem to be falling back with them, but he clearly was not pulling ahead. As the second lap was completed and they rounded the first pylon in the third lap, the Curtiss-Hawk pulled away, leaving the pack far behind. Granny and the brothers yelled in dismay.

Ben told them to give Doolittle a chance, this was a twenty-lap race and there was lots of time for him to make his move. True to Ben's prediction, after the next lap the ZR-2 pulled away from the pack, and it was clear Jimmy was leaving them behind much more rapidly than Page had in the Hawk. The Hawk was traveling an impressive 230 miles per hour, probably averaging over 220 miles per hour. But the ZR-2 was gaining on it at an astonishing pace. By the sixth lap, the Hawk had lapped the pack. By the seventh lap, the ZR-2 lapped the pack, and shortly after that caught and passed the Hawk like it was standing still, and was still accelerating. Jimmy was taking advantage of the superior speed to make wider turns around the pylons, staying safe and not mixing it up with the pack. He didn't need to. His timed speed was 90 miles per hour faster than the Hawk, and a blistering 110 to 120 miles per hour faster than the rest of the field. Averaging 310 miles per hour, he was burning up the course and had the crowd on their feet, leaping up and down and screaming, "Jimmy, Gee-Bee! JIMMY, GEE-BEE!!!"

After a mere thirty-five minutes, the ZR-2 took the checkered flag and Jimmy made a picture-perfect landing. As he taxied toward the victory circle, screams sounded through the crowd, hands pointed toward the course, and alarm registered in the tone of the crowd. All eyes turned to the field, where they saw the Navy's Curtiss-Hawk slowly banking up and away from the pack at a funny angle. Something was obviously very wrong. It continued up and over on the same lazy, banking trajectory until it crashed into the ground, as though it was not being controlled. Response crews rolled. On the seventeenth lap, Captain Page and the Curtiss-Hawk were out of the race in a fiery, spectacular and, sadly, fatal crash. He hadn't bailed out, and was pulled from the wreckage. Ben stood where he was, watching helplessly as the emergency crews rushed out to the crash site, quite some distance away.

"They didn't find the problem, I guess," Granny said, watching with Ben.

"I guess not."

"It's not your fault. You did all you could. They wouldn't have believed the truth."

"No, I didn't do all I could. There must have been something else I could have—"

"You can't just run around telling people you're from the future and that they're gonna die, you know. All you'll end up doing is to get yourself thrown into the looney-bin."

He thought about what he hadn't told Granny. "Don't I know it. But I can do more, and next time, believe me, I will." His eyes grew red with moisture.

History was tenacious and would not allow its course to be easily changed. Maybe it was true; maybe he couldn't be everywhere and do everything and save everybody, but it still bothered him. He now fully understood how profound a situation he was in, how very much it could mean under the right circumstances. What if Captain Page had a family at home? If he did, then their whole life had just been wrecked with that racer out there, while Ben concentrated on the Gee Bees. *I possess the means to change that, to save him, to save them this heartache, and I failed to do so. I'm going to figure out how to use this the right way, damn it all.*

He walked off to calm down. Granny watched him walk off, and knew he wouldn't want to be in those shoes. The crash hadn't been the real issue, though it had served as a reminder of the real issue. It had the same effect on Ben either way.

The rest of the racers made it through the race. Speed Holman in the Solution took Second; Jimmy Haizlip in the Travelair Mystery Ship took third.

Jim Doolittle and the sleek ZR-2 were rolled into the victory circle. After the photographers took photos of him and the ZR-2, the crowds began to mill around with their Brownies, snapping shots to take home. Finally he slipped away with the brothers. He was pleased to be able to report that it hadn't been necessary to push it much beyond half or two-thirds throttle. He'd held back at first to get the feel of her, something Ben had known Jim would do. Jim was scrappy and competitive, but he was smart; he didn't test fate when it wasn't necessary. The Gee Bees had advances that no others had; the planes were faster and more stable in the air, with tamer landing and better handling characteristics on the ground. He knew the secrets, knew how to capitalize on them. Nothing looked like or performed like the Gee Bees.

Soon, race announcers thrilled crowds at the races with their descriptions of the Gee Bee ZR-2 Racer and the famous pilot Jimmy Doolittle at the stick, smashing records, and doing what other pilots only dreamed of doing. Having been hand-fed the word *Aerodynamic* by Granny during interviews, these announcers began using the word when referring to the advanced design aspects of the Granville Brothers' Gee Bee Racers. The crowds ate it up. *Aerodynamic* became an everyday word on the racing circuits. The Granvilles and their marvelous Gee Bee racers would take the racing circuits—and America—by storm.

Lowell Bayles had joined the ranks of the Gee Bee Corporation, so things looked good all around. Lowell liked to fly barefoot to feel the rudder pedals better, and the crowd, having learned about it, loved the idiosyncrasy. Ben insisted that flame-proof safety gear be worn, including footwear, and Lowell started wearing the tennis shoes and flame-proof covers. The newspapers—and therefore the crowds—persisted in calling him "Barefoot Lowell Bayles," so in order not to disappoint them, the addition of flameproof footwear wasn't advertised. Lowell kept his footwear in the plane and climbed in and out barefoot, wiggling his toes to the crowds' delight. A superb race pilot, he soon gained the fame that he had been destined to garner, and before long was as famous as Jim Doolittle. Jim soon had several other pilots in training, the first of them Jimmy Haizlip. Haizlip had been given first choice due to Ben's recollection of him as the one Gee Bee pilot who, during the Gee Bee's "first" history, had by virtue of having survived a Gee Bee crash, recognized that the air technology had exceeded current pilot skills and had written about it. He looked forward with keen anticipation to piloting his own ZR-2, or perhaps a new ZR-3.

The Granville brothers were riding the wave, and doing exceptionally well. Except for a single member of the organization who was having difficulties, they were on top of the world.

Chapter Twenty-Seven

Ben immersed himself in his work. He went to the races for the distraction. But he couldn't forget, and he couldn't get over it. Several months back, things had taken an unexpected turn for the worse.

Not with the racers. The Granvilles were making the Gee Bees a household name. He was delighted that the racers were winning, and when he was at the races he could forget for an hour or two.

It was temporary at best. When the races ended, the gloom descended again.

Ben's troubles came from another direction, a most unexpected direction. He had spent time with Laney for five months, and things had gone very well. A pair of completed ZR-3 racers would soon be "dialed in" by racing several of the smaller cross-country circuits, and they appeared to be ahead of schedule on all aspects of their development.

Jim Doolittle had found them the best sponsor they could have asked for, the Texaco Company. They had been given plenty of money to build the first two ZR-2 racers; fabrication had gone so well that when Texaco's representative came to check their progress and saw the two racers near completion, they immediately authorized another pile of funds to aid in completion. Since they instead of Shell Oil had "acquired" Jimmy Doolittle as a sponsored pilot, Texaco had been quite generous from the start. The Gee Bee Corporation already had enough to finish the ZR-2s, so Granny, Ben, Pete, and Jimmy put their heads together and designed

ZR-3 racers for high-speed long distances, with special attention to be paid to pilot comfort and combating fatigue.

They were certain to be in the money this year; and Ben had looked forward to having a little security. He intended to ask Laney to marry him, and since he could hardly ask her to share his broom-closet, he waited in anticipation, counting the days until he could kneel in front of her and pop the question.

That all changed when Michael Spencer returned home from his stint in the service much earlier than Laney had said. Not in the fall, or even the summer, but a full half-year earlier than Laney had said he would, in the middle of the winter.

Downtown, while drinking and playing pool, he heard about Ben and Laney. Up to that point, he hadn't given her a thought. He hadn't even bothered to tell her he was home. Now, he made a beeline straight for the Perkins house. Within the hour, he had pressed Laney's father for her hand in marriage, and to her utter dismay, her father gave his blessing.

Doc had held high hopes that the Granville's cousin Benjamin would ask him for her hand; the young man had been around to see her just about every night. With his college education and potential, that young man was everything Doc had hoped for, and to his surprise and delight, Laney seemed to be all for it as well. Ben worked like a madman for the Granvilles; the brothers were fortunate that he'd shown up.

But when it came to Laney, his intentions had remained unannounced. No permissions had been asked. It was most . . . irregular. After some time had passed, Doc figured the young man just wasn't the marrying type, and though she had tried, poor Laney hadn't been able to change his mind. He had to admit, she really did do her part this time, and avidly. She had demonstrated on any number of occasions that she could scare off any suitor with ease, but not this time; this young man was welcomed and encouraged. Doc could see the worry in her eyes, she waited for Ben to ask, she hoped for it in the worst way. Laney was no spring chicken; she was already twenty-two years old, and people were talking. Many other women her age would have been married and having children four or even six years ago, though as a doctor, he felt that was too young for safe childbearing.

When Michael showed up and persisted in announcing his intentions, Doc threw in the towel and gave his blessing there and then. What a shame. He wouldn't call it a waste, not out loud. If he had, he wouldn't be able to face himself for giving his permission. He privately hoped that it would light a fire under young Ben and bring him to his senses before it was too late. If young Ryan presented himself and asked, he could rescind the blessing he'd given Spencer, who he didn't think much of.

Things went downhill from there.

Ben got the news second-hand. Mark and Edward ran into the hangar out of breath, and told Ben that Spencer had asked for Laney's hand, and the Doc had said yes. Ben was stunned speechless, and then grew angry and remained quiet and sullen. *Surely Laney wouldn't let that take place, would she?* They'd grown so close, and things were going so well.

Granny expressed his sadness over hearing that, though not directly to Ben. He'd expected it might happen. For some reason, Ben had never announced his intentions. They'd heard it for some time from a number of sources, and the office staff whispered, of course.

The brothers missed the obvious problem. Ben had no idea he had done anything wrong. Being immersed in the design and production of the ZR-2 and then the ZR-3 racers, he'd had no opportunity to discover that. He spent all his time in the old hangar. If he'd so much as gotten his hands on a few magazines or newspapers, he might have had a chance to see how different this society was from his own. He might have recognized his innocent but disastrous missteps and omissions in time to rectify them.

Everything had stacked up against Ben. Laney knew the timeframe had changed but never cleared up her mistake, never told Ben that 'a year from now' had become 'almost anytime between the January thaw and spring.' Nobody had taken the time to explain the small-town proprieties and etiquette of the day to Ben, and Laney hadn't truly understood the depth of his request for her help with their customs during their first conversations. She'd continued seeing him nearly every day, walking, talking, holding hands, and snuggling contentedly. She hid her head in the sand and held onto the earnest hope that he would step up and announce his intentions before time ran out. And throughout those months of time they spent together, she failed to mention to him even once that *in all cases*, he was expected to formally and clearly announce his intentions.

He believed he was being responsible, exhibiting pride and waiting until he had income so they could have a place of their own. He was a product of the year 2010.

In 2010, a dowry was an old, barely-remembered custom which for all intents and purposes no longer existed. In 2010 a woman's father *might* be asked to pay for the wedding, and if he couldn't? Oh, well. The world was a much different place. Most folks in 2010 America thought a dowry was some old European tradition. It was one of the few gaps in the amazing amount of historic knowledge stored within his brain. He didn't have a clue what purposes dowries served in that era.

As if that wasn't enough, he never had a clue there ever *was* a dowry. He'd felt certain that he was making his feelings for her clear. From her perspective, she could tell he had real feelings for her, but for some reason he had drawn a line and refused to cross it.

In fairness to her, she'd brought it up that once and he practically ran away, so on subsequent occasions she was hesitant to broach the subject. Like everybody else, she never put the pieces together, though she knew he came from another time. She assumed that he knew there was a substantial dowry awaiting the lucky man who wed her. She assumed everybody in all of Hampden County knew that. The rumors certainly came back to her saying so. She couldn't understand what was holding him back, night after night, month after month. She didn't piece it together that the only people close to Ben—the Granvilles, Pete, Jim Doolittle—were also new to Springfield, and had no knowledge of her dowry.

She'd spoken with Mark and Edward once, and being the good friends to her that they were, they worried with her and hoped that Ben would announce his intentions. And otherwise they kept it to themselves. They didn't take their concerns or private conversations to Ben. After Spencer returned, they talked with the other brothers and Granny. But not with Ben.

None of the brothers broached the subject with him.

Laney didn't return to work. Ben waited day after day, night after night to hear something from her. Surely she would come by and talk to him about it. She'd never stayed away this long. Ben had no way of knowing that Spencer spent every waking moment at Laney's house, making sure she went nowhere unless it was with him, and he discouraged her from going anywhere near her workplace. No need for that, he said. She wouldn't be working there anymore. She acquiesced to avoid conflict. Spencer barely took time to go home and clean up and change. She waited in silent desperation for Ben to come to her, prayed he would come and stand up to Michael, that he would talk to her father and declare his intentions.

Finally, throwing the propriety of polite society to the winds, she wrote him a letter, beseeching him to come and talk with her father while there was still time. But he never came.

Spencer had expected that, and had plucked her letter from the box long before the postman arrived. She was trapped, without knowledge that her efforts to get to Ben had been sabotaged, and she was under pressure from all sides to take the 'bird in the hand.'

The boys went to her house so they could tell Laney how upset Ben was. Spencer expected somebody to come, and since he had no idea who Ben was, he met anybody walking down the street. Granvilles, especially. He'd come back home just when these boys were leaving last time, and was furious about it, so this time he recognized them and made sure they were turned away. Returning to the shop, their mistake of omission was repeated when they talked to their brothers, but not to Ben.

Spencer had Laney and he was not about to let go of her. Where she went, that dowry went. The way he saw it, that dowry was his. He'd fight dirty to get it, if that's what it took.

Doc and Mrs. Perkins didn't really like him, but were oblivious to his underhanded dealings. To all at the Perkins household, it appeared that Ben didn't care one way or the other. Nobody showed up to say differently.

Because of the potential for tensions, Doc avoided the Granvilles during this time. Every single person who knew Ben had failed him when it came to helping him learn about crucial customs.

It was a comedy of errors, and the result was anything but funny.

Ten days later, Ben heard the news. Laney Perkins had accepted Michael Spencer's proposal. He went out, bought a bottle of whiskey, returned to his room/broom closet, locked the door and for the first time in his life, drank himself unconscious.

Chapter Twenty-Eight

Granny said, "I heard the wedding is today."

Without inflection, Ben said, "Yeah."

"I'm surprised you're here. Weren't you planning on going?"

"Why would I do that?" he said, with no nuance beyond the question.

"I don't know. Perhaps as a gesture of kindness toward Laney? She was always very nice to you."

"Yeah. So nice she dumped me for that Spencer guy," he said, this time with considerable inflection.

"Dumped you? Is that what you think? That's not what happened."

"Oh?" he said, sitting up on his bed, morose and more than a little irate at the thought of her marrying somebody else. "Why don't *you* enlighten me as to what happened, then. Because it sure feels like she dumped me and is marrying some other guy today."

Granny understood why he wasn't happy, but not why he should feel cheated. "You had your chance. Why didn't you take it?"

"What chance didn't I take? I saw her every day at work, during lunch, and then went over to her house every night for five months! I saw her every spare minute I had. If I had an extra two bits, I bought her flowers. I did everything I could with what I have, but *this*. . . ." Ben opened his arms to indicate his neat little broom closet. "*This* is everything I have. And we're only just now winning some races; only just now the money is starting to come in. So I repeat, *what* chance didn't I take?"

Granny frowned. A picture was forming in his mind. One he hoped was wrong, but he didn't think so. Alarmed, he gave Ben a sharp look and asked, "Why didn't you announce your intentions?"

"She knew my intentions," he answered curtly.

"No, I mean, why didn't you formally announce your intentions to her father?"

"Why would I do that? I have nothing to offer her, nothing to marry her with. I wouldn't ask that until I could afford it, Granny. I have my pride, you know."

"Ben, when a man announces his intentions to a woman's father, it's not to ask him if you may marry her *now*, it's to ask permission to court her with the *intention* of marrying her. If the father gives his blessings to you, you may continue to see her, usually without fear of another suitor interloping as you court her. Other suitors will stay away, unless one is particularly determined to vie for her hand in marriage. In that case, the father can intervene in whatever way he feels is best. He can rescind the first suitor's permission. You know all this, don't you? Ben?"

Ben looked as if he had been shot. "If I had done that . . . what you just said . . . she would have married me instead?"

Granny was horrified. "Oh, God, Ben. You didn't know *any* of this, did you?"

Numb, he shook his head. He could barely think. *This trip through time, this never-ending nightmare.* It had stolen love away from him a second time, and once again he had no idea what to do about it.

Granny jumped up and yelled, "Ben, get dressed, we have to get you to that church!"

Ben stood up, the anger gone, but replaced with confusion. He was shaking badly, disoriented, unsure of what he should do.

Granny yelled, *"MOVE IT!"*

Numb but moving this time, Ben shoved his feet into his shoes and grabbed his cane and jacket, and they ran out the door. They cranked up Granny's sedan and climbed into it, and they were off.

Granny needed him to focus, to listen to the crucial information he would need to have. "Ben, you have to go into the church and object. They'll ask you why, and you have to state your intention to marry Laney yourself, do you understand?"

"I . . . I think so." But he hadn't a clue what he should do. He was lost and confused.

Granny, frustrated and furious with himself for having missed such an obvious problem, yelled over the wind and engine. "Oh, Ben, I'm so sorry. You knew so much about us and our racers and our history that we all assumed you knew about things like courting."

"I do know about it, in my time," Ben hollered back. Granny took a corner a bit too sharp and the car bounced up over the curb, then back onto the street. He didn't let off the throttle, maintaining the suicidal pace down the narrow streets and through the snow.

"I'll go in with you; I don't want this going wrong for you this time. I'll speak up for you if I have to. You've got one chance here, if we make it."

"What time is it supposed to be?" Ben asked.

"I'm not sure. No use taking chances, the sooner we get there the better. There it is!" He swung into an open parking spot amongst quite a number of vehicles, and set the brake; they jumped out and ran across the yard and into the church. Ben ran, pumped so full of adrenaline he felt no pain; his cane barely touched the ground.

They burst through the doors and stopped; the church was better than half-full. But it appeared to be a normal congregation. No bride, no groom.

Granny stopped next to Ben. He spoke to the minister, who had stopped when they burst in. "Pardon our intrusion, we thought there was to be a wedding here."

The minister spoke. "If you're looking for the Spencer wedding, I'm afraid it ended over two hours ago. The couple is already married."

Granny looked over at Ben, who was devastated, and shaking. If he never saw a look of pain like that again in his life it would be too soon. He gently took his beloved friend from the future by the arm, turned him around and walked slowly out the door. The congregation was rumbling with comments. Most of the folks there had attended the wedding and knew Ben was Laney's former friend. The whispers cut the air; it was plain that they figured him for the guy who never got around to it. Well, he got what he asked for. Granny heard them all.

And though he would have loved to, he couldn't set a single one of them straight.

The rest of the brothers were driving down Liberty Street when they saw Granny pass them in a big hurry. Not wanting to miss whatever was happening, they had turned around and followed, and were just pulling up.

"Hey Granny! Where's the fire?" one yelled. The others laughed.

Granny held up his hand to quiet them down. He took Ben, devastated and in a daze, and placed him on the seat of the sedan. He walked over to the others and told them the story. The laughter stopped, their cheeriness dissolved into the frigid air. Every one of them had thought for certain that Ben was crazy for Laney, and had not understood his behavior or lack of action. To the last one, they then realized how they had failed him. And in their shame, their hearts broke for him.

Standing next to the church, unseen by the brothers and Ben, the quiet man sadly shook his head. He really liked this young man. But he had a job to do, and he could not interfere. Too bad. He thought, *I would have liked to, just this once.* He'd watched Spencer's manipulations and dirty dealings, then watched him in a *church* as he married that girl for nothing more than money.

Oh, yes, just once . . .

Chapter Twenty-Nine

On their wedding night, they hadn't gone off on their honeymoon. Without a word of discussion, he had driven to his apartment, if it could be called that. It was a single, filthy room, the cheapest in an overcrowded, vermin-infested boarding house in the worst part of town. Once there, he told her that they had no use for such things as honeymoons. Everything Laney had ever talked about, anything she'd dreamed about; he cared about none of it, and told her she was foolish for wanting any of it. He'd started drinking at their little reception from a bottle he'd hidden in his pocket. Now, he started drinking in earnest. Before long, he grew loud, and then abusive.

"I ain't interested in none o' them refined things you're allus going on about. Books and education. Horse-biscuits! I never had none o' that and I growed up jest fine, look at me. I tolerated it before; weren't no use saying much to all that woman-chatter, not when I didn't have no claim on you yet. Well, all that's changed now, *ain't it?*" Then he grabbed her arm because she was looking away from him, terrified. He pulled her close and stuck his face nose-to-nose with hers. *"AIN'T IT?* B'sides, I made it through the fourth grade, that's enough for any man. I know my way around tractor engines and truck engines real good. Mebbe I can't read them manuals good, but I done okay, yes I have. I don't see why you're allus getting so worked up 'bout all those things, because we won't never be able to buy them. Things is tough all over. We're gonna need a passel of kids to run my farm right. You're too damn flighty; and I *intend* ta cure you of that right off. I'll be needin' a wife with a serious mind, one to do what I say. No more talk of this hoity-toity fancy living, y'hear?"

When somebody banged on the wall and yelled at him to keep it down, he tossed her back against her seat, and stomped across the room to pick up his bottle.

Horrified, and frozen in fear, she stayed perfectly still and didn't dare say a word.

Honeymoon nights are supposed to be made of the things of every girl's dreams. When he grabbed her by the arm and dragged her to the bed, the resistance she put up earned her a split lip and a black eye. Her honeymoon night was every girl's worst nightmare.

On the rare occasions he sobered up, it wasn't much better. Now that he'd started, he wasn't going back. Any infraction resulted in a roughing up. Anything more earned her a beating, and he took her at will. His talk of a farm was just that; talk. He was lazy, and slovenly.

He took their dowry money and rented a house instead of placing a handsome down payment on a farm. From that day on, he did his level best to drink the rest, doling out only small amounts to her to buy groceries or pay bills. He rationalized that there wasn't a job around there good enough for him, so he didn't bother trying to find one. It was bad enough when he had to fix a simple leak in his radiator hose. He hated leaving the house to pick up a new hose, but he'd noticed the leak on his last whiskey run. He was getting low on whiskey again, so he walked down to Main Street for both.

Chapter Thirty

"Why do you want to meet Hughes, Ben?" Jim asked.

"I think he can help us with what we're doing. You know him, right?"

"Well sure, I've worked in California and I've done some flying for his company before. He's a bit of a weird duck, you should know."

Ben grinned. "Sounds just like Howard Hughes to me. I'd like to meet with him and have a serious conversation with him; does that sound like something you can arrange?"

Jim nodded. "Consider it done." Howard Hughes liked him. Well, at least, as well as he ever liked anybody, so he felt pretty sure he could arrange that. Whatever Ben felt he wanted to do was okay with Jim.

Ben knew what they needed to do, and Jim had the head for it too. Quicker to grasp the full implications than even Ben or Granny, he had uncanny instincts; he instantly understood what a paradox was and he knew they were all pebbles in the pond. Like Ben, he saw that some ripples appeared to be set in the pond by time itself, and time didn't take kindly to meddling. Overall, however, the broad strokes of their plans seemed to be working to their satisfaction. Ben didn't feel alone in his plans; he had a staunch ally in Jim Doolittle. That made him feel somewhat better about things.

And then there were those problems that nobody could help him with.

He couldn't get Laney out of his mind, but he knew he had to. So, he worked every minute of the day and late into every night. The only problem was, there wasn't enough work right now to keep him busy. Every program they had implemented for pilot training, safety, all the advances in technology, everything worked just as intended. Not much was going on. They'd already fitted one of the ZR-3 racers with a prototype Wasp radial for distance running. Maybe he'd dabble with that. He was trying to stay busy, so he drove down to the Motor Supply store for some clamps. As he waited his turn, a voice spoke from off to his side.

"Well, if it ain't the *loser!*"

He glanced over at the man, who was almost his age, but he'd never seen him before. He looked drunk. Guessing he wasn't the one being addressed, Ben turned back to the front.

Seconds later, the man spoke again, "Hey! You DEAF?"

He had moved up close, and was just two feet away.

Ben turned to him. "Sorry about that. Do I know you?"

"You oughtta! I'm the man who come into town and took that woman right out from under your nose, *boy*," the man said, and loosely poked a finger into Ben's shoulder.

"Michael Spencer," he said, looking into the sullen, red eyes. The man swayed perceptibly from side to side. He was in the bottle, though how deep was uncertain.

"That's right, you *know* my name. I'm taking *good* care of that woman now. She's mine, 'n' don' you forget it!" he slurred, his breath reeking of alcohol.

Ben turned back toward the front, bristling. "Whatever you say, Spencer. It's nothing to me now."

Annoyed that he couldn't get a good rise out of Ben, he tried again. "Well, I wouldn't think so, because she wouldn't be caught in public with no *cripple*. Look at you, using that walking stick like a old man. No wonder she picked me. You ain't nothing but a piece o' shi—"

Ben whirled and used the brass eagle head on his cane to gain Spencer's undivided attention. The sudden blow dazed the man, and he crumpled to the floor. Ben dragged him out the door by the back of his coveralls, where he deposited him on his knees at the top of the landing. He drew back his foot and kicked him in the ribs so hard that it sent him crashing down the steps. He slammed onto the ground so hard he couldn't breathe, and then Ben was on him, kicking and pounding him without mercy. Spencer reeled from the dozens of sharp, well-aimed kicks and punches to his knees, ribs, stomach, and face. He was so dazed that he could no longer cover himself. Ben was everywhere, tearing him to pieces.

Spencer managed to kick him away for just long enough to scramble unsteadily to his feet. They circled each other, and he tried to swing with his right. Ben leaned back and the punch sailed past his face. Grabbing Spencer's wrist with his right hand, Ben drove a lightning-fast left into the exposed elbow. Spencer never saw it coming. His arm broke with a loud Snap. Ben knew he'd inflicted catastrophic damage, and took a step back.

The already-stunned man stopped fighting entirely and clawed and clutched at the all-consuming pain in his shattered elbow, and in that unguarded moment, Ben sent a roundhouse to the side of his unprotected upper throat and jaw. Spencer went down hard and didn't move. But Ben wasn't finished. Not even close. He hated the man for what he was, for what he'd done, for how he'd done it. After the wedding, he'd learned of the methods Spencer had used to keep Laney from him, and it made him see red. Blood red. He'd tried—he had really tried—not to lose his temper, but it was lost, and he wouldn't stop now until he finished what he started.

Before he could start in seriously again on the wretched, bloody, beaten man, hands were on him from all sides, pulling him off. It had gone far beyond a fight; several men had grabbed him to stop the horrific beating from turning into a killing. He wrenched, pushed them, tore away, and dove for Spencer again, delivering more vicious kicks and blows. They grabbed him again, tightly this time, and pulled him off, holding him.

"Easy, son, easy! You're gonna kill that fella. We can't let you do that. You've got to get a *grip* on yourself!"

Still wound tight as a steel spring, it took a moment for his tunnel vision to fade. Ceasing his struggling, he looked around him at the men, and realized with embarrassment how crazed he must have appeared. "I'm sorry. I . . . I lost my temper. Thanks for stopping me."

"Yeah, we figured you lost your temper. You like to have killed that man," the man said, gesturing toward the blood-covered Spencer. "Think you can restrain yourself?"

"Oh, man," he whispered, seeing what he'd done to Spencer. "Yeah. Thanks," he said.

"Don't thank us. We came out to see that fella get what he deserved." The others nodded in agreement. "He got it . . . and then some." Somewhat more quietly, the man said, "But it's done now, so you might want to head on out of here. With a ruckus like this one, I expect the sheriff's been called. He'll probably be along any time."

A couple of the men were helping Spencer to his feet. Before Ben left, he limped over and put his face close to Spencer's and asked, "Got anything else you want to say to me . . . *boy?*"

Spencer, in the first stages of shock, would not meet his gaze. Averting his face, he stared down and away in wide-eyed terror, trembling with fear.

He was done running his mouth. He could barely stand. His right arm was broken at the elbow. He could barely breathe with all the broken ribs. Blood ran from his mouth, his ears, and his eyes were swollen; one was near-shut already.

Ben stepped closer and placed his mouth next to Spencer's ear, and whispered, "Next time, these boys won't be there to stop me. Then I'll give you **everything** you deserve. I . . . can't . . . *wait.*"

Spencer whimpered and backed away from him, a large wet patch growing on the front of his coveralls as he urinated, the liquid trickling audibly as it ran out the pant leg. Trembling, bloody, broken, and now urine-soaked, he was a pathetic sight.

The man speaking for the others said, "Boys, you might want to be a step closer, in case talking isn't all he has in mind. He's mighty quick with those fists and feet."

But it was over . . . for now. Ben agreed; it was time to leave. Picking up his cane, he stopped and thanked the men for stepping in, and turning, limped to the truck.

Unseen by Ben and the others, the quiet man had stood by. As an archangel, one way he *was* permitted to interact with his charge was to inspire him in battle. Though he was an archangel who normally did not relish battle, he was willing to make an exception in this case. As it had turned out, his young charge was more than sufficiently inspired to defeat his challenger with no outside help.

Over the past few weeks, as Spencer had repeatedly beaten and savaged the woman Ben loved, the angel had watched. Furious that he was forbidden to interfere, raging inside against his restraints, forced to remain unseen, it had been everything he could do not to step in and destroy the despicable piece of garbage. Though it could have cost him eternity, he very nearly killed him anyway, and almost certainly would have had Ben not beaten Spencer to within an inch of his life.

Ben drove home, unaware of the quiet man sitting next to him in the truck. Studying the young man he'd been charged with accompanying on his journey through life, the angel realized that this one was different from any of the others.

On the surface, this assignment was exactly the same as his assignments had been for hundreds of years. But this one was nothing like the others. He couldn't remember how long it had been since he had actually *felt* something; how many decades, even centuries, since he had cared. Unexpected or not, this young man mattered to him. The things and people this young man loved mattered to him. True; he had yet to accomplish anything of any real consequence, but there was something about him that touched the angel. More than just the fact that he'd probably saved an archangel from committing a fatal error, though he certainly had done just that. This young man would bear watching more closely, and for the first time in centuries, the angel felt that perhaps— just perhaps—his assignment had some real meaning, some potential.

With a trace of a smile, he said, "Thank you, Ben."

Ben, heard something and looked around, but saw nothing.

Chapter Thirty-One

He drove straight back to the shop and told Granny what had transpired.

"Oh, my. That's bad. I think we can expect some trouble from this, Ben."

Ben nodded. "Yeah. I think you're right."

"For right now, stay close to your room, and let's try to keep the door closed. Do you think you can do that?"

"Sure."

"If the sheriff comes, I'll try to throw him off your scent, but I'm not sure how much I'll be able to do."

"Thanks. I'll keep the room dark. No use advertising."

Granny hurried out back and called the brothers together for a conference. After the conference, Mark and Edward headed out the door and the others scattered. Ben kept working but stayed close to his room. The sheriff never showed that day; that meant all bets were off for the next morning.

At the crack of dawn the next morning, all the brothers were there working, all anticipating the arrival of the sheriff. Minutes later, the sheriff, a big man at six feet five inches, quietly walked in through the rear hangar door. He hadn't driven a car to the front. He was planning to surprise them, and he did.

Granny tried his best to run interference. He explained that Ben was not there; he was off for the day running some errands. The sheriff just nodded down at him amiably and walked around him, continuing toward the rear of the shop, checking every corner and room as he talked. "Do you have any idea how badly that Michael Spencer was beaten? Most of his ribs are broken, he has a broken jaw, a concussion and head injuries, his elbow is so badly broken it'll never work right again, and that's just what we know so far. I need to have a talk with your Mr. Ryan in the worst way."

Finally he came to a closed door.

"What's in there?"

"Oh, that's just a broom closet."

"A broom closet, you say? That's good. I'm told that's where he lives, in a broom closet in the back of your shop."

"Oh, he hasn't lived there for a long time, Sheriff."

"That so?" the sheriff commented, giving him a penetrating look that said he knew damn well that was a lie.

He stepped over to the door, and spoke in a loud voice. "Benjamin Ryan, I'm going to ask you real nice to come out of there. What do you say? Ben?"

Tired of waiting, he grabbed the knob and pulled the door open.

It contained two mop pails and five garbage cans.

"See?" Granny said, trying not to look surprised. The room looked like it had never been occupied.

Outside, the radial engine they had been working on revved up to a powerful thrum, and it soon became clear it was moving. The sheriff turned and listened, then with Granny trailing him hurriedly made his way back through the hall, out through the cluttered shop and out the hangar door onto the runway. He ran outside just in time to see Granny's Senior Sportster lift off and fly past. Next to the pilot's leather helmet, visible above the cockpit coaming, was a brass eagle head.

The sheriff wheeled on Granny, furious and pointing at the aircraft. "I suppose everybody here carries a cane just like his, too!"

Granny, doing his best to avoid confrontation—and the looming man's wilting glare—concentrated on lighting his pipe. "No, no, I'm pretty sure he's the only one."

"*Damn it!* Where is he headed?"

"No telling. He was talking about Hartford, maybe?"

"You tell your Mr. Ryan I'll be back to have a talk with him. Or else he'd better just keep flying."

"Yes, sir, Sheriff, I'll be sure to tell him just that."

The sheriff stomped away.

As the sheriff walked toward the car he'd parked up on the main road, Granny lit his pipe . . . this time with some tobacco in it. He stared at the retreating dot in the sky and wondered where the hell Ben and his Model Y were going. Not that it mattered; as long as Ben stayed clear of this trouble, he didn't care about anything else.

As he turned around, he saw Ben standing next to him, wearing a pair of greasy overalls and a cap, also watching the Senior disappear in the distance.

"Ben!"

"Granny!" he fired back, with an impish grin.

"Well, who the hell was that?" Granny asked, pointing his pipe stem after his departed Model Y.

"Mark. And my cane."

"Where were you?"

"Right here, working on the ZR-3 the whole time. That cane is an eye-catcher, I had an idea he'd be looking for somebody using a cane with a brass eagle head. When he showed up like he did, I slipped on Mark's overalls and cap and then hid in plain sight, while Mark slipped out with my cane and went for a hop in the Senior."

"Where is he going?"

"I don't know. Agawam, probably. We didn't really have time to lay out a flight plan."

Granny wanted to laugh, but things were too serious. Things were in motion. He and Ben needed to figure out their next move.

Ben had already given a lot of thought to that.

Chapter Thirty-Two

Time Flies

Four years ago, Ben had left Springfield. Staying in Springfield potentially held big problems for him. But more than anything, it was time for him to leave. He had a mission to embark upon. Somewhere out there were the people who could help him find a way to achieve his larger goals. So he took the next step and started out full-time on the next phase of his plan to change history.

The day after the sheriff had paid them a visit, Ben left for California in Granny's Model Y Senior Sportster. It was a magnificent plane and he was honored when Granny gave it to him. He was living his wildest dream. He flew a Gee Bee Y almost every day; *Granny's* Gee Bee Y, no less. But it was tempered by the fact that every day he also lived with the bitter taste of the dreams he'd let slip away. With Laney married, there was less than nothing for him in Springfield. Since that day, he'd helped Granny and the boys set up their aircraft service companies, and he was now assured of their success. That success in turn had prevented Granny from embarking upon that tragic flight. Or at least he sure hoped it would, as today was February 11, 1934, and Granny would have been making that landing just about now.

He saw his adopted brothers when he could; at the Thompson Trophy and Bendix races and similar events. Their bond was so strong it always felt as though they'd last been together yesterday.

"Well, I do declare, it's the black sheep of the Granville clan!"

Ben turned at the familiar voice. "Robert! How are you?"

"Well, our Gee Bee Racers are the ones to beat, we're all making good money, and I'm here for the grand opening of two more Gee Bee facilities. I'd say I'm doing just fine, brother!"

They hugged. Robert just loved the business end of things anyway, but was always happier when the numbers were all in black ink. Folks from all over the world were placing orders with the Granville organization to design and build aircraft for them.

"So, the contracts are still coming in?"

"From all over the world, and we're cherry-picking the more lucrative contracts. Your idea to use the most highly-qualified sub-contractors is really paying off. The money's flowing in one direction, thanks to the system you set up for us."

Ben had learned some sound business practices from the time he'd spent working around Ryan Aviation, his Gramps's aviation manufacturing and fabrication concern. Aircraft overhauling and fabrication just happened to fall neatly into his areas of expertise.

"Pretty soon we'll have Gee Bee facilities in every corner of the country. We've got a sterling reputation now, and we're hiring the best men from all over the United States. With people bringing home paychecks again, we're becoming heroes off the racing circuits as well. I don't know why. You and I both know, we've generated—what? A few hundred jobs at most."

Robert didn't think it was something worth placing too much emphasis on, but he saw things from a business perspective. The boost their successes gave a dispirited Depression-era America was priceless. Any business in the public eye that continued to grow and hire men became a fountainhead of hope and a news magnet.

The Granville Brothers and their marvelous Gee Bee racers continued to spark imaginations and inspire Americans everywhere their name appeared.

And now, Ben was opening these two new aircraft centers for them. He'd interviewed and picked the capable crews and engineers at each of the centers himself, so the aircraft centers would flourish with minimal supervision.

A voice behind him, speaking in a distinct Downeast accent, asked, "Who's running this place? Cahn't a guy get any service when he needs it?"

Ben wheeled to see the whole clan. "You're all here. I don't believe it! Boy, you don't know how glad I am to see you!" He gave Granny a bear hug, and then all of the others as well.

Granny looked at Robert and nodded.

Robert said, "Ben, we're not just here to celebrate the grand opening of the new facilities. We had a meeting, and we've decided to present these two new centers to you in appreciation for everything you've done for us. There is a stipulation, and that is that the profits are yours alone, and don't have to be reinvested into the Gee Bee corporation. We voted on it, and we feel that you have already invested more into the Granville brothers than any of us ever will."

"Well, I wouldn't say that . . ."

"You don't get a vote. All you get to do is name your new businesses."

His eyes grew red as he blinked back the mist in them, and he nodded. After a moment, he cleared his throat and said, "I think I'd like to name them Ryan Aviation, to honor my Gramps."

The brothers broke out in applause. Granny grinned and said, "Looks like you're going to need to rewrite the speech for your grand opening today, Ben. Can I help?"

"Absolutely," he said, as they walked. "Hey, what time is it?"

Granny checked his watch. "9:45."

"And what's the complete date?"

Granny knew he was humoring Ben. "February 11, 1934. Why?"

Ben smiled as broadly as Granny had ever seen. "I'm not going to tell you. But . . . you'll live."

The two walked off together, leaving the rest of the brothers to their own amusements.

It was a day of celebration.

Chapter Thirty-Three

When the brothers were with Ben, any mention of Laney was carefully avoided.

He wouldn't go back, even if he could. The law hadn't looked for him for a very long time now. Perhaps nothing had come of it.

No matter. Laney was far away, and he could stand that. Barely. He couldn't be near her. If she was near he'd have to admit she was lost to him, and he knew in his soul that he couldn't stand that pain. And he couldn't trust himself or be sure of what he'd do if he ran into Michael Spencer again. It had come to him after the beating he gave Spencer that if he'd killed him, Katie Lynn might never exist. He couldn't live with that.

So, he lived with a slow-growing dark spot on his soul, with the emptiness he would never be able to fully reconcile his heart to. Almost every day he gazed at Katie Lynn's photo. He knew he tortured himself by doing so. He had no photo of Laney, and this was as close as he would ever get to having one. As far as the photo was concerned, in his mind they were the same woman.

He wasn't crazy. He knew that they were two separate, wonderful women, both of whom he had loved with all his heart. It didn't matter anyway; of the two of them, this color photo was all he had left. As far as wealth and material possessions were concerned, he was now comparatively wealthy. He had Ryan Aviation, which continued to grow even in the ongoing Depression. He had the Model Y Senior Sportster, and he took immaculate care of it. The Senior was a daily reminder of his brothers and still his heroes, Granny and the other Granville brothers. *Ben's* brothers. Aside from the Model Y, he had only one item he treasured; the photo. Every day, no matter where he was, he looked at the photo. He never said a word; he didn't trust himself to say a thing. And so it went, day after day, year after year.

Approaching the manipulation of time and specific historic events from a purely clinical perspective was something he'd figured out. The broad strokes could be achieved through changing the overall balances of existing events. He'd learned this through hard work, focus, and dedication. Although he hadn't noticed himself maturing in the past five years, he had come a long way from being the young man who crashed in Springfield.

Traveling across America, he encountered a country so riddled with depression that folks from 2010 would never have recognized it. He certainly never would have. The first year he left Springfield, the Dust Bowl began, ravaging America's heartland with soil loss brought about by poor farming methods, the long drought and ceaseless wind. He knew it was coming and found he was powerless to change it. He spoke with all of the Agriculture people in Washington, and left them with some recommendations for changing farming methods. There was nothing to be done about the ongoing drought. The new methods might shorten the Dust Bowl, but it would not be stopped. Any efforts to help were hampered by the Depression and lack of money for programs. As door after door was closed in his face, it became clear that his plans to prepare America for Pearl Harbor faced an enemy more daunting than any other: Poverty.

America was broke. It didn't matter how important the situation was; there was an immense country to run and very little money to do it with. Few people or politicians wanted to be bothered with "what-if" scenarios that involved spending precious tax dollars. Every time he brought it up he'd met with the same response, *"The Japanese are our allies, why would they attack us?"*

True enough; they'd lulled us into sleepy submission with their friendship medals and polite, even meek, ambassadors. The clock was ticking. He'd already lived in this time for over five years. *Five years!* He'd believed that twelve years was more than enough time when he arrived. Now he only had seven years remaining and he didn't seem any closer to a solution.

He reminded himself that wasn't really true; a substantial amount of the technology was available now, if he could just start the wheels turning faster. Any warbirds produced now would be tougher, faster, better than those produced during the first history of World War II, limited only by the available materials and the manufacturing processes of the day. He'd already made some important technological advancements with the contract for tire developments with BF Goodrich. With several other technologies, he'd also laid a substantial groundwork. There was much to be pleased with. Cause and effect, do the best you can; move on. Broad strokes designed to shift the balance in ways yet to be seen.

Approaching the manipulation of time and history from a purely personal perspective was another story entirely; and at times it was no less than maddening to him. It was the regrets. Once you've traveled back through time and changed some aspects of history for the better, you look at the pieces that fell beyond your grasp; washed away as the waves of time lapped over them, like ocean waves on the beach, sweeping them from you forever. It's a painful lesson. Time is much like a beach; one tick of the clock, one moment in time when something is available to you, as shiny and beautiful as a shell left on the glowing sand after a wave. Grab it and hold on tight, or not; it's your choice. The wave will come again whether you do or don't. What you do in that brief moment will determine what you are left with.

He'd learned that all too well. He thought, *well, that was then, and this is now.*

Chapter Thirty-Four

Broad Strokes

Two years earlier he'd met Marilyn, a woman who took an immediate liking to him. She was good company. She was also two inches taller than him with her heels on, and usually dressed to kill. For the life of him, he couldn't see what she liked about him. He flew all the time; she'd flown with him once and then pitched fits for two days about what it had done to her hair. She wore nice perfume, he had to give her that. He'd reminded himself all week to order in some flowers for their two-year anniversary, which was—oops—tonight.

He made his approach to Detroit, and made a nice landing. As he taxied toward a huge hangar with a large "H" on the front, the hangar doors opened. As he rolled inside, he shut the motor down and kicked hard left rudder to turn it around. The hangar crew approached and took over as he climbed down and grabbed his cane and gear. By the time he returned, the Senior would be serviced, refueled, and ready for his next flight. He finished his paperwork in the office, ordered flowers for Marilyn, and walked outside.

There he found his driver, whose name was Alexander. He had a last name, but Ben was damned if he could remember it half the time. Whatever it was, it was very British, just like Alexander. Whittington . . . no, Wellington, that was it. Alexander Wellington.

"Good afternoon, Mr. Ryan. I trust your flight was uneventful?"

"Hi, Al. Is that code for: 'So, Boss, I take it you didn't crash and die or anything?'"

Alexander gave a pleasant, tolerant nod. "Indeed it is, Mr. Ryan. Yet I always look forward to your colorful phrasing. It's positively boring when you're not around." The corners of his mouth twitched up ever so slightly; hinting at a reserved smile.

Ben grinned. "I think I was just insulted, but that's okay. You're all right by me, Al."

They were fond of each other. Though other drivers were available, Alexander was the best and Mr. Ryan was very specific about which chauffeur he wanted. Ultimately he hired Alexander full-time, and the man couldn't have been more pleased. Being Mr. Ryan's personal chauffeur included very nice living quarters there within the hangar, and a generous benefits package and expense account. A decent place to live was no small fringe benefit in those times.

"Al, is he on time?"

"I believe you will find him waiting for you upon your arrival, sir."

Ben looked out the window and enjoyed the ride. Today might turn out to be a big day for him. He wouldn't know until he got there. All of this cultivation and nurturing may have come to some fruition. You do what you can do. Broad strokes.

They turned onto East Grand Boulevard and drove until the Packard factory loomed. The facility was immense. Alexander, as always, was prepared. He knew where he needed to go, and dropped him at the appropriate door. Ben stepped inside to hear a familiar voice.

"Right on time, as usual."

"Howard! How have you been?"

"Fine, fine, but busy. The schedule you've saddled me with is grueling."

"You love it."

He laughed. "I do. This is one of the most intriguing things I've ever been involved in. It's stimulating to be here at the dawn of all this!"

"Mr. Hughes! Mr. Ryan! It's great to see you again!"

They turned to see a man bustling toward them. His dress shirt had the sleeves rolled up unevenly, he had his pocket-protector full and pencils stuck over one ear, causing his glasses to skew to one side. Oblivious to his appearance, he was in high gear. Perry was always in high gear. He moved fast, he talked fast, he carried a clipboard; he was a typical shift manager.

"Perry! How goes it?"

"Oh, you wouldn't believe it. . . . *Wonderful,* it's going *wonderfully,* we've got so much going on . . . you'll want to see this, if you'll follow me, I think you're going to be amazed. . . . "

And off they went, hurrying to keep up with Perry as he scurried and wound his way through the maze of the facility, and all the while they listened to him jabber on. He had so much he wanted to say that he never quite finished a sentence, but he was a good man and an excellent shift manager. After some distance they walked into a large, quiet, brightly lit, clean room with white-tile floors, devoid of the machinery that filled the rest of the plant, and enclosed as a quiet area. There they were met by a half-dozen more nervous clipboard-wielding men in lab coats.

Against the back wall was an engine. Supported on a heavy frame, the power plant was quite large, fully eight feet long and three and one-half feet tall. They stopped for a moment to appreciate its apparent simplicity and elegance. This engine was unlike any engine ever made to date. Radials were readily available, and relatively reliable, especially for the day; they were the workhorses that would work perfectly for mass-production cargo planes and bombers. That was not what they sought for the fighters they had designed.

In one of Ryan Aviation's facilities in 2010, in a room much like this, Gramps had an ancient—but still-new—1934 Merlin engine identical to this, on a frame identical to this. Though nobody could fathom just why, Gramps had spent a considerable amount on the best engineers and R & D to develop the potential of what were by then ancient Merlin engines, to develop maximum attainable horsepower. As far as Ben knew, Ryan Aviation had never used them for anything other than horsepower tests and flight tests in various airframes. As a young man, it had been an item of great interest to Ben. He had spent weeks with the engineers learning all about them. His grandfather had never seemed to mind him button-holing the engineers or the lost production time, instead he *insisted* that they spend the time with Ben so he would know exactly what modifications had been made and why.

As that memory surfaced, he realized why Gramps hadn't minded. He somehow *knew* that at some point Ben would be trapped in the past with only his wits. He knew which high-output engines would be available in this era and chose the best of them, modified it, and then trained his grandson to modify it. Moreover, and to the utter mystification of the engineers, the modifications were done entirely with the metals, alloys, and methods which would be accessible to them in the 1930s. Knowledge of this magnitude could make or break their plans. He arrived knowing almost everything about the Rolls-Royce Merlin, manufactured by Packard and used in the P-51s, and knew all about the horsepower advancements and upgrades that Gramps had developed. Howard and he decided to use that knowledge as a base for this power plant. He felt a pang as he gratefully thought, *Thanks, Gramps.* Knowing what he knew now, nobody would ever have to tell him just how much his Gramps loved him.

One of the men stepped up, pointing at the various parts of the engine.

"Good morning, Mr. Hughes, Mr. Ryan. As you requested, this twelve-cylinder Rolls-Royce Merlin has been supercharged with a Wright double-impeller, positive displacement blower. It is intercooled between each impeller through the case jacket, as you suggested, which works well to keep the temperatures down. We originally had your estimated 1900 HP during altitude tests, and then we made the modifications you recommended. Now, we are routinely seeing 2200 HP on altitude tests, and experiencing cooler temperatures and plenty of power during takeoff simulations. Of course, these *are* just simulations, and this is an automotive facility, so we have no airframe to use it in. We're fairly sure you'll find the actual results to be different."

"Do you have any idea of how much it will differ?" Ben asked.

"There could be a potential increase of five to ten percent once the propeller unloads at speed in the air. These estimates of course are conservative."

Howard nodded. "Of course. Have you reviewed the airframe specs we sent you and calculated them against this power plant for speed with the variable-pitch propeller?"

"Yes sir. We weren't certain of the results at first. We thought they must be wrong, but your engineers in California verified them for us.

We've never seen power output like this. In a power-on dive, the fighter should approach six hundred miles per hour."

Howard whistled loudly. "Now, *that* is what I call an engine! How soon can you start a limited production run?"

"Full production capability on limited numbers is available and can begin immediately. We've already done a startup run of twenty-five more engines, from the ground up. Once we saw the results, we felt sure we would be building many more, and we know you like to plan ahead. But Mr. Hughes, once Rolls-Royce learns we are using their engine, won't we need licensing?"

"Leave that to me. Britain is going to need these as badly as we will. We'll offer to teach them our horsepower tips in exchange for our using it only for our defense needs. Then you can sell them these patented modified cases and Supercharger assemblies. Should be downright profitable."

"Howard," Ben said.

"Yes, Ben?"

Ben tilted his head sideways toward the group of men, indicating that Howard might be saying more than he should in their company. Howard smiled and waved away the implication.

"Oh, them. They all know."

"ALL of them?"

At that, the men lowered their clipboards and moved up close to shake Ben's hand. The lead engineer waited until the others had greeted him, and then spoke. "Mr. Ryan. . . . "

"Ben. Please . . . call me Ben."

The leader looked at the other men, who nodded their heads, urging him to continue.

"Ben. We all know your story. To use your knowledge this way is so . . . this country belongs to us all, and we all should protect it. With our lives. We want you to know we're behind you all the way."

He was touched by their sentiment, and thanked them. *So, behind every clipboard is a closet patriot. Who knew?*

Chapter Thirty-Five

The Unveiling

They had lunch together after the Packard plant project. "How are the other projects going, Howard? Were you able to sort out the glitches?"

"Yes. I've made some real progress. But not in all the ways we'd originally planned. I hope you don't mind, but I took it upon myself to change a few details. I've used all my power and influence to try and push something through from the civilian and the military sides. Nobody's willing. The problem is that there's no budge in the country's budget. Without some major financial or security shift, there just won't be any money available for a number of years."

Ben quietly moaned and nodded. "That's the same thing I came up against. If a defense industrialist like *you* can't get things moving on this, who can?"

"It gets worse before it gets better. I've also given up on Chance Vought. They refuse to withhold sales to Japan, mostly because Japan has already made the deal with them. They won't say no to the money in these hard times. But I've come up with an alternate approach. I know this sounds dangerous to you, but I'm proposing that we leave the Zero alone."

Ben was taken aback. He hoped there was more coming.

Howard said, "Here's why. If we're lucky enough to trip the Japanese up on the V-141 and V-143, then where will they go? Along the lines of the drawings you've made of the Zero, I've been able to identify at least fifteen fighters in the U.S. and Europe that the Zero could loosely be based on. You said yourself that there was a lot of controversy about that. It might even have been based on my Hughes Racer, right?"

He went on. "Here's my point; if we leave things alone and they come at us with the Zero you gave us the specs on, we have a known quantity to plan against. If we mess with it, we could be shooting ourselves in the foot. Our new fighters will be so fast and so advanced that those Zeroes won't stand a chance. That's my straight-through-them approach. What do you think?"

Ben pondered the logic for a moment. "That's good thinking. It makes sense. It takes the guesswork out and improves our chances. I didn't allow for other perspectives, or other scenarios. I'll admit it never occurred to me to simply build better fighters and beat the hell out of them. After viewing our supercharged Merlin today, I say yes. Absolutely."

"Good. I've called a number of business acquaintances, and I've run our scenario past them in theory. I think I have most of them sold on our plans. Can you meet us at my offices here this afternoon? I have some things I'd like to run past everybody."

"I'll be there."

The other members of Howard's group had questions, and they were coming fast and furious. Ben was impressed by how sharp these men were, how attuned they were to every aspect of the plan. But of course they would be; like Howard, they were defense industrialists.

"We'd need hundreds of fighters, and hundreds of pilots."

"Yep."

"And you're proposing that we drop your initial plan to convince the US military to re-arm, and build our own air force instead?"

"I prefer to call it a joint industrial endeavor based on America's future military needs. A consortium of patriots, if you will."

Ben liked the idea. A consortium of patriots. He said, "I know how to train the pilots and I know who could train them, but where will we get them?"

"I'm thinking . . . Uncle Sam? Why not, right? If I can swing an aviator training program in conjunction with fighter development. That's the kind of thing the military might spend some of their money on."

"But they don't have any fighters, do they?"

"Sure they do. But not any great number, and they're not very good ones. The P-40s are the best they have so far, and they don't have many."

"Do we have enough money to do all of this?"

"After today's Merlin test results we do, and then some. Am I right, gentlemen?"

The members of the newly-formed consortium nodded; they were satisfied. The funds would flow.

Howard was finalizing the design details for the fighter. It was an exceptionally complicated situation. To put a military fighter into production with no orders having been placed by the military, the consortium would have to manufacture the whole air force on a budget. But, unlike the US government, they had a budget to work with, however limited.

Just to complicate things, Howard had talked about simultaneously building a smaller fleet of a larger version. From what little he'd let slip, it would be equipped with modified wings and spoilers. Perhaps they would get a chance to see the design during today's meeting. Ben was sure he'd probably love it, like everything else the man decided to do. Hughes had a knack for getting to the crux of the problem, while maintaining vigilance over every other possible aspect. He was always miles ahead of everybody, even before anyone else knew there was a crux or a problem.

At the front, sheets covered a couple of easels.

Howard walked up front and began. "We struggled at first, deciding which approach to take with the Japanese Zeroes. We made it simple. We're going to meet them head-on with our new fighter, which, not to put too fine a point on it, should thrash them soundly."

Simple and effective. Murmurs of agreement rippled through the folks in attendance.

"But this doesn't address the flip side of that coin. When they come at us; yes, we can take them on. But in their present configuration, our fighters—and our entire air force, in fact—are purely defensive."

"The Japanese Fleet will be right there, a couple of hundred miles north of Pearl. They'll only be lightly guarded while they spring a sneak attack on us. We know when their first wave will launch—zero six hundred hours—that's 6:00 a.m. for those of you who haven't used military time. Learn how to tell military time; you're going to be using it every day from now on. The second wave will launch at zero seven hundred hours. At zero eight hundred thirty hours, the maximum number of their fighters will reach the furthest possible point from the fleet. That's when their fleet will be most vulnerable. And that's when we can attack them and sink their flat-tops and destroyers."

There was some skepticism among the members about where this was going. Ben sensed it and said, "Howard, this sounds pretty aggressive. Do you think that sinking the entire Japanese Fleet is a realistic goal?"

"Yes, I do. We could sink the critical ships such as the flat-tops and destroyers at the very least, which would cripple their operational capabilities. It'll be complicated, but it can be done. I've approached this scenario a dozen different ways, and here's what I've come up with."

And with that, Howard unveiled the easels. The renderings showed a larger, longer aircraft than the fighter. The wing was larger, with spoilers added. The side-view on the second rendering showed the surprise payload—a massive torpedo.

"Gentlemen, I give you our new bomber. I've taken our fighter, enlarged it to increase carrying capacity and I've added some diving capabilities to it. Our answer and counterpoint to the B5N Kate as described with specs by Ben. It's about twice as fast as the Kate, has a tremendous eight-hour range with drop tanks, as all of our fighters will. Fully loaded, it still has a top speed nearly one hundred miles per hour faster than the Zero, and once it delivers its payload, it can out-fight a Zero. They'll be heavily armored, much the same as the fighters."

Ben gave a low whistle. *What an incredible idea. This bomber is all business, and this plan could end the war right there and then, that day.* Murmurs went through those present. The fighter-bomber was clearly more advanced than anything they'd ever heard of.

"Everything I'm saying is based on the 'first' history Ben brought us; and we need to remember that the attack time is subject to change. So is the date. The plan I'm laying out is based on the 'original' times, days, and dates, as per Ben. We'll discuss alternate scenarios and dates later, and we'll develop plans for each."

"Their first wave of one hundred and eighty planes will arrive at zero seven hundred fifty hours. I propose that we amass three hundred and twenty-five of our fighters directly to the South and East of them by zero seven hundred thirty hours. We come UP and directly out of the sun at them in two waves just as they reach the Island. It's critically important that the first wave concentrates on the Kates and their escorts . . . The Kates are easy to identify—they'll be carrying the torpedoes. They must be eliminated. After our first wave sweeps through their formations, their fighters should break off to counter-attack. That's when our second wave will come in to finish up the Kates, then they take down any planes carrying the 550-pound bombs next. The last priority will be the remaining Zeroes."

"Three hundred and twenty five is what percentage of our fighters?"

"That will comprise about eighty percent of them. With our present plan, that leaves eighty of our fighters in reserve. Here's where it gets interesting. Ben, how many fighters will they have guarding their fleet from surprise attacks?"

"As I recall, right around forty-eight or fifty, plus a handful of scouts."

"Perfect. We'll advance fifteen decoys from a flight of forty fighters into the area at an altitude where they will be spotted, and they can draw the protecting force off in the desired direction, let's say southwest, where we'll have another thirty-five waiting. The other thirty-five will come up from behind and below as the Zeroes chase the decoys. Our forty fighters should be able to handle fifty Zeroes. While the Jap Fleet is busy watching those forty fighters, we'll have another flight coming in here . . . from the north or northeast . . . skimming the wave-tops. They'll be escorting forty of these torpedo-totin' fighter-bombers, and will have the job of protecting them. They should be able to make contact just about zero eight hundred thirty hours, and it should be a complete surprise. Whether it is or not, the fleet's ability to respond should be minimal at best, though they'll still be able to bring their rather substantial anti-aircraft batteries to bear on us. On the deck is still the best place to approach them."

"But it doesn't end there. Back to our initial attack force. Once the first wave of Zeroes is splashed, one hundred and fifty of our fighters will land, refuel and rearm with bombs and drop tanks. They will then cover the sky while the remaining one hundred seventy-five begin to refuel and rearm to meet the second wave of Kates and Zeroes. . . ."

When Howard had finished, the members were silent.

Ben blinked. "Damn, Howard. You take no prisoners."

"No, Ben, not when it comes to protecting my country. I expect the same of every person involved in this project. Questions?"

"That's the entire Japanese Fleet?"

"No. According to Ben, they will have another task force going after the American holdings in the Philippines simultaneously. Very simply put, this plan has to come first."

"Howard?"

"Yes?"

"You're a wild man."

Howard grinned. "Aww, you're just saying that."

"Ben?"

"Yes, Howard?"

"You ain't seen nothin' yet."

Chapter Thirty-Six

Thanks to Hughes's extraordinary problem-solving abilities, Ben's spirits were lifted and he regained some hope for the future. He was in a pretty good mood when he returned home to the hangar. The flower delivery reminded him that he'd better get a move on if he was to meet Marilyn in time to get to the Fox Theatre. If the truth were to be told, he hated going to the opera, but she insisted that it was the "classy" thing to do. She felt that attending the opera helped her chances at work and would help her to climb the social ladder.

Though he cared little about social climbing, he willingly suffered through several hours of torture and culture on special occasions in order to maintain bliss within their relationship. There were compensations, of course. Although ambitious, or perhaps because she *was* ambitious, Marilyn was a warm, affectionate woman. It was rare that his attentions went unnoticed or his generosity unrewarded. He kept several changes of clothes at her place. They were an item. And she could cook. She was a sweet girl, and the fact that she'd turned out as well as she had was a testament to her sweet disposition.

She stayed busy enough that his comings and goings on his big project and businesses didn't bother her. She hadn't enjoyed the best of upbringings, but she had graduated the twelfth grade, no small thing in the 1920s. Ben was more than fond of her, and she was fun to be around. Marilyn's apartment was located in the up-and-coming part of town, and she struggled to pay her rent. Ben sometimes wondered how she would have been able to keep the apartment without his help. He didn't mind, though. He would have been happy to give her a higher-paying job, but she'd never asked him. He respected that. No, it wasn't all he had dreamed of, but she was a good woman. He knew he could have done far worse.

Two hours later, appropriately uncomfortable in his black tux and armed with his corsage, he and Alexander pulled up in front of Marilyn's place. Before Ben reached the front steps, she surprised him by walking out the door, dressed and ready. She had what could only be described as a spectacular body, the lines of which were accentuated tonight by her strikingly beautiful black gown and fox wrap. She spun around in a circle to show him, all sparkling teeth and flashing eyes, then seemed to fairly float toward the car. Alexander was transfixed from the second she walked out, captivated by her beauty. He did snap out of it in time to attend to his duties before she reached the car.

In the car, Ben affixed her corsage, and was pleased to see it complemented her gown and wrap. As they drove across town, she appeared to be a bit distracted. Something was troubling her. Then she said, "Sweetheart, I know you've gone to all sorts of trouble tonight to take me to the Opera. Would you be terribly disappointed if we went someplace for a quiet dinner instead?"

He grinned. *A get-out-of-jail-free card.* "Are you kidding? Not even a little bit. Al?"

"Yes, Mr. Ryan?"

"Do you have any ideas as to where a couple can have a nice quiet dinner for two?"

"Italian, perhaps, sir?"

He looked at Marilyn, who smiled her approval. "Perfect," he told Al.

"Very well, sir. Then Luigi's it shall be."

Minutes later they pulled up to Luigi's. As they headed for the door, a small, ragged man approached them.

He spoke with an unmistakable Irish brogue. "Pardon me, sir, could ye spare anything for a man who's out of work? Anything at all? Perhaps ye have some work I could do? I'm a strong man, and able."

Alexander moved to intercept the man and turn him away. It was an unpleasant part of his job, but chauffeurs were trained for it. Ben held up his hand and stopped Al. At last count there were more than seventy-five thousand people out of work in the city of Detroit. He remembered living in his little broom closet. He'd never forget cooking and eating his meals and drinking his water from those old Pennzoil cans. Life has a way of giving a man perspective.

He saw that Marilyn didn't back away from the man. Ben knew her story. She'd grown up wearing tattered rags and holey shoes, when she had shoes at all. Nobody knew better than her how hard times felt. This man didn't disgust her. In fact, he was quite familiar to her. He could have been her father. Ben saw and felt her concern, her need to reach out. She was real people. He thought, *She leads by example. I should take notice.*

He said, "How much would help you out tonight, friend? Do you have a family?"

"Aye. I've a family, sir. Things are a bit thin for us, but we're not complainin', mind ye. We're always hoping that a job or a bit o' work will be right around the next corner. If ye could spare two bits, I'd be most grateful to ye, sir."

Ben listened to the soft Irish brogue; saw how the man maintained eye contact. "I couldn't help but notice you're Irish. What's your name?"

"Why, it's O'Meara, sir. Sean Patrick O'Meara, and thank ye for noticing."

"Well, Sean Patrick O'Meara, I have a problem, and maybe you could help me solve it."

Sean took a step forward and nodded, looking him straight in the eye and listening closely.

If a fellow man requested his help, then he would get it. No man with the pride to call himself a man would do otherwise. His dear grandfather had survived the potato famine, and had then ventured forth to America to find a better life. He took special care to teach Sean—and his father before him—that times do not dictate who you are as a man. Any man who asked for his help should get it, if he could help him without depriving his family.

"I promised my lovely lady here that I would take her out to dinner. We both know a promise is a promise, so I'll still need enough to do that."

Sean nodded in understanding. A man was only as good as his word. And when you had nothing else, your word was everything. He didn't resent the man for keeping his own money, and anyone could see his lady was a walking vision. He could see the man's quandary, and did not view it as selfish behavior. He knew he was totally dependent upon the kindness of others, and every man had his own problems to contend with. He may not have had any money, but in every other sense of the word, Sean O'Meara was a fine gentleman.

Ben went on. "So . . . I can only spare five dollars right now. If you'd be willing to accept that, I think I can make it up to you tomorrow by finding you a new job. If you'll show up with this card at this address, it would be a big help to me. Would that be all right with you?"

Some life came into the man's careworn expression, and for that moment in time the weight of the Depression and the overwhelming desperation left his eyes. He was breathless for a few seconds. *"Five dollars!* Sir, ye're too kind, this will feed me family and pay our rent. God bless ye, sir." He looked at the card. "Ahh, so it's Mr. Ryan, is it? A fine Irish name too, as if there was any doubt of it. I'll be there at first light, sir!"

"How about . . . noon, Mr. O'Meara? We might get back late tonight. I'm sure you have some food to buy, and a family to be with tonight. I want you well-fed and well-rested when you arrive."

"Noon 'tis, sir, and God bless ye, sir!" He turned, bowed slightly, and tipped his cap to Marilyn. "And madam! Have a lovely dinner!"

And with that, Sean Patrick O'Meara ran off as fast as his sore legs and worn-out shoes would take him, straight for home, excited to be able to tell his dear missus they could buy some food, and to bring her the good news that he'd found work.

Ben watched him run off, and as he did, said, "Al?"

"Yes sir, I'll find Mr. O'Meara something to do around the place."

"Thanks, Al. You're a lifesaver. Oh. Please make sure he doesn't have to walk too far to get to work in those old shoes. If he needs a ride in the mornings, would you make whatever arrangements are necessary? In fact, take him out first thing and buy him whatever he needs for clothes and shoes."

"Of course, sir. Consider it done." Al decided right there and then that he had about the best boss in the whole world. After taking out his handkerchief and wiping something from his eye, he opened the boot, and found his polishing cloth. Mr. Ryan's Packard would shine tonight.

Marilyn found herself so proud to be with Ben every time he did something like that. She could picture her own father running home that way on some rare occasion when somebody had been exceptionally kind to him. Ben could have brushed by that man and saved himself five whole dollars, but he treated the man like he knew him, and left him with his pride. Ben was a decent man. She and Ben didn't have as much in common as they perhaps could have, but he was steady, and kind, and patient, and she could live with that and never complain. And he certainly was handsome. Not in the classic sense. She would say he was a little more along the lines of rugged or outdoorsy. But those blue eyes, they could make a girl's heart skip a beat.

They were given a lovely little table in the back, and Luigi himself came out to make-a-sure ev-ry-ting was-a-just-a-right. He was so round and jovial; they found him irresistible. Dinner couldn't have been any more delicious. After they finished and were enjoying a second glass of wine, Marilyn got to her point.

"Happy anniversary, sweetheart."

Ben raised his glass to hers. "Happy anniversary, Marilyn. It's our two years tonight, isn't it?"

"Yes it is. Do you remember what we talked about?"

"I believe we had talked about getting married if we were still happy together after another year."

"I'm still happy with you, happier than ever. What about you?" she asked, as she tried not to hold her breath, then took a slow breath and held it anyway.

Ben thought about it for just a minute, though he wasn't hesitating. Not much about the prospect was unpleasant. Marilyn was a stunner. There would be few men indeed who wouldn't give their left arm just to have her on their right. She was visual perfection, and she was sweet, warm, and *very* sexy. Marrying her could never be considered losing; he was still winning by anyone's definition. With the passing of years and a house filled with children, their life together could be a happy one, perhaps even filled with bliss. No, he wasn't losing; even if he was not winning all that he'd once hoped to win. He'd accepted it long ago.

"Yes, love, I'm happy with you, too. Very happy. You're a beautiful, wonderful woman. I think you're right, we should start making plans right away."

After he'd thought for so long, Marilyn was surprised at his perfect answer. Her breath left her explosively. She lost her composure and squealed, leaping out of her chair and hugging and kissing him. She was so happy. The hard-luck girl had worked and struggled and fought her way up and out. She'd found her prince. And now, because he'd said yes, more good news was coming. The other tables looked on and couldn't help smiling at this handsome couple who were about to take the leap.

Later that night, lying in bed, Ben had time to think. Funny, he thought, how easily he had sailed through their relationship to this night. He'd never announced his intentions, not even to Marilyn.

Sadly, he had never planned to have any intentions again. If anything, she'd been the one who announced her intentions, the one who initiated every phase and facet. He knew he hadn't put one-tenth of the heart or effort into this as he had with Laney. He had more money than he needed now. Marilyn's father was long dead. He supposed that might have played into it, but no, that wasn't it. Was it the ways of the big city? The effects of the Depression? All of those, certainly, but it was more. Perhaps after all the years growing up poor with people treating her as an inferior, Marilyn's expectations of others had become as worn and tattered as the clothes of her childhood. Other than fidelity, she'd placed no restrictions on Ben, none whatsoever.

When it came to herself, however, she was not so easygoing. She delivered the goods and met all of her expectations. By opening herself up to him in every way and caring for him, she showed him she hoped to take care of him in the future. She left no room for doubt. Though she would never ask it of him, she had every right to expect him to do right by her. He was satisfied with it, even happy about it.

After a long, luxuriant stretch, she draped one long, lovely leg across him and an arm across his chest. She kissed him softly, and nestled her head on his shoulder. Her delicious scent wafted from her hair.

He breathed deeply, and then closed his eyes as sleep found him.

Chapter Thirty-Seven

For the next two months, Ben flew back and forth to California as he worked with Howard on the development of the new fighters and bombers. He arrived in Glendale for a meeting and walked into the offices, where Howard was just starting.

"Right on time, as always!"

"You always say that. I think you wait to start your meetings until you see me landing out there."

"Well, of course I do!"

Both men laughed, and before they sat down Ben was introduced to quite a number of new attendees. The consortium of patriots continued to grow, and whether a scientist or an industry magnate, each new member advanced the plan with their contribution.

At the front, the usual easels were waiting, covered with sheets.

One of the members asked, "I have a question from the last meeting. The first wave of Zeroes is bound to radio back and warn off the second wave."

"Radios can be jammed. We'll be jamming them all, except one frequency, and they won't be able to use that one. That frequency is our own, right, Ben? Why don't you tell them about it?"

"No, it's all yours, Howard. You're doing great."

"Ben brought us a piece of technology from his time. It's a wire-less telephone that uses radio waves and can be carried in a pocket. Everyone has one in his time," he said, and reached into his pocket to show them the impossibly small, flat device, to a chorus of ooohs and ahhhs. "Here it is. We've been working for four years to isolate the frequency and make it usable. What we have come up with isn't nearly as advanced. Hell, to be honest, the battery that powers this thing is presently way beyond what we can do. That's just a fact. But using it as a basis for emulation, we've managed to advance radio technology by decades. We're now able to use our radios without fear of being monitored or overheard. That technology won't exist elsewhere for another forty years."

"Will the Japanese be watching Oahu?"

"Good question. And the answer is a resounding *yes*. There will be Japanese 'tourists' visiting the island. Their job is to report fleet and air activity. I'm trying to establish some rapport with the right people in the military to ferret out as many of these 'tourists' as possible, and deal with them as the situation dictates. That would not preclude providing them with lots of juicy misinformation.

"That leads us to our next item. To date, our fighters have been the biggest secret in our plan. That's no longer the case. Because of those same concerns of spies and plants on the island, we've struggled with the prospect of keeping any air force a secret on Oahu.

"In light of this, our plan has become organic; a living, changing thing that must grow and adapt to accommodate the constantly-changing needs.

"The plain fact is that we can't keep it a secret on Oahu. But that's okay. We'll maintain a presence there, probably fluctuating around forty aircraft. We'll keep these birds notably bare of all armaments; we want them to look like training flights. A few flights of these will be visible all over the big island.

"This is where our first bits of misinformation will be provided to them. Anytime these aircraft are within sight of the islands all pilots are going to be under strict orders to fly them poorly to hide their skills, and to throttle down to make the fighters appear to be underpowered dogs. That will also enable us to move other flights in and out in small numbers, probably twenty at a time.

"The pilots are going to train right here in California at our test facility. Fighter training will be done over the mountains and desert, or out to sea. Once pilots are over there 'in the zone,' their primary responsibility will be to familiarize themselves with the islands and with Pearl Harbor. Their secondary responsibility will be, as we just discussed, making our new fighters look like we have trainers that are as incapable as possible anytime they are within sight of land or ships."

He flipped the page on the first easel. "Molokai Island. It's located off the east coast of Oahu. Whereas Oahu is populated, Molokai has little more than a few settlements consisting mostly of shepherds and flocks of sheep. The Island was used as a leper colony at one time, so most people—even the natives—have little interest in the island. On the most remote northwest part of the island, you can see it's nothing more than a protrusion of volcanic rock and scrub. This scar . . . right here . . . running east to west across the geography gave every indication of being perfect for our needs. We didn't want to make too much of this until our geologists were finished and excavation was well underway. We're well beyond that now and virtually guaranteed of success, so I can tell you about our plans."

He flipped the page on the second easel, revealing an aerial photograph of rocky landscape, then went back to the first easel and flipped another page showing another aerial photo of the same landscape. There were differences, but Ben and the others would not have spotted them without having the first photo to compare them. Even with the photos, they didn't know what they were looking at.

"This horizontal series of scars you see here. Look at this last scar farthest to the south. This is where our work is concentrated. Let me explain what we're doing. First, we blasted and cut down an area all along the front of the rock face, here on the north side of this small lip. We've leveled out an area on this straight line that's nearly six thousand feet long. From there we've blasted southward, straight into the rock face. We've created a cavern that, when it is finished, will be large enough to house all of our fighters and bombers at once, all of our support operations, even our supply transports.

"Adjacent to this is a cavern that will contain offices, living quarters, a hospital and all of the other needs. All told, this complex is over a mile long and cut at least four hundred feet deep into the rock face. Deeper chambers have been added as well. It's impervious to anything they can drop on us, unless they fly it in the front door. It's spread out, so one explosion won't be likely to cause secondary explosions. This, gentlemen, is our REAL secret weapon. Great pains have been taken to maintain the appearance of the rugged natural geography. We had to build a road in . . . here . . . winding through the hills from Highway 420— hardly more than a goat path itself—to bring in the heavy equipment, fuel, and supplies. Now that the airstrip is nearly complete, we've got crews working to make that road disappear. After a year or two of new foliage growth it'll appear to be nothing more than a goat path. We'll keep the heavy equipment right there in case it's needed. Around the airstrip excavation site, the scars that we can't hide will fade as grass and bushes grow around them. Time is on our side with that.

"Aircraft that land are immediately taxied inside and out of view. That's rule number one. Either you're taking off, you're landing, or you're not exposed. The airstrip is so large and long that all materials are now being brought in by cargo transport planes.

"Ben told me about latter parts of the war where the Japanese had dug into the sides of mountains to hide and protect their positions. It made sense. We're going to be on an island and protecting our defenses. We'll be keeping them hidden."

Ben was amazed by this new development. He had thought the new fighter/bomber and plans to attack the Japanese Imperial Fleet were impressive. And they were. But this . . . "Howard, this is mind-bending. I can't even imagine the cost of all of this."

"So far, Ben, it's all paid for. There are more than a few patriots here and outside of these doors, and they're putting their money where their mouth is. Others are contributing in their own ways. Equipment. Materials." He gestured toward a few of the men, who nodded. "Scientists," he said.

"I can't imagine what you could have said to convince them to do all of this. You're unbelievable."

Howard looked at him thoughtfully. Then he half-sat on the desk in the front. He was pretty sure that Ben would understand what he was about to say.

"When Zeroes appear over American soil, we're going to beat them back no matter what. America is going to know they've been attacked, and then, no matter what the cost, our military will arm themselves to the teeth with the best technology available. It's true; what we're doing here will end up costing us . . . probably *scores* of millions of dollars by the time it's complete. Once the Japanese attack, the companies already tooled up for the military contracts not only can, but *will* realize hundreds of millions of dollars. That's the dollars aspect, the people making money from it. They're taking a risk by believing in something first and making an investment in it. It's their way of investing in America."

The others nodded in agreement.

"You don't know what you've started here, Ben. Yes, you hope to save America from a long, drawn-out war with a horrible ending. But you've warned a sleeping nation, and it's awakening. *Some* of the right people now believe that there's real danger. Plans have been drawn for aircraft carriers, destroyers, sub chasers; I've seen them. The logistics are being worked out, and the infrastructure necessary to move the materials cross-country where they need to go is already being put in place."

"How are you managing that without drawing attention to your-selves?"

Howard said, "We may not be able to convince the politicians to re-arm this country right now. But what we *can* do is trick them into lending a hand so that we can re-arm as quickly and efficiently as possible when the time comes. You've heard of The New Deal? Well, that's us. We lobbied the politicians for it, and FDR claimed it for his own. The New Deal is repairing old roads and building new roads, interstate highway systems with stronger, higher clearance bridges 'To plan for America's Future.' FDR can claim it. Our concerns are that it's going to help us by making sure that the materials can go where they need to go."

Such amazing foresight and planning. Ben hardly knew what to say. But the others had questions.

"We can keep our entire force of fighters safe and hidden from view on Molokai?"

"Every last one of them. As well as the pilots, and the crews, and the fuel. Our operation will be as close to invisible as humanly possible."

"Mr. Hughes, how will we know when their fleet is coming?"

"The USA has been developing a long-distance detection system called RADAR, which I have access to. The Japanese don't have this technology. Ben said the present technology actually did detect the Japanese on approach in the 'last history,' but a lot of mistakes were made and their approach was never acted upon. We will be able to improve the RADAR system before then. We hope to have our own people in the crew full-time, and more folks working closely with us in the military."

Ben was impressed. "You've been busy. I'm glad I came today, I had no idea you'd covered so much ground. This is incredible, Howard."

Howard gave a sly grin. "I believe that I told you that you hadn't seen nothin' yet?"

Ben grinned right back. "So you did, so you did. You were holding out on me, but I understand why. Loose lips and all that. Is there anything else?"

"That about covers it for now. What . . . that's not enough for you?"

"Well, it's probably not important, but . . . I was wondering, are we going to name our plan, give it a name like "Operation Takedown," or something like that?"

Howard raised his eyebrows. "I hadn't thought about it. What did you have in mind?"

"Well, a name that vaguely references what we're doing, but doesn't give it away if it's leaked. We're operating from underground, and we'll strike from there like some tarantulas or trapdoor spiders do, so we could go with Operation Tarantula, or Operation Trapdoor."

Howard nodded favorably, giving it some thought. He liked the idea. "Trapdoor. Not bad. Any other suggestions?" He looked out over the others.

Others spoke up around the room. "Operation Rising Sun?"

"Ummm . . . naahhh, that one gives us away." Others murmured in agreement.

"Operation Diamondback. They won't see us until we strike."

"Operation Wolverine. We're going to tear them to pieces."

"Not bad."

"Operation Hourglass. Because time's running out for them."

Ben, who was surprised by a name that referenced Gramps's favorite aphorism, spoke up. "Operation Hourglass. I like that. It gives away nothing."

Howard agreed, nodding. "All in favor of naming our operation 'Operation Hourglass'?"

Enough hands went up to pass it handily.

Howard stood up. "Gentlemen. Welcome to Operation Hourglass." As a smattering of applause ran through the group, he turned to Ben. "Happy now?"

He grinned. "Positively giddy."

Chapter Thirty-Eight

Once the room emptied of everybody except him and Ben, Howard kicked back on the sofa along the wall. He relaxed for a minute or two and looked up at the ceiling.

"So, how'd I do today?"

"You've got a lot of highly impressed people walking out that door, I'll tell you that much."

"They don't count. If I tell them to be impressed, they're impressed. That's a part of being Howard Hughes, I guess. When I *really* wonder how well I'm doing, I have to find a source who gives it to me straight, whether I like it or not."

"Yeah? Well, the answer is still the same. I've never seen planning like this in my life. It boggles the mind. And it all fits . . . all of it. Talk about serendipity; you know, there was a New Deal in the first history. Now, because we moved the timeline up, preparing in advance rather than after the fact, you're going to be able to use it to speed things up. Everything you do helps, Howard. Even if we were just able to shorten the war and not use the nukes, that'd really be something. And we have the potential to save millions of Chinese lives."

"Well, I don't care about them. They're not my problem."

"How can you say that? People are dying."

"Not my people."

"Twenty-five million Chinese *will* die at the hands of the Japanese if we can't find a way to stop them. Twenty-five million, Howard. That's one-fifth of all the people in the United States right now. Do you think for a second the Japanese would refrain from coming ashore and doing the same to us because our skin is white?"

Howard looked pensive. Though he didn't care to admit it, it *did* bother him.

Ben said, "The history books said you were a lifelong racist. So, it's true?"

"No. I just don't like coloreds or Jews," he answered, uncomfortably.

"That makes you a racist."

"I hate Tax men and lawyers even worse," he countered.

"That makes you an American. You can be both."

"I guess I was raised that way," he said, for the first time being candid.

"You're telling me you've never met a black man you liked?"

He thought for a second. "I did have two colored women who took care of me when I was young. I liked them . . . very much, in fact. But when the riots broke out in Houston, I was there. It scared the hell out of me."

"Did any of the rioters hurt you?"

"No. I . . . wasn't actually *IN* the riots. But they weren't far from my house, just a mile or so."

"Did you ever stop to think why they were rioting? Maybe all they wanted was to be treated like men and women, the same as us."

"But they're not the same as us."

"That's bullshit. Because their skin is black or brown? Howard, how would you feel if it was suddenly decided that all people with brown eyes couldn't vote? You couldn't ride the front of the bus, you couldn't use the blue-eyed people's restrooms? Because you're different and we folks with blue eyes have decided you are inferior to us. Tell me, did you give yourself those dark brown eyes? Can you do anything about it? Do they affect how smart you are?"

Howard shifted, uneasy with the direction this was taking. He certainly was intelligent enough to know he was wrong, and painted into a corner.

Ben said, "Maybe I should get to the point I'm trying to make. If some of these fighters were sent to China, we could slow the Japanese down and potentially save millions of Chinese."

"No! Absolutely not. We'd be showing our hand, and we'd lose the element of surprise. I can't do that. I *won't* do that. Our job here is to stop them from bombing Pearl Harbor, and I'm not going to risk our entire plan over some damn Chinese!"

"Damn, Howard! You're infuriating. This whole thing has never been about your plan. It's about doing the right thing for the world. I need you to look at the big picture here. We lose some ships and a few thousand people at Pearl, and yes, that's a lot. But by that time the Japanese have already killed *millions* of Chinese! Can you live with that, Howard? I can't. I grant you; it's risky, but we can't just sit on our hands knowing it's already going on as we speak. Every Japanese plane we shoot down over China is another one we won't have to fight at Pearl Harbor, so it makes a difference."

Howard shook his head. "I don't know, Ben. If we do that, we could compromise all of our plans."

"Our plans have always been about doing something to stop the Japanese, don't you see? Our American boys by the hundreds of thousands are going to be in harm's way once this war starts. It doesn't begin at Pearl Harbor, and it doesn't end at Pearl Harbor. By the time Pearl Harbor happens, Hitler and his Blitzkrieg are going strong. Before he's stopped we'll see the deaths of twenty-five million Russians, two million Polish, six million Jews, a million Allied soldiers—those are ours—do you want me to go on?"

Howard looked stricken. His limited plan didn't account for any of this, and compared to this, his plan seemed puny. He knew what they could win, and he knew that what Ben was asking was not only beyond their capabilities, it was *well* beyond them. "Damn, Ben. We don't have enough to handle a fraction of all that. Our plan—Operation Hourglass—has always been to turn the tide at Pearl Harbor and prepare to proceed rapidly from there with the US Government backing us. *You* came to *me* and asked me to find a way to stop or mitigate World War II. Well, this is the best I could do. And it's hundreds of times as much as our own government is willing to do. You can't ask that much more of me."

Ben's argument was crushed. Everything Howard said was correct, without even bringing race into it. Ben *had* asked him to help stop WW II. *Ben* had made Pearl Harbor the focal point for the plan. With the possible exception of his stubborn refusal to give the black pilots a chance, Howard's brilliant planning had far exceeded any plan Ben could have ever conceived. It was a big world, and Howard's consortium were a small group of dedicated patriots. As much as Ben hated to admit it, Howard was right. They had to pick their battles.

He twirled his cane as he pondered all of these ramifications, and then thumped it decisively against the floor. "You're right, Howard. I'm sorry. I got carried away. You've done more than I could have ever expected here. Can I ask one thing of you, though? I know this one is within your power to grant me."

"Oh, damn. You're not gonna let up on that colored pilots deal, are you?"

"Sure, I'll let it go. Just tell me that you've got plenty already. How many planes will we have?"

"You know that answer. At least five hundred and fifty, more if we can step up production a bit."

"And you already have how many pilots?"

"Ben, it's not that sim—"

"How many pilots?" he demanded.

"Awww . . . shit. One hundred and fifty-eight," he said, now irked over being outmaneuvered for the second time. "All right, all right. If you say I can't pull this off without using coloreds, then I believe you. I used them on Molokai, you know. And yes, *yes,* they did a terrific job. All right, I'll try my best. I'll look into this pilot program in Tuskegee. I'll check into finding qualified coloreds in the military."

"In my time, we call them men. Black *men.* Men that have all the same rights as you and I, the same rights to fight and die for our country. Look, I know this is not a popular subject for you. Try to put aside your knee-jerk reaction to men of other races, and remember the good ones you've known. Black men are just like white men. They can range from real good men all the way down to real bad men. We're looking for the good men. We could not have won World War II the last time without the good ones . . . black men who stepped up and put their lives on the line for their country. Their country is our country, and we *will* need them. Talk to the military about their experimental program for black pilots. They turned out to be some of the best pilots in the whole war. Give 'em a chance. Treat them as equals. You won't be sorry."

"Equals?" Howard was uncomfortable with this, and it showed. He was listening, at least, and that was something. "Ben, I don't suppose there's anybody here who doesn't know how I feel about this." He paused for a moment. "I've trusted you since the first day I met you, and I don't know a better man anywhere. In fact, until the day you showed up I was heading down a path I don't even like to think of now. I'm pretty certain you've given me a new lease on life. I wouldn't do this for anybody else."

"You'd do it for your country, and that's enough for me. It might interest you to know that in 2010, the President of the United States is a black man."

"Really. Is he any good?"

"Depends on who you ask. So-so. I never got to see the outcome."

"Good answer. Maybe you should be a politician."

"Nah. I've got a *real* job."

Howard looked at him for a minute. "You're an unusual man, Ben Ryan."

"Do me one favor."

"Name it."

"Try to find a way to turn the tide on this. All of it, some of it, whatever you can do. All I can offer you is my undying gratitude. But there are twenty-five million living, breathing reasons you should. I was sent back to change things. Until I met you, I thought I had to do it alone. Now I know, I have to ask these things of people like you, but the whole world will benefit. The real crime would be in never trying to do what we could. You might be surprised what you can achieve, how far we can go, if you ask for help from the black, brown, red, and yellow men of America and its allies. Here's an idea; look for some Chinese pilots who want to help their country. I'll bet right here in California you can find some Chinese who are pretty upset over what's transpiring in China right now."

A secretary came in the door with a wire, held it up to show the envelope then left it on a desk and walked out. Howard walked over and picked it up. "It's for you." He handed it over.

"Thanks," Ben said, and opened the envelope. He read the message, reread it and dropped it, grabbed his cane, then bolted for the door. He called over his shoulder; "I'm trusting you with this, Howard, please try," and he was gone. Howard picked up the wire and read it. After a moment of thought, he folded it up carefully and tucked it into his pocket.

Chapter Thirty-Nine

Marilyn was busy planning the wedding. She wanted everything to be perfect. It wasn't that hard to find good caterers and florists anymore, as only the good ones were still in business. And Marcel. Marcel was THE dressmaker, and she had convinced him to create the gown himself, with every little detail attended to, and extracted the promise from him that he would be available up to the day of the wedding for any last-minute tailoring. Ben had no desire for a big wedding, but had given her *carte blanche* to make it as pretty as she liked. She couldn't recall ever having been as excited about anything.

There was a knock on her door. She knew it wasn't Ben. He was off in California somewhere, 'playing with his planes.' This would probably be one of the wedding vendors. She opened the door to find a messenger.

"Telegram, ma'am."

The wire had read:

```
BENJAMIN RYAN
C/O HUGHES AIRCRAFT
Glendale, CA
BEN STOP PLEASE COME ASAP STOP I NEED YOU STOP
LANEY
```

Ben was in the air, flying straight east as fast as the graceful Model Y would take him. He landed when he had no choice; by then it had long since become too dark to fly safely. At morning's first light he was once again eastward-bound.

Before seven he saw the mighty Mississippi pass beneath him. In late afternoon, his heart skipped a few beats, excited to see the rolling hills and the pointed white church steeples of Agawam and his favorite old, familiar Shire Town, Springfield. Majestic as they penetrated the lush New England foliage, the steeples reached skyward and beckoned to him, and they seemed to say, "We've been waiting right here for you!" Within minutes the familiar old Liberty Street Airport with the Granville hangar and grass runway appeared below him. He made a low pass and circled around to make sure the short runway was clear, and then brought her in smoothly. As he taxied up to the hangar, familiar faces began to appear, all smiling. He climbed out of the Model Y, surrounded by his brothers and their backslaps, handshakes, and hugs. He thought, *God, it's good to be back!* He'd been gone far too long, and he knew it.

For a full ten minutes it was excited chatter and question and answer time. They wanted to know how things were going on the Pearl defense front. Of course, there was far too much to tell while standing there.

"Well, I see you've taken pretty fair care of my lady."

He spun around to see Granny sliding his hand over the beautifully maintained old Senior. "Granny!" he yelled, and gave him a big hug.

The talk began to subside, and he gave Granny a worried look.

"Did you send me that wire?"

Granny nodded. "I took her and helped her. Cleve knew where to send it. Come on in, we'll fill you in," he paused for a moment, then said, "You've been gone a long time, Ben."

He looked about. "You're telling me. God, I missed this place, and all you hooligans."

The only brothers missing were Thomas and Robert. Ben looked around the place; it had gathered odd bits of junk and aircraft parts, and a trophy the brothers had built Edward after his recently-crunched Ascender tail-first flyer/Canard effort. Since the ZR-racers were now built and maintained at the various Gee Bee Aircraft centers, the greater part of the hangar now accommodated a larger office section for the Gee Bee Corporation, which now bustled like an efficient beehive. He could see a good forty people moving about in there. He looked, but didn't see the one face he'd hoped to find.

"I would have thought you'd all be scattered across the country, tending to your new concerns."

Granny shrugged. "Thomas and Robert are on the road a lot of the time now, but thanks to some good managers and the system you set up to manage our revenue, materials and payroll, we're home now as much as we're gone. And it's getting better all the time. Your grandfather was a genius."

"Great-great-grandfather."

"Excuse me, great-great-grandfather. I'd like to meet him someday. Have you found him yet?"

That struck a note with Ben. "No, I've never found him, but I have formed a theory. I wish I had time to pursue it, but maybe we can look for him together at some point."

"That might be fun, I'd like that. Right now, though, I think we should get back to the reason for the wire we sent to you. Please understand when you hear this story, Ben. We were made to promise not to tell you anything about it. We wanted to, in the worst way."

"By who? Who made you promise?"

"Laney."

Why would Laney make them promise? "Laney?"

"Laney. Ben, the day you left here, things went crazy. The sheriff was trying to find you. He was over at the Hospital talking to Michael, then he was here tearing the place up and trying to make us account for aircraft and vehicles. It didn't take long for him to find out the Senior was missing, so I was some glad that I'd told you to avoid filing flight plans for a couple of months. About two weeks later, they stopped looking for you entirely. Not because they didn't want to find you, but because they had nobody to file charges against you."

Ben paled. "You mean, Spencer . . ."

"No. No, he didn't die. More's the pity. He got out of the hospital. Laney said he'd been trying to leave from the first minute they took him there. He was crazed; jabbering and saying that you were coming to finish him off, coming to find him, coming to kill him. After the sheriff told him they couldn't find you anywhere, he'd climb the walls trying to run away from whoever was coming through the door. He thought it was you coming to get him. Though he was all taped and splinted up, he was still crashing into things, running into walls, trying to run from anyone who walked in. After about two weeks the doctors concluded he wasn't just hurt physically, he was a mess upstairs. So they decided to move him to the Mental Ward."

He raised a brow and said, "He must have gotten wind of that. He disappeared from his hospital room, and Laney came home to find him packing his things. He was still jabbering when he took all their dowry money, threw his clothes into his old truck, and then disappeared. Left town. Left her with nothing. A couple of days later Laney came in here asking for a job. We gave her back her old job; it was good to have her back with us."

Ben had never had an inkling of all of this. He was appalled.

Granny went on. "She couldn't afford the house rent, and ended up moving back in with her folks. We all wanted to wire you right away; but she wouldn't let us, made us promise we wouldn't. She was worried that the sheriff would find you here should Spencer ever come back. The sheriff already knew that you being in love with Laney was the original reason for that whole episode, so for a couple of weeks he kept a pretty close watch on her; hoping you'd show your face, I'd guess. That worried her. She was determined you should stay away."

Ben knew exactly why Spencer had climbed the walls, why he had left town. He recalled his own words. *Next time these boys won't be there to stop me. Then I'll give you everything you deserve. I . . . can't . . . **wait**.*

Still unaware of the beatings and savagery Laney had endured at Spencer's hand, he felt ashamed of himself, lamented the hardships Laney suffered due to him losing his temper.

He said, "But that was what, . . . five and a half years ago? As bad as it must have been, nobody called or wired me then. How bad are things that I've gotten this wire?"

"She made us promise, Ben. We gave her a raise, we did what we could until the Racers and the Aviation centers started bringing in a good profit, and then we tried to do more. But she wouldn't accept extra money from us. So we did the next best thing. For a while, there were a lot of stomachaches and sprained ankles around here. Then we promoted her into a managerial position. We knew the Perkinses needed the extra cash."

For a moment, Katie Lynn flashed into Ben's mind, her proud refusal to accept money from the Ryans . . . money they had virtually unlimited amounts of, money she so desperately needed for college. Like Granny and the sprained ankles and stomachaches, his Gramps had used subterfuge, arranging for Katie Lynn to win contests and grants to help her out. He felt a twinge in his heart. These two women were not the same woman, but they might as well have been. To protect him from the Sheriff, Laney had made the agonizing decision to live without him. He knew in that moment that beyond all doubt, Katie Lynn was Laney's descendant. The two were cut from the same bolt of cloth. And that he loved her—them—dearly.

"That's Laney, all right. Uh . . . wait. Why did they need the extra money?"

Granny glanced at the others, who nodded and urged him on. "Laney was going to have a baby."

That rocked Ben a little, but only for the few seconds it took him to think about it. She had married the guy, so having a baby was an expected outcome, once you thought about it.

"She's worked here ever since. She had a baby boy, he looks just like her. He's been raised right here in the office, since Laney brings him to work with her most of the time. He has about forty-five aunts and uncles now, and he loves airplanes. Cutest little tyke you ever saw, and he's the apple of his Momma's eye. She named him Benjamin."

Ben looked pleased.

"Benjamin Spencer," he said, trying it out on his tongue. "It has a nice ring to it, doesn't it?" he smiled, and murmured, "Old Ben Spencer. I'll be damned." Gramps often spoke of him. Spencer was indeed Katie Lynn's ancestor, and history is stubborn.

"We all thought so. Of course, we don't call him Benjamin, we call him Bennie."

Ben smiled. "I could've told you that. He'll be Ben soon enough, give him time to grow up."

"Well, that's part of why we called you home. Last week, Spencer showed back up. He's as backward as he ever was, with no job, a bum arm, and a big chip on his shoulder. Seems he saw the photo of you at the air races with Marilyn in the papers, and it talked about Ryan Aviation's offices in Detroit. He realized you weren't even here in town anymore. He came back, went to the Perkins house, said that rightfully, Laney was his wife, and that she didn't work here anymore. Doc was standing there, so she told Spencer she was coming to get her things this time, and that he might want to think twice about coming with her, as he was *persona non grata* around here. When she got here, I took her right over to send you the wire."

"That son-of-a-bitch." Ben said.

"It gets worse. He doesn't have any money, of course, and claims that it's your fault that he doesn't, and without so much as asking, he moved right in with the Perkinses. He stays there all the time, and now he doesn't allow Laney to leave the house without him. The Perkinses are prisoners in their own home. If Doc hadn't brought her over, we might not have found out about this for some time. I stopped by there and Laney answered the door, but then Spencer told her to get inside, and sent me away. And this is the worst part. Laney had a black eye and a bruised face, just like before."

"Just like before?"

"Yes, remember—oh, that's right, you never knew; you left before that. After you left town, when Laney came back to work, her face was all black and blue; he'd beat the living hell out of her. Looks like he picked things up right where he left them off."

Ben was furious; he was seething, and his thoughts were racing. This man was like a plague to Laney. He wanted to kill him, to get rid of him once and for all. He'd been that route before, and he knew it would not work in their favor. He thought it over for a minute, and then it came to him all at once. He knew what had to be done.

"I need a ride, Granny," he said. There was no time to waste.

Whatever it took, he would see to it that Michael Spencer left Springfield forever.

Chapter Forty

Fifteen minutes later they arrived at the telegraph office.

"Why, Ben! Is that you? I haven't seen you for what, . . . five years? How're things going?"

"Cleve Hall. It's sure good to see you again too. I guess you know a little about how things are going."

Cleve was a pleasant fellow, well-liked and trusted by everybody. He wore his visor and arm-garters with pride, and was proud to be the bearer of important news throughout the town. He took his job as seriously as any doctor or lawyer; he was a consummate professional and never discussed anything that came over those wires. But that didn't stop him from listening when folks talked; he'd heard all about Laney's situation.

The smile faded from Cleve's face. "Yes, mos' the town knows about that now. Gettin' so folks aren't safe in their own homes anymore. Anything I can do to help?"

"Yes, Cleve, I think you can. Can you fake a telegram from, say, Detroit?"

Cleve looked hesitant. "Oh, that wouldn't be proper, Ben. I've got my job to consider."

"Well, I can see where that could be bad for you. I'll tell you what. If you lose your job over this, I'll give you a new job at twice the pay. Would that change your mind?"

Cleve looked torn, despite the offer of money. He liked his job. He was good at it, and if he were to be perfectly honest, he didn't know any other kind of work. "I don't know, Ben. . . ."

"What if a woman who is being beaten inside her own home needs your help?"

Cleve looked stricken. Laney was an old friend. He sat up straight, snapped his arms out to clear his sleeves, picked up a sharp pencil and gave it a lick, and leaned over his pad. "This fella from Detroit. I guess we forgot to send his telegram before he left there. I assume it'll need to be delivered right away. Where's it going, and what did it say?"

As they left the Western Union office, Granny looked worried.

"Do you think this will work, Ben?"

"It should. We used small words. If it doesn't, my backup plan will work for sure."

"What's your backup plan?"

"I'll go over there and finish killing that son-of-a-bitch. I'm not going to see Laney live like that."

"That'd work. We probably should try and stick with Plan A for now; you know, try to work within a plan that keeps you out of prison if possible," then he hesitated and said, "There's something else I didn't mention to you before. Spencer has filed papers to have the boy's name changed."

"That son-of-a-bitch."

"You already said that."

"Did I? Hmmph."

Chapter Forty-One

Cleve arrived at the Perkins house twenty minutes later.

Laney answered the door. "Hello, Cleve. Doc's not in right now."

"That's all right, Laney, it's not for the Doc this time, it's for . . . ahh
. . . what in the *world* happened to your face, Laney? Are you all right?"

Just then, the inner door swung back and Spencer grabbed Laney by
the arm. "What'd I tell you? Didn't I tell you not ta answer that door no
more? Git inside!"

He turned and swung open the screen door, and grabbed the telegram from Cleve's hand. As Cleve walked down the steps into the dooryard, Spencer said after him, "You'd do ta mind your own business, mister." He started to close the door.

Cleve turned and responded in a loud, clear voice, "If I learn 'twas
you that did that to her face, I'll be minding my business. Laney's a
friend of mine, and my friends *are* my business."

The door burst open and Spencer approached him in a rage, pushing
his face within inches of Cleve's. "And just what do you think yer gonna
do about it?"

Cleve, who had leaned back a little in the face of Spencer's rage, had
not stepped back, nor did he intend do. His eyes flashed and showed the
anger he was suppressing that moment and he gave a grin, though it
more closely resembled a snarl, leaned forward until he was pushed up
close to Spencer's face, and tapped the envelope in Spencer's hand. Then

he said, "I'll do whatever it takes, and you can believe that. But, you might want to read your Telegram . . . *sir.* I think that should say all that needs saying. Good day . . . *sir.*"

And with that, Cleve turned and walked off, chuckling as he said, "I guess I can forget about my tip. . . ."

Spencer heard that, and his dull, sullen gaze followed the cheeky telegraph man, thinking, *Someday I'll meet that guy in a place where I can teach him a lesson.* He looked at the envelope, and saw his name there. *Now, who in the hell would send ME a telegram?* (He'd never got one in his en-tire life.) He pulled it out of the envelope and began to read it.

There were a fair number of words, so at first he was confused. He looked around. He read it again, read it slowly, carefully, his lips moving and his head bobbing up and down, word for word. Something snapped inside his head, his eyes flew open wide, and he flung the telegram forward and away from him, as though it had burst into flames. He tripped backward and fell, staring in terror at the Telegram as though it might rise up and begin to stalk him. He kicked and pushed at the ground, trying to put distance between him and it, and when his back hit the porch, he reached behind him and grabbed at the rail, then flipped over and scrambled up the steps, tore open the doors and ran inside.

The quiet man crouched and looked at the wire on the ground, and as he read it, another rare smile graced his normally somber features. He flashed inside, still invisible to all except Bennie, and watched over Bennie as Spencer ran in utter terror past Laney, whimpering, jabbering something about "He's coming for me," and flew up the stairs and into the bedroom. He pulled out his duffle bag and with his good arm began stuffing clothes into it as fast as he could. He hadn't but half a duffle full anyway, so by the time Laney reached the top of the stairs, he was tearing downstairs past her, still babbling like a wild-eyed madman. True to form, he ran into the kitchen and grabbed Mrs. Perkins's jar of butter-and-egg money off the shelf, then ran out the door, leaving it wide open in his wake.

As the quiet man looked on, now enjoying the show from his position in front of the truck, Spencer threw the duffle and the jar into the cab of his truck, set the throttle and choke, and frantically cranked the stubborn old truck until it started. Without a moment's hesitation he jumped in, and seconds later he was gone. Inside of five minutes from the time Cleve Hall showed up with that telegram, the only indication that Michael Spencer was ever there was the cloud of dust he left in his wake. It was the last time anybody from Springfield or the whole state of Massachusetts ever saw him.

Laney watched him leap in the truck and drive away. The last time she saw him act like that was after he left the hospital. She was glad he left. If only he would stay gone. Then she spied the man in the dooryard watching Spencer drive away, and walked outside.

"Good evening. May I help you?"

He was a pleasant-looking man, and she immediately sensed he was a kind person.

"Good evening, ma'am. I saw that fellow drop this as he left."

"Oh, thank you. That's so kind of you." She reached out and took the wire from him. Curious as to what it might say, she unfolded it.

The wire read:

```
MICHAEL SPENCER
C/O DR. PERKINS
SPRINGFIELD, MASSACHUSETTS
SO YOU CAME BACK STOP GOOD STOP I'VE BEEN
LOOKING FOR YOU FOR A LONG TIME TO FINISH
WHAT I STARTED STOP YOU STAY RIGHT THERE
STOP I CAN'T WAIT STOP
B. RYAN
```

Laney put her hand up to her lips but couldn't stifle the giggle, which then became a laugh, then a whooping laugh. The whoops melted into a shaking, shuddering grimace as she cried uncontrollably. She sank to her knees and sobbed for several minutes, her shoulders heaving, the unendurable weight of the past five years at long last lifted from her.

"Momma, are you okay?"

Her little boy stood next to her, a concerned look on his adorable little face. His brows were knitted and he was looking straight at her. Just looking at him made her smile. She wiped her tears with her wrists, sniffed, and answered, "Yes, Bennie, I'm fine."

"Then why are you crying, Momma?"

"Oh, Bennie. Because I'm so happy. A dear friend is coming to see me, someone I haven't seen in years." Remembering the man who gave her the note, she looked around, but he was nowhere to be seen.

Bennie's eyes flew wide. This was something he knew about. "Years! How many? I'm this many years old, aren't I?" He held up his hand with fingers spread, then slowly subtracted his thumb, unable to keep his index finger completely straight. "I'm four, right, Momma?"

She smiled brightly through her tear-stained face at her little ray of sunshine, the best thing in her world. "Yes, Bennie, that's right!"

Bennie looked around. He had noticed the flurry of activity in the house, and had seen that bad man run outside. "Momma?"

"Yes, Bennie?"

"Where did the bad man go?"

"He's gone, baby. He's gone."

He brightened visibly. "Good."

Laney smiled again. Life through the eyes of a child.

She stood up and took Bennie's hand. They walked through the yard.

"Momma?" Bennie asked, "Who's coming to see you?"

She thought about the answer. "The man I named you after. He's a very nice man."

"You mean Benjamin Ryan?"

"Why, yes, Bennie. How do you know his name?"

"Oh, I know lotsa stuff about *him,* Momma. Uncle Edward told me I was named after a Hee-ro. I saw pictures of him at your office. But I didn't know he was your friend."

"Oh, baby, Benjamin is a close friend to everybody where Momma works. And you're right, he saved us all. And more than just once."

"Is he nice, Momma?"

Laney's heart raced at the thought of it. "He's *so* nice, Bennie. Momma loves him very, very much," she turned to Bennie to reassure him, "Not as much as you, of course, because you're my sunshine forever. But very, very much."

Bennie smiled to know he was still her number one forever. Then he looked thoughtful. "Momma?"

"Yes, Bennie?"

"Is he my Daddy?"

"That's a hard question to answer, Bennie. I think he might want the job when he meets you. You're a pretty likable kid, you know. But in the end, it's up to him."

"No, Momma. Is he my Daddy?"

She had never been able to bring herself to tell Bennie that the bad man was his father. They were nothing alike, and Bennie hated him. She knew he had always wondered who his father was, but of the seemingly millions of questions he'd asked, this was the first time he had ever come out and asked this question. Perhaps he was smart enough to know without asking. But he was hopeful enough to ask this. She turned and kneeled in front of him, looking at his sweet face. "Baby, he is in my heart."

"He is in your heart?" He sensed that this meant that Ben was not his father, but that his Momma would very much like him to be. That was good enough for him.

"Yes, baby, he is."

Bennie looked thoughtful as they resumed their little walk. "But it's up to him."

"You were listening after all."

"Yup."

"I love you."

"I love you too, Momma."

Chapter Forty-Two

Laney was feeling so much better. Her Mom had cried happy tears when she learned that Ben had sent the wire that scared off that worthless, no-account miserable excuse for a man. Things were considerably happier in the house for the next few hours, and they could barely wait for Doc to return so they could give him the good news. Laney couldn't wait to find out what day Ben would be arriving in town. She hummed happily as she cleaned up around the kitchen.

"Momma?"

"Yes, baby?"

"Who is the man in the brown coat?"

"I don't know, baby. He just gave me that note today. I've never met him before."

"I see him a lot. When the bad man yells and hits you, the man in the brown coat comes in here and shows me where to hide, like he did today. He says he'll never let the bad man hurt me. Then I saw him standing with you when you were crying."

That didn't make much sense to her, so she asked, "Did you see where he went?"

"He didn't go anywhere. He had his hand on your shoulder when you were on the ground. He was walking next to you the whole time we talked."

She stopped washing the dishes, even more baffled as she tried to make some sense out of that, when Bennie interrupted her reverie.

"Momma?"

"Yes, Bennie?"

"There's a man walking up our street."

"That's nice, baby. Is it the man in the brown coat?"

"No. This one walks funny. He has a stick," then after a brief pause, he said, "Nana says no, it's not a stick. It's a cane."

Her heart leapt into her throat. She froze for a second. *He's here?* In a panic, her hands reached up and touched her battered face. She turned to the left and then to the right, in a panic. What would he think of her? She looked a fright!

Mrs. Perkins left Bennie at the screen door, walked in and saw her dithering. Quietly she said, "What are you doing here, girl? You know it's Ben. Go. Go on!" Mrs. Perkins had loved Ben right from the start, and had been furious when Doc had given his blessing to Spencer without even consulting her. She would not sit back and watch this time.

Laney stopped and looked at her mother's happy face. It was Ben. It was BEN! She gave her mother a kiss and gathered up both her skirt and her courage. The hesitation passed and she ran from the kitchen and burst outside. It was Ben, walking up the street toward her with that familiar limp. That wonderful, familiar limp! She ran down the steps and toward him, and then they were together, hugging, sobbing, holding each other's faces and looking into each other's eyes. And both said only one thing, "I'm sorry, I'm sorry."

They sat on the front steps, holding hands, and quiet. They felt their hearts pounding, heard the blood pumping in their ears so loudly that it scared them. Their thoughts raced, and they were scared and excited. Both were aware they'd made such big mistakes, both aware how badly they'd hurt each other. Their own pasts scared them when they thought about the future. And they'd only been reunited for five minutes.

"We've always been this way, haven't we?" he observed.

"What way?"

"Saying nothing while our minds race on the inside. Each of us worried that the other doesn't want to know what we're thinking, or what we want to say."

"Yes, I think you're right about that."

"We need to stop doing that. We need to say things when they need to be said, we need to ask questions when they need to be asked. This . . . whatever it is we're doing . . . it left us without each other for five years."

"How do we . . . change it?" she wondered aloud.

"We just have to do it. I've got things that need to be said to you, so I'll go first. I'm sitting here thinking about all the things I did wrong that caused me to lose you. All the things I didn't say that I should have said. If I had just said a couple of them, you wouldn't have married him, and I wouldn't have spent these past years . . . heartbroken." His voice broke at the end, he could barely finish the sentence, and his lips quivered slightly. He couldn't go on right then, but she knew all he wished he could say.

She laid her hand gently on his leg. "Now let me tell you what I need to say. I was thinking about how much I loved you, and how I never said it, because you had never announced your intentions. I always assumed you were doing that new 'Dating' thing, because you never announced your intentions. Oh, Ben. My Ben. You knew so much about us, about the planes, about the Granvilles, about the history. It never occurred to me, it never occurred to *any* of us that you didn't know how to court a woman in our time. I would have asked *you* to marry me had I realized that."

He sniffed and looked up. "I'd have said yes. Oh, Laney, your face," he said, reaching out and gently touching her purple-and-black cheek. "Are you all right?"

"I'm fine, really I am, it looks worse than it is, and it hardly hurts at all now."

He kissed her cheek gently. "I loved you from the first day I saw you in the office." With the memory, a smile crept across his face. "You were so cute with that big old cast on your leg. And oh my, you did *NOT* want to tell me how you got the broken leg. My heart just went pitter-patter." He grinned ear-to-ear at that memory.

The memory brought a smile to her as well. "That was a day to remember, all right. And you're right; we do need to say things when we're thinking them. And we do need to ask questions. Could I ask you about something?"

"Sure, anything."

"I saw the newspapers from the races, with you standing beside the ZR-3 Racer. I saw that woman with you. She's very, very beautiful."

"Marilyn. Yes, she is."

"A couple of months back I saw the engagement notice in the papers. You two are getting married."

"No, we aren't, Laney." He took her hand. "Not now. I know it sounds strange. She's a beautiful, wonderful woman, and any man would feel lucky to be with her—"

She blurted out, "Oh, she's breathtaking, Ben! I'm so plain. I could never compete with that!"

"You are *not* plain, you're lovely. And you'll *never* have to compete. Of all the women in the world, there's only you for me. End of story. I love you, Laney Perkins, and I've loved you for years, since the day I met you, and I know it sounds funny, but . . . maybe even before that. Please . . . marry me. I'm not going to let you go again."

"I can't, Ben, I'm sorry," she said, scrunching her face up. "I'm still married. This might take a while." Then she smiled a little, wincing.

"I can wait." He said, with a chuckle. "I don't care how long it takes."

"But you can't just ask *me*. You have to ask us *both,* right, Bennie?" She looked up at the house, where Bennie had his little face pressed against the screen in the door, scrutinizing Ben.

"Yup."

"Well, hello, Bennie. My name is Ben too."

"Benjamin Ryan. I was named after you. Uncle Edward says you're a Hee-ro."

"I don't know about that, Bennie. I just do the best I can. Sometimes I help people if things go right."

"Momma says you're her friend. She says she loves you very, very much. But she loves me more, 'cause I'm her sunshine forever."

"Bennie!" she chided, worried that his candor would not be well-received.

"No, that's okay," Ben said. "You're right, Bennie, and I love your Momma right back."

"Only not as much as me, 'cause I'm her sunshine forever."

Managing to keep a reasonably straight face, he raised his finger and pointed it at Bennie. "You sure are!"

Bennie squinted his eye a little at him. "Are you my Daddy? Momma says you're my Daddy in her heart."

Ben turned and looked at Laney. Beet red, and looking down and away, she looked like she felt, and she felt like she wanted to crawl under the nearest rock. But he looked rather pleased. "If your Momma says that, Bennie, then it must be the truth."

"Really?"

"Would your Momma lie to you, Bennie?"

"Nope."

Bennie pushed the screen door open and scooted around it until he was standing on the landing with them. He looked Ben over carefully; one last time for good measure. A few steps to the edge, and he plopped down on the step, nearer Ben than his mother. For a second he looked indecisive, and the next second he leaned back against Ben, looking up at him. He leaned back more, then stretched up and pulled Ben's head down close, and whispered something in his ear. Ben grinned and whispered something back. Bennie's little green eyes lit up, and his expression changed from serious to pleased, and he stood up and shuffled over to the door. "Nana's calling me," he announced, then walked inside.

Laney wasn't quite sure how all that went. It left her nervous. She was unaware that she was wringing her hands.

"He's perfect, Laney. He's a perfect little version of you. I'm the luckiest man in the world."

Laney wrapped her arms around his neck, breaking down again and sobbing and hugging him with all her might. She had her two Bens. She had the love of her life.

She had everything.

Chapter Forty-Three

It looked like Ben would be working an extra week or two with Mr. Hughes in California again. When she got a telegram, that's usually what it said. Marilyn took the telegram and tossed it on the desk to read after she finished her work; but then she noticed it was from Springfield, Massachusetts. Curious about the location, she opened the envelope. The telegram read:

```
MARILYN MURRAY
SKYLINE APTS. APT 32
E. RIVERSIDE DR.
DETROIT MICHIGAN
MARILYN STOP I CANNOT MARRY YOU STOP I'M
SORRY STOP EVERYTHING HAS CHANGED STOP SEE
ALEXANDER FOR YOUR NEEDS FOR THE NEXT YEAR
STOP HE WILL SEE TO EVERYTHING STOP
B. RYAN
```

"Oh, God," she said, sitting down, the wind knocked out of her as surely as if she'd been punched in the stomach.

How did this happen? I worked so hard for so long to get here, fought every inch of the way. Now, in thirty short seconds, I have nothing. How did he figure it out? I was so careful. Marcel, perhaps? No, he wouldn't have given me away; he needs the work and the money. He was grateful to get this job. My marrying Ben would mean a lot more business for him in the future.

She couldn't think of anybody, but it was pretty obvious Ben had somehow learned the truth. *And just like that, Alexander will see to my needs for the next year. That's Ben, kind and decent to the end, even when he figures you out. So I'm just supposed to walk away?*

She deflated, and found she was shaking. That was exactly what she was going to do, because Ben held all the cards. That was just how it was. He didn't owe her anything, and she was fortunate that he extended any parting considerations at all, especially in these times. The irony of it struck her full-force, because lately she'd thought she might have been falling in love with him.

She checked her hair, and pinned on a nice hat. In the mirror, she checked her still-perfect figure. At twenty-seven, she still had her looks and would somehow find a way to get through this. It wasn't as though her plans had never fallen flat before. Another adjustment or two and a little lipstick, and she was done. Picking up her clutch as she headed out the door, she said to herself, "Okay, Alexander, let's see how many of my needs Mr. Ryan has authorized you to take care of for the next year," and tried to sound angry.

Her moment of bluster changed nothing. She felt like a scared young girl who could not be sure what the future now held for her.

She had good reason.

Chapter Forty-Four

"THINK about this, PLEASE. Ben, YOU have the knowledge to succeed where others have not. Remember that NOTHING in history is set in stone. What you know is more powerful than anything on this earth."

"Ben? Ben darling, wake up. Ben?"

He sat up with a start, covered in sweat. Laney sat on the edge of the bed with a worried look on her face. "Are you still having the same dream?"

"Uhh . . . yea . . . yeah. Same dream. Same guy. Sorry about that."

"Don't be sorry, dear. With all the responsibilities on your shoulders, sometimes I don't know how you manage to stay sane. You take on too much."

That struck him funny. "Yeah, I take on the whole world." He gave a quick, sardonic laugh and decided that it was time for him to roll out. He threw back his covers and started to move.

"Ben Ryan! You get right back in that bed and cover yourself up. What kind of a woman do you think I am? We are not married yet. Such behavior!"

He slipped back under the covers, chuckling about it.

He'd bought a large house in town, not far from the Perkinses' place. Now she and Bennie could have plenty of room in their own place.

Upon Laney's insistence, he announced to her parents that he would be living in the other wing of the house in his own bachelor's quarters until such time as Laney's petition for divorce could be granted. Not about to mess up again, he took it upon himself to announce his intentions to marry her, and asked for their permission. The Perkinses were delighted to give their blessings.

Relieved and happy to have Laney safe, loved, and well cared-for, they were more than tolerant of the new living arrangement. And they were happy to have their house back. Doc would never again put peer pressure and public opinion ahead of Laney's safety and happiness, and the townfolk were made aware of the hell Spencer put Laney through, and how Ben rushed home to rescue her. In an unprecedented move (and without any mention of a dowry they no longer had), they turned a blind eye to what might otherwise have been an awkward situation, and made it clear that they expected the same of others. The blessings flowed from them and the entire town, and many locals showed up to help with the move to the new house.

Laney was astonished to learn she had a driver and a car. Ben insisted that technically, since they shared Charles, he wasn't hers. Charles wasn't as much fun as Al, but he did come highly recommended. Ben chose him for two important qualities; he was loyal to a fault, and he was tough. Neither of the two revealed to Laney that, first and foremost, Charles was a bodyguard. He knew what Michael Spencer looked like, and Ben had made it very clear what was expected should he ever try to approach Laney. Charles knew the treatment that Laney had suffered at Spencer's hands. He wouldn't hesitate to reduce Spencer to a pile of broken bones on sight. He liked the new family placed in his care, the brand-new Packard, his hefty paycheck, and his new, rather large, beautifully-furnished apartment.

When Ben hired a housekeeper, Laney was irritated with Ben and insisted that she could clean her own house. She protested to Ben that he did too much for them, that a housekeeper was too much. When the sweet woman arrived, however, Laney found she just adored the woman, and so did Bennie. Ben had heard about and sought out Mrs. Gruber, a childless, middle-age, recently widowed woman in desperate need of a job and a place to live. He knew very well that Laney continued to take care of much of the housekeeping and helped the woman all day long.

The two women grew close very quickly and did most everything together. He tried to keep a straight face when he said that once they were married, she would be in a position to fire the woman and could do as she pleased. He knew that Laney would need company during his long stays in California. Laney had gained some insight into what made him tick, and she realized that her sweet Ben was just doing what he did . . . saving people, taking care of people. Helping people.

When Laney barked at him to get back under the covers, it was less about propriety and more her way of telling him that Mrs. Gruber was nearby. Just last night, Laney and he had enjoyed a candlelight dinner and some wine. The evening had ended with them holding one another in breathless, joyful, loving bliss, and looking deep into each other's eyes. But, as he so often said to himself, *that was then and this is now. Besides, I suppose our housekeeper needs to think we're respectable.*

Mrs. Gruber knew better than that, and she knew two young folks in love when she saw them. They were a wonderful couple to give her this good-paying job and a beautiful apartment in one wing of the house, and it did her heart good to see Margie's girl Laney and little Bennie happy and safe. The Ryan household was as a house should be . . . filled with warmth and love.

This morning, Ben had to kiss Laney farewell. He'd stayed longer than he should have, and he had to get back to California. Howard had requested his presence as soon as he could get there.

No telling what kind of trouble Howard was getting himself into with Operation Hourglass. And as always, Ben couldn't wait to find out. The man loved a challenge, and you could never tell how he would meet it. It wouldn't be boring; that much was guaranteed.

As he pointed the Model Y westward, his thoughts were on the repeating dream that plagued him. The dream had persisted until finally he comprehended its intent. Now, it scared him. From the start, there had been aspects of this quest where Ben felt the quiet man asked too much of him, even if the requests had never actually taken the form of words.

Coldly calculating odds, deciding who lived and died; that terrified him. In that respect, Ben was nothing like Howard. On this chessboard, the players died screaming in agony, and in his dreams he imagined every scream. Operation Hourglass really was an apt name for it. He just wished he could be sure whose time was running out.

He now knew what would have to be done, and he hated knowing it. Every part of him violently opposed it. When Commander Spock had said, "The needs of the many outweigh the needs of the few," it had seemed . . . logical. And when the movie was over, he'd tossed his popcorn bag and soda cup in the trash and had gone parking with Katie Lynn.

But that was then.

Chapter Forty-Five

Marilyn's cab pulled up in front of Ryan Aviation's hangar. She'd never understood why a man of his wealth cared to live in a nondescript apartment inside a working hangar at an airport. He'd told her it felt like home, whatever that meant, and declined to comment further upon it.

In the office she found Alexander, filing some papers with the help of a little man who held an uncanny resemblance to Snuffy Smith, right down to the overalls with the baggy seat. She recognized Mr. O'Meara at once.

He welcomed her in his familiar, soft lilt, "Well, good day to ye, madam, and what can we be helpin' ye with this fine day? Ahh, if it isn't the lovely Miss Marilyn! And if I may be so bold as to say, lookin' as fine as Ireland in the springtime!" He pronounced it "Ayreland."

She blushed a bit. O'Meara was a dear little man, as sweet, good, and kind as they came. He could always put a smile on your face and make you forget your troubles. "Mr. O'Meara, it's so nice to see you again! How is that family of yours doing?"

"Thanks to the blessins o' yourself and Mr. Ryan, me family is doing wonderful, and I thank you for askin' after them. I trust you're doin' well yourself!"

She opened her mouth to respond, but just then, Alexander interrupted their chitchat and ushered Marilyn into a conference room.

Being ushered into a quiet room when you're totally defensive can be unsettling, even unnerving; and Marilyn felt both as she sat down.

"Miss Murray, may I offer you some coffee? A pastry, perhaps?"

"Thanks, Al. Yes, some coffee would be nice." At least he was being civil.

He poured her a cup and offered cream and sugar. "I was most distressed to hear the news. I hope this will not have an adverse effect on our friendship."

She almost raised her eyebrows in surprise, but thought better of it. *Friendship? Oh, well.* "No, of course not, Al. I feel the same as always about . . . uh . . . you . . . and . . . I."

He breathed a sigh of relief. "Oh, smashing. It can be most uncomfortable chauffeuring folks when there is tension between you."

"I . . . uh . . . Al, I don't understand. Chauffeuring?"

"I'm sorry, Miss Murray, I've forgotten my manners. Here, I've assumed you knew all of this, and how could you? I'm pleased to say that I will remain your personal chauffeur until further notice. Essentially, nothing has changed. We will continue to maintain the telephone in your apartment, and help with your rent as needed. Call me whenever I am needed, and I shall be there."

She was dumbstruck. *That's easily worth twice what I make. Why would he still provide me with that?*

"Mr. Ryan has instructed me to provide you with discretionary funds to meet all your needs and pay your bills. You may continue to spend as much as you typically spent before. Rest assured, no actual limits have been placed on you. It is Mr. Ryan's wish that you are comfortable during this difficult time."

She thought, *So, he does know. That's what I needed to be sure of. Okay, let's see how this goes.* "So, you're saying that Mr. Ryan is taking care of everything."

"Yes, Miss Murray. You need but tell me what you require," he said, and sat down next to her, rather than across the table.

She felt herself falling apart. This was so much to bear alone, and his expressed desire for friendship, unexpected though it might be, combined with his closeness and struck a chord within her.

"Alexander, I don't know if I can do this alone. I've never had a baby before. I'm . . . sca . . . oh, Al, I . . . I may need a friend as I go through this," she said, and began to tremble. Frightened and overwhelmed, she turned, and with a broken sob, buried her head in his shoulder. He hesitated, then put his arms around her, and held her as she wept.

A baby. He hadn't expected that, but the wording of Mr. Ryan's telegram did cover all of this, which seemed to indicate that he knew all about it.

Al had one small wish, one hope . . . that the care he took of her might draw her attention.

One could hope.

Chapter Forty-Six

Ben left immediately for California, stopping only once for the night, where he picked up some goods he would likely need in Glendale. The next afternoon, he arrived in the offices to find Howard with two men; one looked familiar, and one did not.

The unfamiliar man wore a military uniform, and spoke first. "Is this the fellow who's stirring things up?"

"Yes, sir. I'd like you to meet Benjamin Ryan. Ben, this is Colonel Leslie Groves. And this is Robert Oppenheimer, a scientist and professor from Berkeley. They're a little surprised to learn that they're going to be working together in a top secret program six years from now, and I brought them here to talk to you about it."

"You remembered them both from me talking about it?"

"You know I record, transcript, and reference everything around here. Paranoia has its advantages."

"It's interesting that you should bring them here right now—"

"Ben, I know that this is something you didn't want to do, but we're out of options—"

"I know we are. You're right." He turned to the men. "Colonel. Robert. Thank you for coming." He shook hands with them.

The Colonel said, "What's all this about? I've been hearing your name everywhere I go, Mr. Ryan. The scuttlebutt is that you've singlehandedly mounted a national defense against the Japanese, who incidentally are friends of the US. You claim they are going to attack Pearl Harbor?"

"That's correct."

"And where did this valuable intelligence come from that lets you know more than the US military?" Condescension fairly dripped from his words.

Ben didn't like the attitude. He looked at Howard.

Howard said, "They arrived shortly before you did. They're not up to speed."

Ben nodded, and looked at the Colonel. "The history books, Colonel Groves. But let me say something here first. I don't have time for too much more government bullshit, so you can believe *this;* I don't care whether you believe me or not. I was sent back here from the year 2010 to save millions of lives. Not just American lives. No race, color, or nationality was specified. The unlikely pairing of you two resulted in the development of a simple device, more powerful than any destructive force on the face of the earth. One bomb detonation levels an entire city. It was used to end World War II. The difference here is this; I wasn't going to call you in here, Colonel. You're superfluous and unimportant to my plans."

Groves gave a derisive snort. *"Your* plans? World War II, you say? This just gets better all the time. So, the Japanese are going to attack us and World War II will be the result, and Mr. Oppenheimer and I develop a weapon that ends it?"

Ben's volume increased with that. "That's a bit oversimplified, and you left out the part where sixty-one *million* people die before you succeed. But essentially, yes; that's correct."

"Well, I think I've heard enough. Gentleman, good day."

Howard looked at Ben. "Ben, this is the best way. . . ."

He rolled his eyes skyward and relented, though he was patently unenthusiastic about it. "All right, all right. Colonel, there's proof. I can tell Mr. Oppenheimer something right here and now to make him a believer. Or at least make him hear me out. I still want to restate my position that we don't need the military, Colonel, though for some reason Howard thinks we might."

Robert had been listening raptly, and he was willing to hear Ben out. It was a good teaser; he wanted to know where it was going. "I'm listening."

"Black holes do exist, and in 2010 we have proof of it. You were right. Or, rather, you will be."

Oppenheimer was stunned. Indeed, for some time he had believed it, but to date it was all theoretical. He'd made notes, scribbled some theories, but hadn't published anything at all. There was only one way this Ben Ryan could know this.

He turned to the Colonel and spoke, "He's telling the truth."

"What's a black hole?"

"It's irrelevant, that's what it is. But it got my attention and I believe he is who he says he is. I do have one question. Mr. Ryan, why are you carrying a soccer ball?"

"This? I brought it for you. I was going to go and see you as soon as I got here. Howard, as usual, was a step ahead of us all. You'll need it. Here." He tossed the ball to Robert, then turned to the Colonel with an icy look and said, "Notice that I didn't get anything for *you,*" then turned back to Robert. "It's a representative model of what you spent years trying to figure out. In 2010, knowing how to build a nuclear weapon is commonplace. In fact, with the Interne— . . . uh, with the study materials available in my time, any high school student could learn the basic designs in an hour."

Oppenheimer was stunned. He'd been working on fission and fusion in relation to power generation. He recognized the potential for it to be used as a weapon, something that, like Ben, he was diametrically opposed to. His own estimate of the timeframe for these developments stood at twenty years, yet this man claimed it was not complicated.

Ben continued. "You're presently working with a Cyclotron and small amounts of radioactive materials in your lab at Berkeley. You're researching the enrichment of certain radioactive elements for various aspects of your work. For brevity I'm only going to talk about three of them here. U-238, U-235, and U-239. For the simplest and easiest version of this type of nuclear weapon, called a gun-assembly, you would need U-235. Of the three isotopes, that's the most difficult to accumulate any significant amounts of. Because of that, because it'll take years to implement a full enrichment program, it becomes highly impractical for our uses. The next is U-238, which is plentiful, but unsuitable for this use. Last, and probably the most important for our needs, is U-239."

Mesmerized, Oppenheimer sat and listened as Ben casually listed off Top Secret isotopes from his lab, and then moved on to the requirements necessary to achieve critical mass for a successful nuclear chain reaction. Then he listened to the story of how their team on the Manhattan Project had solved the problem. Or historically *would* solve the problem.

Chapter Forty-Seven

". . . and that's where my gift to you comes in."

Excited, Oppenheimer stood up. Studying the ball, he carried it across the room. "Of course! This ball represents the configuration of the outermost layers. The black and white panels would be explosive segments, all detonated at once to uniformly crush the layered inner components together, achieving critical mass before the fission can bleed off! Genius!"

"Yes, you are. You designed it. I had to provide the company with ball technology from the future to have this ball custom made for you, so I hope you appreciate that this is not just any soccer ball. The black and white panels are a good model, and you can use whatever is handy in this timeline for the compressive charge. Gelignite or Nobel 808, whatever the newest plastic or putty explosive is right now."

"We can do better than Gelignite or 808, I assure you, Mr. Ryan," Groves interjected.

Ben raised an eyebrow, still oozing coldness toward the man. "Oh? You're still here? I was under the impression that you didn't believe me, and that this project would be proceeding without you, Colonel Groves."

"Let me make this perfectly clear, Mr. Ryan. I don't believe you. But if there's a snowflake's chance in *Hell* that you actually have the ability to create a weapon of this magnitude, you will not be doing so without the involvement of the US military. Am I making myself clear?"

Ben snorted and stood up, about to deliver a snappy retort, when Howard stepped in between the two. It was time he weighed in. "Colonel Groves, you may be used to having your own way, but you're standing in the offices of Hughes Industries. We are an independent defense contractor, and as such, we may create any weapon of any type with impunity, and here's the most important part: *Without the involvement of the US Government.* You want to play in this ball game. I'll decide who is allowed on the playing field. If you want in on this, you'll have to fulfill certain requirements."

Groves' face turned red. Indeed, he was used to calling the shots, and he'd dealt with this Hughes character before. He didn't like him much. And he didn't like his snotty friend with the cane at all.

He and Hughes were a lot alike; territorial, ruthless, ambitious, and focused. The difference was that the IQs in the room on this day surrounded Groves and dwarfed him like a mountain range. And he knew it. The ball literally was not in his court.

But it could be—if he was careful and picked his battles. "Let's hear them," he growled.

Howard knew these military types; the man's growl was simple posturing. He couldn't get anywhere without Hughes's help, and he wanted Howard to think he could. But he could bring something to the table, something that Howard obviously wanted.

Ben stepped back to watch. He could see Howard was in his element, and had a plan of action.

Howard continued, "We've been self-funding the development of weapons, aircraft, and a support system for the defense of our country, because whether you believe it or not, our country will need all of it in the worst way in the coming days. Our government and military have displayed a notable lack of interest until now. We need funds for development and production of this and our other current projects. We need pilots, lots and lots of pilots," he glanced at Ben with the faintest trace of a grin, and continued, raising his fingers one-by-one, "and we don't care what color they are . . . American, Chinese, Canadian, UK, French, or Australian. And a pilot program, including the Tuskegee program, if you've started that. In exchange, we will involve the military in our plans in a consultation capacity *only*. You, Colonel, will be specified as our preference for the government's military liaison. We'll need current intelligence to help us plan our moves. We will make all decisions regarding weapon deployment. After our program has run its course—and we alone will decide how long that will be—we will turn over the weapons program to you. Hughes Industries will remain the sole manufacturing contractor."

"But the program will be turned over only under permanent civilian control and oversight," Ben interjected.

Howard said, "Correct."

Groves ceased his posturing; he knew the deal was fair. To acquire a weapon of such magnitude, military leaders would twist a lot of political arms right off. They'd do whatever it took. He knew he could make a conditional agreement on this, right here and now. Hell, a Sergeant with knowledge of this weapons program could probably make this conditional without fear of reprimand.

"You have yourselves a deal, gentlemen. Mr. Ryan, Mr. Oppenheimer, put your heads together. You're going to be making a presentation to some very powerful people. Dumb it down . . . it's critical that they feel they understand it. Concentrate on the yield, what it can do, and soft peddle how it works, the nuts-and-bolts part. If you come across the way you should, I'll take it from there. I know the people who can get you an open-ended, flexible funding arrangement. Mr. Hughes, before this comes to pass, I want to meet with you and the members of your defense consortium to talk dollars."

He paused for a few moments, then said, "Understand this, gentlemen. Before this is over I'll be the least powerful person you'll have to deal with, and you will need my help with all of it. Remember, if your presentation fails, there goes the funding, there goes our deal. None of us want that." He couldn't resist a quick bit of posturing at the end.

"We'll remain cognizant of that, Colonel," Howard replied. "And please try to remember that should this deal fall through, we will protect this project and will remain in control of it, even if we have to move it offshore. Don't put this independent defense contractor in the position of having to auction off this . . . this . . . what's it called again, Ben?"

"Thermonuclear weapon."

"Thanks. Of having to auction off this thermonuclear weapon to the highest bidder. As an American, I'd take that personally. But I'd still auction it off, make no mistake about it."

Grover gave a surly grunt and struggled to maintain his composure. He'd never met somebody who could push his buttons like this. He hated this guy. But the guy was good; he had to give him that. Hughes and Groves both were aware that this gave Groves exactly what he wanted; the directorship of this program, which would mean an instant increase in rank to full bird Colonel, maybe higher.

He looked straight at Howard, who had already fixed a cool gaze on him, and said, "I'm sure we'll be successful in our mutual endeavor, Mr. Hughes. I look forward to it."

Howard smiled at him and stood up, extending his hand, friendly and relaxed once again. "Then we have a conditional agreement, Colonel. We'll get started on this end, and we should be able to have a presentation ready in about two weeks. Is that good for you, Doctor?"

Robert nodded, he was in. Howard looked back at the Colonel. "Let us know where and when."

Groves made his goodbyes to the others and headed out the door.

Chapter Forty-Eight

Ben settled down with a fresh cup of coffee. He and Oppenheimer had watched Groves and Hughes play their unique game of chess. "You wouldn't actually consider auctioning off the weapon to the highest bidder, would you, Howard?"

Howard turned and stared at him with a severe, wild-eyed trademark Howard Hughes look. "Shit, no. What do you think I am . . . *crazy?*"

Ben jumped up, choking, coughing and red-eyed, and looked around for something to mop up the coffee he'd just squirted out of his nose. He decided as he wiped; it might be better to leave that question unanswered.

After he finished his clean-up, Robert sat down with him, and asked, "Please, tell me about this weapon. Tell me about this situation, too. I'm intrigued by every aspect of it. To be honest, I'm surprised I was involved in the development of such a weapon. How did that come about?"

"I'm not entirely sure of your motivation. In fact, I don't think you were ever sure of it. You were haunted for the rest of your life because two bombs you assembled with your own hands were used to level two cities and kill two hundred thousand people. You criticized the US for not warning the Japanese adequately. You felt that had the warnings been more explicit, it might have been different."

"Do you feel it might have changed things, now that you have had the advantage of historical analysis and retrospect?"

"No, it wouldn't have. The Japanese of this time are an unyielding people. Everything is done for the glory and good of their country and Divine Emperor. To have heeded a warning would have shown fear. Showing fear was treason. Our warning was dire and foreboding; we told them exactly what it could do. After dropping the first bomb, we waited three days for some response before dropping the second, but got none."

"So, you feel that this episode of history will repeat itself?"

"God, I hope not. That was the first and only time nuclear weapons were ever used in anger. I'd like to think that we can learn from history's tragedies and mistakes. Howard has already established control over the where and when. I think we can blend the present and the future—my past—and find a reasonable answer. If the Japanese are not stopped soon, twenty-five million Chinese will die by their hands. They're already dying by the thousands, perhaps millions now."

"My. You've given this a lot of thought."

"I wouldn't have brought you into this if I'd felt there were any other options. Nobody is more opposed to Nukes than I am. These bombs are world-destroyers. I hate to be the one to say this, Robert. If the only way we can save half a million Americans, twenty million Chinese, and a million Japanese is to kill two hundred thousand Japanese, it's easy to see that's equitable. Me? I want to save everybody. I want there to be no more wars. That's not the reality. This is." He tossed Robert the soccer ball.

Robert looked at the honeycomb designs comprising the ball, envisioning the structure of the weapon. There would have to be more dialogue, but for now he'd made up his mind. "So, I should not view it as many thousands of lives lost?"

"It's not a win-win scenario, but even using it, a million Japanese lives are saved, and maybe fifty, sixty million other lives are saved. And by having it, we might be able to avoid using it."

"You make a compelling argument, Mr. Ryan."

"Ben. Call me Ben, everybody does."

"All right, Ben. When do we start?"

For the next two weeks, Ben and Robert worked together every day. Ben ran off occasionally to answer one or two of Howard's questions, or to give his opinion on some aspect of Operation Hourglass. Before the two weeks were up, their team had put together a presentation that they felt would hook military leaders and their political counterparts. Howard viewed their presentation, and made a few suggestions to help sell it. The changes were quickly incorporated.

Then, they waited for word from Groves.

Chapter Forty-Nine

In the evenings, Ben and Howard liked to sit with cool drinks and look out over the ocean from the deck of the relaxation room off of Howard's office on the top floor. It helped to take the edge off.

"Ben, do you mind if I ask you a question?"

"Not at all."

"You've told us all about the future, so many aspects of it. But you've never once brought up the subject of my future. Why is that?"

There was no way he could tell him the truth. "Because for individual people, the future hasn't been written yet. Look at the variables we're introducing into your life. How could I possibly predict how your life will turn out now?"

"I didn't ask you to predict how my life will turn out now. I want to know what was so bad about my life that you don't dare to tell me about it. I want to know why you avoid the subject." Damn little got past Howard.

Ben had prepared for a question or two, other than that, he had little good to tell him. "I already told you that you were a racist. I guess I can tell you a few more things. By the time you died, you were worth more than two billion dollars."

"Tell me more. More than that. It's important to me, Ben. I want to know who I was, how I was viewed, how I acted. You owe that much to me. Look at all I've done here for you."

He was right.

Ben hadn't realized he'd been holding his breath until he released it all at once in a whoosh. "You were kind of . . . crazy. You had lots and lots of women. You made more films than you did planes. You were all about domination of everything and everyone. You had tremendous amounts of money, but I think you lacked purpose or direction. The Howard Hughes of recorded history was almost the opposite of the Howard Hughes I know as a friend. When I came to you, I cared only about using your money to find a way to complete this . . . this *quest* I'd been given. I didn't care who *you* were. That's all changed, Howard, and so have you. You have purpose, and look at you. You're vital, you're energized, and probably the most unexpected thing, a real humanitarian."

"So, I wasn't much of a person."

"No, not much at all. I like this timeline. I like you. You're okay, Howard."

"Do you see that man in me?"

"I see that man in me, Howard. We all have the potential to end up . . ." he hesitated.

"Finish the sentence."

"All right. We all have the potential to end up going in the wrong direction, taking a wrong turn somewhere along the way. That's why we need friends, they keep us on track."

"I don't have any friends. I trust almost nobody, and I find myself wanting to hide sometimes."

"You have a lot of money and you're well-known. You can't just walk down the street like anybody else. You can't trust people because of the same reason. You tended to be reclusive in your first history, for the same reasons. I can understand that. But you have friends, and I'm one of them. I don't care about your money. I've had money before, and I know how unimportant it is to the things that really matter. I care about what happens to you. I don't talk about your first history because the way things are going, it won't turn out that way. Do you remember Granny, the oldest Granville brother who comes out and visits me here? Two years ago he was supposed to die in a plane crash. I swore I would never let that happen. I swore I'd burn the plane before he got in it. All it took was changing his direction."

"Like you changed mine?"

He thought a moment before answering. *"Just* like that."

Ben walked into Howard's office and slapped the paper down on his desk. "What the hell is this?"

Howard glanced up from his paperwork, then down again. "Looks like a wire to me."

"That's just what it is. Now, why in the *world* would twenty million dollars just appear in my bank account out of nowhere? Howard?"

"Don't make such a big deal out of it. It's my way of saying thank you."

"That's half of your entire worth!"

He waved his hand like it was nothing, and casually added, "Nah, it's not even a third. Do what you want with it. I'll never miss it, I promise you. It's yours."

Ben sighed. "You're crazy."

He didn't even look up. "I thought we established that the other night."

"Ahhh . . . *Jesus!*" In utter frustration, Ben turned and walked out, shaking his head and waving the paper over his head like a white flag. He tried not to laugh as he hollered, "All right, all right, I give up. But you haven't heard the end of this!"

Howard never looked up. He grinned a little, and quietly said, "Spend it in good health, my friend." He just loved the "my friend" part. Sometimes, just sometimes, you find yourself in a good place.

Chapter Fifty

Oppenheimer knew everything he knew about the bomb, and still the man wanted him there all the time. *They've assigned a whole team of scientists to him,* Ben thought, *so what the heck does an egghead like him still want with a nothing-special guy like me?*

In truth, Robert liked his company. He liked hearing about the future, about where he was headed. Ben, uncomfortable with that, normally tried to avoid that type of discussion and finally had to close the door on "future talk" unless it was bomb-related. He'd already been trapped into talking about Howard's future, now here was another historically tortured soul asking how his waning years were spent.

Who could know how they'd turn out? *He* certainly had no idea. It was like a kid asking for a fairy tale before bedtime. If he told somebody about their future, it was another fairy tale. It might as well have been a story he made up in his own mind, because he was here to change that story. Ben began to have his fill of being swami to the stars. Anything non-bomb related was politely declared off-limits.

The presentations had gone off without a hitch and funding had been approved. Thanks to the leg-up Ben's knowledge had provided Robert, the design aspects were already complete and production on a prototype was well underway. Howard already had plans to add a significant number of fighters and bombers to the mix, and could hardly wait to show him what he'd been working on.

"I gave a great deal of thought to your recommendations. Our first one hundred government-provided fighter pilots have graduated, and it just so happens that they coincide with a recognized need. So, we're shipping fifty pilots and seventy-five fighters to China, to fight the Japanese and gain experience with Japanese tactics, and test the tactics we've been giving them."

"You're sending planes to China? But I thought—"

Howard held up a hand to stop him. "You were right, and I was wrong. It *is* my job to find a way. Nobody's going to say that millions died on *my* watch, while I looked on and did nothing. We've got a lot to do, I need your help and I want your thoughts on it. I want to make sure we aren't forgetting anything."

Ben said, "Okay, shoot," and sat down across from him.

"We've equipped the China fighters with a variety of armaments to see what works best under what conditions. And we've equipped a good number of the fighters with cameras. The film is going to be flown back out on weekly supply transports for review."

Ben said, "Make sure you ship boatloads of ordnance and aviation fuel up front. Just getting them there won't be enough. Once the Japs know we're supplying the Chinese, the shipping lanes are sure to be threatened. Land, air, or sea, they'll try to sever the supply lines. It could move up the attack on Pearl Harbor. It doesn't matter that we're going in there as a mercenary unit, because we'll be primarily an American mercenary unit."

"We think alike. I've already made arrangements for a massive amount of ordnance, fuel, and spare parts to be sent over at the same time. We're going to fully stock the warehouse there, and maintain a high stock level. If shipping is interrupted for any period of time they'll already be stockpiled. When they learned that there was a chance that they might be sent against the Japanese with the mercenary forces, we had a great number of qualified Chinese men respond in our search for prospective Chinese pilots, enough for a whole class in two different schools. I gave the green light to move them into the program immediately. Our plan is that they should fly with and then relieve the American pilots in China as soon as possible."

"That's great news. If we can populate the forces there with primarily Chinese pilots, it could buy us some time, or get us off the hook entirely."

"My thoughts exactly."

"Are you painting a shark's mouth on each of the fighters?"

"A shark's mouth? Why?"

"Well, technically it's a Tiger Shark's mouth and teeth."

"Tiger Shark, eh? That's a good name for our fighters. It's perfect; I think we should use it."

"The AVG is called the Flying Tiger squadron."

"The AVG?"

"The American Volunteer Group. Here, I'll give you an example. Have the fighters—the Tiger Sharks—painted up like this. The pilots will appreciate it."

"Like that? That looks mean. Nice. Okay, I'll get them going on that."

"I have a question" Ben said.

"Ask away."

"Where do you think our new nuclear capability is going to lead?"

Howard thought for a moment. "Whatever we do, I know the US will develop these weapons anyway, so it satisfies me as the defense contractor. If you're asking me how I feel they should be used, the answer's easy. You've convinced me that we should never use them at all, not ever. Let's place strict regulations on them, and let's make a pact between us to do all we can to avoid ever using them."

"I'm all for that. Agreed."

"Good. So we'll let Robert and Groves do their thing, and we'll go back to concentrating on our pet project. I intend to win Pearl Harbor, and things are really coming together. I've got a planeload of people going to make a progress check on Molokai Island, and I'm curious myself. Photos just don't show you everything you want to know. Are you in?"

"Heck, yeah. I was starting to get bored with all this talking. I want to do something hands-on for a change."

"Have you taken any of the fighter training yet?"

"I've familiarized myself and gotten the basics down. I'm able to fly them with no problem. I could handle one in a dogfight and probably come home alive. How about you?"

"Are you kidding? I'm in one of those babies every chance I get. Wringing one of those out is one of life's little pleasures. Can you believe how fast and responsive they are? I'll admit it. I'm tempted to climb into one on December 7 and go hunting."

"Just tell me you'll resist that urge. We're going to need you in the war room. We . . . uh . . . *do* have a war room, right?"

Howard laughed. "Yes. We have our main operations center in the mountain, and several other relay centers to move information back and forth, plus your repeaters."

"I can't wait to see this."

Chapter Fifty-One

Two of Hughes's DC-3 corporate passenger planes sat on the ramp. Only a few items remained on the pre-flight checklist. In the early morning sunlight, the dew that covered their aluminum skins glistened.

"Are you ready to see what we've worked so hard to build?" Howard called out. Ben waved and headed over.

"You're here on Hughes One, with me."

"Hughes One. Well, La-Tee-Da. Aren't we fancy?"

"See, that's what I like about you, Ben. You're a real ass-kisser. So, shall we?" Howard swept his arm toward the plane and bowed.

They climbed aboard, and a dozen faces greeted them as they walked forward.

Ben looked around. "There are no more seats left."

"You're riding in first class. Ahead—through that bulkhead."

He walked through, and found himself in the cockpit.

Howard pointed to the left seat. "Best seat in the house. Get strapped in and we'll get rolling."

Ben shook his head and a smirk formed as a thought crossed his mind. *I'm probably the only guy in the world who would willingly strap himself in a cockpit with Howard Hughes for a 2400-mile trip.* "I'm not checked out on multi-engines, you know. You'll have to give me a crash-course, if you'll excuse my terminology."

"Not a problem, my friend. By the time we get there, you'll know all about this bird."

Ten minutes later they were climbing and westward bound. Destination: Molokai Island. The DC-3 was exceptionally smooth and quiet. Once they'd reached altitude and leveled out, Ben asked, "So, tell me about this lady, Howard. She doesn't look like a normal DC-3."

"See those engines? They're our new Magic Merlins. They add about two hundred pounds to each side, but the pods are now streamlined and we've doubled the horsepower. A four-bladed prop handles all the power and minimizes prop length. As it turned out, the vari-pitch fighter props were perfect for the job. It was an easy conversion, smoother than I anticipated. Cruise speed on this airframe was 130 knots, about 150 miles per hour. With the upgrades, we're cruising . . . well, you tell me how fast. That gauge right there."

"Jesus. Is this right? It says we're cruising at 260 knots. That's . . ."

"Three hundred miles per hour; you got it. With the four added drop tanks we'll be flying non-stop to Molokai Island in just eight hours. No worries of losing a cylinder; these water-cooled Merlins are solid as a stone. I had the exhausts baffled slightly and pointed them down and behind us, which dramatically reduces the noise levels."

Ben chuckled. "I guess I *am* in first class. So, what does *this* do? I haven't seen this before. . . ."

Ben learned all about the conversions to the Merlinized DC-3. The eight hours passed before they knew it.

"Molokai Island. Thar she blows!" Howard pointed something out to him that looked like nothing more than a dark speck in the endless ocean.

"Where? Ah, I see it. What's our landing vector?"

"None needed in clear weather. Bank left and go south for two minutes, then bank right and proceed straight to your visual right side of the island, reducing your altitude. You'll be landing visually at about six hundred feet and flying straight onto the runway. I'll guide you in."

He switched on the radio. "H-1 to H-2, fall back to give us room to land. Then follow us straight in. We'll continue further down the run way before we touch down, to leave you room. You can land as soon as you feel you've acquired the runway."

A voice came back through the headphones. "Roger that, H-1. Will do."

"I thought you hadn't been here before?" Ben said.

"I haven't. But we've filmed the approach from every direction for pilot training. Didn't you sit in on the approach simulations yet?"

He glanced over at Howard, a bit embarrassed. The films were so grainy he'd assumed their benefit would have been minimal. He hadn't watched them.

Howard sighed. "You're killing me, Ben."

He chuckled and turned to Howard. "*What?* Where'd you get that from?"

"You're always saying it. I guess I liked it."

"Great. Nice to know I'm polluting the timeline with my 2010 speech patterns," he mumbled.

Howard said, "Okay. See those cliffs ahead? The wall going straight up the side of it, do you see it? Just align yourself with that wall and fly right alongside of it, close enough so you're not entirely comfortable with it. That's it. Look at that, straight down the runway. Nice job. Remember, in this big-bottomed gal you're an easy twelve feet off the ground when you roll on."

Howard knew Ben was concentrating on flying, so he attended to the landing checklist. "Deploying flaps. Green light . . . on both. Visual confirmed. Dropping landing gear. One Green. Two Greens. Good to go. Reducing power. Visual approach. Take her in, Ben. I'll be right here on my yoke, okay?"

Ben was getting the feel of the massive lady. This wasn't his graceful, responsive old Model Y. The DC-3 flew gracefully, but handled like a river barge to his touch. Fortunately, the plane could virtually land itself. His approach was almost straight onto the runway, and thus far it had been flawless. The cliffs seemed to go on forever, and Howard gave him small tips to make adjustments. Out of the corner of his eye, Ben saw the caverns running alongside the plane. They appeared to be just off the wingtip. The wheels touched the ground before he expected them to, when he was about twelve feet off the ground. Howard was already dancing on the pedals, keeping it rolling straight and true.

He saw a man in the distance with flags. The caverns ran the whole length of the runway, and there were camouflage nets hanging in front of some, making those caverns nearly invisible from the air. At the farthest end they reached the flagman, who guided them inside the last cavern entrance. The cavern here was easily thirty or thirty-five feet tall, and when the DC-3 rolled inside, he couldn't see much. He removed his sunglasses, and caught his breath. There was enough room in this section alone for dozens of DC-3s, or more likely, their C-47 military counterparts. There was lighting on the ceilings and walls, and people hurrying about.

After the other plane rolled inside, they disembarked. He climbed down the ladder and looked around, and felt miniscule in the cavern. "Howard, this is amazing!" he said, his oooohs and aaaaahs lost in all the others as the group gathered around.

Chapter Fifty-Two

Tiger Sharks

Howard briefed them. "Gather round, everybody. Gather round. Like the runway, these caverns extend over six thousand feet along the side of this mountain. That's about six and a half times the length of the Titanic, to give you some perspective. The bus should be here within a few minutes. Look around, but stay very close. Don't bother the workers. Simply put, don't speak to anybody who hasn't spoken to you."

Ben wandered over to the walls and inspected the marks from the drilling, blasting, and carving out. The caverns had been excavated from solid rock. The amount of labor and equipment required to excavate the place must have been staggering.

The "bus" arrived; a jeep towing two frameworks that looked like hay-wagon frames. A bench ran down each side of the frames, and workers sat on the benches and bounced along. Two buses ran up and down the caverns at all hours of the day; one never had to worry about having to walk long distances. The immense complex was well over a mile long.

When the bus stopped at their cavern, designated Sector 12, workers climbed off, and Howard ushered the new arrivals aboard.

The driver dismounted and addressed them. "When we reach Sector 6, which we call Ops, you will be given passes that must be worn in plain sight. Please pay close attention here. I cannot emphasize this strongly enough. DO NOT lose your passes. Keep them in plain sight. Should you fail to do so, security measures are in place here that will make it very bad for your health. You have been warned. If you are found without a pass showing you will be asked to produce one. If you produce one, you will immediately be taken back to the transports. You will remain there under armed guard until the next transport departs, and you will never be allowed to return. If you cannot produce one, you will be immediately taken outside and shot. That was *not* a joke. Are there any questions?"

Not a hand was raised, and for once, there was no talking going on.

"Okay, let's go, driver."

Ben leaned over to Howard. "You guys really like shooting people, don't you?"

Howard shrugged and nodded. "Yeah, and you'd think with a setup like this we'd have had a lot more. I've been disappointed so far."

"I can see that. That's a bummer."

"Bummer? Slang?"

"Yeah. It means you're bummed . . . umm . . ."

"No, I get the meaning." Howard said. "I like it. If you think I'm bummed, you should see my Marines. All they've gotten to shoot so far was a big bird that got in here and wouldn't leave." In the seats immediately around Howard, they cracked up laughing as he related the story.

The bus moved down along the front of the cavern, and as they passed the first bulkhead, rows and rows of fighters came into view, stretching far into the distance, with crews everywhere working on them. It looked like an ant hill. Something caught Ben's eye, and his jaw dropped in surprise. Every single fighter had been painted with a massive mouth and rows of huge, sharp teeth. *God, they look mean.* "Tiger Sharks!" he yelled. He chuckled and his grin went ear-to-ear. He turned to Howard, who had been watching him to see what his response would be. He too, had a big grin. *What a character.*

There were clearly far more of the Tiger Sharks than they had originally planned to build. "My rough count is around seven hundred planes here, how is that?"

"More than seven hundred! And more to come!"

"But, how in the world did you manage that? I thought we were working on a budget."

"You didn't really think I needed all the government money I specified to design something you already knew how to build, did you? The manpower and equipment required was a small fraction of what we quoted. I instantly put half that money into increasing production here. Call it my—no, call it *America's*—investment in America. I also beefed up the pilot programs to increase pilot output by nearly double. We're going to need lots of pilots."

Ops was just as Howard had described. Armed guards took up position around them. Very large guards who looked like they meant business. A clerk at a table interviewed each of the new arrivals, then provided them with a pass to be worn hanging around the neck and a stern warning to display it at all times. Ben and Howard went first. They were given their passes, then routed behind the clerk and around the corner, following the hallway. No sooner did they round the corner than they were shoved backward by two pistol-wielding men, who pinned them against the wall with one hand and demanded their passes. They inspected the passes carefully, then stepped back and one of them said; "You may pass." Passes were held out in front by the others, and pass inspections went smoothly from there.

"Call it a hunch, but were those two of your former Marines?" Ben asked.

Howard nodded. "We have a need for tight security here, and we have a hundred of them. All came highly recommended."

"They get my vote."

The group gathered inside of the next room. "Okay, folks, I'm going to take you into the heart and brain of this operation, our Operations Center. Stay close to me, and don't talk to anybody who doesn't talk to you first. Understand?"

Heads nodded vigorously; after their 'warm' greeting they were getting a feel for the place. The group stayed close as they moved upstairs to a large, square room. Each wall was about sixty feet long.

"Welcome to Ops. We can see 360 degrees from here. The walls are hardened. This glass is three inches thick. An aircraft could explode right next to us and we'd be safe. Piped-in air, self-contained everything. The staff can live in here if need be, and continue to direct operations remotely for some time . . . even under siege. All wiring and pipes in and out are encased in several feet of concrete. Not invulnerable, but we did everything that could be done."

"We have backup generators in hardened areas, and we have six tons of batteries, always charged and ready. This room could run for a week on that alone. It's important to remember that realistically, should we come under siege, we might last a number of hours or a day at most. For all intents and purposes, it couldn't be any more secure. And we need to be honest about it; most battles would be over within hours, and we'd almost certainly be able to hold out that long."

"Here in the center of the room you see our relief map of the Islands and the surrounding area, extending as far as three hundred miles out, especially to the west and north. We can show ships, task forces, single aircraft, and flight movements. We can track our own transports coming in. Everything we need to command this battle is right here in this room, gentlemen."

Murmurs and comments ran through the group as they moved on with the tour.

Chapter Fifty-Three

"If there are no more questions, let's break for some chow. We'll show you to your quarters after chow, and you'll have the evening to relax and socialize. They'll be playing a movie tonight, *The Dawn Rider,* a John Wayne western.

"You are allowed outside on the runway, but should any aircraft appear, no matter how close or how far away, you will *RUN*—not walk—back into the nearest opening and out of sight. If you cannot run, then you will not go outside. If you wish to smoke after dark, keep your lighter covered. No smoking near the aircraft. Questions?"

There were none, so they traveled the length of another hallway cut deep into the recesses of the mountain. It opened up into a mammoth cavern that, except for the forty steps carved from the passageway to the floor far below, clearly had not been carved out by men or machines. The walls were smooth.

It was an ancient volcanic magma chamber, and a big one. The chamber was a chow hall, theater, gathering point, and served a variety of other uses. The acoustics were amazing. They'd stumbled upon it while excavating for a planned community chamber and chow hall. It was a real piece of luck and had advanced the project an entire year. The walls were moist and glistened with bits of quartz, perhaps mica, reflecting or refracting the ambient light. It gave the feeling of having a night sky inside the chamber all the time. The subtle spectacle brought a peaceful atmosphere to the place, making the chamber a perfect fit for its intended recreational uses. It became a popular place for the off-duty personnel to relax and decompress. The movies were shown at the far end. Food was served around the clock. And for the most part, it was tasty.

Howard looked thoughtful as he held up a forkful of meat he had speared. "A lot of chickens died to build this place." At least it wasn't 'mystery meat.'

"What makes the starlight on the walls and ceiling, Howard?" one of them asked.

"We haven't had it analyzed. It's probably some form of quartz."

"Maybe they're diamonds."

"I wouldn't mind recouping some of my costs, but I won't hold my breath on that one."

Ben said, "I'm fading fast. I think I'll head for my quarters and turn in."

"Me too, I'm beat. Just remember, this place is built for war. It ain't the Ritz."

Ben nodded, then wondered something aloud, "Do you own the Ritz?"

"No. I don't own any hotels. I was thinking about buying some in Las Vegas."

"You did really well with that."

"I did? Hmmm. Thanks."

"Just remember, hire some black men this time. Hire some Hispanics, some native Americans, some Chinese. . . ."

Howard didn't answer, so Ben followed his gaze. The rest of the group had been watching and listening. None were eating.

He wasn't saying anything that didn't need saying. He stood up. "That goes for the rest of you, too. What makes America great has always been the diversity of its people. Hire some men of color, you won't be sorry." He waved to Howard. "Mr. Hughes. Gentlemen. I'm off to hit the hay."

As he walked away, the group remained silent. As he reached the top step and turned into the passageway, he heard the silence break. The group launched questions at Howard, as though there was some secret to be learned from Ben's words of wisdom. Howard said that everything Ben told him was true, that the whole project wouldn't have gone nearly as well as it did had he not heeded Ben's advice to hire on a great number of blacks, Hispanics, and others. "Blacks, that's what they call the coloreds in Ben's time. He says they're called African-Americans too. Native Americans are what they call the American Indians. Things are going to change, and we might as well be ahead of the curve. In fact, in his time the President of the United—"

Ben walked out of earshot, smiling and shaking his head. Maybe there was some hope for Howard after all. He walked out into the big chamber, headed for his quarters. The lighted hangar area was lighted just enough that at this time of night it had an eerie feel to it. All along the front of the cavern the blackout curtains were rolled down to keep the lights from being seen from anywhere outside. He absorbed what he saw, stored it in his mind. *This is the result of my trip through time. For what it cost me, it has to make a difference. It just has to.*

Chapter Fifty-Four

After a reasonably comfortable night, Ben and the others gathered for the rest of their tour. Several of the Martin PBY's had arrived from Oahu. The PBY's were search and rescue planes, essentially flying boats, slated to be repaired and upgraded, readied for action. Two of them had already been "Merlinized," retrofitted with the Magic Merlins. Some of the fighter pilots were bound to be shot down. These could be put to good use retrieving the downed pilots in record time. The wings, fuse, and attachments had to be reinforced to handle the stresses of twice as much power. These would lift off the choppiest seas, and fairly leap off smooth seas.

The repair bays were amazing. As expected, a few runway mishaps had occurred, and Ben watched the men working on the Tiger Sharks. He felt a pang of longing, remembering those early days back in the Granville's shop at the old Liberty Street field, watching the brothers work together and the enjoyment he had being able to work with them. It brought back a moment when he was a kid, lying in bed, having the same pang, wishing he could be there with the Granvilles. As he pondered that, it struck him that he'd been granted his fondest of childhood wishes, though he had to travel two or three lifetimes to do so.

In spite of the time travel and being forced to stay in another era, even having to walk with a cane; he was a lucky man. He had been afforded the opportunity to do the right thing, to really lay it all on the line.

He saw two of the mechanics scratching their heads and talking. They were having some difficulty with the Merlin they were working on. He wandered away from the group and over to the two men. He listened to them for a minute or two. During a lull in their discussion they noticed him.

"What can we do for you, Mr. . . . Mr. Ryan?" one said, reading Ben's pass.

"I was listening to your problem and thought maybe I could be of some help."

"No, sir. We're trained Merlin mechanics, I doubt you would even know what we were talking about."

"That so?"

"Sorry, sir, but I'm afraid that's so."

"Okay. Then I'll be on my way. But . . . once you've lent all the expertise you have to what you're doing, pull that Supercharger apart and replace the impellers. One of them has gone bad, and I guarantee you, that's the cause of your power loss. Did the pilot have a prop strike?"

The two mechanics stole uneasy glances at each other. Both had the sudden feeling they'd challenged the wrong man. After an awkward pause, the mechanic admitted, "Yes sir, he nosed over. We just replaced the damaged prop assembly yesterday, and couldn't get any power out of her after that. Say, wait a *minute*! "B" . . . You wouldn't happen to be *Benjamin* Ryan, the Magic Merlin guy, would you?"

"One and the same, fellas."

"Holy Shi— yes, *Sir!* We'll get right on that blower, sir. If you say that what it is, then that's more than likely what it is. C'mon, Jackson, hand me that spanner."

Ben grinned as they snapped to. They seemed to be pretty nice fellows. "I have a thought. Would you like to know why that happened that way? Call some of the others over, and the group of you could spread the word, and next time a plane won't go down for a week with a simple prop strike."

"That'd be great, Mr. Ryan. These *are* pretty new to us; we'd like to know as much as we can." He beckoned several of the other crews over, and introduced them to Ben.

"Okay, let's do this." He pointed with the tip of his cane. "You see this puffed-up housing here? That cools the recycled air from this. One weakness in this setup is that when a prop strikes, the sudden stop combined with the impeller's momentum will as often as not shear one of the solid worm drives between the crankshaft and the blower . . . here. The engine restarts all right, but with the blower broken, it's not getting even a sixth of the air it needs. And as you've seen here, nothing looks broken. But it's designed to be repaired easily through this access plate. If you know what you're listening for, you can hear it make a noise like a—"

Behind Ben, Howard and the consortium watched him talking to the mechanics, answering questions, laughing, and having a great time teaching, and they in turn having a great time learning. Dozens of other mechanics were migrating over and joining Ben's impromptu Merlin seminar. He'd already rolled up his sleeves. They'd peeled back both shrouds and dropped the belly-plates as he pointed and thumped this or that with his cane, walking them through the advances that made these Magic Merlins . . . well, magic. The mechanics were enthralled with Ben's common-sense explanation of the workings of the Merlins.

Howard decided to leave Ben right there. *He was so wrapped up he wouldn't even notice the group leaving. He's a natural, and he's right where he belongs. He deserves a little time off, and it's easy to see this is his idea of fun. He'll get to see all he can stand of this place in the coming months.*

"Hey, you!" Howard said, summoning a Marine. "See that man down there talking to those crews? You belong to *him* now. Wherever he wants to go, you take him. He has no restrictions. He's the reason you're here. He's the reason we're all here. Just keep him safe, no matter what. Got that?"

"Yes, sir, Mr. Hughes. Anywhere he wants to go. No restrictions and keep him safe, sir. Got it."

"Okay, folks, c'mon, we've got some ground to cover."

Chapter Fifty-Five

Ben shivered. *Brrrr. It's frigid over these Rockies this morning. Probably should've waited until later, but I haven't been home to see Laney in months. I'll live until I can drop down the eastern slopes.*

He'd climbed into the Model Y and headed east the day before, and had made it as far as Salt Lake. Back in the saddle at first light, he'd found the mid-October air above the early-morning Rockies to be brisk, to say the least. As noon approached the sun was higher, the air was warmer, and he was reducing altitude and settling in for a nice run in some clear weather. By mid-afternoon he made Troy, Ohio, where he landed at the Waco aircraft company. He taxied the Senior up to the building and climbed out, stretching his stiff limbs. For a thirty-two-year-old, he was sure having a lot of stiff muscles lately. Ahhh, fleeting youth. He grabbed his cane and walked inside, and there he saw it. His Waco UMF. Not rebuilt. Built for the first time, brand spanking new, with one notable change. He'd had them repair and install his original radial. They'd even painted this lovely lady to match the . . . 'original.' Or was *she* the original? It was a mind-bender. Once they'd straightened out the twisted metal frames, they'd had near-perfect patterns to use, they even knew where to weld and where to bolt, where to drill. The first UMF had left the facility on schedule, over six years ago. And now, here was his old girl, built at long last, right down to the VIN number.

"Ben! Good to see you!" It was Ed Weaver, the man who had come out to pick up the hulk of his original UMF.

"She's perfect." Ben said, running his hands down the sleek white paint.

"You were right about it all, Ben. I don't understand how it all happened, though. Look at this." He brought out a piece of the horizontal stab from the crashed plane and there, etched into the metal, was some writing. *Ed—It's true—you built this—do what he asks —Ed*

He looked at Ben and said, "When I saw this, I knew it was real. I etched this one's frame too. I compared the two after I did it, and they were a perfect match. It gave me goose bumps."

"Yeah, this can be tough to wrap your mind around sometimes. How many have you sold?"

"About . . . forty-five to date. They're real popular."

"You sold eighteen in the first history. They became classics later, after you closed up shop. The Waco Classic Aircraft company from my time built beautiful, perfect replicas. They'd sold over one hundred and twenty of the YMFs by 2010. Of course, all that could change now. Look how many you're selling."

"Well, *your* original, gen-u-ine Waco UMF is all ready for you. The motor's purring like a kitten, the oil is fresh and she's been checked out and retightened a dozen times. She's one hundred percent. I hope you like her. So, what do you want us to do with the Model Y for now?"

"Do you do rebuilds?"

"We sure do. But Ben, you have your own aircraft rebuilding companies, why do you need us to do it?"

"Oh, you don't want to do it?"

"I didn't say that. We can always use the work, there are mouths to feed."

"And now because you'll be rebuilding her I don't have to figure out what to do with her. Let's say I pick her up in the spring? Rebuild the engine too, new everything. Take your time, Ed, do it right. Right means *perfect*. I don't want her left outside or under a damn tarp—not ever. She stays inside and dry, whatever it costs me. Send me a wire or call me when you need more money. This envelope has enough to get you started on the rebuild in good shape. And this envelope here has the amount you specified for purchasing the UMF. Did I get that right?"

Ed counted out the cash and smiled. "Yep. That's exactly right. Thanks for the work. Thanks for everything, Ben."

"No. Thank *you* for giving my baby back to me. You're the only one who could have done it. Well, I'd love to stand and talk shop all day, but I have a sweet little thing waiting for me in Springfield and she just won't wait. Could you have the men get the old girl started and warmed up for me?"

Fifteen minutes later, Ben eased his antique—or rather, brand-spanking-new—Waco biplane into the air, and was eastbound. By central Pennsylvania, however, the declining sun and the brisk autumn air had him shivering and looking for an airport to land for the night.

He found a place to land and a place to stay for the night, and was back in the air at 9:30 a.m.; not an early start. The hard frost that had forced him to land the night before left him with stiff muscles and bones. He didn't feel up to another frigid couple of hours. Late in the morning, the spires of home could be seen surrounded by the endless flaming fall foliage as they welcomed him home. Soon Liberty Street and the familiar old Springfield airport came into view, and then he was taxiing up to the Granville hangar. He showed off the Waco to the brothers and they talked about it; like him they were teased by knowing it *was* the actual wreckage he had been pulled from, and it would be again someday . . . maybe? He shook hands, hugged and laughed, and then offered his opinion that they weren't nearly as pretty as Laney. He was headed straight home to her. Granny gave him a ride and wished him well. He promised they would get together and do some serious visiting the next day, and made his way into the house.

"Daddy!" Bennie cried out and nearly bowled him over.

Ben grabbed him up and held him in the air. "Let me see what you look like. Gosh, Bennie, you're getting so big I can barely pick you up! You look wonderful!"

"I know," Bennie said, beaming as his Dad placed him back on the floor.

"Where's Momma?"

"Upstairs with the baby," he said, and thundered ahead to lead the way.

He must have heard the little guy wrong. He hadn't been gone *that* long. *The things kids say.* Bennie ran upstairs ahead of him to tell his Mom.

"Momma! Momma! Daddy's here! Momma!"

He laughed and continued his steady climb up the stairs. With his bad leg, stairs weren't his forte. As he reached the top, Laney rushed down the hall and held onto him as though another five years had passed. He gave her a soft, loving kiss, and she looked into his eyes, smiled, and tucked her hair over her right ear. "Oh, sweetheart, I miss you so when you're gone."

"I miss you too. The only place in the world I ever want to be is right here with you."

"You don't know how glad I am to hear you say that," she said, and called over her shoulder, "Mrs. Gruber, could you come out here?"

Mrs. Gruber, looking very happy, walked out into the hallway, carrying a bundle in her arms. "Hello, Mr. Ryan, it's wonderful to have you back home again. We all missed you."

Apparently they'd been babysitting. "Hello, Mrs. Gruber, it's great to be home. Whose baby is this?"

Laney, still holding him, looked up at him. "Ours. Isn't he cunning?" she said, using the New England term often used on children and sometimes puppies or kittens to mean 'cute' or 'handsome.'

He looked in her face to see if it was a joke. She looked quite serious.

"No. I haven't been gone *that* long this time!"

Her eyes shifted off to the side, then back to him. She had a devilish gleam in her eyes, but he didn't pick up on it when she said, "I probably wasn't as clear about that as I could have been. He's *yours.*"

Ben felt an instant of panic, after which he decided he'd better clear the air. He looked straight into her eyes. "Laney, I swear to you, I would never cheat on you. Never in a million years. I don't know anything about this."

She fought the smile. "I know you don't, darling. And I'm not angry at you for anything."

He felt the knot of panic start to release, but not entirely. "Oh, good."

"In fact, I'm pretty pleased with you about something," she said in a sing-song voice, her eyes dancing and twinkling as she looked up at him. She took a step back, and he saw it. Laney was pregnant.

He didn't know what to say at first, and then his eyes opened wide with delight. "Laney! You're pregnant! We're going to have a baby!"

Bennie and she corrected him at the same time. *"Another* baby."

He felt confused. He looked confused. To the point of being over-whelmed.

Laney, still enjoying the moment, reached out and took him by the arm and gently steered him downstairs. She kept him from asking too many questions by bringing him up to date on nearly everything else, and saving the best for later. "How about some dinner, darling? You must be starved. Let's get you something to eat, and then we'll talk so you can make some sense of it all. I can tell you one thing. It's been any-thing but boring around here for the past five months. You simply will not believe half of it. But everything is fine. That attorney you hired for me was worth every cent, though I'm now a woman of scandal, good-ness knows. Divorced, unmarried, pregnant *and* living in a man's house. Oh, how they are talking all about the town, you can just *imagine. . . .*"

Still on overload, he let her guide him to the dining room, and as she droned on, he listened—more or less.

His headline news of the new Waco and the twenty million dollars had been bumped to the back page.

But, lunch was delicious.

Chapter Fifty-Six

After dinner, they retired to the parlor and Laney waited until he was seated and comfortable before relating the story of the family's newest addition.

Ben encouraged her to elucidate. "All right, Dear, I think I can probably handle whatever this is."

Laney, still smiling her mysterious Mona Lisa smile and enjoying the complete upper hand, started to tell the tale. "A couple of months ago, a couple showed up at the door with this baby. The woman was beautiful. Oh my, but she was breathtaking! The man didn't say much, but they finally got to their point and said that this was your child, and they were here to bring him to you. It's a boy."

"And you never questioned it, you just took the baby?"

She knit her brow, "Benjamin Ryan, do you think I am daft? Do you think I don't have a brain in my head? Of course I questioned it. Now, do you wish to hear the story, or are you going to keep interrupting me?"

Before he could answer, she went on. "Well, I recognized the woman straight off. You don't see somebody like her and just forget her. It was Marilyn."

Ben's head snapped up. She had his attention.

"The baby is yours, Benjamin, he looks just like you. Marilyn wanted to leave the baby with you. She doesn't want him and she wanted to make that very clear. She hoped that you would want him, but she said that her year was about up and that you'd know she couldn't take care of him after that in any case. The man was named Alexander. He was very proper, and I think he was British, too."

"Oh, Alexander is my chauffer! He's a good friend."

"Oh. Well, your good friend asked Marilyn to marry him, and she accepted. They're married now, and she looked very happy with him."

He grinned, impressed with Al's actions, and was excited for him. "Way to go, Al!"

She was surprised to see him so enthusiastic about Alexander and Marilyn. "You seem quite happy about it."

"I am. They're both wonderful people. I couldn't think of a nicer couple. But I don't understand about the baby, I'd think they would want him."

"Well, he's yours, don't *you* want him?"

"Well, I suppose, yes, I do."

She wouldn't accept that. "You *suppose?*"

"All right, yes, I do want the baby; of course I do, he's mine. But . . . I don't want to take him from his mother."

She pressed her point. "I promise you, she wanted to leave him here with you."

Ben thought it over. "Then . . . I suppose it's okay, but I still would like to make sure there were no misunderstandings. I'd be proud to raise him, but I think there's one condition that you and I must agree on."

Apprehensive, she said, "Yes?"

"She's his birth mother, and if she ever wants to come and visit him, she has the right."

No! Marilyn gave him up! Oh, he's right. I know he's right. And he did say yes. She'd gotten herself worked up, worried he might say no. Though she couldn't imagine him not wanting to raise his own child, as good a father as he was to Bennie. She insisted, "All right, but she can't take him anywhere unless we both agree to it."

"Agreed, as long as it's reasonable. So—it seems I have another son. What is his name?"

Laney smiled that little smile again. "What else?"

He rolled his eyes upward. "Oh, no, don't say Benjamin!" He

thought, *Shades of George Foreman*—and rolled his eyes in mock despair. He wouldn't have minded anyway.

Laney tittered gleefully. "No, silly! His name is Alexander."

"Whew. Dodged that bullet. That's a fine name."

"Alexander Benjamin Ryan."

"Ouch!" *Oh, well, just a flesh wound.* He grinned. "That's a fine name. Do you like it, Laney?"

"Oh, yes, very much. Mrs. Gruber, could you bring in our new son?"

Mrs. Gruber came in, cooing and cuddling the little one, and Bennie walked beside her, holding onto the blanket. He was helping.

Ben asked, "Bennie, could you sit on my lap first? I'm going to need some help to know how to hold him."

"I know how. Here I come." Bennie climbed up on his lap, and watched as Mrs. Gruber carefully handed Benjamin his new son. Then he gave his Daddy detailed instructions on what he should do to make sure the baby's head didn't fall off, and other helpful hints.

Now that he was up to speed and holding his new son, he beamed with pride. "Bennie, you're going to have to give Alexander some help as he grows up. He doesn't know how to be Momma's sunshine like you do. Can you help him be Momma's little bit of sunshine, seeing as you're the oldest brother and the man of the house when I'm gone?"

Bennie's eyes opened wide as he realized he was still the first son and Momma's sunshine forever. And the man of the house—when Daddy was away, of course. "I sure can!"

Ben smiled at Laney and said in his best Downeast accent, "You're right; he's cunnin' as all get-out."

Bennie helped, and Ben cuddled and cooed his little boys. No man could ever ask for more. A while later, Laney snapped a photo of the three of them, fast asleep in the chair.

Chapter Fifty-Seven

Ben had been busy for days, running errands and sending off wires. After that, he called Alexander on the telephone.

"Al, is that you?"

"Yes sir. It's wonderful to hear your voice. I trust you have been home and that you heard the news?"

"Yes, I have. That's why I'm calling you. Al, I have a very serious question for you, and I need a serious answer. The baby, little Alexander. Did Marilyn give him up because she couldn't afford him, or because she didn't want him, or because she thought she couldn't win if she fought me for him? I want you to think very carefully before you answer, Al. And I want you to remember that if she wants to keep him, I will provide for them . . . for life. I had no idea she was pregnant, or my arrangements would have reflected the situation. I'm sorry that I put all of that responsibility on your shoulders, my friend."

"You didn't know? That answers a number of questions. But no worries, the wording of your telegram was quite adequate, Mr. Ryan. It enabled me to provide her with the finest of care throughout her pregnancy. Since you left me in charge of everything, I was personally able to see to all her needs. I assure you, you were . . . quite generous. I left nothing to chance."

Ben laughed at the way Al worded that. "That's my Al; you've got my back as always. And I see you've always had Marilyn's back as well."

"Yes indeed, sir. It was no trouble at all. I don't have to tell you what a remarkable woman she is."

"You certainly don't. You're a good man, Al. You took what could have been a very bad situation and saved the day. I owe you for that, more than I could ever say, and I promise you, I will make it up to you. And by the way, I hear congratulations are in order. You are two of the finest people I know. You both deserve to be happy. Which leads me back to the question about the baby, Al. I'm serious."

"Mr. Ryan, Marilyn wished for you to have the baby. She wants a baby from a husband and a marriage. As enamored as I was with the child, she was adamant about it. I could not sway her decision. For the record, sir, I tried. I wanted to keep him. I apologize if that offends you, but it is the truth."

"I'd expect no less from you, Al. Are you two living in the hangar?"

Al was silent for a moment, hesitating before answering. "Yes, sir, we are. I apologize for taking such liberties with your generosity, but her year was about to run out, and her apartment—"

"Al." Ben interrupted. "Don't say another word, and don't you dare apologize for doing the right thing. I understand that you two are in love. The hangar is where you live. I have a thought that should help out with the situation for now. First, extend my support for another year, with the same guidelines, as a small gift from me to you both. Second, my quarters there are several times as large as yours. Please—move yourselves into them right away, with my blessings. Keep all the furniture. Put my personal papers and such into boxes and run them over to my office at Ryan Aviation."

"Oh, sir! We couldn't possibly—that's too much!"

"That's nothing for as dear a friend as you are, Al. Not to mention for a woman you love as much as Marilyn. Nothing's too good for her or you, my friend. Get started on that right away, would you?"

"As you wish sir, but I'm . . . uncomfortable about it."

"Don't worry, Al, nothing comes for free. I have some work for you to do, and I need you to go and look into it as soon as you've finished relocating to your larger digs. Have you got a pencil? I need you to contact Fred Deakins over at the Realtor off East Grand. Do you know where that is?"

"Deakins Realty? Yes, sir, they sell the higher-end homes in and around the city, I believe."

"You got it. I've already contacted him about finding me a fine home in the low-upper range, with about two "reallys" before the nice and two "reallys" before the expensive, but not three. I know that's more of my colorful phrasing, but I think you understand about what I'm looking for."

"Yes, sir, and as always, your phrasing is a refreshing change. You have always had impeccable taste, yet not utterly extravagant. Beautiful but not beyond functional, along the lines of your Packard. Does that sound correct?"

Ben liked that description. "Just so, Al. Just so. And, if I could impose upon the two of you, I'd also like to ask you to have Marilyn help in the search. She has wonderful taste. Take your time and be thorough, then let me know when you find a place that you both agree is the nicest one of the bunch. Can you do that?"

"It would be our pleasure, sir. And sir?"

"Yes, Al?"

"I don't believe I've ever taken the opportunity to properly thank you for my job, and for your never-ending generosity. It has always been my privilege knowing you and being in your employ, sir."

"Nobody likes an ass-kisser, Al."

"Indeed, sir."

He chuckled. "You're the best chauffeur in the business, you know that, Al? I miss you all the time."

"As I do you, sir. I look forward to chauffeuring you once again after you've purchased your new home here."

"I look forward to it as well, Al. Well, I've got to get going here."

"Yes, sir. I shall be in contact, sir." And with that, he hung up.

Ben was happy to have that deal in the works. Things were happening fast. He wanted to get as many issues settled as possible.

Chapter Fifty-Eight

Alexander and Marilyn loved the search. They had a wonderful time touring all the fine homes, and they dreamed about where and how they'd live if they had plenty of money. It was more than fun; it was exciting. But they had to admit it; the search had come to an end. They had found the perfect place, and there was no denying it.

'Grand' was the word that described the estate at 1200 Beacon Boulevard, in every way possible. The newest of everything was in the house, which was by anybody's description a mansion. And there was one more feature that had occurred to them during their search. Of necessity, of course. The domestic staff and chauffeur would need a place to live. This estate came replete with a carriage house for the former owner's staff and chauffeur. It was a grand old carriage house, a sizable residence all by itself, also with the finest of everything. They rationalized that a man as wonderful as Mr. Ryan would want the perfect home with the perfect facilities for his staff as well. Never mind that at the present price it added $25,000 to the price instead of the average additional $4,000 for a carriage house. That was the price of perfection. There were any number of substantially more expensive homes available, but tours of those yielded none that were both as beautiful and functional as this one. Another valid point they could make; none of the others were nearly as well-maintained. Mr. Ryan valued well-maintained things above all. It wasn't mentioned—and since he'd asked them to find a place that *they* felt was the best, it probably didn't need to be mentioned—that Marilyn and Alexander had fallen in love with every inch of it. There was little money to be found, making it a buyer's market. The owners—their finances ravaged by the market crash—had lowered the price for the third time, desperate to move it, with not so much as a nibble.

There was that nagging worry in the back of Alexander's mind that living this near to Ben might be a problem to Marilyn, with her first baby growing up in the main residence while her others grew up in the carriage house.

He had broached the subject once they included carriage houses in their search, but Marilyn never even flinched. She'd grown up a practical woman. Difficult, and sometimes heartbreaking situations were just a part of life. They had always been a part of hers, to be sure. They couldn't be certain they would still be able to live in the hangar, which, after living there she had to admit was very comfortable, not to mention cost-free. Ben's return to the hangar had always loomed as a possibility, and with it the potential complications of the situation.

Ever the practical one, she felt it was important that they do whatever they could to ingratiate themselves to Mr. Ryan (and she still referred to him as Ben, which Alexander found disconcerting). Their fervent hope was that he would continue to keep Alexander in his employ. Times were hard. She was right, and he had to admit it. But it worried him, and he didn't want to admit that he harbored these fears. Though he'd managed to sock away a pretty decent bit of money over the years, he feared Marilyn would leave him if he lost his job. It all boiled down to her. He didn't care about money. He still couldn't believe she had said yes and married him.

To her, marrying Alexander was just as surprising. Irony of ironies, after all her plans to climb the social ladder, she'd fallen completely head-over-heels in love with this sweet, attentive chauffeur who had lovingly cared for her through every minute of her pregnancy. Al had no way of knowing this, as they'd never discussed it in depth, but the aspect of having or not having money and the prospect of being poor mattered little to her; she'd been poor before. With somebody who loved her—and somebody she really loved in return—at her side, she could be poor again without complaint. She loved and adored Alexander. They would get by.

Alexander only viewed it one way, and well he should have. He had won the lottery of love.

He contacted Fred Deakins with the news that they had finalized the search for Mr. Ryan's new property. He gave the address, and Deakins fell all over himself being helpful when he learned which property it was. It never failed to amaze Alexander how some people acted over money. He contacted Ben, and the price negotiations and paperwork started.

Two weeks later, Ben called Al and asked him to grab all the spares and drive the Packard out to pick him up.

Chapter Fifty-Nine

It was a long trip east. Alexander used up three of the four spares, so he was thankful that Ben had reminded him to bring them. He pulled into the yard and parked next to a brand-new, gorgeous gold and brown Packard. As a chauffeur, he coveted it instantly. Not just any new car, it was a Packard—and a thing of beauty. Mr. Ryan's taste, as always, was exquisite. He couldn't blame him for not wanting to drive this new Packard out to Detroit through the snow and slush, though as a matter of pride Alexander would personally have washed it from top to bottom, underneath and inside and out, until one could not tell it had ever even been on the road.

By the time Al climbed out and stretched his legs, Ben had come out into the snow and greeted him with a warm hug. Had anybody else tried to hug him, Alexander would not have allowed it. Not to mention the critical need for maintaining decorum. But his feelings for Ben were warmer than for most folks. He ranked at the top of his list of good and decent folks. Ben ushered him inside. It was getting dark, and Alexander was hoping they wouldn't be leaving tonight for the long trip back. Three days was a long time to be in the driver's seat. Still, always the consummate chauffeur, he braced himself for the possibility.

Inside, he met the family. Laney was a sweet, wonderful woman and he could see how Ben would have thought the world of her. In his eyes he saw just that, and was gladdened to see how she held Ben's heart. He'd never seen Ben look at Marilyn that way. Not even close.

Al was delighted to be able to see and hold little Alexander, and he felt a pang when he handed the babe back. The same pang he felt when they'd left him there. He was growing so!

They all settled in the living room, and he was offered the easy chair next to Ben's. It placed him in an uncomfortable position. As domestic help it was not proper to assume familiarity with your boss and your boss's family, and he stated just that. Ben laughed at Al's by-the-book rule readings, and Al's objections were shouted down with hearty hugs and laughter by Laney and Ben and Bennie. He was told he was family and not the help. He was still a bit cautious, until Mrs. Gruber came into the room with little Alexander and sat in the easy chair next to his. When no reprimand was forthcoming, Alexander remembered whose house this was. Ben's. Ben had always just been Ben, unaffected by money and wealth. The best boss in the world, and to Ben he was just plain Al. He released the breath he hadn't realized he was holding, and settled down into the plush easy chair. He thought, *This is nice. I could get used to a chair like this.*

They talked about the trip, and Laney was mesmerized. She just *loved* listening to Al's proper British accent; it was an elegant style of speech, and he was eloquent. Once they established that the trip out was relatively uneventful—two or three flats on a long winter trip in those days was minimal—the talk waned, and the warm, comfortable silence of the old house relaxed them all. But Ben had one more subject to cover.

"Well, it looks like the old Packard is in fine shape. You've done a great job of keeping her in tip-top condition, Al."

"Thank you, sir. Although one would never know it looking at her now, she was pristine when I left Detroit."

"No doubt in my mind, none at all. Well, I'm glad you brought her to me, Al. Because I'm going to be keeping her here. And Al, I'm sorry, but I'm no longer going to be able to keep you in my employ after today."

Alexander was stunned. He hadn't expected this. Mr. Ryan must have been more upset over his marrying Marilyn than he'd been able to detect on the phone. But he looked so happy with Laney! Well, he supposed it was to be expected. Now he would be returning by bus. *Oh, my. How depressing.*

"Al? Are you all right? Are you with us?"

"Oh . . . oh, yes, sir. Sir, I deeply regret anything I might have done to have caused this situation. It has always been my distinct pleasure to be in your employ," his voice quavered.

"Well, it's just not possible any longer. You're going to have other things on your mind pretty soon. I've got a couple of things here for you to sign, and then we'll be done."

Al sighed in resignation. "Yes, let's get this over with."

He didn't notice Laney smirking in her chair, trying to cover her mouth with her hand. *Ben is such an imp,* she thought. *Poor Alexander!*

"Okay, first thing here, Al, I need you to sign this. You saw the new Packard in the dooryard? These are the ownership papers for it. Sign right . . . here. Of course, you'll have to move out of the hangar by the end of the month."

Al nodded, still stunned by his sudden firing, but he went ahead and scribbled his name on the line. This meant he was homeless. No, worse. This meant he and Marilyn were both homeless. He was confused and upset. "I don't understand, sir."

"That's your new car, Al. I know how you love Packards."

"It's a lovely car, sir, but please, does this mean I am still employed? I'm a bit confused."

"Nope, you're still fired, and this is your brand-new Packard." Ben looked cheerful. Almost . . . happy.

Alexander was lost. Something was happening here, and for the briefest moment he thought perhaps he started to smell a practical joke. If it was, he was much too confused to figure the rest of it out. He had no choice but to see where this went. Somehow, the dreaded bus ride home had just left the table. That was a move in the right direction. He hoped.

Ben went on. "This is your severance check. Please sign here on this paper that says you received it."

Severance pay. He was fired. He signed the paper. Things weren't going in the right direction at all. What's next? At least he'd have some money to drive the . . . new car . . . home. Home . . . the hangar . . . where he couldn't live after this. Where-the-hell . . . his head was spinning.

"And this paper will need to be signed as well in several places. Sign here . . . Alexander . . . Wellington . . . that's right, and there . . . good . . . and right here . . . perfect."

Al wanted to cry. His voice shook, then broke. "Mr. Ryan, I'm afraid I am at a total loss here. Please . . . I beg you . . . I would do whatever was required to remain employed."

"Now, why the hell would a multimillionaire want to drive my silly ass around?"

"Sir?" That was it. Al was no longer confused. Al was toast. He dropped his head in his hands.

Everybody burst into laughter. Al looked up in misery and confusion, so far beyond lost he couldn't have described it for anybody.

"Al! What's the matter with you? Don't you read anything you sign?" Ben asked, barely holding back his laughter.

Alexander was afraid to answer, or even to move. His pleading eyes went from one of them to the next. Laney was covering her mouth and her red face, either laughing or crying, and he couldn't tell which. Finally, Ben took some pity and handed him the papers. "What's the first paper for, Al?" He demanded briskly.

"For the . . . new Packard, sir?"

Ben laughed. "That's right, and it's all yours. Here are the keys. So, the next paper?"

"For my severance check, sir?"

"Ever-so-correct, my ever-so-proper-and-British friend. And the amount of your severance check is . . .?" And he handed the check to Alexander, who looked at it. He couldn't read it for a moment or two, because he was still so upset by being fired.

"Yes, sir. It's . . . it's . . . whoa." He stopped short, forgetting even to breathe. "This can't be correct."

"READ IT, AL!" Ben yelled, laughing as he did.

"T . . . T . . . Two million, five hundred thousand dollars, sir?"

"Sounds about right. I'd say that makes you a multi-millionaire, Al. What do you think?"

Al could barely speak. He was starting to get it. The fun was at his expense, but Ben was paying for it all. "I believe it does, sir," he agreed, though he didn't trust his own perceptions right then.

"No more SIR, you don't work for me anymore. I'm Ben from now on."

"Yes, sir. Err, B . . . Ben."

"Okay, Al, last paper, here we go. Focus, now."

Al had to work to move his eyes off all the numbers on the check, but they kept drifting back again and again, as he kept thinking he *must* have read it wrong.

Then he turned to the last papers as Ben requested. "It's a . . . a deed . . . for the property at 1200 Beacon Boulevard. It says . . . it's . . . mine?"

Ben nodded. "It's yours, Al. You picked it out yourself."

Picked it out? He hadn't . . . then the address clicked. He jumped up. "Sir!"

Ben stood up. "Ben!"

"Ahh . . . Ben! This . . . this can't be right! This was for *you!*"

"You don't like it? You picked me out something you didn't like?"

"Yes, sir . . . I mean no, sir . . . I mean . . . oh, *shit.*"

"That's oh, shit, *BEN.*"

Laney and Ben burst out in hysterical laughter and came over and hugged Alexander, who was just coming to the realization that he was not only unemployed, but very, very wealthy. As well as the owner of a regal home that reflected his new-found status. Red-faced, grinning and shaking his head he said, "Oh, shit, Ben."

Even though his boss had fired him, he still loved the man.

Chapter Sixty

Several days later, after a wonderful visit with Ben and the family who had now made him a part of it, Alexander prepared to return to Detroit. Bennie made uncle Al promise that he would come back and visit soon, and bring his pretty wife with him. Maybe they'd have babies by then, right? Laney and Ben had held back their amused grins through his whole visit as the little guy peppered him with questions about where he lived and why he talked so funny. Bennie could be exhausting. Al loved every minute of it, and hated the thought of leaving. Ben and Bennie came outside in the snow as Al prepared to leave. Ben twirled his cane for Bennie, who always thought that was magical and giggled with glee.

They stood together and waved as Al drove away in his new Packard, bound for home. Bound to tell the woman he loved that they were wealthy beyond their wildest dreams. He and Marilyn would be living in the mansion they'd fallen in love with. He found himself amused at the thought of having his own chauffeur. No more living in the hangar.

Then he thought of dear Mr. O'Meara, and a smile slowly formed on his face when the thought crossed his mind that it was about time the O'Meara clan—who he and Marilyn had formed a close attachment to—had a decent place to live. *We will need to find a staff. Mrs. O'Meara works as a housekeeper. Shaun worries all the time because Delia has to ride*

261

buses across the city just to get to the few low-paying jobs she can find. And Shaun has mentioned a number of times that he dreams of being a groundskeeper for a fine estate, and planting his own small garden in some hidden corner. There's a large area right behind the Carriage house that would make a lovely, grand garden.

Yes, the carriage house sounds perfect, doesn't it?

Time to pay it forward.

Chapter Sixty-One

Ben and Granny enjoyed their visits for several months, until winter's grip had broken and spring prepared to spring forth. A day rarely passed without the two getting together for their chats. Granny's office was their favorite spot, perhaps because the shop was a sort of home to both.

Granny had mirrored Ben's investments. He was quite comfortable and would be wealthier still in the future, though thanks to Howard's generosity toward Ben, not nearly on the same level. It mattered little to them. Neither man cared about accruing wealth beyond what it would take to keep his family well cared-for in the event of an accident or death. Both had far exceeded that.

Granny had kept close tabs on the progress of Operation Hourglass, and he'd given the situation much thought. "So, how is your search for pilots going?"

"Not bad at all. We estimate that we'll have more than we need at this rate by December of '41."

"I hate to be the one to bring this up, but what happens if the time-tables are moved up, say, a year?"

"December 1940? We'll go with what we've got. If we can retract the pilots from China in a timely fashion, we'll be okay." He hadn't really answered the question. "No. We probably wouldn't have enough for all the planes. But we'd have enough to win, I think. Maybe."

"Say December 1939?"

Ben grew quiet and somber at such a scenario. "Late this year? Two

263

years early? I . . . I don't know; my first impulse is to say that I might as well have not come back in time at all. I don't think we could stop them, but—"

Somebody knocked at the door.

"It's open!" Granny hollered.

Cleve Hall walked in. "I've got a Telegram here for you, Ben, I stopped up to the house and Laney said you were down here. Sounded important, so I thought I'd best run it right down to you."

Ben looked at Granny. "He's bucking for a tip, wouldn't you say?"

Granny grinned. "I'd say he earned one."

"Now, I said nothing of the sort, gentlemen."

Ben said, "That's okay, I still owed you a good one from when you got stiffed that time."

"Jesus, no, it was worth it just to stand on the corner and watch that fool start running around like he did."

They all laughed. But Cleve was mighty brave to stand up to Spencer like that, and Ben wouldn't forget it anytime soon. This man was good people, and a good friend in his book. Digging in his pocket, Ben forked over some bills. "Thanks for taking the time to find me. Oh, and Cleve?"

"Yes, Ben?"

"I've contacted some people and we're going to be starting a new telephone company here. Telegrams are going the way of the dinosaurs, my friend. I need somebody to run this company, and I'd like you to do it. You were there for Laney when she needed it, and from that day I swore I'd be there for you."

Cleve was stunned. The telephones had taken so much business from them, he'd wondered how he would make a living in a year or two. "Oh my, I've been worried about that for some time now. That's very kind of you, Ben."

"I'm tripling your pay, Mr. Hall. My general manager's pay should reflect his position."

"You're really not joking about this, are you?" Cleve asked.

"Couldn't be more serious about it, my friend. I'll need for you to start right away, as soon as you can give notice to your employer. I'll send you off to learn whatever it will take to bring this new utility to our town. It'll take some time. You'll have an expense account, and a company car and driver. Springfield is going to need good telephone service for the city to grow. Do we have a deal?"

"A . . . a car and driver?"

"Comes with the job. Are you in?"

"Well, jeeze, I s'pose I can't say no to that. If you're offering, I'm accepting."

"I'm offering." Ben stood up to shake his hand. "Then we have a deal. I'll make arrangements, and I'll make sure you have one year's salary as a signing bonus in your hand before the week is out. You'll need a wardrobe to reflect your new position as well."

Cleve thanked Ben. "Well, I'd best get on back. Ben. Granny. Thanks so much." He touched the brim of his cap and he was off.

Granny asked, "Do we need a telephone company here?"

Ben was distracted by the envelope and not too concerned about opening a telephone company or the expense. "Gee, I sure hope so, because it looks like I'm opening one. Hmmm. Sounds important, eh?" Ben said, curious as he popped open the envelope.

The telegram read:

```
BENJAMIN RYAN
SPRINGFIELD, MASSACHUSETTS
HAVE RUN ANALYSIS ON STONE YOU SENT STOP
STONE IS A HIGH QUALITY DIAMOND WORTH
THOUSANDS STOP WOULD LIKE TO PURCHASE IT
FROM YOU, DO YOU HAVE MORE? STOP PLEASE
ADVISE ON DISPOSITION OF STONE STOP
BOSTON - NORTHEAST GEOLAB SERVICE - WM AMES
```

He chuckled, and handed the wire to Granny.

"What stone?" Granny asked.

"I pulled a stone out of the chamber wall on Molokai Island. I sent it in just to see. Howard's going to get a kick out of this. I guess I'd better forward this to him."

"Before you go, I need to talk to you about something."

Ben sat back down. He didn't want to leave anyway. "Sure. I'm not in a hurry. Whatcha got?"

"I'm thinking of going into fighter training."

"Granny, you have two kids. Let the single guys do the crazy stuff."

"You're taking it, and you've got three kids, if you count the one on the way."

"I'm an engineer. I have to fly the Tiger Sharks to make sure they do what they're supposed to do."

"Okay, tell me you won't climb into one on that day if they're short on pilots, and I won't bring it up again."

He knew he was cornered. "Yeah, okay. Look, there's something you don't know. I worked from the minute I got here to make sure you stayed alive. You died in a plane crash on February 11, 1934. I was going to burn the Model E before you climbed into it that day, if that's what it took."

"Yes, I heard the rumors that I died the first time around. Talk gets around. But I can't let that rule me. Lots of men will fly those Tiger Sharks. Some will die. Lots will live. I'm going to be one of the men flying them, and just like every other day I'm going to do my best and hope I'm one of those who come home. From the very first day I met you, I've known that there was something between us, as though you were one of our very own family. You're the best friend I've ever had, Ben. I've known from the first day you told us the country needed fighters that you'd be piloting one of them on that morning. And one other thing. I've known that I would be there as your wingman, that you'd *need* me as your wingman. Don't take that from me."

Ben pointed a finger at him. "All right, but if you go out and get your fool self killed, I'm never speaking to you again. Got it?"

Granny beamed and pulled out his pipe, tapping it out on his desk. "When do we leave?"

"Anytime we like. I have unlimited access to the Tiger Sharks and the training programs. I hope you get the mean instructor. He'll kick your ass."

"The mean instructor?"

"Yeah. Short guy. Don't let that fool you. Tougher than nails. Goes by the name Doolittle. See, right now, you're thinking: *Hey, I'm a friend of Jimmy's, he'll be a great instructor, this'll be so much fun!* When you get there, Colonel Doolittle will kick your friendly little butt all over the place and whip it into shape. This is serious, high-pressure training, and the trainers are *not* there to make friends. You still up for it?"

"Sounds scary. I'm in."

Chapter Sixty-Two

"You ready?" Ben yelled over the Waco's engine. "Now's the time to back out!"

Granny gave his toothiest grin and a thumbs-up, then adjusted his goggles and wrapped himself tightly in his scarf and extra coats. Technically, it was spring, but it was plenty cold and damp, and they knew the Rockies would be frigid this time of year. Off they went, bound for fighter pilot training, with a quick stop-off in Ohio where Ben planned to pick up a completed Model Y Senior Sportster.

When Ben landed in Troy, Ohio, he hadn't said a thing to Granny.

"Come with me, we have some business here."

Granny followed him inside, and there was the Y, gleaming under the lights.

"Oh, my. That's my . . . that's the Senior, isn't it? It's like new."

Ben nodded, also pleased with the results. As promised, the Y was completely overhauled and detailed to perfection.

"Ben, I don't think I've ever seen it look quite this good. They did a fantastic job."

"I had them take her apart and completely overhaul her. The engine is totally rebuilt, and they've broken it in, readjusted it, and changed the oil again."

Ed Weaver came over and shook hands, and said, "I hope you're pleased with the results." He gestured toward the Y and said, "You know, for some time I was pretty keen to fly a Gee Bee. *That* is one of the nicest flying planes I've ever had the pleasure to fly. Now that she's all done and the new engine's broken in, I hate to give her back to you. You take good care of her, y'hear?"

"Granny'll take good care of her, I promise you that, Ed."

"Ben, thanks for all the work you sent our way this winter, it made a real difference for us. I'll send the boys over to get her warmed up and ready for you." He shook hands again and rushed off.

"What do you mean, Granny will take good care of her?" Granny asked.

"I mean that the Senior was your plane, your pride and joy, and then you just *gave* her to me to help me out when I was in trouble. You never said a word about it, never asked for a thing. So the way I see it, she was on extended loan from you until I could get myself something else. Well, look at me, I've got my own Waco back, safe and sound, and brand new again. I thought that you should have your Senior back in exactly the same condition."

"You know," Granny said, "I've been afraid to ask you what had happened to her ever since you brought the Waco home. I thought that maybe you sold her—"

For a moment, Ben thought Granny might cry. For a moment, Granny himself thought he might cry.

Then he climbed into his Y, and his eyes lit up. He had always loved his Senior. He was as excited as a little kid to have the chance to see it and fly it in sparkling brand-new condition.

Westward bound again, toward Glendale they flew.

Chapter Sixty-Three

Ben walked into Howard's office.

"I'm going into the bomber pilot training program."

"I thought you might. Here's a question, then. If the man heading up the bomber program could be anybody in the world, who would you want?"

"Billy Mitchell," he said. He didn't even have to think about it.

"Give the man a ceeegar! Not bad, you got him on the first try."

"You actually got Billy Mitchell in on this? I don't believe it."

"No, I didn't do it. Jim Doolittle told him how you said he was right all along. I guess that hooked him; he had to come and find out what was going on here. I don't think I could have convinced him to leave even if I wanted to, which I did not. He wanted to use nothing but bigger bombers, until he studied our torpedo-totin' Tiger Sharks. He's in. Loves them in fact, and he's working hard at determining how they can best be used. But he still wants to use the bigger bombers."

"Will we have access to any B-17s?"

Howard looked at him like he was daft. "Weren't YOU the one who told me the Japanese flight approaching Pearl was mistaken for a flight of B-17s scheduled to arrive that morning?"

"Oh, yeah. I forgot about those. Mostly because they were never involved. But right now, at this point in time, there's only about a dozen of them, period. You're thinking that you might want to load that flight with bombs and 'divert' them to pay a visit to the Japanese Fleet?"

"It crossed our minds," he said with a smirk.

"I love coming in here and finding out what that devious little mind of yours has been up to. That's not just a good idea, it's a great idea."

Howard handed him a form he'd just signed. "Here you go, I've got you going into the Torpedo Bombers."

"Great. And Granny came to train in the fighters as well. Can you find him a place?"

"Sure. You two go get yourself situated, I'll get Jim and Billy in here, and they can fill you in about the details. Your timing is good, the next school starts in three days; after that, you two will be on your own for a while. Come by and we'll all get something to eat tonight."

Granny, Ben, and Howard had dinner and talked shop late into the night, and the night after that. For several months after that, Ben saw very little of Granny, who was busting his butt to keep up with the other military types in training. The Tiger Sharks were unbelievably fast, faster by far than anything in the Bendix races, the Gee Bees included. Only upon flying them did Granny have a real idea of the power and technology available to the aviators of the future. For the times, the radial engines were fast and powerful, and were his favorites.

That being said, the modified 'Magic' Merlins put out power beyond anything he ever imagined. Thanks to the superior design aspects, the Tiger Sharks had excellent landing tendencies, and when he advanced the throttle he could feel himself being pressed hard into his seat. The G's it pulled and the vertical acceleration could make a pilot gray-out. Fortunately, their flight-suits had been built with advanced pressure features (modeled after future jet-pilot suits) to keep their blood in their heads and torsos. It kept them sharp when they needed it most.

Granny loved it, and paid strict attention. And Ben hadn't lied to him. If anything, Jim Doolittle was tougher on him than the others. During a brief visit with Granny, Ben explained that Jim's job was to make sure he became a skilled enough pilot to come back alive. Reassured, he worked even harder. Before long his confidence increased, and he was amazed to discover what he and the Tiger Shark could do together. He soaked up strategy. Like every other fighter pilot in the school, he learned exactly what a Zero and a Zeke could do, and what they could not do, and exactly what threats they posed to the new Tiger

Sharks. They knew what the Tiger Sharks' strengths were. It was hammered into them that their greatest potential enemy could be a single bad decision.

If they knew their enemy inside and out, if they didn't take their enemy for granted, if they gave no quarter and expected they would be given none, they stood the best chance of coming home. A Zero could not outrun them or catch them, but a Zero had a tight turning capability. A Zero could not withstand an accurate frontal assault, because a few 20- or 50-calibre bullets into their radial would down them. Anywhere the Zero was in relation to them, they knew their own strengths and weaknesses, and the Zero's as well.

It was more than tough; it was grueling. The training flights were exhausting. At first, flying the Tiger Sharks in mock combat exhausted the new pilots so quickly that they could barely stand up without wobbling after thirty minutes total flying time. That wouldn't do. The first wave would likely take a minimum of forty-five minutes of all-out combat, pitted against the best-trained battle pilots in the world, and then the Tiger Sharks would have to land, refuel, and do it all over again.

Training progressed and they grew accustomed to the Tiger Sharks, to the forces and stresses upon their bodies. They exercised and hardened up. By the time training was complete, they knew themselves, their fighters, their enemies. They could fly in combat for two hours straight and still be ready for more. By July 25, they were ready.

With Ben's bum leg, if Howard hadn't used his influence, they wouldn't have allowed him to train to fly the bombers at all. But he graduated fighter/bomber school. Ben ranked as the most accurate bomber pilot they had trained. He was proud to receive his wings, and he would be able to perform his duties with full confidence. He would lead the bombing attack.

Granny graduated at the top of his class after a less-than-auspicious beginning. He refused to quit, and like Ben, he prevailed. He announced that he was going to be Ben Ryan's wingman, and just let anybody try to stop him.

Nobody did.

A few days later, Ben and Granny walked into Howard's office, and he smiled broadly when he looked up and saw their wings and flight suits. "Well, I see they finally made men of you! Sit down! Sit down!" He put the papers he was working on aside, and reached into his desk.

"I have something here you should see. Our AVG group in China has been a big success, and during their continued presence we've learned a lot of things that have made our training schools much better. However, for the past year there have been some serious diplomatic upsets over it. The AVG is a mercenary force, but since a number of the pilots are still American, the Japanese have been calling it US military opposition. Recently, they've made threats of reprisal. The sons-of-bitches are getting their fannies kicked in China and it's pissing them off. Our Tiger Sharks are tearing them up, and they hardly get a shot in before they're going down in flames. It's demoralizing to them. They can't make any headway, and they've been driven back by the Chinese, who have been inspired by our presence. We made a difference. We saved countless lives." He looked at Ben and nodded slightly, and gave him a look that said, *You were right. You were right about all of it.*

He picked the papers up and shook them. "Now for *this* . . . the US countered the accusations with this official statement four months ago, and I quote, 'The Japanese presence in China is unwarranted, and their killing of hundreds of thousands, possibly millions of Chinese citizens, is both abhorrent and contemptible. If the Japanese do not take it upon themselves to withdraw without delay, it shall forever remain a black mark of disgrace upon Japan's honor. Effective immediately, all oil sales to Japan are to be discontinued.'"

Howard threw the paper down on the desk. "Pretty much the way you called it all along, Ben. Which leads me to my next question. In 1941, didn't the US cut off oil sales to the Japanese?"

Ben looked thoughtful. "Yes. I think it was . . . yes, in May. It was their main reason for attacking us, to prevent us from interfering with them reaching other oil stores in the South Pacific. We'd never had any intentions of doing anything to stop them; we severed oil sales because we refused to be associated with their actions in Indochina. But they didn't believe that."

"Well, here's where this leaves us," Howard said. "I'm certain that we've been a great help to the Chinese, but it's entirely possible that we may have cut off our own noses to spite our faces. It's now two years too early, and the US just cut off their oil in April, not May. Gentlemen, we may have the makings of a real crisis here. Our pilot program has *not* turned out enough pilots yet, and that is the one natural resource we cannot find enough of. If they're true to form—and so far they've done *exactly* as Ben predicted—then they'll be attacking us later this year." He shook his head and said, "God help us; we're not ready, and they're coming."

Ben and Granny looked at each other, and both remembered the conversation they had just a few months ago, in which Ben said, *"Late this year? Two years early? I . . . I don't know; my first impulse is to say that I might as well have not come back in time at all. I don't think we could stop them—"*

Howard said, "I'm calling an emergency meeting."

Chapter Sixty-Four

He called the meeting to order. "Ben, you know the history, so you know them better than we do. Can you give me your thoughts on what you'd expect of them?"

"They're already lying to the US, pretending to be our friends. They'll maintain diplomatic relations and talk about friendship right up until they attack. When they attacked, they declared war a couple of hours *after* the attack started, because their diplomatic staff members weren't able to decrypt and prepare the announcement in time. Even if they'd been able to, they were ordered to present it to us only at the moment of the attack."

"So you're saying . . ."

"There will be no warning. Many of their officers studied in America; they know our customs and they will capitalize on that, using our own customs against us. They attacked right after Thanksgiving because so many military personnel go home on leave for the holidays between Thanksgiving and Christmas. For that whole month, Pearl is a fairly sleepy place. Add a Sunday morning into the mix, and the remaining sailors—who were out on the town Saturday night—are sleeping it off. My guess? They won't leave Japan before November twenty-fifth, certainly no earlier than the twentieth. On the far end, no later than December twentieth." He walked to the wall with the calendar on it. "If I had to bet my money on it, I'd bet that they had their reasons for leaving right on November twenty-sixth in 1941, planning to arrive and attack on December seventh, a Sunday morning. I see nothing that would indicate that their reasoning and motivations might change, just because it's 1939. Do you?"

There was some talking and whispering, but nobody thought differently.

"Let's go with the indications that Sunday morning is an integral part of their plan. This 1939 calendar shows Sundays on the third and the tenth. I'm going to throw my dollar in the Pearl pool for a December tenth attack. My reasoning is that they don't want to set sail until the Americans are preparing for the holidays, same as last time. To attack on the third they'd have to leave before Thanksgiving, and risk drawing attention to themselves."

Heads nodded, clearly all were in tacit agreement with his thoughts so far.

"They *are* going to attack. It's no longer if; when is the only question. We've severed their main oil supply, *AND* our planes and pilots have shot down bunches of their planes in China and set their plans back. They're more pissed off this time than the last history. They're coming."

Howard sighed, "And we're coming up short."

"Well, what have you got so far?"

"We're still at least a hundred and twenty pilots short right now."

"Ouch. What about us? Our class that just graduated?"

Howard got up off the desk and went around back for pen and paper, scribbling. "Yeah. Good. That'll bring us just below a hundred, say about ninety. It fills all the Torpedo Sharks and makes the torpedo-bomber mission a go, which is critical to everything we're trying to achieve here. Hmm . . . if we can get the pilots back from China, we'd have probably about forty-five more able bodies. We're still coming up . . . about forty-five, maybe fifty pilots short, damn it."

"What about Tuskegee? Can we get some more pilots from there?"

He shuffled through some other papers in the pile. "Yeah . . . wait a sec . . . here we are. No, my numbers include them, they're graduating in the next couple of weeks. The next batch of pilots will graduate from there . . . in November. So that's another thirty."

"I can live with being twenty pilots short, Howard."

"Me too. We're closer than I thought. Not too bad. Now, if we can get those transports in and out of China without them being shot down. They'll be gunning for us."

Granny said, "How about this? Leave five pilots there using drop tanks and escort the transports as far as they can. We'll likely get a good forty back in time."

Somebody asked, "What about detecting the fleet when they leave Japan?"

Howard said, "I have watch-boats disguised as trawlers fishing off the northern isles. Wherever there are any islands, I've placed island watchers. Those are some brave men, I'll tell you. They're dropped off with minimal supplies and a radio. At least our frequency is undetectable to them, which reduces the danger to the watchers and the trawler crews."

His mind was already reeling, grappling with the staggering must-do list of logistics that needed to be addressed. "Okay, I think we've established that this is the breaking point; it's time. For the foreseeable future, all vacations are suspended across the board, and we will remain in a state of high alert. We'll notify the pilot training schools that they should advance training as much as they possibly can or risk missing their window of opportunity. Maybe we can get one extra batch from each in time. Even a few from each would put us where we need to be. We can't count on that, though."

Ben said, "For right now, this is the best we can do. We *are* running a *lot* more fighters than we planned at first, *plus* we have a full torpedo-bomber flight. That alone is a huge strike force. They haven't developed any numbers of the B-17s yet, so there will be none at our disposal. That's going to hurt us some. But I think . . . I think we'll be okay. You've done an incredible job, Howard. Everybody, let's keep all lines of communication open. Keep talking to one another. I'm going to let Jim know right away. If anybody has any ideas at all, no matter how cockamamie, let's run them past each other."

Many voices spoke up this time and said, "Agreed."

After the others left, Howard walked over. "Oh, Ben. About the diamonds. After the war, we'll mine them out and I'll split the proceeds with you."

"Sounds like a plan. Let's make sure we're alive to implement it."

"Amen, brother. Amen. Your mouth to God's ear."

The quiet man, leaning against the nearby wall and listening to them, nodded in silent agreement. *Good idea.*

Chapter Sixty-Five

November 29, 1939 - 0600 hours

The conference room was filled to capacity when Howard called the meeting to order. "I'm sorry to call you all in so early, but the time has come. We've received multiple reports that the Japanese Fleet has set sail on a southwesterly course. We will monitor them, but we have to assume that this is it; the timing can't be a coincidence. Our Sunday the tenth is three days later than Sunday the seventh in 1941, and now they've set sail three days later than they did in the 1941 history. Operation Hourglass is to be put in full effect *now*. Jim, call in any pilots with enough training completed that you feel they can handle a Tiger Shark. They may fly or stand by as backup. There are two dozen Magic DC-3s out on the ramps. They'll run around the clock, moving necessary staff, pilots, Doctors, nurses, and last-minute supplies to Molokai. The operation plans are a GO. Make it happen, people. You are the ones who have made this all possible. You know your jobs. You're in charge now. Let's move!"

Ben, Granny, Jim, and Howard watched everybody leave. Howard leaned back against the desk, and crossed his arms. "I guess we're going to see if we're any good at this, now, aren't we?"

Nobody said a word for a moment, until Granny spoke. "Yeah. Oh, Ben. There's a wire here for you, it just came in."

"Thanks." He popped the seal and pulled the telegram out. He started to read it, and then he jumped up from his sitting position on the desk. He looked at his two best friends and yelled, "*It's a girl!*"

Shouts of congratulations and excitement went up, and they slapped his back. Elated, he read on, *"Mother and child are doing fine. I'm keeping an eye on things here for you, boss. Congratulations. Cleve."* With eyes glistening, he said, "A girl. I've got a baby girl." He looked at Howard. "Do I have time to send a return wire?"

"Absolutely. Here. Write it down, and we'll send it right from here. And Ben, you can go home, you know. Go on. We've got this."

"He's right, Ben. We've got it covered."

Ben looked at these two characters he'd gone through so much with, and felt his chest tighten. Because of them, he could hardly remember the feeling of being stranded here in this timeline, alone. He knew they meant it; he could go home right now.

He nodded, finished writing out the return wire, and handed it to Howard. He slipped his jacket on, picked up his cane and gave it a twirl, and as he walked toward the door he spoke over his shoulder. "I hope you three are packed, because I'm calling dibs on the cockpit. Last one to the planes has to sit out the whole attack!"

Howard observed, "I do believe he's coming anyway."

"I think you're right," Jim said.

Granny said, "Yeah. Hey, wait! Hey, Ben, it's my turn in the cockpit this time. Hey! Come back here!" he hollered as he ran after Ben.

As it turned out, none of them rode in the cockpit, and none of them left until the next day. This time, Howard refrained from pulling rank or using his authority. The plans were being executed by well-trained people; he didn't have to control every detail. Instead, as Ben had recommended, he concentrated on other things, and stayed in the back with Jim, Ben, and Granny, covering and rehashing issues relevant to the upcoming operation. He left the pilots in charge of their own aircraft, and he gained eight hours of in-depth discussions with other key personnel present. By the end of the ride, he'd gleaned a nice cross-section of what he had for a team.

He couldn't have been more pleased or proud.

Chapter Sixty-Six

December 10, 1939 – 3 a.m.

Molokai Base, now on high alert for over a week, bustled with activity and resonated with the sounds of the mighty Magic Merlin engines. Flights arrived and departed several times each hour, and the flight crews worked around the clock with Ordnance, attaching bombs and filling fighter ordnance in the Tiger Sharks. When Operation Hourglass commenced, they would be ready.

Ben couldn't sleep more than a few hours. He rose, dressed, and went to get something to eat. He wasn't too surprised to find he had a lot of company; he wasn't the only one who couldn't sleep. He went into Ops and found Howard there. "Are you still up, Howard?"

"No, but I couldn't get much sleep. Too excited. Santa Claus is coming, you know."

Ben grinned. *What a nut.* "Whatcha doing?"

"We've been monitoring the radar, and the Japanese Fleet is very nearly at the exact spot you indicated, about 275 miles north and west of Oahu."

"So, it's on."

"Oh, yes. We knew they were close, so yesterday I started sending notices to Washington advising them that the Japanese fleet was nearly upon Pearl Harbor, as we had warned. They've sent a number of urgent messages to Pearl. But for some reason, no action was taken. There's some idiot asleep at his post, more than likely. So, three hours ago we sent a flight out to bomb Pearl Harbor."

Ben yelled, *"WHAT?"*

Howard laughed and held up his hand. "I knew you'd say that. Come over here. There's a large sand bar—here—away from the fleet, but not far from it. I had them buzz the fleet and then drop some bombs on the sand bar and an old fuel barge that ran aground right here; it's pretty much empty, but not entirely. Lots of explosions and fire, but nobody near it. At the same time, a couple of dozen Tiger Sharks buzzed the ships and fired their guns off into the open harbor. We made a hell of a racket and then flew off, and now for some reason, the fleet's leaving the harbor with orders to head straight south. Our flight is already back in the hangar and they're being refueled and re-armed."

"And it went like clockwork," a voice said. They looked up to see Jim walk in, still in his flight suit.

"You led that raid?" Ben asked. He knew the answer.

"Thought I'd get warmed up a little early, take that edge off. I'm feeling pretty relaxed now," Jim said, with a grin. "The most fun was landing by the tiki-torches out there. This place was never designed for night operations, so we had to improvise. Good idea, Howard."

"Well, Doolittle's Raiders bombed Pearl Harbor this time around. That's an interesting twist," Ben said, with a laugh and a shake of his head.

"Let's leave this one out of the history books, if you don't mind," Jim said.

"What about the spies watching the harbor? That much noise would have alerted the whole area."

"We've identified all the spies and all the possibles. All of them were quietly rounded up during the last few nights. They're being detained in a safe place until they can be 'questioned.' Besides, any who might be left, I doubt they could communicate right now anyway."

"No Pacific fleet in the harbor. You're a genius."

"I think it makes up for the pilots we lost when they shot down that transport."

Ben agreed. Tragically, they'd lost one of the transports bringing the pilots out. A flight of Zeroes spotted one transport not long after the five escort Tigers had returned to base. The lone transport was easy prey. Losing twenty seasoned Tiger Shark pilots was a tragedy of enormous magnitude, both to their cause and in terms of human lives lost.

Granny had arrived, and heard most of the news. "Only you would bomb Pearl to save the fleet, Howard. A tad unorthodox, some might say. Not me," he shrugged, "but some. Is there anything else we should know?"

Howard glanced at the clock. "We have two and a half hours before the main briefing; it will be held out on the runway at zero five hundred thirty hours. All personnel are to attend unless they cannot possibly leave their work, and there's not much of that left to be done. Tell them all to make sure they don't miss it."

"Ben and I can spread the word. We'll see you there."

"Ben. Granny."

"Yes?"

"I want you two front and center with me when the briefing starts."

"Can do."

Chapter Sixty-Seven

Zero five hundred thirty hours.

All personnel were on the runway. On the far side of the runway, Ben, Howard, Jim, and Granny stood on the wing of a DC-3, where a loudspeaker system and microphone were set up. Between the pilots, flight crews, Ops staff, Ordnance, flight support, and all the rest, there were thirty-two hundred men and women waiting for this briefing, waiting for the final stage of Operation Hourglass to commence.

Howard said, "I'm going to speak first. After that, Ben, I'd like you to say something to them. Would you do that? Try to be inspiring."

"Sure. Inspiring. Right." *No pressure.*

"Well, here goes." Howard tapped the microphone, and the tinny tapping sounds bounced off the cliff walls.

"Hello, men—and women—of our special task force. This is the day we've talked about for years. The moment we've all worked and waited for. We've detected a large force coming in from the north. Our country needs your help in stopping an enemy at our very gates, an enemy that has already launched fighters and bombers against us, an enemy intent on the destruction of our Pacific fleet. The American fleet has left Pearl, so you pilots attacking their air forces over Pearl, your objective is to shoot down *any* Zeros or Kates you get in your sights. See Colonel Doolittle if you have any questions. Fighter-bombers, your objectives remain the

285

same—to attack the Imperial Japanese Fleet. Let's stop them and send them back where they came from, or else send them straight to Hell!"

Loud cheers came up throughout the crowd, and a smattering of applause. It didn't last long, and Howard handed the microphone over to Ben, hoping he could lend a bit more inspiration. "I warmed them up for you."

Ben grinned. "Thanks." He turned to the crowd. When he spoke, his words were metered, spoken a few at a time, as though to let them echo down the line and sink in before the next few. "My name—is Benjamin Ryan. Most of you—know who I am—and I know many of you. Every one of you—knows your job. We've trained long hours together. Here today, we have assembled a force—a force—the likes of which the world has never seen. American men—from the north and the south—are fighting—*together*—to protect our country. Men of every color—from many countries—have joined forces—to keep this terrible threat—from crossing the thresholds into our homelands. Patriots from three continents—and a half-dozen nations—have placed their lives on the line—to protect their homes—to keep their families safe—from these interlopers. I—have never been prouder—in my life."

The crowd remained silent. Their fear was palpable. They knew the enemy was out there, and they felt the urgency, and knew the dangers they faced. The blood was pumping.

He continued. "Make no mistake. This—won't be easy. The cost—may be high. Some of us—*will*—pay the ultimate price—for protecting our countries. You—me—*any of us*—could fall in battle today. Those that remain standing—*must* carry on. We cannot quit. We cannot let our fallen brothers die in vain. We *must* protect our families—their families—our homes—and our countries."

Not a single sound emanated from the crowd. "Are you with me?" he yelled, and raised his hand to cast his own vote. Thirty-two hundred other hands went up at the same time, and then they cheered, and the cheer became a roar, and the roar became a battle cry. "Then, let's-send-them-*packing!*" Ben yelled into the microphone, whipping his fist into the air. The men scattered for their planes and their posts, and after several moments of watching the sea of men flow in all directions, he dropped his arm and turned to Howard. "So, how did I do?"

Howard held up his hand and rocked it from side to side. "Eahhhh, mediocre at best."

Granny said, "Yeah, it could have used a little more zing, don't you think?"

They turned and watched the surging mass of men, some still yelling, all moving with purpose. "Yeah, that's what I thought, too," Ben said. "Yours was good, I thought," he offered to Howard, without much conviction.

"Yeah. I practiced it."

"It was good."

After another moment of watching the inspired troops, Granny said to Ben, "It would be my honor to be your wingman, Ben."

"Mine, too," Howard said.

Jim said, "You're needed here, Howard."

"The hell I am. You're the ones who tell me to delegate all the time. There are a dozen people in there—no, *dozens*—who know the plan and the backup plans. With one inspired move we've managed to move the fleet to safety. Technically, we've already achieved our primary goal. But now the fight is coming and we're short on pilots. Jim is heading the Harbor defense, and I'm not going to see you get your tail shot off just because there weren't enough wingmen to protect you. If you say no, I won't like it, but I'll stay here. It's up to you."

Ben thought about it. *Nothing since the day I arrived has gone quite according to plan. This strange, quirky man has been a fierce and unstoppable friend. Who am I to say no to this wild-eyed genius now? He's never once said no to me. He's believed in me, seen to it that my plans were brought to fruition in the face of unbelievable adversity and insurmountable odds.*

He shrugged. *What is there to decide?* "Gentlemen, we have a mission to fly. Would you do me the honor of being my wingmen?"

Chapter Sixty-Eight

Ben's group formed up and assumed their east-northeasterly heading. In order to achieve surprise, they needed to come from an unexpected direction. They knew all directions to the south of the Imperial Fleet were being closely watched. The only possible exceptions were north and northeast. They wanted to try to come in from as far north as possible. Because of Howard's advances in production methods and the extra funds funneled in from the bomb program, the forty torpedo-totin' Tiger Shark fighter-bombers were each protected by two dedicated fighters, not one. Howard and Granny remained glued to Ben. The forty fighters on the right side of the group had red tails. That was Ben's idea. The pilots who had graduated from Tuskegee were named the Tuskegee airmen by Ben, and he had all their planes painted with red tails. When they asked him about it, he'd just said, "Some parts of history are just too cool to be messed with."

They skimmed the waves to stay invisible. No fighter or bomber group likes to make an approach on the deck. Sure, they had the element of surprise on their side; but they also left themselves exposed to being surprised and jumped by enemy aircraft patrolling the skies high above them. The Jap-frequency jammers had been activated at zero six hundred fifty hours, so a Jap patrol wouldn't be able to see and report them, but they could still be jumped. Heads were on swivels, and eyes were strained.

Thanks to their special frequency, the bomber flight could talk freely and communications could be maintained. They'd traveled to the north and east of the Imperial Fleet and hadn't been spotted so far. They were feeling pretty good about the plan when they started to make the slow curve to their left at zero eight hundred hours.

"Heads on a swivel, guys, eyes everywhere, they could come at us from anywhere."

If they could engage the fleet at zero eight hundred thirty hours or a little later, their chances would be the best. With the massive torpedo Ben was hauling, he was using up a lot of fuel, but his fighter-bomber had been designed with bigger everything, including drop tanks and gas tank. Some enterprising ordnance crew members had painted the torpedoes with Tiger Shark markings, and they looked particularly mean. One could almost picture them tearing through the water after their prey.

He'd given a nervous laugh taking off with his. As freighted down as he was, the damn thing required a lot of runway to lift off.

They'd practiced with fake bombs and torpedoes, but the fake torpedoes weighed a fraction as much. He lodged a complaint with the big boss, who conveniently was flying right alongside him, and was assured they'd address the situation before the next war.

Right then, a few bigger issues loomed on the horizon . . . literally. At zero eight hundred thirty hours, traveling almost straight south, they had to be in close proximity to the Japanese fleet. They now faced the same hazards as the enemy would face approaching Pearl; the bright morning sun was in their eyes. Specially devised pin-hole glasses helped them search around the sun, but it was still hard to see well.

"Contact! Twelve o'clock. It's the fleet!"

"Oh, Damn! Contact! Contact! Ten o'clock high. Zeroes! Looks like about forty of them, and they see us. Here they come."

Forty Zeroes! This is bad. They were supposed to have been drawn off! He looked up and to his left, and spotted the Zeroes banking for a run on them. His stomach tightened. His mouth went dry.

Howard took charge of the fighter escorts. "Escorts, release your drop tanks. Port-side wingman from each bomber stays and protects, the starboard wingman goes with me! *Let's **get** 'em!*"

He accelerated away with the red-tailed fighters, moving away from them at amazing speed, driving their Tiger Sharks head-on at the Zeroes, blasting away. Zeroes peeled off, and some were already smoking. The Tiger Sharks tore through the flight of Zeroes. One Zero exploded in flames when his gas tank ignited, and tumbled in a ball of flame into the sea. The other one burst into black smoke when some rounds trashed his engine, and he spiraled downward, trying in vain to regain control without an engine. He pancaked into the water just seconds later.

Half a dozen Tiger Sharks on the outside of the group banked hard and acquired some Zeroes that had banked off. The Zeroes were vulnerable and trying to attain an offensive posture. The Tigers tore through them and flamed two of them, took the wing off another, and the tail separated on the fourth. Eight or ten down, thirty or so to go. And at such low altitude, there was nowhere for the Zeroes to dive or run if they got in trouble. But that went both ways.

Ben was trying to remain focused on one of the big flat-tops, their primary targets; without flat-tops, the Japanese could not hope to continue to prosecute the war. Things were happening fast all around him; he knew he might be splashed before he could accomplish his goal, perhaps forced to drop his torpedo and pray it hit something while he turned to fight. They'd been trained to focus on the target and get into position, and he wasn't giving up. He looked up and saw the sky; abuzz with dozens of fighters. *They look like an angry swarm of hornets. More than half of those hornets are ours, though.*

Several Zeroes broke away from the fight and sprinted straight for the bombers. The more seasoned Japanese pilots knew the threat that torpedo-bombers posed to their ships, and one was making straight for his lead bomber. He held his course; it was critical that he held his course, and the other bombers would follow his lead. So far, they'd all held on and stayed in formation. He was certain the Zero pilot had him in his sights. At the last second, the Zero was blotted out by something, and Ben heard the pumpf-pumpf-pumpf-pumpf percussive sound of the Zero's guns. Then he realized what had blotted out the Zero. Granny had placed his Tiger Shark directly between the Zero and Ben's bomber; taking the full brunt of the attack with his own fighter.

"Granny! You all right?"

"Yup! I've only got holes where I'm supposed to have them! Keep on straight, brother, you're doing fine! Let's sink us some flat-tops and destroyers, boys, whatayasay?"

Several voices together yelled, "YEE-HAH!"

Ben glanced around; he could see some of the Zeroes banking around for another run. He checked and saw a hole where one of the bombers in his group had been. The warships were growing larger and they'd be in range in less than a minute.

"Okay, boys, pick your targets, split up, and head for them. Somebody line up with me on that big flat-top. If me or my partner fall out, somebody jump in. If you're hit and you're going down, release your torpedo immediately; take that shot while you can. Those flat-tops have got to go down!"

Several acknowledgements followed as the men coordinated, but he was occupied watching a Zero coming straight at him. He could see its guns flaming as it fired, then the Zero exploded in a brilliant fireball and tumbled into the sea underneath them as a Tiger Shark streaked down past them in a hard bank right over the top of him, nearly dragging a wingtip in the water as he headed back into the fray.

Howard's voice crackled over the radio, "I told ya Santa was coming, didn't I?"

Ben gave a quick laugh that bordered on hysterical. *I was wrong, Howard is just friggin' nuts. Thank God.* "Just one of life's little pleasures, eh?" he quipped.

"Can't get enough!" Howard yelled, flying straight back into the thick of it.

The ships loomed large now, no longer in the distance. All were making hard turns to minimize their silhouettes as targets.

He let the others know. "Bombers, the fleet is turning, repeat, the fleet is turning. Bank right now, compensate for their turns!"

He banked off in the direction of the turn; he'd have to fly a big "S" pattern to get into position, but his bomber was fast, and that flat-top was slow. If he could stay in the air, he'd have it. Of course, staying in the air was the tough part right now. He was halfway through the S when a massive explosion rocked his bomber. He looked and saw his wing bomber had been shot down. By the sound of it, his wingman's torpedo must have taken a hit and set off. His own wing looked tattered out toward the tip. He was lucky he hadn't been downed by the blast.

One of his group yelled, "They've got us bracketed with that AA fire! Ben, you okay? That looked pretty rough!"

Ben yelled, "It woke me up, that's for sure. Keep going! Somebody fill this hole! This flat-top has to go down! The closer we get, the harder it is for them to lower their Ack-Acks that far. I want to hear that there are a few of you on every one of those flat tops. How many do you see?"

"I counted seven, maybe eight flat-tops."

"So did I, but I was a little busy right then."

"Seven or Eight? Damn it all. That's one or two more than there should be. They brought a bigger force this time. Okay, two on each flat-top, two on each destroyer, whoever's left over spread out and help out on any flat-top; those won't be easy to sink!"

Another bomber settled in beside him. "Moncrieff here, laddie. Lait's show them how it's done, shall we?"

Earl Moncrieff's rumbling, rolling brogue always made Ben smile, and this time was no exception. "I couldn't imagine anybody else helping me finish the job, Earl!" The tough-as-nails Scotsman was one of the UK flyers in Ben's bomber group.

Together they completed their S turn, and lined up straight across their noses was the biggest flat top of the entire carrier group. The buffeting from the AA fire was tremendous, but as Ben predicted, it was above them now. They were "in the zone."

"We're on this flat-top, Earl! Ready? RELEASE! Drop tanks too, if you want to go and get into a fight!"

Their torpedoes splashed. Releasing his drop tank, and relieved of the tremendous weight, Ben yanked his suddenly-nimble bomber-turned-fighter up and over the flat-top. He had the option of heading straight back for base, but he wanted to give them a little of their own medicine.

"You're askin' a Scotsman if he wants to go get into a fight?" Earl yelled, and he wasn't the only one who laughed as they dropped their tanks.

As Ben banked and yanked it back around, his plane was slammed upward and everything became bright orange and black for a second. Then he was in the clear. He looked back and saw the flat-top breaking up, its fuel and ammo had exploded, and the fireball had been so large his bomber had momentarily been caught in it. Fires raged the whole length of the ship. Both torpedoes had found their marks. Their flat-top was going down.

A few bumps reminded him that the fight was the safest place to hide from the AA fire; they wouldn't shoot at their own planes in the fray. As he gained airspeed, he lined up on a Zero he caught looking the other way. It spotted him, banked away and tried to run, but there was no running. He overtook the Zero in the climb, moving nearly a hundred miles an hour faster. He maneuvered until it was in his sights, and poured a trail of shells toward it. The powerful fifty-millimeter cannons kicked and stuttered, and the fighter shuddered as he focused on tickling the stream of tracers into the center of the Zero. The Zero disintegrated; the wings folded and it simply fell from the sky. No fire, just bits and pieces tumbling toward the sea.

Granny's voice crackled through. "Not bad, sonny. Let me show you how it's done!"

"Granny, you're okay! Yeah, go ahead and show me!"

Granny's Tiger Shark rocketed past Ben's slower bomber, and lit into not one, but two Zeroes. He stitched a straight line through both of them in a single pass. The left wing split away from one and it tumbled down and away, out of control. The second wasn't disabled, however, and it banked tightly toward Granny's Tiger, which was banking for a return pass. Ben saw this and banked hard to line up on it. The Zero continued to focus on Granny. Just before it would have been in position to fire upon Granny, Ben managed a steady burst through it from bottom to top, just behind the pilot. The tail separated from the front, and the two halves fell away.

Out of nowhere, a fusillade of bullets tore through Ben's bomber, sending splinters and dust whipping through the cockpit. "Jesus! Damn it! I'm taking fire! Got one on my six!" he yelled, banking away in a direction where he hoped Granny might get a line on the Zero behind him. Whoever this guy was, he was good, because he couldn't shake him with his best maneuvers. Bullets tore through his fighter again, and then again, and he knew he was in trouble. The armor plating was the only thing that saved him each time.

"Straight ahead, Ben, hold it straight ahead," a voice whispered to him. The voice was familiar, and he held a straight course. Out of nowhere, a Tiger Shark came from straight ahead of him and screamed past him front-to-back, just above and to his right, all fearsome red mouth and white teeth, seemingly within inches of him, guns blazing the whole time. It involuntarily filled his heart with terror. He was glad the Tigers Sharks were on their side, and as it flashed by him and he followed it over his shoulder, he saw its wing actually strike the tip of the Zero's rudder. The Zero had splintered from the rounds poured into it. A split-second later the Zero, which had stopped firing, started a roll and exploded into a massive fireball. Bits and pieces spiraled lazily down toward the sea. No parachute. The pilot was dead.

"You okay?"

"Granny? That was you?"

"I'm your wingman, aren't I?"

"Whew, thanks. Yeah, somehow I'm still okay."

"That's what I said when I blocked for you. This armor plating is great. You did good, holding that steady course while I lined up on him."

"Yeah, thanks for telling me to fly straight ahead."

Granny was silent for a moment. "I didn't tell you anything, I just saw you were setting him up for me and took him."

"Who said that to me, then?"

"I didn't hear anybody say anything to you, Ben."

"I didn't either," another pilot chimed in.

Then he remembered the voice. "It was the quiet man."

"Yeah?"

"Yeah."

"Well, his timing is good."

"I'll say."

"*These* guys are good. It's scary."

"Yeah. They are. Just not good enough. Do you see any more?"

"Nope, it looks clear now. I think that's the last of this bunch. Let's head for home."

"I'm with you."

Some of the red-tails had been unloading on other ships after the torpedoes released, and had destroyed a lot of tonnage. They joined Howard and Ben for the return to base, and one look back told the story.

Behind them they left half the Japanese Fleet sunk or sinking, and a number of others on fire and in imminent danger of sinking. As near as he could tell as he left, looking through the billowing clouds of black smoke that filled the air, not one flat top was left afloat. Out of forty torpedoes, at least thirty-six had found their intended targets. Two bombers were shot down on their approach, but one released. Those three remaining torpedoes missed their intended targets but still struck ships. One of them was a fueling tanker, now raging out of control, the smoke and flames filled the sky, and the sea was an inferno for a thousand yards in every direction. Thirty-nine out of forty. Their rigorous training had paid off.

On the way home they encountered a number of Zeroes returning, most of them smoking badly and struggling, barely airworthy and unlikely to reach their fleet. His first impulse was to let them go; they had nothing to land on and no fuel to go elsewhere. Those pilots were doomed. Howard and some of the others felt differently; they engaged every Zero they saw and sent them down in flames, as did a number of the other Tiger Shark pilots. They were determined that not one Zero would make it back to the Japanese Fleet.

Ben suggested that they pick one or two Zeroes and escort them back a ways, then leave them alive to tell the tale of how American pilots filled the sky and shot most of them down with their terrible shark-faced fighters, then surrounded and followed them to make sure they beat-feet out of there. Probably as much because the fuel for the bomber flight and the escorts was running too low to play around with, the idea sounded good to the others. They came upon three Zeroes that weren't smoking and looked like they could make it back to the fleet. The Zeroes offered no resistance, so a pack of the red-tails turned and flew above them, below them, behind them, and off their wingtips, bracketing them and letting them know they owned them. They escorted the three back for a couple of minutes. Then they peeled off homeward again and caught back up with Ben. Perhaps those three would be fished out of the drink next to the ships, and would tell their stories. Ben was glad that they didn't have to die; not right then, at least. The hapless Japanese pilots that had escaped death here would likely perish soon enough.

"Contact! three o'clock! There's a large flight heading this way." Heads snapped to attention; they all knew they were dangerously low on fuel. Fighting another battle would mean ditching in the ocean soon afterward.

"You sure? Can anybody ID them?"

"Good news. Looks like ours. Must be the red flight. Red leader. Do you copy?"

Red flight was just what it sounded like. They were a full flight of red-tail Tuskegee airmen that had been sent out to draw off the Japs protecting the fleet.

"Roger, red leader here. We're on our way home."

"We thought you were supposed to draw them off for us."

"Roger that. We drew off about sixty of them. Those boys gave us a run for our money, but we splashed them. Took us all this time until just a while ago."

"They must have brought a much larger force this time. That explains the extra flat-tops."

"White leader, how did you do? Any flat-tops left?"

"We're pretty sure there are none left. Did you lose many?"

"We lost a handful. Not bad against sixty of them. Those boys were fighters, and they could fly."

Ben was experiencing worsening mechanical problems. The coolant temperature continued to climb steadily, and they were still 160 miles north of Oahu. And the oil pressure was dropping. He wasn't going to make it. "Granny, Howard, uhh, do you see any leaks on my bird? I'm having a few issues with cooling and oil pressure. I thought maybe you could tell me if you see anything."

Howard said, "We've been looking at your bird all the way back, Ben. I think we've all been thinking the same thing."

"What's that?"

"That there ain't a reason in the world that bird should still be flying."

Chapter Sixty-Nine

Ben's plane gave a sick lurch as if to confirm their assessment. He tried to keep it light. "No reason it should be flying? You don't say. Why's that?"

"Most of your rudder and fin is gone, chewed right off. Half of one of your horizontal stabs is gone. There's a big chunk of turtle-deck missing. A lot of metal sheeting is missing from under your right wing; I can see framework. And your lower shrouds for your coolers are gone. I think I see liquid coming off of it."

"No, really, do you see anything? Anything at all?"

Several chuckles came over the com.

"Naw, you'll be fine. You, uhh, *did* bring your Mae West along for the pool party afterward, right?"

"Life vests clash with my wardrobe, they're *way* too clunky to bring to a fight."

More chuckles from the others.

They were scared.

Howard thought, *You can look over and find a hole next to you in the middle of a battle, and somebody fills the hole, and you don't think about it after that. No time for it right then. But when the fight's over, you're going home and you have a single buddy whose plane is shot all to hell, and all you can see in the whole world is ocean. Everywhere you turn there's nothing but water. Now, this guy . . . this guy you have time to be scared for; and you'd do anything to help him. Except, there's nothing you can do for him.*

Silence.

He asked, "Uhh, how long do you think you've got, Ben?"

The bomber kicked alarmingly as it coughed again, voicing its opinion. "I dunno. If I wait until the engine seizes, I might auger in hard. If I don't wait until then and fly her onto the water, then I suppose I ought to get started right here soon."

"Aw, shit. Er, roger that."

"Moncrieff here," the Scotsman said, the r's rolling from his tongue.

"Go ahead, Earl."

"I think it's time you move doon near the water. Follow him doon and help him make a good water landing, one man on each side. Those water landings can be a wee bi' tricky. One of you lads go up higher and try to radio for help."

Ben spoke, "Sounds good, there, Earl of Moncrieff. By the way, you did good out there today."

"As did you, young Ben, as did we all. See you back a' base."

"I'll be back in time for tea, Earl. Count on it."

Granny said, "I've got your left side."

"And I've got your right," Howard said.

"Good thing I learned how to swim."

They were terrified, having to leave their friend there in the ocean, alone and exposed. But everybody was low on gas, especially after playing with those Zeroes.

"Guys? Would you tell Laney something for me?"

Neither spoke. They couldn't speak right then.

"Would you tell her I want to name my baby girl Cassiopeia? Like the constellation."

Granny could barely speak. "Sure. Cassiopeia. Like the constellation. I'll tell her, Ben." He choked on the last couple of words.

Howard came on, his voice raspy too. "God damn it, tell her yourself. Now let's get you a bath so you'll be clean enough to send you home to her."

Several nervous bursts of laughter came over the com. Everybody was scared for him. As Ben settled toward the surface, so did all the members of his group. Several red-tails cut their speed and dropped their flaps, some banked off, dropping way back. Somebody would need to verify if he was able to get out.

Howard said, "Better pop your canopy back, Ben. You'll want to get out quickly. She won't float long, shot-up the way she is."

"Good idea. Ummm. Damn it. I can't get the canopy open."

"Keep trying."

"I am. It's stuck tight."

They were just over the water. His engine was red-hot and failing . . . he didn't have enough power to go up again. He was committed to the water landing.

Granny's voice crackled through. "Flaps, Ben. Focus."

Ben was holding on, as the plane settled. He'd tightened his harness and secured everything. He mumbled, "This is good. I needed this. I was rusty on panic."

"What?"

"It's Richard Dreyfus . . . oh, never mind. Here I go."

Granny threw back his canopy and said, "Me too. Howard, you remember to tell Laney, just in case."

"Granny! No, it's too dangerous!" Ben yelled.

They struck the water at the same instant. Granny had kept his right wingtip just off Ben's left, and when the tremendous shock was over, he shook it off and climbed out. He unsnapped his parachute harness and dropped it off his back as he ran down his wing, dove into the water, and swam a short ways to Ben's bomber, which was settling some already. He clambered onto the wing and scrambled up to the large canopy. Ben was working furiously at the inside, with no luck. Granny could see where some rounds had ricocheted off the track and pinched the window slide. He pushed hard. It would never open. The wing was already settling below the water. The plane was rapidly filling up and was about to go under. He yelled, "Cover your face!" In desperation he splashed back down the wing a couple of steps, ran forward and leaped into the air, kicking with both feet on the side of the canopy. It popped loose from the track on his side. He regained his feet and pulled back on the canopy, but it refused to slide back. The plane settled further into the water. He grabbed the side of it and lifted with all his might. With a muffled 'pop' it gave way, and flipped onto the water over the far wing. Ben was free, but the fighter was going down.

Granny yelled, "Your harnesses, release your harnesses!" He reached in and tried to help.

Ben handed him his cane. "Take my cane!"

"Forget about the cane!"

"Take it!" Ben yelled; and he did.

He managed to get his harness to release, stood up, unsnapped his parachute, grabbed his orange seat cushion and threw it out for floatation. Then he grabbed his Mae West. No sooner did he finish tying it on than the plane sank away beneath them, and was out of sight within seconds. The two were left floating on the surface.

"Whoa. Chilly," Ben said, bobbing in the water.

"Whoa yourself, Mr. 'take my cane, . . .' here, *you* hold your cane now while I swim over before my seat and Mae West sink on me."

"Hey, my best friend in the world gave me that cane! It goes where I go," he complained as he grabbed his cane. He stuffed it through a couple of the ties on the Mae West, then paddled to his seat and dragged it over with him to the still-floating fighter while Granny got his gear out of the cockpit and strapped on his Mae West.

Fortunately, the fighter's wings and other areas were designed with sealed air compartments to keep the plane afloat or delay sinking. Ben's fighter-bomber was much heavier and could not have remained afloat for long even if its wing bladders had not been turned into swiss cheese like the rest of his plane. They sat on their cushions on the wing and waved to the brave red-tail pilots who had held back for the extra couple of minutes to make sure they were safe, and who now had to depart with— at best—marginal fuel. They were the last of the group to fly out of sight.

Inexorably, the Tiger Shark settled in the water, and a short time later it finally sank from beneath them. They floated, straddling their flotation seats. Perhaps the seat cushions weren't as good as surfboards, but as floatation devices they were not half bad. Most of the body was held out of the water, which made a real difference in the cold water. Aside from the utter desolation, it was kind of peaceful.

Granny looked out over the endless ocean. "Best seats in the house, don't you think?"

"We had to fight for them. They must be."

Chapter Seventy

To the north they saw a darkening of the sky. It was eerie. There were so many of the Imperial Fleet's vessels on fire that the black smoke visibly darkened the sky, and could be seen from nearly a hundred miles away.

A while later, they heard Merlins in the distance.

Granny said, "Hey, here comes our ride. That was fast. What time is it?"

"Well, if you must know, this watch stopped at 10:03."

"So, it's time for a new watch."

"Yup."

"Did Laney give you that watch?"

"Yup."

"Boy, is *she* ever gonna be pissed."

"Yup."

"Don't you ever shut up? Talk-talk-talk, that's all you do. Give it a rest, would ya?"

The engine sounds grew but nothing came into view. As the volume increased, they wondered what they were hearing. Then Ben realized what it was.

"That's not for us. That's the second wave against the fleet! Three hundred and fifty Tiger Sharks, loaded with bombs."

"I forgot about the second wave. Did we leave them any?"

"Enough, I think."

They watched the Tiger Sharks fly over. Ben thought, *Wow, you can say, "three hundred and fifty fighters," and sure, it sounds like a lot. When you're actually watching three hundred and fifty fighters, flying with purpose to take on the Imperial Japanese Fleet, it's humbling. They don't blacken the sky, but they sure do gray it out. I can feel the noise in my bones as they're passing over.* He said, "I think they're late. By maybe an hour."

"I'll bet they had a tough time whipping the Zeroes. Those guys we fought only had forty Zeroes to our eighty, and they gave us a bad time. We thought we were pretty good, and we were. They were better. But our Tiger Sharks were the best. Tougher than nails."

"Speaking of nails, I think I broke a couple trying to get my canopy open."

"Poor baby."

"How many of our bombers stayed in the fight afterward? They account for another forty; that made it as many as one hundred and twenty to their forty."

"About half of them stayed and fought. But only half the fighters engaged the Zeroes at first, the rest were babysitting the bombers."

"And I for one was glad to be babysat. How long did that whole deal take?"

"Maybe seven, eight minutes during your acquisition and approach. Maybe fifteen, twenty minutes after you dropped your torpedoes before we splashed the last of them. So, I guess a total of maybe twenty-five or thirty minutes. Man, some of those guys were good. That guy who was on your tail, he was something else. If you hadn't set him up for me, he might have gotten you."

"Thank the quiet man for that. He whispered in my ear and told me to hold my course. Oh, and I should probably point out, that guy *did* get me." He held out his arms and looked around at the empty ocean. "See?"

Granny cracked a smile. "As Moncrieff likes to say, 'Point taken, laddie.'"

A while after the large group had passed from their hearing, they heard Merlins again. This time they could hear the unmistakable harmonic resonance of twin engines on one plane. Soon after that, they slid off their flotation cushions and raised them above their heads, waving the bright orange to be seen by the Martin PBY crew. They heard the sweet sound of the engines changing tone, and just a few minutes later the lovely seaplane was idling up to them, with none other than Earl Moncrieff at the hatch offering a hand to help them inside. They both laughed when they saw him. He didn't know what was so funny. Americans. They were a tough lot, though.

The PBY crew had flown right to their location. When they ditched, Earl had marked a spot on his charts that he was sure was correct, and they had found Ben and Granny "close enough to spit on" the spot he had marked.

"It sure is good to see you, Earl. Thanks." Ben shook his hand.

"I'm glad you're not hurt, young Ben. Carry on, lads, carry on; we've more men yet to find. If you're feeling up to it, Ben an' Granny, you can lend a hand."

Moncrieff had taken the time to dot his charts anytime he saw one of the boys go in the drink, and his estimates had been amazingly accurate. Almost all of them were found. Some, but very few, were found dead. The important thing for the searchers was that they were found, whichever the case. The search and rescue/recovery efforts went well, and after returning to base, refueling and picking up fresh spotters, the PBY crew took off to continue their work.

A voice spoke from behind them. "It's about time you two slackers got back here. I thought you were going to miss all the fun with your day at the beach."

They turned to see Howard walking toward them, his arm in a sling.

Ben looked at the sling. "You put your hand someplace it didn't belong?"

Howard looked down at it, chagrined. "Yeah, one of those nips got a lucky shot in. Straight through the meat . . . here . . . but yikes, it's sore as hell. I'm off the flying roster."

"What a wuss."

"Hughes always was a complainer."

"We saw the second wave go over. Any reports?"

Howard nodded. "They're starting to come in now. They did a ton of damage, but the AA fire was intense at first. We're getting reports that they sank a great number of vessels. We're waiting for more details."

"Did they have designated targets?"

"Same as you did. Sink the biggest ships you see. The flat-tops and destroyers first."

"I don't think we left any carriers afloat, from what I could tell."

Howard said, "I spotted one still afloat when we left, but it was listing to one side pretty hard. It looked like it was about to go bottom-side-up at any moment. The next reports should give us something more to go on, and once the camera footage is developed, we'll have the whole story."

Ben was pensive. "So, do you think we accomplished our goals, Howard?"

Howard nodded. "Yes, I do. I think there was a much larger fleet sent this time than your history had. And we had to fight a lot more Zeroes and Kates than we'd planned on. At least two hundred more, all told. And there were nine flat tops, not six."

"Nine! That's almost all of their carriers! We counted a quick seven or eight out there. How did we do?"

"Over Pearl? Jim said it was rough at first, the Jap pilots were seasoned fighters and they got in a lot of hits, but Jim began barking orders and our pilots remembered their training. They started communicating and setting the Zeroes up for each other, using all the plays from the playbook. After that, they started dropping like flies. They tried to break it off, but Jim thought it was downright rude of them for trying to leave our little shindig so early. They couldn't outrun our fighters. Our boys caught them in a few minutes and finished them off. We had our fighters all refueled and rearmed when the second wave came in; Jim said we took them head-on."

Relating the details was exciting for him. "*Our* Tiger Sharks, Ben. The fighters you and I developed together. They were tough as nails, and the armor plating was perfect. We lost some planes, but most of the pilots whose Tigers went down got out without a scratch. And I don't have to tell either of you how well the flotation bladders in the airframes worked, and the flotation seats too."

"No you don't; they worked great. We did okay, then."

"We did okay."

"Well, then," Ben said, taking and releasing a big breath. "Next stop, Japan."

"Japan? Why?"

"Because these people are too damn stubborn and proud to surrender without having absolute proof that we'll annihilate their entire country if they don't. I need to talk to Yamamoto."

"Are you sure? Look at what we've done, they can't ignore that."

"You don't think so? They can, and I'm betting they will. Oh, they know we've beat them, and almost for certain they'll seek diplomatic solutions and offer us bullshit like another worthless non-aggression pact as a counter-offer to our demand for unconditional surrender. We're planning tests at The Nevada Test Site pretty soon, right? Let's get Japan to bring a delegation there to see it."

"But we don't know that it will work yet."

"It'll work. It would've worked a month after we started, if we'd had enough isotope material. Ask Oppie. Let's try to bring in a Russian delegation and a German delegation too. No flunkies, high-ranking officials with clout only. Can you do all that?"

Howard shrugged and said, "Sure, if they'll come when we ask them to. But why?"

"To avoid other upcoming events. One of them is called the Holocaust."

"Okay, Ben; you've got it," and he added, "I trust you'll tell me about that too?"

"Absolutely. Careful what you ask for, though."

The second wave returned not long after. The entire base was on pins and needles, waiting to see whether a third wave would be necessary. As it turned out, it was not.

Of the entire Imperial Japanese Fleet, only a handful of small ships remained, and the Tiger Sharks left those few ships to do what they could about the impossible task of rescuing thousands of souls from the water. By the time they departed the decimated fleet, the AA fire had ceased entirely. The Tiger Sharks circled the vessels with impunity and made photo passes before leaving.

Operation Hourglass had succeeded beyond their wildest hopes.

Having received word that the hostilities had ended, Howard relayed the crippled fleet's location and desperate condition to the Japanese through Washington. The capitol was already abuzz with the stories of the massive dogfight above Pearl Harbor, and the hundreds of crashed Zeroes dotting the surrounding landscape. Washington instructed the Japanese to send rescue vessels to save those they could. They made it clear that this was to be considered America's last offer of mercy. Further hostilities would be met with the utter and complete annihilation of the hostile forces. America would send two delegates to speak with the Emperor, or at the very least Yamamoto . . . to discuss America's demand for unconditional surrender and Japan's future.

The president gave a surprisingly familiar speech about it being a day that will live in infamy, about Japan's treachery having been met with the American spirit, and our forces sending the few that survived straight back to Japan. Howard snorted.

Chapter Seventy-One

Japan refused to surrender, as Ben expected. Then they refused Ben's delegation outright. No trip to Japan.

The good news was that they'd put all their eggs in one basket; they'd sent all their destroyers and aircraft carriers to attempt a massive attack on Pearl, and had not favored the alternate plan that included simultaneously invading the Philippines. *No Bataan death march,* Ben thought. But they steadfastly refused to pull out of China.

Since they hadn't surrendered, their refusal to leave China was expected. They would need a large amount of raw materials to replace the ships and aircraft they lost.

That would not be allowed. Three hundred Tiger Sharks, pilots, and massive shipments of ordnance and parts were flown and shipped immediately to China, where they proceeded to push back, corner, and crush the already dispirited Japanese army, quickly reducing their forces to wretched and starving ragtag isolated groups, hiding where they could. Hardened veteran soldiers, they fought hard, but their fighting capability was reduced to unsupported infantry and near-depleted ammunition. Within a few weeks they had no air force with which to repel the Chinese forces should they attack, and attack they did, and with a vengeance; but unlike the wretched Japanese soldiers, the Chinese were fully supported by the terrifying, screaming Tiger Sharks from above.

America was up in arms. As Howard had predicted, it now became critical to all of America that the military should arm itself properly to protect the country. Howard's consortium had provided the effective military might to fight off the Japanese attack. They now became the go-to providers for rapidly arming the military, and with the funds flowing liberally, they happily obliged.

The military took credit for much of Howard's hard work, claiming to the public that it had been a joint program involving them at every step of the way. Ben was furious; Howard laughed. Ben couldn't understand how he could just sit back and let them lie like that. Why, they'd contributed nothing until Howard twisted their arms with the bomb program.

Howard explained that he said nothing because they had to pay him to say what they said, and they had to say it to save face with the American people. They paid handsomely for the face-saving, and for providing the American military with these amazing Tiger Shark fighters. Not hundreds of fighters this time. Whole factories, building thousands and thousands of them. Howard first presented them with a hefty bill for their share of the mythical "joint program" costs in the Operation Hourglass program, which they paid without asking a single question. The consortium as a whole made a handsome profit, and his net worth tripled overnight. He made another deposit into Ben's bank account; so large this time that he now (by far) exceeded Howard's former net worth. Ben pitched another fit in Howard's office, ending with the two of them laughing so hard that they could barely breathe.

American men lined up to enlist in all the services. Many wanted to be fighter pilots after learning the story of the Battle of Pearl Harbor. Indeed, more pilots would be needed to rearm America to its full potential.

Ben and Howard were summoned to Washington, to explain how they'd known all this was going to happen in advance. In a closed-door session arranged by some of the highest ranking military and political leaders of the time, the two explained where and when Ben had come from, and how he had repeatedly attempted to talk to politicians and military leaders alike about this.

The individuals present loudly questioned whether any of that was true, because . . . well, quite frankly because somebody's head was going to go on the chopping block if this was the truth, and nobody wanted it to be theirs. So the officials tried to imply that the two were liars.

Ben, frustrated with the form the questions took, finally unloaded on them.

"I tried to tell you fools all about this for ten years, and you closed door after door in my face. You are the ones responsible for having allowed Billy Mitchell to be persecuted for his foresight and his patriotism. You need to face it; you have egg on your faces! You *know* you have egg on your faces or this wouldn't be a closed-door session. I think that the media should be invited to attend, don't you? I have nothing to hide, and there are a number of things—provable things—I believe they'd enjoy knowing. You have no objection to that, do you? You don't have anything you'd like to keep hidden, do you?"

A man sat to the side and listened, and after Ben unloaded on the stunned panel, the man stood up and quietly put an end to the session. He looked at the panel leader and nodded, and it was over. Ben and Howard were taken to another room, where a man identified himself as a White House aide. He asked them to accompany him. They were taken by limousine to the White House. There they were ushered into a waiting room with a pleasant secretary, who offered them beverages. Finally a door behind her opened, and a man looked at her and nodded.

She turned to them. "Mr. Ryan, Mr. Hughes, would you please follow me?"

They followed her inside, and found themselves standing in the Oval Office. They felt a fair level of intimidation. They were directed to a sofa and asked to sit and wait there. Ben was scared silent. Howard, as usual, still had time for a wisecrack.

"Oh, boy. *Now* you did it, we're in big trouble this time. It's all your fault."

Ben, already nervous, started to crack up, trying not to laugh, but not too successfully. "Howard! Behave!" he hissed in a whisper, hoping his friend would take it seriously.

"Yep. Straight to the principal's office. The BIG principal. You did it. It wasn't my fault."

Ben started giggling, horrified that he couldn't stop laughing. "Stop it! You're killing me here. Please!"

Just then a door across the room opened up, and in rolled a man in a wheelchair, pushed by the aide that had summoned them, and then by the man who had nodded and stopped the inquiry. Ben forgot all about giggling and stood up, as did Howard. Franklin Delano Roosevelt was wheeled behind his desk, where he dismissed his aide. After placing a few things on his desk and moving a few things off of it, he stopped and looked at Ben and Howard.

He raised his hand and gestured toward the two chairs in front of his desk. "Gentlemen, will you join me?"

Ben and Howard walked over and sat in the two chairs without a word. Howard didn't appear to want to offer up any more wisecracks, much to Ben's relief.

The President pointed to Ben. "You are?"

"B . . . uh, B . . . Benjamin Ryan, sir."

"And I'm Howard Hughes, sir. I'm honored to meet you."

The President looked Howard up and down severely, as though sizing him up. Then he looked back at Ben and said, "It's I who should be honored, gentlemen. If Mr. Ryan's historical account of the "other" Pearl Harbor is at all accurate—and I believe it is—you defended our country from a terrible attack on our fleet at Pearl. Your Operation Hourglass saved us from a big black eye and a protracted war with the Japanese. The only thing that ended up burning in Pearl Harbor were downed Zeroes." Then he looked deadly serious. "I do, however, have a question." He raised one eyebrow, still frowning.

Ben spoke, "Yes, sir, we'll be glad to answer anything."

"Maybe you will be, maybe you won't. Was it YOU that dropped those bombs in the harbor at 1:00 a.m., and strafed my ships?" The emphasis on the word "my" was unmistakable.

Somebody had let the cat out of the bag.

Ben turned to Howard. "This one's yours," he said, his face deadpan. He didn't have the urge to giggle at all. But he sure wanted to see how Howard handled this one.

Howard's face turned a dark shade of red. "Uh, yes sir. I had tried for six hours to relay messages through Washington to Pearl to have them move the fleet, and nothing was happening. We needed the fleet to be out of the harbor when the Japanese forces arrived, in case we couldn't stop them. I'm sorry, sir, I didn't think we had any other choice. We were desperate."

While looking at him with fierce eyes, FDR's severe demeanor suddenly melted into an amused smirk. "Hah! I *told* you so!" FDR said, slapping his desk and pointing at the other man. "I'd have paid *money* to see the look on Kimmel's face when those bombs went off and those planes strafed the fleet." He turned to Howard, still smiling, but then the smile turned back into a frown and he squinted one eye. "I assume the guns were pointed away from my ships. . . ."

"Oh, yes sir, out into the water. No danger at all, sir."

Once again, FDR looked pleased as punch. With ebullience and the confidence of a man who was sure everybody knew he was running this shindig, he said, "Gentlemen, I have done something unprecedented in my Presidency here today. I have cleared my schedule for the rest of the day." He grabbed his wheels and backed the chair out, and nodded to the other man, who came and took the chair from there, steering it out to the area with the sofa. As he passed the sofa he reached out and patted it. "Come! Come!"

They sat down on the sofa, and some refreshments were brought in for them all, and FDR leaned forward. "Now, start at the beginning, Benjamin, and don't leave anything out. Tell me everything, how you arrived in our time, how you knew what you had to do. Tell me the whole story! Don't stop until you've finished!"

". . . and that's the one event I really am hoping to avoid, and you can see why."

FDR, who had been swept up in the story Ben brought him, sat quietly. For such a young man, this Ben Ryan carries a heavy, heavy burden. It's as though every life lost in this war would be counted against his soul. He saw strength in the young man, the maturity in weighing the needs of the many against the needs of the few. Even as the President, he knew the conflict he himself would face having to consider two hundred thousand Japanese lives to be the few, weighed against millions of lives. Now I understand why he showed Oppenheimer how to build the

Atomic bomb. And I understand his reluctance. It could be left to me to decide whether it will be used against the still-defiant Japanese. "So you designed this bomb because you could not be sure you could make them surrender unconditionally using any other means?"

"Yes, sir."

"In your opinion, have we exhausted our options yet?"

"No, sir, we can still fight them conventionally. But the first time it happened we lost tens of thousands of men taking dug-in Japanese positions on remote atolls in the South Pacific. It doesn't make sense to lose that many men or to allow the Japanese to continue killing millions of Chinese when we can stop them without fighting protracted battles. They won't surrender, but we can't let them continue."

"And knowing the horrors of what you would be unleashing, you would still find it to be a viable solution, Ben?" FDR was new to this situation and really wanted to weigh Ben's opinion here. This young man has put years of thought into this. And human lives are precious to him. I like this young man a great deal.

"I'd hoped to visit them and talk to Yamamoto, and bring him and some high-ranking members here to see the weapon detonated, so they can truly understand what it is we might be forced to do. But they've severed diplomatic ties."

FDR sat back in his wheelchair, and looked impressed. "You carry the weight of this whole country on your shoulders, Ben . . . and Howard. But you don't have to carry it alone. They haven't severed all diplomatic ties; no country does that in time of war."

He glanced at the other man, who pulled out a notebook and walked over. FDR turned to the two and said, "This office has been idle long enough. I'm going to shoulder some of this load from now on. Let me see what I can do with it. May I ask you to wait around Washington for a week or so, while I explore this situation? We will of course provide you with accommodations and take care of all your needs. I may need your advice, and I would like you to be handy."

"Yes, sir, it would be our honor."

"Yes, sir!"

Chapter Seventy-Two

"I thought you said you were going to give him a piece of your mind? And when he nailed you for bombing Pearl, I thought you were going to have a stroke. I don't think I've *ever* seen you speechless before, Howard!"

"Turns out he's a pretty nice guy, after all, wouldn't you say?"

Ben laughed. He looked out the window; traveling by train was new to him. Five days after speaking to the President, they were told that a Japanese delegation would be arriving and transported to the Nevada Test Site in four weeks, as would Russian and German delegates. He took Howard home to Springfield for the holidays. Ben couldn't wait to meet his new baby girl and see his family. They also visited Granny and the Granville brothers, all home for Christmas as well. When they traveled back out, mid-winter flying was getting too cold for him. He was having problems with his circulation and muscles, so they decided to try the train.

A car met them in Las Vegas and drove them out to the test site, where Robert Oppenheimer was running around, attending to all the details in order for the test to go as planned. They stayed out of the way and looked around the place, although there wasn't much to see. Winter in the desert, on an old military installation. Brown, and cool.

Two days later the Japanese delegation arrived, but to Ben's disappointment, Yamamoto was not among them. The lead delegate was a resident military attaché named Tamichi Kurubiyoshi. Ben realized he might be able to remember Tamichi, but none of the other names would stay with him. Tamichi spoke English, thank goodness. Ben had learned a basic greeting. He bowed slightly to Tamichi and said, "Konichiwa."

Tamichi was pleased, and returned the greeting. Few Americans bothered with gestures of respect or to take the time and effort to learn a word or two of Japanese. He immediately liked this young American, and was surprised to learn that though he walked with a cane, he'd been a torpedo-bomber pilot in the recent conflict. Ben asked him if he would like to take a walk, and Ben told him how he had arrived knowing their exact locations and plans, as well as being an aeronautical engineer from 2010 with the knowledge of advanced avionics, etc. Tamichi was stunned to learn all of this, and wondered out loud why Ben would reveal it to him so readily.

"I'm trying to prevent the annihilation of your people, Tamichi. We had hoped that Japan would surrender after being soundly defeated at Pearl Harbor. We left thousands of your sailors alive and didn't sink the remaining ships, and we sent word to your country to send help for your defeated fleet. We did this as a gesture of goodwill."

"Please understand, Mister Ryan, in Japan it was taken as a gesture of condescension and viewed as weakness, an unsound decision made by poor strategists."

"Condescension to be certain; Japan came at our country with a sneak attack. As to poor strategists; we could have killed them all, to the last man."

Tamichi stated matter-of-factly, "We *would* have killed them all."

Ben would listen to the voice of Imperial propaganda only as long as he felt it was still productive. It already wasn't. "Could. Would. Tamichi, here is what WILL happen to your country if they do not surrender. If you leave us no choice, we will do what I am about to tell you. It's not a threat. I have done everything I can to prevent the use of this weapon of mass horror and destruction on Japan.

"It is a bomb. A single one of these bombs will level one of your largest cities instantly. When it detonates, the thermal flash it will create is the temperature of the inside of the sun. Anybody within a thousand yards will be vaporized. Do you understand what vaporized is? Good.

Anybody beyond that will be consumed instantly, leaving human carbon statues. That will continue out past a mile. After that, flesh, hair, skin, and eyes will melt away. It will instantly ignite everything within an eight square mile area of city; the entire area will start burning uncontrollably. People will have no place to run. They will try to run to the rivers to escape the flames, but the rivers will be filled with thousands of bodies.

"Just when you think the worst is over, a sickness will follow. The people will start vomiting, the lucky ones will die quickly, the others will develop purple sores. Many of the children who survive will not be able to reproduce. You cannot in your worst nightmares imagine the horror and devastation this weapon will wreak upon Japan. Tamichi, I know the Japanese are proud people with a history of being fierce warriors. Your culture is too precious to suffer such devastation, and I have sworn to do all I can to stop this."

He let it sink in for a moment, then continued. "But you are leaving us only two choices; the first choice is to allow the Japanese to kill another one, two, or ten million Chinese and drag the United States into a war. Even after you're clearly beaten, you refuse to surrender, and cling to your 'Divine Empire' and 'manifest destiny' beliefs. Before it's over, the conflict costs us hundreds of thousands of lives.

"The second choice is to drop these bombs on your cities. You need to understand this. I will authorize the use of as many of these bombs as it takes to ensure Japan will never do this again."

Tamichi displayed righteous anger at such impudence, but he sensed these were neither threats nor empty words. Just honest assessments. *But such a weapon would surely have already been used, yes?* "Mr. Ryan, I have my doubts about such a weapon. If you have it, why have you not used it? It would give you a decisive advantage against us if what you are saying is true."

Ben snorted. "We already *have* a decisive advantage against you, Tamichi; I just led the attack that sank your whole God-damned Divine Imperial Fleet in a couple of hours. But those were soldiers. What I'm giving you here is an opportunity to save hundreds of thousands of Japanese people who are going to perish at the push of a button. You believe you came here to negotiate. You think you're about to do what you did the last time we had you cornered, after millions of Americans and allies died fighting you. You plan to offer another non-aggression pact and restoration of trade relations. That's bullshit, my friend."

He turned to Tamichi. "I'm speaking to you very informally today, because I am not a negotiator, and I want you to hear and understand every word I say. There was a rumor after the attack on Pearl Harbor happened in the 'first history' that Yamamoto said, 'I fear that all we have done is to have awakened a sleeping giant, and filled it with a terrible resolve.' Or something to that effect. Well, Tamichi, he *may* have said that, or he may *not* have said that. But it's true. Both times Japan sailed their Imperial Fleet to Hawaii and launched a surprise attack, they awakened that sleeping giant, whether you want to admit it or not. And I'm speaking for that giant right now. We don't negotiate. We're not here to negotiate, and you were not invited here to negotiate. Your delegation was invited here for one reason only. You are here to witness the detonation of a very small version of the thermonuclear weapon that will be used on Japan's cities if you fail to surrender immediately. The first time we dropped these bombs on you, your armies had already slaughtered tens of millions in your expansion of the Divine Japanese Colonial Empire." He fairly spat out the last four words.

"Japan is *not* going to kill millions of Americans and Allies this time. Before we allow that to happen, we will wipe the island of Japan from the face of the earth. Every last one of you."

Tamichi looked . . . intimidated.

"The terms are not negotiable, they remain the same; we have demanded, and we expect, unconditional surrender. You are here, the Russians are here, and the Germans are here, and we have only one thing to say to all of you. The hostilities end now, or we will end them, and the cost to you will be dear; more dear than you can imagine in your wildest, most horrific dreams. You are all here to witness the detonation of a single, very small thermonuclear weapon."

He stopped and turned to Tamichi. "If you do not believe me, if you doubt my resolve to protect my country and its allies from all enemies, then go home and wait to see what happens. Here is a paper, saying everything I said to you already. Take it and study it, and tomorrow after we go to the range, I will answer any of your questions. And please remember, this detonation will be an extremely small test; a tiny fraction of the yield of the larger bombs we have prepared to drop on your cities. We can build them with a hundred times the yield of the weapon you will see tomorrow."

"Domo arigato." With that, he bowed slightly, turned and walked away. Now he was going to have another informal talk with the Germans and then the Russians, and let them wait all night to see what the weapon can do. He wanted them all to have the holy hell scared out of them *before* the weapon was ever detonated, and he wanted them to need a change of drawers after witnessing it.

Chapter Seventy-Three

"Now I am become death, the destroyer of worlds."
Bhagavad Gita, Hindu Scripture

"Are you ready for this?" Howard asked, as he and Ben headed for the chow hall the next morning.

"I am. But I'm hoping that these guys are totally unprepared for what they're about to witness here today."

Howard said, "What about me? I've never seen it either."

"Prepare to be scared shitless, my friend. This no toy; even a small one like this levels a whole city in ten seconds, vaporizes many of the residents, and kills most of the rest. It's the worst thing you can imagine in your mind, multiplied by fifty. I'll be the happiest man in the world if we can avoid using it as a weapon."

After chow, they were issued protective gear, which in 1939 to 1940 was comprised entirely of a pair of dark goggles. He decided he'd have to do something about that in the future. For today, though . . . they were perfect.

They boarded a bus for the range, where they met the delegates from the three nations. Each delegation was issued a bunker with one guard as an escort. It was Ben's idea to separate the delegations. There they each waited until the countdown started. Ben and Howard were in the bunker with the Japanese, much to Howard's distaste. Ben made sure everybody had their dark goggles on and were ready to watch. Nerves grew short as the countdown commenced.

When the detonation occurred, it felt as though the noise had been sucked from the air. Then the noise and the shock wave hit full force at about the same time, knocking everybody backward with the violent wind that whipped through the view-slot into the bunker. Ben looked at Tamichi. The man froze in horror as he watched the mushroom cloud climb to fifty, then sixty thousand feet in seconds, and as he witnessed the ring of fire radiating out from its center. After a time, Tamichi looked his way, shaking uncontrollably, his mouth still pulled back into a horrified grimace. He was traumatized; it still showed on his face, his eyes open wide and his mind overwhelmed with pure terror.

Ben looked at him. "Tamichi, can you understand what I'm saying?"

A torrent of Japanese, screaming in utter terror, gushed forth from Tamichi and the rest of the Japanese delegation. Ben knew these men were not warriors; they were paper-pushers and had never felt fear like this. His own heart was pumping fast, and like most Americans in 2010, he had seen nuke film footage of tests like this a hundred times, maybe a thousand. And now Ben himself knew; the film footage didn't remotely compare to viewing a live detonation, to feeling the earth shudder and shake, to seeing the air itself whipped, burned, consumed. He gave them a few more minutes to regain their composure before speaking again.

"Mr. Ryan."

"Ahh, you're better now, Tamichi?"

"I am . . . distressed."

"I should say. I must emphasize again that, in comparison to the devices we will use to force Japan''s unconditional surrender, the yield of this device is extremely low. This device is very, very small. As you can see, the larger devices will level cities, and depending on where they are when it detonates, people will be vaporized, or burned horribly, and all will be poisoned by the radiation."

Though Ben had told him before, and emphasized the words over and over, they were only now sinking in. Tamichi was awestruck. "That was a very, very SMALL version?" he asked, terrified that he had in fact heard it correctly.

"As small as we could make it. We can easily make them one hundred times as powerful. The larger ones, of course, are the weapons we will be forced to use on your cities. Please, *please* do not force us to do this to your country, Tamichi." He stood quickly, indicating he was leaving. "Thank you for attending this demonstration. You will be provided with film footage to take back with you. Domo arigato." He bowed slightly.

Tamichi Kurubiyoshi, to his credit, translated and relayed Ben's answer to his delegation. The color drained from their faces, their terror beyond their abilities to conceal. Wide-eyed, they too bowed to Ben, and he turned and left the bunker. Howard left with him.

"I think that went pretty well. I think we got our message across. What do you think?" Ben asked. "Howard?"

He looked at Howard. Like the delegates, his face was colorless.

"Howard! You okay?"

Howard slowly turned and looked at Ben. He still looked stunned. "Jesus **Christ**, Ben."

"Yeah?"

"We can *never* use those weapons . . . *ever.*"

As he spoke, Ben saw Oppenheimer running up to them, wringing his hands and looking as distraught as Ben had ever seen him. *It won't hurt for Robert to hear this, either.*

"Howard, you need to put this in perspective. C'mon, steady up, now, I need you to focus, okay? Okay. Both of the bombs we dropped on Japan killed a total of about two-hundred thousand people. Remember that number. That's a lot of people, isn't it?"

Howard just nodded. Robert nodded too, and continued wringing his hands.

"Let's look at some other numbers now. In China alone, the Japanese killed twenty-five *million* people, and several million others fighting the war and so forth. Twenty-five million is *one hundred and twenty-five times* as many people as our bombs killed. The Japanese *willingly* killed at least one hundred and twenty-five times as many people as were killed by our two bombs. They did it to expand Japan's Colonial Empire, for domination. I need you to understand this, Howard, and Robert; I need you to see this perspective. I'm against using nuclear weapons if at all possible. But I won't flinch over using them here. Right now, right this very minute in time, the Japanese have already killed a dozen times as many as our bombs did before. We could drop *a dozen* on Japan and I wouldn't have an ounce of guilt. We didn't even have to warn them. Not the first time, and we don't this time."

Howard blinked. "Damn, Ben. *You* don't take any prisoners, do you?"

"Not when it comes to my country, Howard. You with me?"

Howard nodded, but he still looked white and badly shaken. "All the way, Benjamin." They all started walking again. "Can we really make them a hundred times that powerful?"

"No, not yet. A handful, maybe ten times that powerful, we could do. But they don't know that."

"So, you lied to them."

"Yep, and I'd lie to you or anybody if it meant I could save hundreds of thousands of their people's lives."

"You still care about them, knowing what they would have done?"

"These people have a magnificent, beautiful, ancient culture. I'd like to get all their cutthroat politicians and military leaders responsible for pursuing their "Manifest Destiny" in one two-mile circle. Ask me if I'd drop a bomb on *that*. It's *always* the politicians. Take away the wars, the conflicts, and their people are just like our people."

"I see your point. I guess I never thought of it quite that way."

"Spend some time with some of them later, when we're not killing each other. You'll find that fathers worry about their kids, kids love their grandparents, people need jobs. People are the same everywhere."

"I'll do that, if you leave any of them alive. So, what's next?"

Ben grinned at the comment. "We have the same talk with the Germans and Russians; see if we can get them to cease hostilities. I think we've given them some incentive. Twenty-five million lives at stake here as well."

Robert found his voice at last. "Oh, God, Ben, what have we done?"

Ben turned to Robert. "So, it shook you up as badly as I thought it might."

"Howard is right, Ben, we can never use these!"

"That's the plan, Robert. We brought them here today to scare them into using some common sense. Do you consider this a better warning than we gave them the last time?"

"Yes. Much better," he admitted. Nevertheless, he was distraught.

"I know I never talked to you about yourself in the other timeline, Robert, and there's a reason. When somebody interviewed you after the bombs were dropped, you looked like you were ashamed for having made them, like you might break down and cry any second. You quoted some Hindu scriptures: *I am become death, the destroyer of worlds.* You were in abject misery over it. I hope what we did here today will keep you from having to go through that."

"I pray it works," he said. "I don't know if I could bear the burden."

"Just remember, Robert, I'm the one who designed these bombs, not you. It's not your burden to bear this time."

Oppenheimer's eyes searched Ben's, looking for something there, hoping he'd find something there that would speak to him, sooth his tortured soul, perhaps convince him that this was the truth. Finally, he said, "From your mouth to God's ear. Well, I'd better get back. Gentlemen," and hurried away, still wringing his hands.

They watched him leave, and then Howard asked, "So, what're your plans with the Germans and Russians if they don't comply?"

"As soon as Japan surrenders, I'm turning that responsibility over to FDR. Ideally, they'll face the same as the Japanese. I've already told them that if they use it they should target Hitler, and explained why. But I'm certain we've done what we came to do. It's time for me to be with my family. I have a new baby girl and two fine boys, and they need me."

"You should. You deserve it."

"What are your plans?"

"I guess it was going to come to this sooner or later, eh? The planet is a safer place, and Ben Ryan finally steps down from saving the world. Me? I'm doing what I do best, thanks to you. I've got a lot of planes to build, and we're launching the new Essex and two other aircraft carriers next month. All because of you."

"Yeah? This soon?"

Howard slapped him on the shoulder. "Yeah."

"Can you name one the USS Ben?"

Howard looked at him, and a smile crept into the corners of his mouth. "Jesus," he said, chuckling as they walked away.

"No, seriously. The way I see it, they could; all it would take . . ."

Chapter Seventy-Four

The Japanese surrendered three weeks later. Their delegates returned to Japan, described what they had experienced, and showed the films Ben sent home with them. Their war machine ground to an immediate halt. It was a certainty that the Americans were not posturing. There had been no warning when, like locusts, they had swarmed the fleet north of Pearl, laying every major vessel to waste. Imperial policies dictated that no warning was owed or expected. As delegates, their own countrymen had witnessed firsthand the detonation of this instrument of total destruction. The fear and angst that haunted their eyes and minds and left their hands shaking was only amplified by the mind-numbing film footage they carried. The young American's promise of total annihilation was no empty threat.

Their soldiers were withdrawn from China, Thailand, Korea, Malaysia, all over Indochina; anywhere they had encroached. Their instruments of war where left to rust, wherever they sat. Anything that was not necessary to travel back to Japan was abandoned. Overnight, the Japanese Colonial Empire dissolved, collapsing in upon itself. Japan once again became a small island nation, isolated from the world, dependent upon outsiders for many of their needs.

As in Ben's timeline, they were required to melt down all instruments of war. They had to start again with nothing. This time, though they may have felt they were being poorly treated, they had *NOT* lost a million soldiers and citizens, and had *NOT* lost a single city to thermo-nuclear weapons. Upon Ben's recommendation, FDR set a future precedent by announcing that the US would render no aid to them. They set a policy that aggressors would have to implement their own recoveries. This was eminently fair, as victimized countries like China and most of Indochina had to pick up the pieces of their own countries. The cash-strapped US needed its money for domestic issues. Magnanimous in victory, they established trade relations with Japan, and stated they would in time buy products manufactured there.

The detonation had also scared the bejesus out of the Germans and the Russians, who pulled back across borders into their own countries, cautious not to incur the wrath of the young man with the weapon of ultimate destruction and the golden Eagle-head cane, the young man who spoke softly for the USA, who implemented plans that destroyed the Japanese Fleet and ended the war with Japan practically overnight. The young man rumored to be able to see the future, to know of any plans of war they might make.

FDR's delegates met with Ben, then traveled to Germany and Russia, where they managed to establish and maintain an uneasy peace in the region. Sporadic skirmishes, posturing, and border disputes would occur, but a second World War never did break out.

Germany would once again struggle with the limitations formerly placed upon them, and had no choice but to learn to get along with other nations.

Adolf Hitler, in the early, undiagnosed stages, faded into obscurity as the advancing syphilis rotted his brain. Slowly, trapped inside the tortuous madness of the insidious disease, he died, inch-by-inch, a forgotten madman. His madness and he died with only each other, and left Europe, Britain, Russia, and Africa relatively intact.

Chapter Seventy-Five

"So, this is where you grew up?" Granny asked.

Ben nodded. "Our house was right over there, and Gramps's house was right over the hill there."

"You're planning on buying all of this area?"

"It's available right now, so I'm pretty sure that it's me or nobody. I know exactly how both houses were set up, so, yeah, I'm going to get started on it. See that long, flat area there that runs along the hillsides?"

"Over along there?" Granny pointed.

"Yep, right there. That'll be made into our grass runway for the Waco. The hangars will be built against the far end."

"Wow, nice setup. With the runway positioned north and south, that ridge should block a lot of wind from the side."

Ben looked at the beautiful, untouched land, marveling at its beauty and now seeing the care and planning that had gone into their estate to retain the greatest part of that beauty. "I'm going to take it a little farther, I think. I'm going to buy all the land around here for Bennie. His descendants will become farmers; maybe Bennie will be one, who knows? I really want the Spencers close to the Ryans in the future, especially the ones I know and love."

"You mean Katie Lynn?"

Ben grinned at his closest friend. "I mean Katie Lynn. We used to talk about how she wished their spread had been laid out differently.

329

Their land was a number of smaller parcels spread around the country-side. I'm going to build a big ranch and house for them right over there, and buy the land all around it so that it's centralized. I also plan to make sure that it'll remain theirs forever."

"Don't forget the white three-board fences," Granny insisted with a grin. "Miles and miles of them. They helped make you the man you are today, Ben."

Leaning on his cane, he rolled his eyes and groaned at the memory of how his Mom developed his work ethic by having him paint those miles of three-board fence to "earn" his Waco.

After a few more moments enjoying the beautiful parcel of land, Granny asked, "You never *did* find your great-great-grandfather, did you?"

"As a matter of fact, I think I did. I found him in the mirror," Ben said.

"How can that be? Is that even possible?"

Ben shrugged and said, "How can *any* of this be possible? But it happened, didn't it? The quiet man didn't exactly overload me with information I could have used. But my Gramps always used to say, "Time travel is the realm of angels and their hourglasses." I'm pretty sure that was a hint designed just for me."

Granny pondered that, nodded, and said, "Who do you think the quiet man was? I've always wondered."

"I have a theory, but you might think I'm crazy," Ben said, dangling the carrot.

"I'll bite. Go ahead; this, I've got to hear."

Ben took a deep breath, as though wondering where he should start, and said, "It's what I just said. I think he's an angel, like an archangel. Think about it. The way I see it, it would take a powerful being like God to make the rift in time that sent me here. Or perhaps one of his angels. A powerful angel; an archangel, I'd say. Then the quiet man shows up and just as quickly, he vanishes.

"If he sent me, then who sent him? Who told him how much he could and couldn't say, and why? I'd seen him several times before that, talking to my Gramps. In fact, standing almost where we're standing right now. I saw him here, eighty-one years in the future, then next

330

thing I know, there he was, right there at your shop on Liberty Street. I know that was years ago, but the part that sounds really crazy is that I know he's never really left me, like he's been here the whole time. Who else would do that? You know, stay with me the whole time, except for an angel? I can't see him, but he's here, Granny. I can *feel* him. I always have."

Granny raised his eyebrows, "Right now?"

Ben nodded. "Right now."

"If you say he's here, Ben, then I believe you. I told you once that I'd never doubt your word again, and I never have."

As the pair walked away, the quiet man looked out over the fields, hills, and tall pine trees, and took a deep breath of the cool, fresh air. *Ben could feel him.*

After basking for a few moments—perhaps a bit selfishly—in the satisfaction of that feeling, he turned to follow them.

Chapter Seventy-Six

Over the next year, all three parcels of the Ryan estate took shape. The Spencer farm and house were included, and would someday be Ben's legacy to Bennie. Where local jobs had long been scarce, for several years to come, the Ryan project would ensure that any local man willing to work had a good job. As the Ryan family grew and flourished, in the process, so did Springfield. Late in the summer of 1941, the Ryans, Charles, and Mrs. Gruber moved into the bigger house. The house nearer the hangars, which someday would be his grandfather's home, was used for on-site tradesmen to live while they worked, as was the farmhouse for the future Spencer spread.

Ben continued to keep tabs on world events, and visited Howard every year to see what wondrous new things he'd developed. Howard started a medical division for research, as he felt that the drug companies only researched in ways that were self-serving. Howard, as shrewd and perceptive as always, felt that their goals were focused on perpetuating their drug sales and profiting from the misery of others. Ben found this to be a wonderful new goal for Howard to pursue of his own volition, and was delighted to be able to tell him that he had in fact done the same thing in his 'first' history. Sadly, those visits ceased when the pain in his joints and muscles increased to the point where travel of any kind became too difficult for him.

The quiet man had told Ben, so he knew from the start that he would spend his whole life there. But it hadn't taken another thirty, forty, or fifty years, as one might have expected. Only seven years after the battle of Pearl Harbor, Ben found himself confined to a hospital bed with severe health problems. The doctors couldn't diagnose his ailment. He looked like he was well into his eighties, and he was quite literally falling apart. The X-rays they took showed nothing. He only grew worse. His skin degraded in a very strange fashion; each morning they would have to brush sand-like material off of him and off of his bed. The doctors were baffled and after months of testing, they admitted that there was nothing further they could do to help him.

Granny came and sat with him every day. Sometimes they talked. Sometimes they didn't say anything. Ben and Granny were like that. Either way, they were near each other. Soon after the Doctors told him they could do nothing further, Ben made up his mind. "Laney. Granny. I think that I would like to be in my own home for what's coming. Could you arrange for that?"

Laney and Granny agreed with him, and by the next day Ben was back at the estate, which seemed to perk him up. He seemed happier and more vital. Howard came east as often as he could to visit him, and told him that he probably hadn't noticed, but his bank account was a lot larger now. Howard told Ben he had signed over ten percent of Hughes Industries and would be continuing to make regular deposits of even more millions to Ben's account. With a devious grin he said, "I just wanted to stop by and piss you off with the news."

Ben smiled at his dear friend. "Howard, the money never meant a thing, and you know it. Friends like you and Granny and the brothers, you're what has made me such a wealthy man. Laney and my babies . . . they're the real riches. Please, my friend, try to find some of that for yourself."

Howard looked down at his failing friend, and his normally hard, brown eyes welled with tears. "I *have* found some of that for myself. I have wonderful friends, because of you and Granny. I'm a wealthy man. I may never be as wealthy as all this." He gestured at the folks and family gathered around. "But few people are ever *this* lucky. I'm lucky just knowing you, Ben." He picked up a fragile hand and held it with both of his. His friend was dying, and his heart was breaking. He sat a long while, both of them silent. After a couple of hours, he said his goodbyes and made his apologies, and departed for the west coast.

Laney sat down with Ben. "He's a strange man, isn't he?"

Ben held her hand. "He's a good man. Lonely. Brilliant. Isolated by his money, driven by his ambition. Hard for people to understand. But he's my friend, Laney, my very dear friend."

"He's very fond of you too. There's no doubt of that."

Bennie came over and sat by them. "Dad, are you hurting much today?"

He lied, "Not so bad, Ben. Not so bad."

"Dad! You called me Ben!"

"You're getting older now, Ben. You know, I was called Bennie too, when I was young. That changed when I became a man. I think pretty soon you're going to become the man of the house. Think you can handle that? Until then, we'll just have to call you young Ben."

Young Ben would be sixteen this year. "Sure, Dad, you know I can. You taught me how."

"I know you can. I'm very proud of you, Ben."

"Thanks, Dad. I love you."

"I love you too, son."

Both knew that the time was fast approaching when they would not be together to express that to each other; accordingly, they rarely missed an opportunity to do so.

After a few quiet moments, young Ben asked a question that had been bothering him. "Dad, how come you never changed my last name to Ryan?"

Ben smiled a wan smile; he'd expected this question would come. "Because there's a girl, a *beautiful* girl who looks just like your Mom. She'll be born oh, about fifty years from now, and her name is going to be Katie Lynn. Katie Lynn Spencer. She'll be your great-granddaughter. She's going to need her last name so a young fella, not much older than you are now, can fall in love with her. My Gramps will talk about you and tell that young man stories about how wonderful old Ben Spencer was. You're going to need that name, Ben." His eyes moistened as he recalled his Gramps. It seemed a lifetime ago.

Young Ben raised his eyebrows. "Wow. Those are really good reasons. Thanks, Dad."

Alexander was almost nine years old now. Too young to know all of Ben's story yet, he didn't really understand the reasons for his Daddy being in the bed all the time, only that he was always in the bed. He would make small talk with Ben, and then run off for a while, and then return for more. Mostly questions and answers. Ben loved it; he was just the same when he was young, and it made him think of Gramps, seventeen years ago. The roles were reversed now. Seventeen years. Could it have been that long?

Cassie was just like her mother. Bright as the sun, everything interested her, and lord, how that child could talk. She just adored her Daddy. Just seven now, she and her doll often climbed up on Daddy's bed and talked for a half-hour straight, until Laney took pity on him and lifted her down. It wasn't that he didn't love to have his baby girl up there talking to him. But the pain was intense most of the time now, and at times it became nearly unendurable. Laney could see it in his eyes, just as she saw that he loved their little girl with his whole heart. As much as he loved her Momma. And Momma had no doubts about being loved.

One morning came when Ben was particularly bad, and Laney placed a call to Granny.

"Hello?"

"Granny, it's Laney. I'm sorry to bother you this morning, but I think . . . I think it may be time. Can you gather the family?"

"I'll take care of it, dear. We're on our way." He hung up, and made a few calls, after which he and Alta left for the Ryan estate. When he arrived, his brothers and their wives were already pulling up in their cars. They'd all come back home when they heard Ben's time was near. Adopted or not, and a fictional cousin or not, he was a cherished member of the Granville family. They would all be there, no matter what.

As they quietly entered the house, Mrs. Gruber was busy cooking and offered them something to eat and drink. It would be a busy household today, and a good housekeeper knows that grieving people forget to eat.

That whole end of the house was filled with close family and friends, and they alternated between visiting with each other and hovering around Ben, who was awake, but failing. He faded in and out, and some moments were more lucid than others. They softly talked about the families and whatever was new in town. Ben woke occasionally, and once he commented on how the brothers had all matured into such fine men. He loved them all, just as much as they loved him.

There was a knock on the door. A man entered and said he had come to talk with Benjamin Ryan. Yes, he said, Ben knew him, and yes, he knew Ben was very sick. He was ushered into the room, and walked over to Ben. A gleam of recognition showed in Ben's eyes. The brothers all recognized him too. He was wearing the same brown jacket. They also saw he hadn't aged in all the years since they last saw him.

"You're the man who was standing in the yard," Laney said.

"Yes, ma'am. It's good to see you again."

They made room next to Ben, and as the quiet man took the seat, young Ben walked over and took him by the hand. He looked at the boy and said, "Hi, Bennie, good to see you."

"You too. I knew you'd come. And it's Ben now."

The man nodded. "You're Ben now. Got it. And who is this?"

"That's my cousin, Lee Granville. He's nine."

"It's nice to meet you, Lee. You're Robert's boy, right?"

Lee, shy at first, nodded and stepped forward to shake his hand. "Yes, sir. You must be the man in the brown jacket."

The man raised an eyebrow and glanced down at his jacket, and the corner of his mouth curled up in a bit of a smile. "That would be me," he said, and shook Lee's hand.

At that point Ben came around again, this time a bit more lucid, and he looked at the man. In a raspy, breathless voice he said, "Nice touch."

The man looked a bit confused. "Nice touch?"

"Yeah. Knocking." He grinned weakly. The quiet man smiled back.

Ben asked, "Hey, quiet man, I've got a question for you."

The man raised his head a little. "I'll answer it . . . if I can."

"I've always wondered. What's your name?"

"Rafe. My name is Rafe."

"Rafe. That's . . . that's short for Raphael. Like Raphael, the arch-angel?"

"Just like that. Exactly like that." He smiled gently. Ben really had figured it out.

"Well. I'm pleased to know you, Raphael . . . Rafe. Now we're friends," and his eyes moved to young Ben, who was still holding Rafe's hand. "What do I always tell you?"

"You say that time travel is the realm of angels and their hourglasses."

"That's right. I want you to keep telling that to your brother. Raphael here, he's going to visit you and Alexander and Cassie from time to time, to make sure you know about certain things, okay?"

"Okay, Dad. Rafe visits me a lot, anyway. I like him," he said, and smiled at Rafe. During this assignment, though not allowed to appear or to fraternize with Ben beyond their single meeting, Rafe had discovered he liked Bennie. So much so that, since nothing specifically forbade it, he used that loophole to continue visiting Bennie long after there was any need to protect him from Spencer. But there was more to it than that. Since he had none of the Ryan DNA, young Ben was the natural choice to become the next to liaise with Rafe.

Ben was comforted by the knowledge that his family had always been watched over. He looked at Rafe and asked, "You here to pick me up?"

Indeed, he had come personally to take his charge home. He gave a barely perceptible nod, just enough that Ben saw it. "I, uh, I came by to tell you why you're dying of old age at forty-one."

"I figured you'd be by to fill me in."

"Remember how I told you that the part of your makeup that held you together couldn't hold up to a return trip?" Ben blinked and nod-ded weakly; he remembered.

"The radiation from your work with Oppenheimer started this, and the additional radiation from the recent X-rays have set off a chain reac-tion in you. The weakened bonds are breaking; it can't be stopped. You're reverting back to the form you were reduced to as you passed through the temporal rift. I'm sorry, Ben."

"So, I'm turning back into this?" He rubbed his fingers together and they watched the 'sand' fall away.

"Yes. That's about it. Nobody else had ever made it this far, so it took a while to figure it out."

"Ahhh . . . so, I'm *not* the first one. I didn't think I was."

"No. Not even close." Rafe's brow knit in compassion as he saw the pain Ben was in. He leaned close. "Ben, I can't even tell you. You did *so well*. You saved over fifty million people."

"Then it was all worth it," he said. With his last bit of strength, he reached out and pulled Rafe close. Shaking with the effort, he looked directly into his eyes and he said, "You're done watching over me. You watch over my family now, Rafe. You keep them safe for me." Tears brimmed from his eyes.

Rafe reached around Ben and laid him gently back onto his pillow, and his eyes and smile said what Ben needed to know, and brought peace to him. It would be done. "You're the bravest man I've ever met, Benjamin Ryan."

"An archangel thinks I'm brave? Hmmm."

Two hours and fifty-seven minutes later, with all his brothers and their wives, his dearest friends, his children, and his wife there to see him off, Ben Ryan closed his eyes and passed away.

Rafe disappeared a few seconds later. He had a job to finish. Nobody saw him get up, or vanish. A few minutes later, only Laney, young Ben, and Alexander were aware that he'd ever been there.

Chapter Seventy-Seven

Pete Sanford didn't like his job. At least the Dugan Funeral Home was steady and it paid well. His friends, who weren't much in the way of friends anyway, teased him about his job. He knew they were a lazy bunch who held no jobs themselves, and would have taken his job in a second. He was lucky. Except for having to work in a cold, refrigerated room, it wasn't particularly difficult. When the deceased were brought in, he cleaned them up and did whatever was required to make them look presentable for initial viewings. He was busy last evening when they brought Mr. Ryan in, so he hadn't had a chance to get to him yet.

At least, that's what he told himself. The guy owned the telephone company. But he knew what else the guy was rumored to be; he had supposedly come back through time or something like that. Those were probably just whispered rumors and gossip, but what if they weren't? Maybe the guy wasn't human at all. He'd found all sorts of other things to dabble with, leaving Mr. Ryan on the table with a sheet over him all night and day, waiting to be cleaned up and made ready for viewing.

A door opened percussively at the far end of the hallway and a voice carried back to him. "Peter, are you finished with Mr. Ryan yet? The family is here to say goodbye." *Uh-oh.* He'd dabbled himself into a corner. He knew what "here to say goodbye" meant. They were here for an informal viewing to see that their family member was being well-taken care of, cleaned up and so forth.

"Not quite. I've been busy, so I just got started on him! Give me a few minutes." J.R. Dugan, his boss, knew that was code for "Not even close, I'll have to scramble to make him look anywhere near good enough."

As Dugan talked with the family to buy him some time, he scurried around and got things ready. He threw on his rubber apron, pulled the washer overhead and grabbed some sponges and washcloths, and a few towels. He could make this a fast one. He pulled back the sheet, and groaned. "What the hell is *this?* They told me the guy died in his bed."

The man in front of him looked like he'd died from being buried in a sand dune. He was covered with sand; it was everywhere. Though it was pretty creepy compared to what he'd hoped to find, sand wasn't that bad and should wash right off. He unbuttoned the man's pajama shirt, and began to lift him to remove the shirt and get started. All at once, from head to toe, the man dissolved into a pile of sand. The man was gone. Just . . . *gone.*

He froze. All he could think was that he was in some pretty big trouble, though he had no idea what he'd done wrong. What should he do? "Oh, *shit!*"

This was *way* more than he was paid to deal with, and he knew it. Wheeling and running for the front, he called his boss aside. After some terse whispering, he convinced the man to come see for himself.

J.R. had seen it all in his many years of undertaking, and he couldn't understand Peter's babbling or panic. He excused himself and hurried to the back to get things back on track, while Laney and Granny waited in the front.

When, a few minutes later, the eternally-calm and composed J.R. Dugan emerged, his face showed one thing. Panic. He was sweating bullets, and if 'spooked' could be an acceptable term to use to describe a funeral home director, then he was *spooked* . . . and then some. He had no choice. He walked over to Laney and Granny, and his voice quivered as he tried to remain calm. "Mrs. . . . Mrs. Ryan, would you please accompany me to the back now?"

He led them back to the preparation room, where poor Peter stood pressed against the wall and countertop, keeping as much distance as he could between himself and . . . whatever was on the table. The director, helpless to do anything else, told them the truth. "Peter was preparing Mr. Ryan for viewing, and when he went to move him, this is what happened. Mrs. Ryan, please understand; we have no idea how this could have happened."

Laney and Granny walked over and saw the pile of sand. "Oh," she said, and exchanged a knowing glance with Granny. She turned to Dugan and Peter, and beckoned them over. "Do you know Benjamin's story, Mr. Dugan? Peter? Most folks in town have heard it, and it's whispered about quite a bit. Ben came to us from the future."

Dugan and Peter nodded, they'd heard the stories.

This pile of sand just yesterday had been her beloved Ben. She gently reached into the pile of sand, scooped up a handful and let it sift through her fingers. Her voice grew strong. "Well, gentlemen, the story is true, as you can see. These are the sands of time, and time has reclaimed my Benjamin. Would you do me a favor, and be so kind as to box this up as ashes? I believe that would make an acceptable story, and leave all of us in comfortable positions. Don't you think?" she asked as she raised a furtive eyebrow to them; a single gesture that spoke volumes and implied that they were all in on it, so they might as well play along. She went on. "Nobody else would believe it anyway. This ring . . . is to be placed in with the sand. We *will* check to make sure it's in there."

"I guarantee it, Mrs. Ryan," Dugan said, relieved. Weird story or not, the man's wife was not frantic or upset, the situation was explained, and he was off the hook. Crisis averted. Back to being the ever-calm, reassuring funeral director. "It would be our distinct pleasure. I'll make arrangements to modify the details to accommodate . . . a cremation." He turned to Peter, who was still pretty shaken. "Peter, get started on Mr. Ryan, while I show Mrs. Ryan our urn selection. Remember the ring."

They turned and walked off, leaving a very, very unhappy Peter alone with 'Mr. Ryan.' For a full minute, he didn't move. He hadn't signed on for weird stuff. But things were still lean all over; he knew others would take his job, macabre or not. "Yes, sir," he mumbled as he carefully re-moved the clothing from the sand. He picked up and looked at the ring that Mrs. Ryan had pointed out, a gold rectangle with a raised set of intricately carved platinum wings.

"Nice ring," he said, and tossed it into the pile of sand.

Chapter Seventy-Eight

The deep, cozy feather mattress wrapped around him like a cocoon. She ran her fingers through his hair, and he stretched long and lazy, enjoying it. Still half-asleep, he yawned and mumbled, "Morning, darling girl." He blinked a few times to clear his vision.

The soft morning light cascaded through the windows onto her tumble-down red hair. It glowed like a halo in the soft morning light, and her gentle voice coaxed him from his reverie. "Good morning, Mr. Ryan," she said, cuddling close to him for warmth. He loved her green eyes, her freckles, her red hair. Her smile that took his breath away. That one tooth that didn't quite line up with the others.

Wait a minute. He lifted his head and looked at her. "Laney, you look so . . . young. You're beautiful!"

The smile melted from her face, and she sat up. "What? Just who the hell is Laney?"

Ben blinked. He looked at her, then looked around, and when his gaze found the headboard, he stared in disbelief.

There, carved into the wood of the headboard, were the heads of two moose. He was in the Moose room at the Lodge at Moosehead Lake. Could it be? He looked at her again, scarcely able to believe it. His voice quivered as he asked, "Katie Lynn, is it really you?"

"Of *course* it's me. Who else would it be?"

Dazed, he looked around. He'd woken up in this room with Katie Lynn the morning before the storm. This was the last morning he'd ever seen her. "It's over. It's finally over. I'm back home with you." He grabbed her and held her so tight that she could barely breathe. After a half-minute or so, he eased off, and she felt he was shaking.

"Did you have a nightmare? Are you all right, Ben?"

"I . . . I'm all right, I think." He sat up, swung his feet off the bed and started to look around, feeling for something up by his pillow.

"Did you lose something?"

"No, I'm just getting my cane."

Alarmed, she hopped up off of her side of the bed and hurried around to his side. She grabbed his shoulders, put her face close to him, and shook him. "Ben!"

Surprised, he pulled his face back. "Yes?"

"Wake up, darling. C'mon, you're dreaming. Wake up. You're here with me, and you don't use a cane."

"Well, of course I—" and he stopped. He slid off the edge, placed his feet on the floor and stood on both of his strong, young legs. "Of course I don't. Thanks, sweetie. Sorry about that." He didn't know exactly what to say, so he decided to wing it. He went with what he remembered about that day. "Well, I guess we'd better get a move on. We've got to get you back to school, and we've got some wedding plans to make."

She grabbed his arm and turned him toward her again, looking closely at him, and emphasizing her words with more shaking. "You are *really* starting to scare me, Ben. Are you sure you're awake? Are you sure you're all right?"

"Sure I am. Why wouldn't I be?"

"Oh, I don't know. Maybe because I finished college a year ago, and we've been married for almost a year now?" She held up her hand to display her wedding ring, then grabbed and lifted his hand to show him his. "That must have been one hell of a dream you were having."

He was a bit overwhelmed, but all things considered, not particularly worried. He sighed, and thought, *Welcome to Paradox, you've been here before.* He sat down again, and taking a deep breath, looked out the window overlooking the lake. "You have no idea," he said, half-sighing, and looked at her. "But I'm okay now, I promise you. Just a little confused. I'll be all right."

"Are you sure we shouldn't get you to a doctor?"

"I'm sure. Positive. But I don't think there's any way around it, love. We need to talk, and it's going to take a couple of hours *at least* for me to tell you everything I need to. Let's get some breakfast, and I can tell you the whole story while we sit by the lake."

"All right. Is this something I should be worried about? Is this Laney why we need to talk?"

"Laney is Elaine Perkins Spencer, your great-great-grandmother. And there's nothing to worry about. Nothing at all." He looked her in the eye. "I love you, and I will until the day I die. I know that because I've already done that. Nothing will ever change that."

Looking back into his eyes, she smiled, and tucked her hair over her ear. She wasn't following everything he said, but she saw the love in his eyes, and he promised to explain, so she said, "Then let's get some breakfast, I'm hungry. I'm looking forward to hearing whatever this is."

The lake was a beautiful shade of blue, and the sky was perfect. As the morning wore on, cool breezes off the lake brought a soothing element to some otherwise complicated dialogue.

"So, *you* were the Benjamin Ryan responsible for stopping the Japanese at Pearl Harbor. Not your great-great-grandfather that you were named after."

"That's right."

"And *you* married my great-great-grandmother?"

"Right again. *After* your great-grandfather Ben was born, of course."

"Of course. And—Howard Hughes was one of your best friends, and Zantford Granville was your very best friend? And Howard is the reason we're so rich?"

"You got it. The two best friends any guy ever had. But Howard, he could be a real pain. He was always sneaking millions into my bank account." He shook his head in mock disgust.

She struggled to suppress a grin, amused at how that irritated him. "And you walked with a cane because your . . . biplane . . . fell on you."

"That's right. Well . . . part of it fell on me, anyway."

"Well, I knew you owned fifteen percent of Hughes Industries, but I never knew the story behind it."

"*Fifteen?* That god-damned sneak. It was supposed to be *ten* percent," he said, chortling as he shook his head as though he'd just lost another game of chess. *Oh, well.* With Howard, it amounted to about the same thing. "Ahhh, Howard. What a nut."

"He sure was. He spent billions and billions on research facilities, and he advanced medicine in ways it might never have gone. He's a great man, and well-loved."

Ben gave her a dubious look. Back through the looking glass. "Howard? Well-loved? Howard Hughes?"

"It's often said that he's done more for America and the whole world than any single human being, though he says that's not true. He said during an interview that there was somebody who had set the example for him. He says he was carrying on the work his friend had started." Her eyes widened with understanding. "*You're* the friend he talks about, aren't you?"

He was confused. "Maybe. But you're saying, "he says," and, "he talks about," like he's still alive."

She looked sad. "Oh. No, love. He just died last year. I'm so sorry. He was one hundred and four years old. He's buried down in Springfield. That's where he asked to be laid to rest, next to your . . . your . . . next to you. That explains what he did, then."

He was hurting, reeling with the knowledge that Howard died so recently, but he tried to keep up. He asked, "What did he do?"

"He left it all to you, everything. Everybody thought he was crazy, but his will was specific. We all thought maybe he was senile, or maybe he had it in his head that your great, great grandfather was still around. You both have the same name, and you . . . well, you're alive. He liked you so much, he knew us both from the time we were little, and he loved it when we came to visit. And we visited a lot. So nobody really questioned it when you got it all. You own Hughes Industries. All of it now, not just fifteen percent."

He chuckled, and shook his head in good-natured resignation. "No, he did *not.*" *Checkmate again, old friend.*

"He most certainly *did.* You're worth five *billion* dollars, hubby of mine."

"*Jesus!* He always was a real pain in the ass," he crabbed, and she heard him whisper soft and low, with a catch in his voice, "God, I wish he was still alive." He looked at her, his eyes misty. "Could we visit his grave?"

"Of course," she said, and laid her hand up to his face, stroking his cheek lovingly. "We can do anything we like. We're the Ryans, love."

"So you believe me, then?"

"Of course I believe you. I have a lot of questions for you, though."

Over the course of the morning he delighted in rediscovering just how easy Katie Lynn was to talk to, what a sweet and devoted woman she was. No wonder he'd loved her so.

Hand in hand, they walked toward Main Street. Reaching their car, he said, "I don't recognize this make of car, but it's magnificent. What is it?"

"It's a Packard. The Ryan family has a large interest in the company. This is one of this year's first releases."

"That's right, I remember helping them do a big restart after the battle of Pearl. Boy, I like it. A Packard, eh? Nice," he said, running his hand down the fender.

"Al would have *loved* this baby."

Chapter Seventy-Nine

They arrived in Springfield and stood in the cemetery, overlooking the lush, green, rolling countryside and the town. The spires of the old church steeples rose in the distance through the trees. Laney had found a breathtaking place to lay him to rest. There was her headstone, next to his. She had lived until 1981. His sweet, wonderful wife had died five years prior to his birth. He read the inscription. *"Elaine Margorie Ryan, Beloved wife of Benjamin Ryan."* Because it was supposed to have been a one-way trip, he had never envisioned standing here like this, and was wholly unprepared for it. He grimaced, struck all at once by the sharp pain and loss. Tears filled his eyes. He covered his mouth as his lips quivered.

"Oh, Ben, this must be so hard for you."

He looked at her pretty face, into her eyes, so very much like Laney's, and remembered. "She said the same thing when she first saw your photo."

She slipped her arm through his, as Laney had so often done to comfort him or to talk with him. "Will you tell me all about her?"

He nodded in affirmation, unable to speak for the moment.

They arrived at the next stone.

Katie Lynn read the stone. "Benjamin Francis Ryan, Cherished husband of Elaine Ryan. He saved the world. He came and went with the sands of time." The meaning came clear to her. She whispered, "So it's true. It's really . . . all true."

"Yes."

"Oh, Ben."

Now that the shock had worn off, he managed a shrug, indicating that he felt as much acceptance as grief. "As you grow older, you lose friends and people you love along the way. I fought in a big air battle and lost a number of friends. As you grow feeble, you recognize the cycle of life at work. I know I seem sad, but I said my goodbyes as that Benjamin Ryan sixty-four years ago."

They slowly walked down the line. Alexander. Cassiopeia. They were here. Benjamin Spencer.

She said, "This whole area is both of our families' plot. All of our ancestors are here."

"You mean, all of my descendants."

She placed her hand over her mouth, realizing the depth of his statement. "Oh, my. You're right."

They continued to stroll along, and on the other side of his stone was another familiar name. Ben smiled. "Howard Hughes, friend of Ben. 1905 to 2009." He blinked back the tears, then he laughed a little. "Well, I'll be—he had a soccer ball etched on the stone. What a nut."

"Everybody thought that was pretty strange. Do you know what it's about?"

"I sure do. It's for me. It's a good story. I promise, I'll tell you all about it."

"Look at this. Edward. His wife. Mark, and his wife. Most of the brothers are here, aren't they? Oh, look. Alta, and . . . ahhh, here we are. It's Granny. Zantford Granville, loving husband of Alta. 1902 to . . . hmm, it's blank. Somebody screwed up."

"No, they didn't. Zantford is still alive. He lives right here in town."

"No, that's impossible! He'd be over a hundred and five by now."

"He turned one hundred and eight this year, sweetheart."

"Granny's alive?" he said, astonished.

"Uh-huh. He comes up here a lot, and sits in front of your stone, and talks to you. Sometimes he just sits. At least, he used to, when he still could get around some. He's a very nice man, and he always fusses over you and me." She stopped, and looked off in the distance, remembering something. She looked back at him and smiled. "*He* calls me Laney sometimes too! He says I remind him so much of her, it's like she's standing right in front of him." She turned to Ben, looking at him for a long moment, and then she spoke. "You really did it. You lived a whole lifetime last night. No wonder you're so different today."

"Am I? I'm sorry, love. I . . . I don't know what I can do about that."

"No. Nothing. Don't be sorry, and don't change a thing. I like it. It's like you're you, only . . . only more so. The best parts of you are even better. Come on, sweetheart, we need to go somewhere."

Off they went into town, and down on lower Park Street they pulled into the driveway of a large house. "Do we live here?" Ben asked.

She gave him a worried look. "This is going to take a lot of work isn't it?"

He shrugged. "All I can tell you is that in our other life, I loved you more than anything in the world. I'm going to have to tell you all about that life as well. We're going to have to help each other get up to speed." A thought occurred to him. "Did you grow up with money?"

"Sure, lots of it. Why?"

"You were a hardworking girl raised on a farm."

"You got that part right, but our farm is more of a ranch . . . it's bigger than your spread. We had plenty of hands, and it was right next door to yours. We grew up together."

"I know about your farm, I planned it that way, but damn, *THAT* is something I wish was in my memory. *We* didn't meet until our teens."

They reached the door, and knocked. A woman answered the door and recognized them both, calling them by their names. She scolded them mildly because they knew they didn't need to knock. They walked inside and she left them to find their own way. Katie Lynn knew the way. They came to a room and she entered. "Hello, Mr. Granville, it's Katie Lynn and Ben."

A wizened man sat in the chair. He was ancient, and frail. But his eyes were lively and they lit up when they saw Katie Lynn, and also when he saw Ben. "Come in! Come in!"

They entered, and Ben saw Granny. He knew the eyes at once. He walked across the room, and he kneeled in front of Granny, and looked into the eyes of his dear old friend. "Granny, it's good to see you, my old friend."

Granny heard his family name being used and the new tone in Ben's voice, then he saw the recognition. He'd known this young man and this young woman for many years, and he'd waited so very long to see if his Ben might return home. It had kept him and Howard alive for sixty-five years. He knew Ben would not recognize him until he made his trip back, if he did make a trip back. Howard had almost lived long enough to see it. Granny had made it. Not by much, but he'd made it. He took the young man's hands, and his eyes searched Ben's, looking back and forth for something. "Benjamin, is that you?"

"It's me, Granny. I made it home."

Overwhelmed with joy, Granny started weeping, and held out his arms, and hugged Ben with all the might his frail, withered body could muster. Ben held him for some time, until the old man stopped sobbing and regained his composure. Finally Granny grabbed him by his arms and pushed him back, and Ben leaned back to help. "Let me take a look at you. You look wonderful. Walk across the room for me again, would you?"

Ben stood and walked across the room, and the old man waved him back to his side with a big smile. "You walk a whole lot better now, don't you?"

Ben laughed. "No more cane, Granny. I'm fit as a fiddle."

Granny, shaking with the palsy of extreme age, held his arms up a bit. "Me, too!" he beamed at them. They all laughed.

Granny looked at Katie Lynn, and somberly held her gaze. "And now you know, young lady."

She walked over and took his hand. "You could have told me all about it, Mr.—"

"Granny."

"Granny, you could have told me all of this."

"I thought about it. I wanted to. But we couldn't be sure he would return," he said, and raised his eyebrows. "It was supposed to be a one-way trip." He looked off somewhere, remembering. "But the sand." He looked back at her. "Howard and I just had a feeling he'd gone home again."

Ben asked, "The sand?"

"Sit down, sit down! I'll tell you all about it!"

They pulled up chairs, and Granny told him how his sand-generating "condition" became total and complete the day after he died. They talked about how Ben was going to have to re-learn his earlier life from scratch, how everything was different. Granny gave him some broad strokes about history since he'd left. How the world—following Howard's lead—had learned to work together so that all the people in all the countries were fed, and wars were nearly nonexistent. How he and Howard had remained close friends. How they both had made sure Ben's children and grandchildren, and young Ben himself, for that matter, knew how to fly anything with wings. Howard spent the last several decades of his life in Springfield, in the arms of the extended Ryan, Granville, and Spencer clans, all of whom had lovingly laid claim to him as a cherished member of their families, making Howard truly as rich as he had ever hoped to be.

There was much to talk about, but at one hundred and eight years old, Granny could endure only short spans of activity before tiring and needing to rest. They helped his caretaker ease him into bed, and promised to come back every day and visit and talk.

They sat in the car afterward, and Katie Lynn could see it was taking its toll on him. "We're going home, and we're staying there for as long as it takes for you to get yourself acclimated to everything," she said, "and that's final."

"Okay. Good idea. But . . . I still want to visit Granny every day."

"Like you used to."

"Yeah." He smiled. "How'd you know that?"

"Granny talked about you all the time. It always sounded like he was talking about *my* Ben. Sometimes he even slipped and said you did this, or you did that, as though you were the Ben he was talking about. Some of the stories were interesting. You certainly were well-loved. Do you think he was getting me ready for this?"

"In his own way, I suppose he might have been."

"Did you two really have to ditch your planes out in the Pacific Ocean, over a hundred miles from land? Were you really stuck in your bomber?"

Ben recalled that day. "Yes, that's a true story. Granny saved my life."

She looked at him in silence for a minute. They'd grown up together and were married, and now they hardly knew each other. "You're the boy I grew up with, and the man I married, but at the same time, you're not. We're going to have to get to know each other all over again, aren't we?" she asked, a little worried.

"Yes. And no. Not in our hearts, love. Just in . . . some other ways." He looked at her lovely green eyes and grinned. "I'm kind of looking forward to it."

Her eyes lit up again, and she tucked her hair back over her right ear, causing his stomach to jump a little with excitement. "Me too," she breathed.

He smiled at that. Then he asked, "Am I a good husband, Katie Lynn?"

"The best." She smiled at him, and he saw the love in her eyes.

Chapter Eighty

Katie Lynn was a godsend. While his "flu" kept him home for the next two weeks, she went over to his Mom's house and borrowed home-movie video tapes and DVDs for him to 'have something to do' while he was sick. A monument to organization, Mom already had them handy and categorized, and ready for use. She sent them all home with Katie Lynn.

As he watched himself growing up in another life, he realized he was through the looking glass again. He learned more about Katie Lynn as a child than he ever had in his previous existence there. And to his utter amazement, he watched himself having fun growing up and doing things with his father. His father was alive! And there he saw Howard and Granny with him in the hangar, placing him in the cockpit of his grandfather's antique Waco biplane. So, that's why he and Katie Lynn came home from Moosehead in the Packard. It made sense. The Waco still belonged to his Dad. Of course! *Good trade,* he thought.

It was dizzying, learning his whole life over in just two weeks. Katie Lynn urged him to go easy on himself. He'd get there. They would use the flu excuse for his being out of sorts and not remembering things well right now. He might have to say, "Oh, sorry about that," a lot, but in the big picture that meant nothing. Thank goodness he had his visits with Granny; that seemed to help a lot. He cried a number of times back at home when he was overcome with the realization of how short his time with his beloved, ancient, frail friend would be. He watched all of the home videos several times, until he thought his eyes would fall out of his head, and finally decided he was ready, or close enough. Besides, he was pretty sure his Dad and Gramps would be okay with it, though he wouldn't know until he talked to them. But looking at his Dad, he saw something. He had a feeling.

He and Katie Lynn drove over to Gramps's place. His Dad was supposed to be there, and so was Mom.

They walked through the house and she walked off to find his Mom when he found Gramps dabbling in his family room. Some things never changed.

"Ben, good to see you! What's new? I heard you had the flu. Feeling better?"

"No, Gramps, I didn't have the flu. I just got back."

"Oh? From where?"

Ben held up his hand, the ring facing Gramps. Gramps did the same and they nodded. "I went, Gramps. I've gone there. I'm done."

Gramps raised his eyebrows, surprised. "You went for the quiet man? You're done?"

Ben nodded. Just then, his Dad walked through the door, followed by Mom talking to Katie Lynn. "So, you're privy to the family secret, you're one of us women of mystery now?"

Katie Lynn said, "It would seem."

Ben looked confused. "Mom? *You* knew?"

Sheila gave him a big hug, then held him at arm's length and looked him in the eye. "I'm Mom. I know everything around here! None of this can be done by just one person. The women of this family have their part to play in this, too. I made sure you had plenty of home movies, to know who you are. In some timeline somewhere, I gave birth to you, young man, and you're my responsibility."

Dad looked a little surprised when Ben hugged him hard and held on for a time. Then he hugged his Mom again. He and his Mom had grown up together. He'd missed her terribly.

Gramps still didn't believe it. "How long did it take you?"

"It took me seventeen years. I died at forty-one."

"When did you go?"

"Two days after my twenty-fourth birthday."

"What? Last week?"

"That's right."

Gramps looked surprised, but some inner knowledge told him that it was true, so he accepted it. "Hmm. I'm surprised you had to go. I never had to. Neither did Danny."

"Yes, you did, Gramps. So did Dad," he said, with certainty.

Gramps shook his head. "No, I didn't. I think I would have remembered that."

"I don't think you're supposed to. You did your time. You both did your best. Gramps, once you passed down what you learned to Dad and me, you forgot it."

"I must have. I don't remember any of it."

His Dad said, "Neither do I. I'm positive I didn't go."

Sheila said, "You went, dear. Trust me. You went." She looked at Katie Lynn and rolled her eyes upward.

"Men," she said, and they chuckled. Katie Lynn wasn't exactly sure why they were rolling their eyes and chuckling, but she reasoned that she would before long.

Ben said, "Yes, you did, Dad. Your A-10 warthog crashed in a storm in Iraq, you never came home. Mom and Gramps raised me from the time I was five years old. That was when you went."

"Iraq? Why would I be flying in Iraq? I've never even been there."

"It's a long story. It took me almost two decades to figure it out."

A voice spoke behind them. "I'll need those rings, gentlemen."

"Ahhh. The quiet man, Raphael. Right on cue." Ben said. "Before I give mine to you, Rafe, I have one question. Will we remember it?"

"Good question." Rafe gestured at the older Ryans. "For the most part, they already don't. They remembered for long enough to prepare the next in line, but then it faded from them. You remember now. Soon you'll start to experience vivid dreams of yourself doing things you are sure you never did. That will be your memories returning from the temporal displacement. More and more, you'll forget being in the past."

"So I'll remember growing up with Katie Lynn here in this time?"

"It's your time. The memories are yours."

"That's great news. Thanks. But . . . I'll forget the life I lived back then?"

"Yes."

"Okay. Then you're not getting the rings back. Not until I tell them the story."

Rafe sighed. "You always were the stubborn one. The rings—"

"You always were the pushy one. You told me I couldn't come back."

"I said *living matter* couldn't survive repeat trips. As I recall, you were dead."

"How did I get back here alive, then?"

"You returned to the point of origin. Or I returned you, more or less. Okay. Yes. That's the only part where you're allowed one little . . . miracle."

Rafe stopped. He had an idea. They could see he was hesitating. He said, "Let me ask you this; would you like them to remember the story you tell? Would YOU like to remember the story you tell?"

"Yes, I would. Very much."

"Then you have to remove the rings first. You'll remember everything that happens after that. You'll remember telling them the story. But one thing won't ever change; in the course of time, you'll no longer remember having been in the past."

The three Ryans looked at each other. The eldest Ryan removed his ring, then flexed his hand as though it had been set free. Dad did the same. Then Ben removed his. It felt strange. They laid them together on the counter. Rafe reached for the rings, then stopped, his hand just above them. He looked indecisive for a moment, then withdrew the hand. He removed his own ring, laid it on the counter, and turned to the Ryans. "Could I ask one favor of you? Before I take them back, could I hear you tell your story? It would mean a great deal to me."

"Sure you can. But you were there the whole time, and we both know it."

A smile played at the corners of Rafe's mouth as he said, "Is that so?"

Chapter Eighty-One

The older Ryans sat down, and gestured to Rafe to come join them.

With the invitation to sit down and listen, it was not lost on him that he was welcomed rather than reviled for only the second time ever on this assignment.

"Wait!" Gramps said, and hurried out of the room. He returned with a video camera. He showed it to Rafe. "Will this work?"

"It will. But I won't show up."

"Really? Too bad. You're like one of the family now."

Rafe was entering undiscovered territory; learning more about humans and love all the time. Sometimes the small things were the most important. So small that he needed to get this close to understand. Something he had taught others long ago came back to him; *you're never too old to learn.* Could so much time have passed since he brought knowledge to others?

Gramps set the camera up on the counter across the room, and sat down, mumbling, "I could do with some popcorn," but he stayed seated.

Ben walked across the room. On the wall, several old, framed black and white photos that hung there caught his eye. In the first he saw himself, older, asleep in his easy chair with Bennie hugging him, asleep on his right leg, and little Alexander bundled and asleep in the crook of his left arm. He loved that photo. He loved that Laney had taken it. In the other, he stood in front of the old Waco when it was new. In front of him stood a young boy. Ben smiled. He remembered the day that photo had been taken.

Gramps said, "That's a photo of my grandfather, and my father is the boy standing in front of him."

He turned, still smiling, his eyes still glistening. "No, Gramps, that little boy standing in front of me isn't your father. That's young Ben Spencer, Katie Lynn's great grandfather. Ben Spencer was named after me. At the time this photo was taken, your father was just a baby. This was taken not long after this other photo, where I'm holding your grandfather Alexander, and Bennie was asleep on me."

"That's you? And that little boy was old Ben Spencer? I loved that man, Katie Lynn. He was like a second father to me. He and Dad were always close."

Ben said, "I asked Ben to make sure of that. He was Ben's brother."

Gramps's brow knit in confusion. Katie Lynn looked confused as well. Ben smiled and held up his hand. "Don't worry, I'll explain."

He glanced at the photo, and spotted the ancient cane hanging on the wall above it. The varnish had aged and cracked, and the rubber tip was nearly worn off. At the top he saw a tarnished brass handle carved in the shape of an eagle's head. Gently, reverently, he lifted it from its hangers. It felt good and familiar in his hand. It was then Katie Lynn remembered how it alarmed her when he searched for "his cane" that first morning. She now believed him, but seeing the pieces fall together with her own eyes made his journey that much more real. In some ways, it made her worry about who Ben was now; he was not the man she married, and yet, he was indeed the same man. She saw both. In other ways, she was excited about this man, who had seen so much, yet who left her with no doubts about his gentleness and undying love for her.

Gramps saw the cane and said, "That belonged to my grandfather. I was told he took it everywhere he went, had it until the day he died. When you were just a baby you loved to play with that cane. You would pick it up and yell, 'Ganny!'"

A grin spread across Ben's face as he was struck by how old it looked. Over his shoulder he said, "Yeah, kids have trouble with r's."

As he turned around, he twirled the cane. It felt the same, and the grin stayed on his face. He looked at his grandfather and held it up. "Do you mind?"

"Be my guest."

Katie Lynn said, "I see you found your cane."

He grinned, sporting quite the satisfied look. "I did, didn't I?" After giving it another twirl, he leaned one last time on his old familiar friend, and began.

"Let me tell you about the greatest bunch of guys in the world; the Granville brothers. You probably think you know a lot about them, but you don't. The word genius doesn't even begin to describe them. But the oldest, Zantford, my friend, my dearest friend, is called Granny by those close to him.

"I flew through a time-storm, a temporal rift, to get there, and crashed the Waco outside of town when I arrived there in June of 1929. Granny found me. The Granville Brothers couldn't afford a cast, so old Doc Perkins trussed me up with what they had handy; some splints made from pieces of wood and strips from an old blanket. The boys built me a pair of crutches from wing spars. My leg was so badly broken that when it healed, I never walked right again. So Granny gave me this cane. . . ."

Katie Lynn, Mom, Dad, Gramps, and Rafe, the quiet archangel, all settled in for the afternoon. It was another one-way trip, a story to be told one-time only. And there was no doubt in any of their minds. Every single word was true.

Epilogue

Before young Ben Ryan came along, none of Raphael's charges had ever wanted to know his name. None had so much as asked. When Ben called out and asked what his name was on the day he vanished out behind the shop, Raphael—Rafe—found himself tempted to break the rules, to reappear.

Instead, he'd followed orders and accompanied Ben through his life, watching as he struggled against heartbreak and adversity. Raphael, inspired by Ben's dedication and focus, was touched by the way he tried to do the right thing, even when the cost to him was dear.

Raphael was astonished to realize that young Ben Ryan had the heart of an archangel. Not just any archangel. Like Raphael himself, Ben's heart was unique. This human was a warrior with a fierce heart, consumed not by a love for battle, though he was a most capable warrior. His fierce love for this broken Eden and every soul it contained brought the wall around Raphael's heart tumbling down, and renewed an ancient cynic's love for a fragile, struggling young world. By displaying a surprising capacity for love, and calling forth the incredible beauty that dwells deep within these oft-blackened human hearts, Ben restored a lost angel's faith in humans and humanity.

The simple truth opened Rafael's heart, released the love trapped within it, released the unimaginable beauty he had hidden away for eons. His eyes radiated a new light that shone as bright and full of promise as the face of his all-knowing creator.

Such a simple truth.

He had not been sent to help Ben Ryan.

His beloved creator had sent Ben Ryan to help his Raphael.

For indeed, the creator could have allowed the humans to take any course they wished, and it would have signified nothing more than a blink in the eye of eternal time. When the humans obliterated fully sixty million of their kind, the creator did not grieve. Humans as a species were still young, still learning the profound ramifications of their greatest gift, free will; and as such were prone to any number of iniquities.

Much time would pass before they decided which path to follow; extinction or enlightenment. Given everything they needed to achieve either, they would decide their own destiny. Angels and archangels had their purposes, but at no time had they ever been intended to influence that outcome. These were special circumstances.

Humans are well-loved by the creator, but they are not the creator's first creation, nor are they the creator's first love; a mistaken belief they so often enjoy in their youth and arrogance. Archangels hold that position, and other angels are a very close second. It doesn't matter where the humans rank.

Raphael's assignment was never intended to correct historical errors. When Raphael's heart broke in grief over the humans' actions and the subsequent lives lost, the creator could not abide by that. For a number of centuries, he allowed the cessation of time while his most-loved creation healed and found himself again, while the creator sought to restore his precious archangel to his former radiance. In this, he was successful, thanks to the human Ben Ryan.

You have doubts. That's to be expected. You say, "This story never happened, those sixty-one million people died, and are still dead." True enough, today and now, but how would you know or remember that should you wake up tomorrow knowing only that we never had a second great war, that we work together and live in harmony with other nations? How could you know that one grief-stricken angel and a handful of humans with good hearts joined forces to make that difference, to give this fragile world just one more chance to find a better path?

Did you ever expect to see something, and were surprised when you found something different? Of course you did; we've all done that. Did you ever ask yourself why you expected something else? Perhaps it was a memory imprint that wasn't entirely wiped away when one ripple crossed another in the pond of time and changed history. Perhaps you still contain a shadow of who you were before things shifted. Maybe it takes time to remove all traces. Maybe it takes time to recover every trace of who you are now. When nobody knows, one plausible theory is as good as the next.

How many of us have seen a single shoe lying somewhere and had to resist the impulse to see if it might fit? With several pairs of shoes at home and a good pair on our feet, where else might we have been, in what other time might we have lived, and how impoverished were we that a rejected, forlorn shoe should now entice or compel us to explore its potential value?

Maybe we're reincarnated. If we are, are we always reborn into the future, or will some of us be sent back to learn more about living in the present or even the past first? Is that how déjà vu occurs?

Is it our business to know any of these answers? I'm probably not the one to ask, as I fear we walk the path not of enlightenment. I can only tell you the two things I've been told.

- Time travel is the realm of angels and their hourglasses.
- I'm never to remove this ring. Not for any reason.

An Interview with
Lee Granville

JS: This interview was granted me by Lee Granville, son of Robert Granville of Gee Bee fame. Lee, thank you for giving up a big chunk of your day; you are indeed a gentleman, and I am overjoyed to find you are a Gee Bee fan like me. You kind of have to be a history buff to do what I'm doing here.

LG: Yes, I'm afraid so; this is pretty ancient history now.

JS: But for those of us who love everything about airplanes, it's pretty exciting stuff.

LG: I've seen that, the interest just keeps on going. I'm surprised just how many people still remember Gee Bees, considering how long ago it was. I go to any sort of aircraft gathering, and almost all the people know just what a Gee Bee was.

JS: Oh, yes! The Gee Bees are distinctive. I've flown radio control planes for many years, and anytime a Gee Bee Model shows up it generates a lot of excitement. I've owned a few myself; kind of hard for me to resist.

LG: Yes, I went with my father (Robert Granville) up to Oshkosh several times. All you had to do was mention your name and they were all over you. I myself had no direct connection with the Gee Bees; I was just a very small child when the airplanes were being built. I remember playing around the shop and hanger when they were working.

JS: So you were born in . . . ?

LG: 1936.

JS: That would have put you there right around the time of the QED, or a bit later?

LG: Yes, I showed up in more of what you'd call the aftermath of the Gee Bee Corporation's bankruptcy, there were more corporations formed that mostly comprised of the same people, most of the bothers and the engineers and so forth. The times were terrible for the purpose as far as financing.

JS: From everything I hear and from what I could gather, these guys were scraping a living together the whole time.

LG: Yes, that's right. Now, early on, before they got into the racing, they were doing quite well for a while, and they decided to build some bi-planes first. They built eight or ten biplanes in the period of a year or two. I suppose I should point out that because of my age, I have very little firsthand information; everything I say here is just repeating what my father told me.

JS: Well that's as close to the horse's mouth as anybody on the planet is going to get at this point, I believe.

LG: (Laughs) Well, I guess that's true! Not very many left to . . . (pause) . . . not very many left at all where you could find any information.

JS: Do you have any brothers or sisters left?

LG: I have my brother Robert, he's my younger brother. He was far enough from that whole situation that it never touched him at all. He was completely out of it, he was born during the war, in fact, he was born on the day they dropped the bomb on Hiroshima.

JS: So you can remember THAT day pretty well.

LG: Yes, we sure can. But that just goes to show you he had no timely memories. Right after the war, my parents pulled up stakes and moved us down to a town right outside of Bridgeport, CT. That's where my Dad went to work for Chance Vought. My Dad was absolutely totally and mentally exhausted after the war, he was a foreman of one of the depart-ments. He had 150 people under him, it was an enormous section, and they worked seven days a week. He was in production, one of the things his section built was the turtle-deck for the Corsairs, the area of the plane that sits behind the pilot's head and shoulders that runs back down to the tail. They worked with any employees, and they used anybody they could find, with the men gone off to war they had a lot of women, a lot of minorities from down south, and it was his job the find out what they could do and where they could do the best job and still meet all their specifications and so forth. It was an exhausting job for him.

JS: Oh, I would imagine.

LG: Because of national security, the factories were all completely blacked out, and it would be months and months at a time when he never saw the sun. With fourteen and fifteen hour days, get there in the dark, go home in the dark.

JS: I've had a schedule like that for a brief period. It was tough. I can't imagine doing that for the length of the war.

LG: At the end of the war, Chance-Vought combined with somebody like American Airlines and moved their operations down to Texas, and Dad decided not to go.

JS: I also have a lot of questions about the brothers, both together and separately. I'm interested in each of them as characters. As an author writing a fiction piece, I'm sure I could make them be anybody I wish for them to be. But as a die-hard Gee Bee aficionado it just appealed to me to try and find out who they are and what they looked like on any typical day, what they liked to do and how they liked to be, what they were prone to do. I'm looking for the scuttlebutt, anything that can bring some depth to the character that I hadn't brought to them before. In fact, I've done a lot of the writing in this novel involving the Granville brothers and so far I've written each brother as I thought he would be, using everything from all the materials I've ever used to research the Granville brothers, and from there I've just used my intuition and impressions.

Let me bring you up to speed so you can understand what the book is about and how the Granville brothers become mixed up in it.

LG: Okay, I'd like to hear that.

JS: I've given you a quick run-through on some of this before I came. This twenty-four-year-old kid from the Springfield area comes through a big storm in his Waco UMF and crash-lands in the Springfield area in 1929, and he's found by the Granvilles when they go to check out a reported crash from the night before. He's familiar with their history and can see from the minute he gets there that they're not keeping up with what history reported, they're behind schedule. All the time he's still trying to figure out where he is, how he got there, how he's going get back, until a stranger shows up and tells him it's a one-way ticket, he's there for life, and then disappears just as quickly and mysteriously as he appeared. Well, it seems the brothers were around the corner peeking and eavesdropping. . . .

LG: I like that.

JS: I want them to be human, because I think that's who they were. I have no proof, but I'm convinced of it.

LG: They were . . . very much so.

JS: They come up to the young man and say, we believe you now, but then we always did. What can we do to help? And the kid says; "You can build the R-2 FIRST!" and he walks away.

JS & LG: (Laughing)

JS: And here's where I inject a little humor for the Gee Bee fans out there. I have Mark and Edward looking at each other and asking: "What's an R-2?"

JS & LG: (Laughing)

JS: So, I kind of twist it around at times and have a little fun with it, but the whole book moves toward Pearl Harbor and revolves around the fact that the United States faltered and failed miserably at maintaining any level of air superiority, even though the air racing and these men of sheer genius like Granny Granville with his incredible intuitive aeronautic tendencies, and Pete Howell were making HUGE advancements, sometimes on a monthly basis. The Japanese have no such compunctions, and it's even said that they acquired the technology for their Zero from Howard Hugh's racer. The whole time the kid is there, the clock is ticking and the US is moving toward Pearl Harbor.

LG: Funny you should mention that, because it just happens that I know a lot about that.

JS: Pearl Harbor?

LG: No, I know how the Japanese got their hands on the technology to build the Zero. I know EXACTLY how it happened.

JS: (stunned look) Uh . . . you DO? Really?

LG: Indeed. This is another story I got directly from my father. In the years leading up to the war, the Japanese were trying to find the right design for their main fighter aircraft. Despite the fact that no fighters were being put into production by the United States, there was still a lot of designing going on, everybody wanted to have designs ready to compete with. Chance Vought had been working on a prototype fighter, it was not a large frame but it flew very well. It was powered by a Pratt & Whitney radial. My father worked on the development of that design, and he told me all of this. After some testing, they found that they had two big issues with this design; it was too light and fragile for what they were looking for. Second, by the time they added armor plating, this bird would not be able to support armaments and the weight, it would slow it down too much, so they decided to scrap it. We were still on good terms with the Japanese, and they came to look at the prototype and bought it just as it sat. They took it back to Japan, took it apart piece by piece and retro-engineered it. They even built their own radial, with the parts machined exactly the same as the Pratt & Whitney. Then they mass-produced it. That plane became the Zero.

JS: What did they do about the fragility and the weight problem?

LG: I don't think they did anything. It was a small fighter and the Japanese were struggling to find enough metal, so the small Zero was ideal. The Zeroes were not given a lot of armor plating. For a long time until we caught up, their speed kept them out of the crosshairs, so their fragility was not a problem until then.

JS: Goodness. That one item alone made traveling all the way to interview you priceless. That's . . . that's amazing! Thank you so much!

LG: My pleasure. I'm glad it's something you can use.

LG: I think you really would have liked their personalities if you could have known them, as far as writing your story is concerned, because they were a unique bunch of characters, and I knew all of them. Except for Zantford. I never got to know Zantford; of course everybody always called him Granny. He died in 1934, about two years before I was born.

I did know his son Robert. They were ordinary, but they were geniuses, every one of them was a genius in some way. It's incredible, because they came from this little town called Madison, NH, it was a little village.

JS: I know where that town is!

LG: They grew up on a little hardscrabble farm, and five brothers and two sisters comprised the family. Zantford had to be a genius of the highest order, and I have no idea how that would have happened, genetically, because it doesn't show up in any of the earlier generations, as much as I've been able to find out. But I'll tell you, there was some kind of combination of genes there, and by the time he was five years old he was extraordinarily gifted mechanically and working with his hands. He could make and do all sorts of things. I can remember in the old house, which is still in existence where they grew up; when I was a kid there were still all kinds of toys and things which he had made, one of the things I found remarkable was that he'd taken a long block of wood and hand-carved it and made this block of wood into a continuous wooden chain . . . at six years old.

JS: Wow, sounds like he had determination as well. That's a project!

LG: He did, he had determination and he had vision, he could visualize these things that nobody else could see.

JS: That's great. I've written him as a man of vision.

LG: He was ten or eleven years old and he acquired an old Model T Ford and he converted it into a portable saw rig. He had NOTHING, no money whatsoever to work with, it was all seat-of-the-pants, scrape-it-up and find a way to utilize it engineering, and this thing worked perfectly. That's what he used to earn some money with. He was just a child, if a man had done it you might not have thought so much about it, but he was just ten or eleven years old. He drove it down the road and took on custom sawing jobs for firewood, that sort of thing.

JS: Oh. I thought he'd just taken the power train and built this on blocks.

LG: No, he found a way to leave the power train intact for driving the rig.

JS: Talk about problem-solving!

LG: The whole farm over there was just FULL of his inventions and contraptions. When he was about sixteen, he felt there wasn't a lot of future for him there in Madison so he moved to Boston. By the time he was seventeen, he was the youngest Chevy Dealership owner in the United States.

JS: Highly entrepreneurial.

LG: A gifted mechanic, a visionary, and an entrepreneur. He could see what he wanted to do, and he knew just how he wanted to do it. Even from a very young age. Shortly after that, when he was eighteen or so, he decided he was going to start taking flying lessons. About that time, he enticed his brother Tom to come to Boston and take over the auto dealership, at the time Tom was probably about sixteen. Tom came on down and took over the dealership while Granny pursued his dream of learning to fly and then started working on planes, and then he started to build them. Right after Tom took over the dealership, Robert . . . my Dad . . . came down to help him run it and to have a job. They were all doing pretty well at that point. You need to remember that not one of them made it past the eighth grade, and I'm not entirely sure that all of them actually made it to the eighth grade. None went on to high school.

JS: You hear about that happening a lot back them.

LG: I'm sure it was very common. Well, Granny got his hands on this big old truck, a great big thing, and he converted it into a repair shop on wheels. He specialized in chasing aircraft to wherever they'd landed or crash-landed, something like that, and repairing them so they could be flown back home. Or if they couldn't be flown, he'd take them apart and load the pieces into the truck and take them where they needed to go. If it had anything to do with airplane repair, he'd do it. That's how he got his start in this. They worked out of the truck, low overhead and so forth, and for several years they pursued that. Then, in his early twenties he built his first experimental biplane.

JS: Was that on floats?

LG: You're talking about the Performer, that was the only one on floats, but it did receive a lot of attention, so there are a lot of photos of it. They were unique at the time; they had side-by-side seating arrangement, and Granny had all the controls rigged so that you could unlatch the controls and move them from one side to the other and latch them down again. He built a number of those bipes and sold them.

LG: These guys were all "Type A" personalities in the strongest sense of the word. They didn't suffer fools gladly under any circumstances. They were always looking right straight ahead, they were profane and irreverent in their speech and so forth.

JS: Growing up in New England and spending literally years on a farm myself, I think that must come with the territory.

LG: Oh, sure. That doesn't make them bad people, they were result-oriented and they knew what they wanted. They worked right on it and they found ways to get it.

JS: Now, Thomas, what could you say about him as a person, what was his personality?

LG: Thomas was a little more reserved I think than the others, and for a long time after the others went into the airplane work he ran that dealership. He was also a meticulous craftsman; later in his life he became the chief welder for Command helicopters. In fact, much of the first Command helicopter was built in his garage. He could fix anything, anything at all, and usually with very few parts. He was a little less outgoing than the others, but he was a very nice guy and a great family man.

JS: Which leads us to your Dad, Robert.

LG: Dad probably of the five was the least mechanically gifted. He was a good workman and a good craftsman, but he wasn't a genius in the sense of engineering like some of the others were. When he joined the business they all told him he wasn't much of an aircraft mechanic and he'd have to be the bookkeeper, so he did the bookkeeping, acted as the materials purchasing agent and lining up materials and maintaining the stock and the inventory, and so forth.

JS: That was his forte, he did well at that?

LG: Yes. When he wasn't doing books he worked on the aircraft as well.

JS: Sounds like he might have been detail-oriented.

LG: Oh, yes he was, and because of it he wasn't as fast as the others, but he was meticulous. He was a good worker all of his life.

LG: Moving down to Mark, the next brother down the generation list. Mark was something of a genius on his own; he designed and built aircraft on the side which were completely different from what the Granville brothers were doing. He'd find an old building or garage and build something of his own, using leftover parts and whatever he could get his hands on. He took the old parts of an Aeronca and rebuilt the plane sort of backward, with the wings and motor in the back and the elevators in the front. He named the Ascender. One thing you probably won't read in the books is the name the brothers all gave it . . . the ASS-ender.

JS & LG: (Laughing)

JS: That's great!

LG: He flew that thing for hundreds of hours, and it was a marvel all around the airport because nobody had ever seen anything like it. It was well before the days of anybody turning engines around, anything like that.

JS: They call that type of plane a Canard now.

LG: Yes, that's right. It may have been the first canard built.

JS: The first Monoplane Canard, anyway. So Mark had his own level of genius, outside of the box, as they say. I guess you might say that he was outside of the box that the others were already outside of!

LG: Of all of the five brothers, I think he was the biggest character of the bunch. (Chuckles) He was just an amazing guy. I just looked up to him when I was a kid. He would cuss and swear and stomp around, but he was always doing something, he was a "Type A" all the way.

JS: In the book I've got him buddying around with Edward, like you'll often see with the two youngest boys in a family.

LG: Yeah? Edward was a genius in his own right. He designed an airplane or two, but it was later on. He was younger; he was quite a bit younger than all the others, something like three or four years younger than Mark. That made him kind of the "kid brother" of the group. But later he became the head of the experimental department for Pratt and Whitney, so it ended up that he was a big-name executive toward the end of his career. So, he went farther than any of the others as far as organized working for somebody else.

JS: What would Edward's job have been within the Gee Bee organization; Odd-jobs man or . . .?

LG: Edward was a gifted welder. All of them were quite good at it, in fact. In those days, everything was done with gas welding; it was all oxy-acetylene, and the fuselage and all the structural parts of the aircraft were welded and it had to be done right.

JS: I used to enjoy gas welding, there's really quite an art to making good welds every time.

LG: I know he was really gifted in that department; if they had an important job they'd give it to Ed. Even though he was only fifteen or sixteen at the time.

JS: It sounds as though they all knew what each other's strengths were and they just knew, they didn't have to delegate.

LG: I think that's true, and I think it went well with such a very loose-structured organization, and I think they got along so well and assigned jobs just by conversing and keeping the communications going. They were all straight-shooters, there was never any slyness, they said what they meant, and they were all honest.

JS: Okay, physical attributes. I'd like to add a little depth and give the readers a mental photo of each brother if I could. Zantford—Granny, there are lots of photos of him around, there are a significant number of them, in fact, and so I can get a good idea of him. But there are not a lot of photos of the others around.

LG: I can tell you this, they were all very slim guys; the most my father ever weighed in his lifetime was 140 pounds and he stood five feet ten inches tall. That was about the same for all of them, they were all built very much alike. They were all energetic, all fast moving, all moving in top gear most of the time, so they stayed slim.

JS: Was there a lot of food to be had at that time? Or were they slim from going all the time?

LG: Well, in the case of the Chevy Dealership, Granny did quite well at that time, but he was always moving. That's just how he was, that's how they all were. On top of that, he always had something new, some expectations, some wants, some new goals, usually things that most people would throw up their hands and not even aspire to. Things got kind of lean from time to time in Springfield, I don't know exactly how lean. They were always taking the money they made and putting it back into whatever they were doing. When they built the first biplane they did it nights and weekends in a garage, like that. They were looking toward building racing planes and being on the cutting edge of the racing world, but they didn't have the physical facilities where they were, which is now Logan Airport.

JS: Didn't they want to get into the air races in Springfield?

LG: It's somewhat more complex than that. They were looking for financial backing so that they could get into this, and there was a man in Springfield named Tait, he was in the dairy business, I guess you'd call him the H. P. Hood of the day. He had a daughter named Maude Tait. She was a pilot, and she's flown some of the Gee Bees at the races.

JS: Oh, sure! Yes!

LG: She flew the Y. Granny went out to meet her father, I'm not really sure how it went, but by the end of the day the brothers got a telegram telling them to pull up stakes, we're moving to Springfield, lock, stock, and barrel!

JS: The meeting went well.

LG: Yes, it did. At that time, they sold the automobile dealership and all of them moved to Springfield. Tait owned a big part of the Springfield airport, and he had a place that they could fabricate their racers.

JS: From what I can tell, that was a grass field, and not very long.

LG: It was grass, and something like two thousand feet long. Those Super-Sportsters had a real bad time landing there. Taking off from there was no problem, they had plenty of power. Most of the time the pilots were supposed to land the Super Sportsters across the river at Bowles airport in Agawam, which had a much longer runway. Do you remember the R-1/R-2 hybrid?

JS: That's the one they extended eighteen inches, right? I sure do.

LG: I think it was Lee Minor flying that hybrid and he tried to land in Springfield and he came in too long, the plane went right off the end of the runway, skidded through the grass and into a ditch, which flipped the plane in a somersault over the fence, and it landed on its gear in the roadway, wrecked.

JS: That was their last chance, right?

LG: Yes, they had run out of resources and their backing was pulled.

JS: Now, later on . . . the QED . . . there's a plane you don't hear much about.

LG: It was built for Jacqueline Cochrane, who was scheduled to fly in the London to Melbourne race. She was an Amelia Earhart type; she had a lot more publicity than she had flying skills.

JS: I think the same was said of Amelia too.

LG: Oh, yes. Well the first leg was from London to Italy, and they did very well. The second leg they had to fly over the Alps and she had never done any of that cold-weather flying, she was woefully unprepared and she liked to have frozen to death on that leg of the race. The co-pilot landed it.

JS: I heard they carried her from the plane.

LG: After that she walked away and never looked back, so it must have been pretty bad. The family sold the plane to a family where the father was a high official in the Mexican government. They'd flown it successfully a number of times and he was in a race from Mexico City to Washington DC and back. He set a new record flying to Washington; that leg went perfectly. When he took off over the Potomac and the engine quit. An investigation showed a grease rag had been sucked into the carburetor. The plane was shipped back to Mexico.

JS: I think we've covered everything on my list. Lee Granville; Thanks very much for everything you've told me here. . . . This is the Skowhegan History House, here in Skowhegan, Maine?

LG: Yes, this is an 1840s house that's been restored and preserved as a museum; it's called the Skowhegan History House.

JS: Then I'd like to thank the Skowhegan History House as well, for providing us with a lovely place to have this interview. Lee Granville, thank you for your time, it's the most fun I've ever had doing an interview!

LG: Thank you!

Acknowledgements

I would like to thank Lee Granville for taking several hours to interview with me. Lee's father was Robert Granville, one of the five very real Granville brothers fictionalized within this book. Lee is one of the last remaining people who have firsthand knowledge of his father and uncles, and his interview presented me with and offers us all a rare glimpse into who they were as men, and what drove them.

I've often heard people say, "Oh, if just a few of those things hadn't happened to them, things might have been a lot different." I've had the same thoughts myself. So, who among us, in my unique position, could resist giving the Granville brothers a chance to do-over the 1930s? Their drive and their genius is the stuff of legends, and I hope I've managed to bring across their personalities in this story as well.

Lee's interview is the only true non-fiction in my book. Thank you so much, Lee.

More than anything, this is a story. It's fiction, full of what-ifs and better luck. I hope you have as much fun reading it as I had writing it. Just as the time-travel implies, it could all have changed had just one or two of those things gone differently. I think you'll like the surprise I have in store for you. I have included the transcript of my interview with Lee Greenville, who provided me with wonderful, concise bits of the personalities of each and every brother. I've gone to great lengths to depict each brother as accurately as possible, using Lee's information whenever possible, and of course, as the fictional storyline allows. Outside of those boundaries, this is ultimately a work of fiction; so I made the rest up.

Within *Angels and Their Hourglasses* you'll find among the subject matter; World War II, the Japanese, and the detonation of the atomic bomb. As this book was about to be published in its original eBook format, I was stunned to learn that the Japanese had suffered a tsunami on March 11, 2011, which subsequently triggered a nuclear disaster when one of their nuclear power plants had a reactor that went into meltdown. Occasionally God sends a message to coarse folks like me—normally the last to look to the heavens—to stop the presses and pause for a moment of hope and prayer.

My heart goes out to the people of Japan, with my best hopes and wishes, and this thought: On this earth, we are all connected. That's why we shed tears for people we don't know.

There are some folks I'd like to thank, for their help with this book, and otherwise.

The Museums in and around Springfield, Massachusetts. Thanks for letting me hang around the Gee Bee and Granville brothers exhibits.

My deepest thanks to **Erika Q. Stokes** for her hard work editing and formatting *Angels and Their Hourglasses*. I watched in awe as my ugly duckling transformed into this swan. Erika has more knowledge of book editing and publishing in her little finger than I have in my entire body.

Al Kennedy, for being my reader, for slicing-and-dicing me without mercy. For asking, "What are they, having a yard sale on this word today?" You have a keen eye, my friend.

Ande Binan, graphic artist extraordinaire who hails from my "other home;" Maine. Your artistic interpretation translated into mind-blowing art for my book cover. I thought I knew what I wanted, until I saw what you'd envisioned and created. You rock!

My dear friends, from whenever and wherever I've lived; who laugh when I steal their names and their likenesses for my sometimes wild and crazy characters. For making me laugh when they ask me to make their characters sillier or meaner, or the hit man nastier or more frightening. Who never get mad and always seem to get a kick out of it.

Oh yes, Cleve. I did it. You're in here, and you're already such a character that I didn't have to make you more of anything.

Tim and Tom, should you ever read this; the two youngest and closest brothers, Mark and Edward, were loosely based on the two of you, long ago and far away. I'll let you decide which was which. And as always, we can tell them apart. =)

Above all, I would like to thank my wonderful wife Sharon, who puts up with me like nobody else; and I'm no picnic. Who encourages me in everything I do (mostly). Who warms her feet on me at night (without fail). My love. My anchor. My North Star. I'm blessed.

About the Author

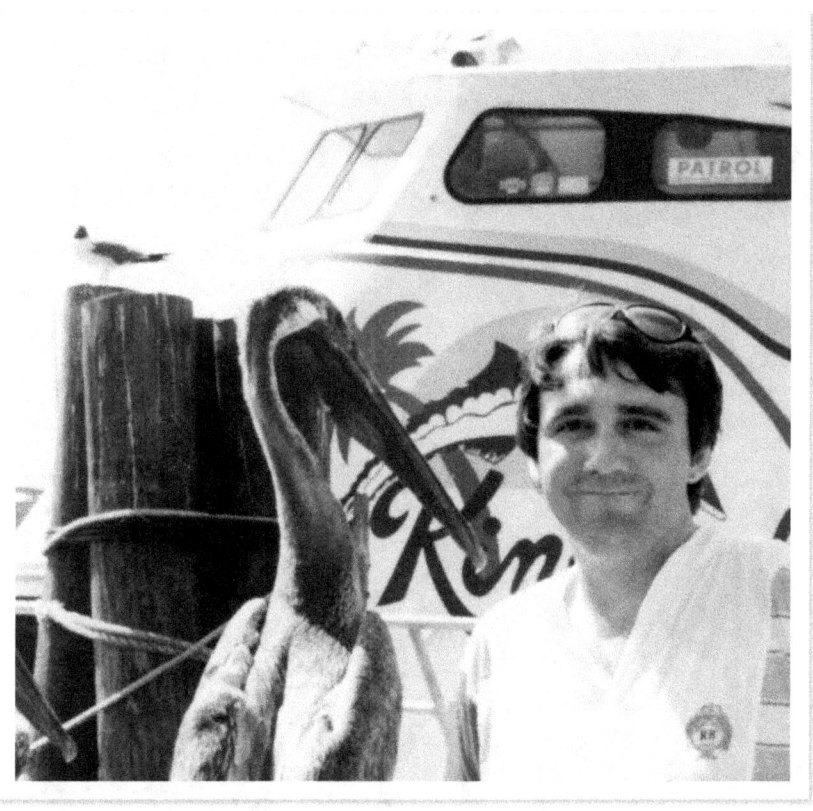

J.M. Surra has called the Bangor, Maine, area his home for twenty-five years, and now splits his time between there and San Antonio, Texas. He is the award-winning author of *Angels and Their Hourglasses,* which was released to numerous five-star reviews and won the Global Award for Popular Fiction.